ALSO BY DARCY COATES

DEAD

OF

WINTER

DARCY COATES

Poisoned Pen
PRESS

Published by Poisoned Pen Press, an imprint of Sourcebooks
P.O. Box 4410, Naperville, Illinois 60567-4410
(630) 961-3900
sourcebooks.com

Library of Congress Cataloging-in-Publication Data

Names: Coates, Darcy, author.
Title: Dead of winter / Darcy Coates.
Description: Naperville, Illinois : Poisoned Pen Press, [2023]
Identifiers: LCCN 2022061970 | (trade paperback)
Subjects: LCGFT: Thrillers (Fiction) | Novels.
Classification: LCC PR9619.4.C628 D44 2023 | DDC 823/.92--dc23/eng/20230105
LC record available at https://lccn.loc.gov/2022061970

Printed and bound in the United States of America.
LSC 10 9 8 7 6

1.

Snow in my mouth. In my nose. Burning my eyes as winds buffet me about like a scrap of cloth tangled on the mountainside.

Kiernan screams for help. His voice is raw, cracking. He holds my hand with a grip so tight it hurts. I suspect it would hurt more if I weren't so numb.

"Stay with me, Christa," he repeats, and his words are dragged away by gale-force winds. "Don't leave me."

Snowdrifts rise up to my knees. We're struggling, clawing our way across a landscape we can barely see. I don't know where we're going. I don't think Kiernan knows either, and that thought is terrifying.

Nothing around us is familiar. I can no longer see the sun or which way the summit is or whether there was ever a path under the snow we're stumbling through. All I can see is white, interrupted by pockets of black rock jutting out of the empty void. The landscape is inhospitable. Jagged and harsh, inhumane. Not even the wildlife wants to live here.

My black jacket has turned gray under a coating of snow. My heart thunders, each pulse bruising the back of my ribs. I can barely breathe. My scarf keeps sliding down to my chin, exposing my face to the brunt of the snowstorm. My nose burns. I imagine blood vessels bursting and spreading a web of red lines across my skin.

I pull the scarf up again, trying to hold it in place, but then my footing slips on the uneven terrain and I stumble. Kiernan clutches at me. He tries to pull me back up, but we've been fighting the snowstorm for too long and we're both exhausted. Instead, he drops to his knees beside me.

Not much of his face is visible, just a slim line between his neck gaiter and thermal hat, revealing squinted eyes and pale skin. Ice flecks cling to his brows and lashes.

"It's not far," he says. The wind howls around us, deafening, and he bends close so that I can hear his voice. "We only need to go a bit farther."

He's said that before, nearly an hour ago.

It wasn't supposed to be like this. No one had expected the storm. Or how rapidly we would lose the path once visibility dropped.

Kiernan tugs at me, his gloved hands slipping off my jacket as he tries to pull me up. "Come on, Christa." Another pull. "Not far."

I'm so exhausted. My exposed skin is either numb or burning. I scramble to rise, and Kiernan pulls me against himself. "There we go," he says, or I think he says, under the gale. His hand runs down my arm until it finds my hand, then he grips it, and I grip back as fiercely as I can.

We're perhaps a hundred miles from civilization. My view from the tour bus window showed sparse hiking trails, but no houses. No shelter. Nothing but endless stretches of unforgiving wilderness: craggy, dark rocks and infrequent, anemic pine trees. The mountain range rose ahead of us and cut across the skyline like a broken knife. We are truly, unbelievably alone.

We're going to die out here, I think, and the fear turns to acid on my tongue.

"Hello!" Kiernan yells into the void. "*Hello!*"

I'd screamed with him at first, pushing my voice to rise above the howling winds until it cracked in the cold air, and I couldn't even hear myself. Now, it's all I can do to stay on my feet. Stay moving.

The scarf slips again, and it feels like my skin is being scraped off by sandpaper. I turn my head away from the gale and Kiernan notices. He tugs his own scarf off his neck. Out of the two of us, he was the better dressed. The better prepared. He'd grown up in an area not too different from here; he'd known how temperamental it could be.

He reaches the scarf toward me. I shake my head. *You need it.* His hand finds my jacket lapel and pulls me closer as he loops the thick merino wool around me.

"Don't fight me on this," he says.

The scarf doesn't just sit around my neck but covers the lower half of my face, almost blocking my eyes. It smells of damp and Kiernan's breath and sweat. My own hot breath blows around my cheeks with every exhale.

Kiernan bends to put our heads at the same height. He's still wearing his neck gaiter, pulled up to cover his nose, but it looks too lightweight without the scarf. Crystals have formed around the corners of his eyes and I can't tell if it's an effect of the sharp wind or whether he's fighting back tears.

"We need to stay together," he says. "This way."

The landscape is changing around us, growing up vertical, the jutting black shards of rock rising high past our heads. The snowdrifts are deep around them, and every step is a fight. A horrendous sinking sensation forms in the pit of my stomach. This isn't even remotely like the area where the bus was forced to halt. We're moving in the wrong direction. I try to call to Kiernan, to tell him we need to turn back, but my throat is stripped raw and my voice escapes as a reedy whisper, inaudible even to myself.

Uneven walls rise to my left, crusted in ice. An endless expanse of white stretches to my right. Clumps of snow tumble away from my boots and vanish into it. I press back, pushing closer to Kiernan, grabbing at his arm to warn him we're on the edge of a ravine. He sees my gestures.

"It's okay," he calls, and his voice sounds thin and broken under the wind. "We just need to get around this. Stay close to the wall. Don't let go of me."

I've never seen Kiernan terrified before. It feels like an alien emotion for him. Something unnatural, something that doesn't belong.

But still, he's moving forward.

I grasp his hand and try to pull him back. It's too dangerous. We need to retrace our steps. See if we can find out where we turned wrong and which path will lead us back to the tour group.

He calls something to me and leans forward again. I shake my head, but he doesn't see it. His shoulder brushes along the rough stone as he moves close to it, holding himself as far from the ravine as he can.

I can't get him back. Which means I have to follow.

The ground feels uneven, though it's hard to be certain with the snow as thick as it is. I mimic Kiernan's motions and press against the bare stone face, my glove running across the rough surface to guide my movements. The snowstorm is so thick that I can't tell how close the cliff's edge is. I can barely see the snow around my legs, white and blurred under the flakes funneled in by the wind. At a certain point, I can't see the ground at all any longer. There's no clear edge. No sharp line to warn me how close I am. Just a fade into nothing.

Kiernan is moving fast. I can feel the desperation in the angle of his shoulders and the thought returns to me: *We're going to die here.* I wonder if that idea has occurred to him yet. Whether he's dwelling on it.

Hot air gusts out of my mouth, trapped in the scarf, and brings pins and needles to my damaged skin. I feel as though I am suffocating, but pulling the scarf away won't bring any relief.

I still can't see the edge of the ravine to my right, but the ground under my feet is tilting toward it. I press hard against the rocks to my left. My boots are slippery on the ice. Kiernan is pulling ahead. I try to call to him to slow down, but my voice comes out as a whistle.

The wind races across the bare rocks, trying to pry me away from them. My heart is pumping ferociously, and I've never been so hyperaware that the heart is a muscle because it feels like it's on the verge of snapping.

Kiernan turns to say something. I catch a vowel, but the rest of his words are torn away.

I'm watching his face, not the ground, as I step forward. My foot plunges into the snow and fails to find anything solid beneath.

If I'd been less exhausted—if my reflexes had been sharper, if I'd been more prepared—I might have been able to pull back. Instead, I plunge down, my mouth open in a gasping cry that never quite materializes. Snow gets into my mouth. My arms stretch out, fingers reaching for any kind of purchase, but they only find fresh snow, crumbling and delicate.

I feel myself sliding away. Toward the edge, toward the void. I claw and kick but it's like grasping at air.

A hand catches mine. Kiernan, his eyes huge and wild, clutches at me.

It's not enough.

Pain arcs up my arm as I slip out of his hold. He grasps for better purchase, taking the glove and a strip of skin off the back of my hand before I fall away.

I don't even have the breath to scream. My face is to the sky, my back to the empty white void beneath me as I plunge, carrying a wave of snow in my wake.

2.

Crimson bleeds across the white.

My eyes sting. My lungs ache. Spasms of pain rise through my leg and hip, but when I try to twist to relieve it, I find I can barely move. Everywhere I look is white, dotted with red, and I realize that, although I feel the press of ice against me, I'm no longer experiencing the driving force of the winds.

I'm under the snow.

That thought sends a jolt of terror through me. I push, thrashing, before falling still again. It's difficult to breathe, and I can feel the air inside the scarf growing stale.

I've heard that skiers who are caught in avalanches often perish because they don't know which way to dig to get themselves out. Trapped under layers upon layers of freshly churned snow makes it nearly impossible to tell which way is up. The advice is to spit: see which way your saliva drips, then dig away from it.

My mouth is bone dry, and I've barely started to work my tongue around looking for moisture before realizing I'm a fool. The spit will just absorb into Kiernan's scarf, which is cinched so hard around my face that I can barely move my lips.

I can see light, though. Not much, but a little, filtering through the snow. I reach one hand toward it. The snow shifts around me, heavy, and then my hand breaks free and feels the bite of icy air.

I begin struggling again, clawing and kicking toward the surface as the snow presses in around my face and tries to suffocate me. I'm already drained. Every extra inch of effort feels like nails being pushed into my muscles, but I fight and fight and eventually get my head free of the snow.

My lungs are on fire as I hang there, my head and the tips of my shoulders out of the snow, and suck deep, gulping gasps of fresh air in through the scarf's layers. The storm is immense. Even when I squint my eyes open, I can't see anything but a hopeless expanse of white.

White and red. My hand reaches out of the snow ahead of me. The skin was torn when Kiernan tried to catch me. Streaks of bright crimson run down its back and disappear into my jacket's sleeve. It's stopped bleeding, though, I think; the blood is already drying as the wind tears across it. I don't feel much. That whole hand has started to go numb, and the fingertips are a frightening white.

I try to twist to see the area around me. If there are any landmarks, the snowstorm hides them. If there are sounds, the howling winds swallow them.

What happened to Kiernan?

Did he fall as well?

Icy air burns my lungs as I breathe deeply and then scream, as loudly as my cracked voice will allow: "Hello!"

I don't think he could hear me, even if he was close. My body aches at the thought of moving, but I force myself to begin struggling again, crawling out of the snow an inch at a time. I reach the surface and collapse, my lungs heaving for air like a racehorse pushed too far.

I try again, even though I know it won't do any good. "Kiernan!"

The wind funnels into my eyes, making them weep. Twinges of pain continue to rise from my leg and hip. I don't think it's bad—a sprain or a pinched nerve—but it will make walking harder.

The temptation to rest and regain my breath is sinfully attractive. I know I can't afford it. I'm already very close to freezing. If I sit, even for one or two minutes, I doubt I will ever get up again.

And so I roll onto my hands and knees, the numb fingers plunging into the snow, then groan as I finally make it to my feet.

I stagger in slowly widening circles. The snow is over my knees and I have to fight to gain each inch of ground, but I can't overlook the chance that Kiernan came down the cliffside with me. The narrow walkway was treacherous, and my own fall dragged clumps of ice free from it. If he fell, he could still be under the snow, struggling but unable to escape.

The hole that I surfaced from is still visible but quickly being filled in by the driving wind. I circle the area until I'm certain there are no other piles of snow where a person could be trapped.

Jutting rocks mark the base of the slope I fell down. I can't see the top. I try to scramble up the surface, but the slope increases within a few feet and I slide back.

My teeth are chattering. It's growing harder to feel my arms and legs, and my feet threaten to skid out from under me.

I need to get back up there. The brutal cliff face continues to the left and the right. It's impossible to tell how far. I turn left.

Strange sounds come through the roar of the gale. They blur in and out until it's impossible to know whether they are man-made, animal, or the whistle of wind passing through narrow gaps in the rocks. Sometimes, they sound like screams. Lasting longer than human's lungs could manage, they shriek and shriek and shriek.

My feet stumble with nearly every step. I look back to judge how far I've come, but the tracks I'm leaving fade into the uncanny white within moments. The cliffs are no longer at my side. I don't know when I staggered away from them, but I did.

Something dark rises up on my other side. Human-shaped but indistinct, I think I can make out the width of a torso. Energy flows back into me and I force my way through the rising snowdrifts to reach it.

The shape resolves into a tree, its lower branches stripped off by the winds, and I want to scream.

I'm going to die out here.

The thought is circling me like a vulture. Before, it was a fear. Now, it's almost a certainty. I will walk as long as my legs carry me, and it will not be as far as I want them to. Once I collapse, I will have maybe an hour, if I'm lucky, before my body folds under the strain of the cold and drags me into a sleep I won't wake from.

The tree fades behind me as I move away from it. A dark ridge teases at the edge of my vision. Without any other markers to keep my path running straight, I aim for it.

At first I try to tuck my gloveless hand between my other arm and my body to protect it, but every stagger and scramble forces me to pull it free again, and eventually I just stop trying.

The screams rise out of the whistling wind again and again, always lasting too long, lingering until they hurt my ears. I don't know how long I've been walking. I can feel my consciousness bleeding in and out, even as I stay upright and continue stumbling forward. I was trying to find Kiernan, but I have no idea which direction he might be in any longer. The landscape rises and collapses in unpredictable patterns. For all I know, I could be going in circles. When possible, I choose a downhill path, though it never lasts as long as my numb legs would like.

A new sound breaks through the howling wind. My mind is so numb that it takes a moment to register. I lift my head. My mouth aches from the dry and my eyes burn. There is nothing to see ahead except the hazy, pale void. I pause, my breathing ragged, as I listen.

The sound comes again. It's sharper and higher than the wind. Man-made. A whistle.

I don't even have to force my legs to move this time. They stumble forward, carrying me blindly. I could be facing another cliff edge, and I wouldn't even know. But the whistles are growing louder, and my mind is empty of anything except the blind desire to reach the source.

Dark shapes flicker in and out at the edges of my vision. Pine trees.

More than before. They cluster erratically, bent at uncomfortable angles, their roots clinging to the thin soil as though to spite the environment they've found themselves in.

And then, past them, a darker, broader shape. For a second it looks like another wall of stone rising out of the ground, but then I realize it's too sharp, too straight. A building of some kind.

And inside the building is a light.

3.

Blackstone Alpine Lodge.

It's supposed to be closed. The weather this time of year is too inclement, the roads too unreliable, to ferry guests in and out.

We're going to have the whole place to ourselves.

The private tour bus rocks uneasily on the narrow road. I clutch the brochure in my lap. The photo on the front shows a beautiful weathered stone building with wooden trim. It's huge. Less of a lodge and more of a manor. During peak season it could probably house two hundred guests. Small text inside describes lake views, skiing opportunities, and the wild deer and goats that roam the region. Those descriptions are punctuated by photos of snowcapped pines and beds with deep red covers.

Beside me, Kiernan is trying to hold his energy in check. He's been buzzing since this morning, sorting our bags, holding us to our itinerary, helping the tour guide pack the bus. He must have noticed I was clutching the brochure a little too hard. His hand snakes out, delicate, and brushes the back of mine. I like that he always does that—asking, instead of demanding, to hold my hand.

I spread my own fingers in response and feel some of the anxiety bleed out of me as he threads our hands together.

When I first met him, I thought he might be too much for me. He had so much joy, so much enthusiasm for life, all of it bright and fresh and unblemished.

I...

I was a mess. I don't know how else to put it. Each day felt like a fight to earn the right to be happy, and they were fights I lost more often than won. The things that energized Kiernan drained me—cooking breakfast, going shopping, choosing a movie. For Kiernan, even the mundane seemed like a chance to discover something new and good. For me, they were hurdles, scraping my shins every time I failed to clear them.

Kiernan's thumb grazes over mine. A reminder: breathe. Relax.

I try.

I haven't trusted anyone in a long time, but against my better judgment, I've started to trust Kiernan.

This trip was his design. He'd grown up in one of the small towns below the mountain range and had told me about the years he spent exploring the craggy rocks and windswept patches of trees. The landscape has, in a way, become built into his soul. And he wants to share it with me.

Somehow, this feels more important than just a vacation. As though this is some kind of *next step* for us. Four months should be way too soon for a proposal. My friends, the few I keep in contact with, would have told me to slow it down. But there was something in the way Kiernan talked about the trip—a hint of nervous excitement in his smile, a flash of intention in his eyes—that made me think I might not be wrong.

The bus is a charter, with plush, mostly clean seats and large windows. It's not quite half-full. Kiernan and I are near the back, which gives me a chance to watch our companions. I count eight. Nine including Brian, the driver and coordinator.

Kiernan picked this trip specifically to avoid the crowds. He found a private tour with only a handful of other attendees. We'll have two weeks at Blackstone Alpine Lodge with very little stress. At least, that's the goal.

We are an eclectic bunch from what I can see. An older couple sit in the row ahead of us, talking softly. To our right, a young blond woman with pale skin and severe features leans against the bus's side, staring through the window at the ragged landscape flashing past. Two rows ahead of her is a man with his hair styled into an undercut that's so precise it must have been done professionally.

Near the bus's front, two men—one old, one perhaps a couple of years younger than I am—sit in silence. Father and son, I suspect. Then, two other women, on opposite sides of the bus: one young, with pale hair cut shoulder length and deeply tanned skin, writing in some kind of journal or notebook, and one older, pale and with gray hair cut so short it stands up in spikes on top of her head.

As though she can sense me sizing up the bus, the woman in front of me turns around in her seat. Her hair is dyed brown, with hints of gray showing at the roots, and her eyes are shrewd as she glances me over.

"Huh," she says. "You've got one of those faces."

My voice is a whisper. "I'm sorry?" *One of those faces you want to punch? One of those faces you love to hate?*

She swirls her finger around her own features, which are broad and bold: a large nose and a square jaw with the earliest hints of jowls. "The kind of face that feels familiar. You haven't been to Louisiana in the last few years, have you?"

I manage a laugh, even though my heart is going a little faster than I would like. "No, never. Is that where you're from?"

"Yep. Me and the hubs. Though he travels plenty. Trucker, you know."

On cue, the man next to her turns. Despite the chilling temperatures, he wears a baseball cap. His white beard is cut into a Vandyke style, a block of hair that rings his lips and vanishes underneath his chin. I've heard that married couples who live together for long enough can sometimes start to look alike, and I can see that theory in action. Their faces have a similar square shape, with fluid-heavy skin under their eyes and hints of rosacea across their noses.

"Steve," the trucker husband says, and thrusts his hand over the back of his seat. Kiernan dips in quickly and shakes the hand in my stead, something I'm grateful for. "My wife's Miri," Steve continues. "When we first heard about this trip, I thought I was going to get to do some hunting. Take home a ten pointer. But they wouldn't let me bring my gun."

"Probably not too many deer in the area at this time of year anyway," Kiernan says. He's friendly, but I know he doesn't like sport hunting. "And the lake will be frozen over, so no fishing either."

Steve groans, and it's as he turns away that I see he's wearing a vest. Embroidered on the back is a design of a large fish leaping out of the water, a hook barbed in its mouth, with the line looping back toward a distant fisherman. The news about the lake must be an extra blow.

"You'll find something to do," Miri says, fond but unsympathetic. She gives me a wink. "It's our first proper vacation in nearly ten years. We need to get some spice back into this marriage one way or another."

I chuckle, even though I'm left feeling uncomfortable in ways I can't quite explain. Miri and Steve seem friendly, but the hairs on the back of my arms rise.

There's a change in the bus's rocking, tilting motion. It slows, its motor rumbling. I crane to see over the backs of the seats.

Through the windshield, I can make out a patch of the road. There looks to be something bulky and dark ahead.

"Trouble?" a man asks, but everyone is facing away from me and I can't tell who's spoken.

"Might be. I'll take a look."

I like Brian, the tour guide. He's cheerful, almost chirpy, in a way that doesn't feel manufactured. As he checked us off the bus's roster at departure, he reminded me faintly of Kiernan: not just in stature—tall, on the slender side—but also in his attitude. As though this trip was as much an adventure for him as for us.

"Hang here a minute," Brian says. He climbs out of the bus and closes the doors behind him.

Kiernan cranes to see. "We can't be at the lodge yet, surely?"

"Nope." Steve, the man ahead of us with the fish embroidered on his vest, is pressed so close to his window that his breath mists the glass. "Looks like there's a tree down."

Other people in the bus are rousing. "What does that mean?" the woman with short gray hair asks. "Are we going to have to turn back?"

The bus's doors creak as they open and Brian bounds inside. He's still smiling, but the sting of cold air has left his skin blotchy. "Okay, quick update. A pine's come down over the road."

"Can't we get through?" Miri asks. "Don't tell us the trip's canceled."

"Absolutely not." Brian claps his hands. "I have a chain saw and cartons of fuel for exactly this kind of situation. It'll take a moment to chop it up, but we'll make quicker work if I can get some volunteers to help."

The older man near the bus's front rises first. He's massive, easily six foot four, and shaggy gray hair hangs down to his shoulders. His jacket stretches taut over his back as he moves. The teenager at his side seems to be trying not to make eye contact, but the older man taps his shoulder—not roughly, but not gently either—and the teen shrugs and stands.

"I have a bad back," the lady with spiky gray hair says as the man with the undercut hops up to follow Brian.

Steve huffs out a breath and pats Miri's leg. "Time for the men to get to work."

At my side, Kiernan reaches for his jacket. "You could stay here," he murmurs to me. "Take it easy for a bit."

"No, I'll come." After a day of sitting, I'm almost looking forward to stretching some muscles. Plus, the bus's insulation isn't designed for the snow. With the motor off, the cold is already beginning to seep in. Kiernan looks happy and waits while I get my own jacket and scarf from the overhead storage.

We shuffle out of the bus, and I realize no one is staying behind. Even the gray-haired lady with the bad back didn't want to be left there alone.

The icy air flows around me, and I rush to zip up my jacket. Kiernan, following behind me, passes me two of the knit gloves I'd packed, and I gratefully pull them on.

The sky, which was a relatively crisp blue early that morning, is now a bitter, pitted gray. The mountains are beautiful. The jagged peaks stretch for hundreds of miles in each direction. I can barely see them now as clouds roll like a stormy ocean suspended above our heads, and I glance at Kiernan for reassurance that we're not about to be caught in a storm. He's focused on the roadblock ahead of us, though, and I hunch to pull my jacket higher around my throat as I follow him.

Trees grow on either side of the road. They're not exactly dense, but there are enough to make visibility poor. One of them—its trunk thicker than a man's torso—has collapsed across the road. Green-tipped branches have splintered off, scattering in a halo around it.

"It looks bad now, but we can clear it, no problem," Brian says, walking sideways so he can speak to us over the whistling wind. "If we're efficient, we can be at the lodge before dinner. Take care of your back, okay, ma'am?"

"Blake," she says, but her coat has a fur trim that covers her mouth and muffles the word. She's pulled a beanie over her spiky gray hair. She's short and blocky, and shows no intention of approaching the tree. Not far from her, Miri turns aside to shake a packet of cigarettes out of her pocket and lights one.

"I'll cut the tree into logs," Brian says. "With a couple of volunteers, we're looking at about an hour, maybe an hour and a half. Anyone who isn't in the mood to haul wood is welcome to stay in the bus, or you could take the opportunity to enjoy your first day in the mountains and take a look around. Just don't stray far. I have insurance for you all, but I don't want to have to use it."

Cold wind snatches at my back. I look behind us. The clouds seem to have gotten denser and darker in just the couple of minutes we've been outside.

Kiernan's not looking at the rocks, but at the slope leading upward. "How are you feeling about a walk?"

I smile. He was born close to this very ridge of mountains, probably no more than a few hundred miles away. Areas like this must feel like a second home to him. "Yeah?"

"I can see a gap in the mountains up there." His excitement is rising. He takes my hand, an eager grin showing his teeth. "That means there's probably a good lookout close by. Do you want to try to find it?"

Some of the other guests are already moving away from the bus. They're mostly following the road, either stepping over the tree to explore farther up the path or wandering off to the side to get a closer look at the plants, their hands in their pockets and their shoulders hunched against the cold.

"That sounds nice." It's been a long day, and all of it has been spent in the bus with near strangers. The idea of having an hour of quietness, particularly with Kiernan, is too tempting.

"Brian!" Kiernan calls. "We're going to see if we can find a view of the mountains. We'll be quick."

"Sure, no problem, just don't wander too far."

"Okay?" Kiernan asks me, his hand warm on mine.

I say, "Okay," and try not to shiver as the first snowflake touches my cheek.

Kiernan is a fast walker but stays patient with me as I stumble over tree branches and rocks that have been hidden under the snow. It's hard to tell if we're following a walking path or if we're now into wild terrain. I don't like how far we've walked from the bus. But Kiernan has always had a good sense of direction, and I'm letting him lead the way, even when I begin to lose my orientation.

"Shouldn't be far," he says, breathing heavily through his smile. "Look—clear sky ahead!"

I can't see any clear sky. Just the thickening, darkening clouds growing low and pendulous around us as the snowflakes come faster and thicker. I wish I'd brought a heavier jacket. Even the scarf feels scant as the wind picks up.

How long have we been walking? I glance behind myself. The slope is a ragged mess of sharp rocks and trees. It's already growing hard to see the path we took. *Brian said the bus would be ready to leave in an hour. If the weather's turning bad…if the bus is at risk of becoming snowbound…how long could they afford to wait for us?*

"Kiernan—"

I catch myself. He looks back at me, and there's so much fondness in his eyes that it breaks my heart. "Are you okay? Can you put up with the cold for just a bit longer? I want to find the perfect spot. I want to show you something beautiful."

There's not much I can do except nod. He reaches out and takes my hand, and we step deeper into the endless white together.

4.

My mouth tastes bad—sour and gritty, with a tang of blood. My hip still aches. There are small pains everywhere: in my feet, in my calves, in my hands, in the muscles in my face.

But pain means life. It means I'm out of the numbing snow.

The room's blurry. It's not just because my eyes won't focus; the lights are low, leaving it bathed in shadows.

Someone crouches beside me. Kiernan? I blink. No. A woman. Her face is very pale. I recognize her: she sat on the seat opposite us on the bus, facing the window, her blond hair pulled back into a stark ponytail. She looked bitter then, and she looks bitter now, her delicate features pinched as she manipulates my hand.

"That's frostbite," a voice says, and it sounds muddy to my ears. "We should amputate."

"No," the woman says, and that's all she says. Figures shuffle in and out of my peripheral vision. I strain, fighting through the fog. A pulse of fear runs through me. Did they find him? Is Kiernan here?

A familiar form shifts near the room's opposite corner. It's Kiernan. The relief is intense. He's near the back of the group, facing away from me. I don't understand why he's not closer. I want to see him. I need to make sure he's not hurt.

He's standing and conscious, at least. That should be comforting. Instead, a small twinge of doubt squirms in my stomach. I try to shift my legs and feel stabbing pains cut through the muscles. The woman working on my hand must have felt me moving, but she doesn't say anything. She doesn't even look up to meet my eyes.

The sense of danger, of wrongness, grows worse. A premonition that something bad is coming. Like a storm threatening to break.

I've learned not to ignore that feeling. The last time I tried was on August 8. And the cost it exacted was extreme.

But Kiernan is there, running his hands through his hair. It should be enough. But he still won't look at me. He's almost as far across the room as he can get. I open my mouth to call to him, but my voice is barely a whisper, and it drains the last of my fading energy. I slide back to unconsciousness.

My dreams come as ragged, vicious things. Not fantasies but memories, crowding one over another and biting me as they pass. Kiernan clawing at my hand as I slip over the edge. In reality it was over in a second, but in the dream it lasts for minutes, his fingers sinking through my flesh in his desperation to catch me.

Then his voice, playful, happy, as we fight our way through a clump of fir trees: "We just need to get through this patch. I bet we'll be able to see the entire valley from this high."

When his voice came again, the excitement had faded into uncertainty as the gentle dusting of snow thickened into something more insidious and the wind picked up. "The road was over here, wasn't it?"

And then, true fear sparked through as what we'd believed was our return path culminated in a dead end. "Stay close to me, Christa. We'll get back. Just stay with me."

My fingers twitch at the memory. I'd tried. I'd tried so hard.

A new voice, not a memory but something fresh and invasive, cuts through my dreams. "Turn that damn phone off, will you?"

A male voice responds. "It's not hurting you."

"Have some respect." The first voice again. "A man's dead out there."

A dead man? I struggle to surface from the lasting traces of sleep. My brain feels sluggish, like I'm drunk. It's hard to move. The room swims, and my eyes fix on the figure near the room's opposite side. Kiernan is bent over a small wooden table, working on something. He's still there. Thank mercy.

I try to call to him, but my voice comes out as a croak. He turns.

Not Kiernan. The tour guide. Brian. Same frame, different hair color. My subconscious had noticed, had tried to warn me, but I'd been too exhausted to realize what it meant.

A fresh stab of fear enters my veins. It's enough to get me to scramble to sitting. I've been mostly undressed; my clothes are hung to dry on the wall beside me. Only my underwear is left.

"Kiernan?" I manage, and this time the word is barely understandable.

I'm struggling to make out the shapes in the room. It's small and crowded, and the lights are so low that I can barely tell the figures apart from the furniture. They're all the people from the tour bus, though. I see the young girl with shoulder-length hair, clutching her journal to her chest. The older man, tall and shaggy, looking more like a bear than a human. The teenager, studiously staring at the wall.

They're all there, spaced about, some standing, some sitting on the few chairs that are available, others sitting on the floor. The space, which I took for a bedroom at first, appears to be a cabin. The walls are made of wood. Furniture, all rough and handcrafted, makes the place feel claustrophobically small.

I can't see Kiernan.

No one is answering me. Most of them won't even look at me. I try again. "Where's Kiernan?"

"Oh, honey," a voice says, and I recognize Miri, the trucker's wife, sitting nearby. She has her wool cap in her lap and is fidgeting with it. "It's a miracle you made it back."

No. No.

I twist around. My bed is on the floor, made of old blankets and spare coats. There's a window over my head. It's narrow and dull, the glass in need of a clean. I claw onto my knees to see through it. Snow has caked over the glass, leaving only small gaps.

My knuckles—the knuckles on my intact hand, at least—bulge as they hold on to the windowsill, keeping me upright. The other hand is swaddled in dense bandages. Spots of red bloom through the layers. The bandages run from my wrist and around my fingers, turning that hand into a club, and while I can use it as such, I can't move any of the muscles or joints underneath.

Patches of the world outside fade in and out of sight. The storm continues; it batters against the glass, rattling its frame and whistling as it squeezes through gaps. Trees flicker into sight, their branches straining and their trunks bending painfully under the onslaught.

And Kiernan is out there somewhere.

"Miss Bailey?" Brian's voice is tentative, as though he thinks I'll crumble under anything louder. "Christa? I'm so sorry—"

"Did you find his body?" It's the worst question. The sort of thing that, in any other situation, I might have wrapped in softer, cushioning language.

There's no time for delicacy, though. I need the answer. I need it faster than anyone seems to want to give it to me.

Brian crouches. He braces his forearms on his knees. His lips work, slightly dry and tacky as he feels out his answer.

I repeat myself, louder and harsher, my voice cracking. "Did you find his body?"

"No," Brian finally says.

I feel as though I am stepping back from a cliff edge. I let go of my grip on the windowsill and instead reach for the clothes hung above my makeshift bed. They're still damp. I struggle to pull them over my goose-flesh skin.

"Christa," Brian says, and the words are wrapped in that horrible, careful tone that's reserved for funerals and bad news delivered in hospital waiting rooms. "We searched for Kiernan for as long as we could. I'm so sorry, but—"

"He's out there," I snap, kicking sore legs out as I fight them into the pants. The pale skin is mottled with fresh bruises. "Help me look for him."

Brian doesn't respond. The others are horribly quiet. Most of them still won't look at me, as though I'm doing something shameful, something they don't want to see. In the gloom, I can make out the gleam of diverted eyes and the shadows around twisted lips, but not much more.

I have my pants on. My sweater is crooked but close enough. I grab the jacket last and stagger up from the makeshift bed. My feet feel as though I'm walking on knives. Stabbing pains travel from them and into my thighs.

"Christa, you can't go outside." Brian rises with me. I don't listen as I search for the door. It's not easy to find in the gloom, but I locate it just a few feet away. Brian catches my arm before I can open it. "Please, stop. It's a small miracle that you're even alive right now. We searched for you and your partner for nearly eight hours, until we were close to hypothermia ourselves. If you go back outside now, you're courting the very real danger of dying."

"Kiernan's out there." I never yell. I'm very close to it now. "His—his clothes were warmer than mine. He grew up here. He knew how to dress for the cold. He's—he can make it."

Brian's own voice rises. He's not angry, though; he's frightened and trying to compensate for it. "You've been unconscious for hours. It's night. Visibility is close to nil and the temperature's dropping with every minute." He pulls in a shuddering breath. "Please, trust me. If I thought there was any chance we could find him, I would be trying. More than anything, I want to keep you guys safe. But that includes protecting the people inside this building too."

He sees the look on my face and takes half a step closer, his voice growing still softer. "I've sent out an alert to the emergency responders. They'll bring in proper search parties and helicopters as soon as they can."

"When will that be?" I'm not going to back down. "Tonight? With this storm? Or tomorrow sometime? You said yourself that it's getting colder with every minute. If he's still alive, we can't just leave him out there."

Brian swallows. He breaks eye contact first.

My face burns. I thought I was too dehydrated to cry, but tears trail over my cheeks. "You can give up on him. I won't."

"Christa—"

"I'll go with her," someone says. I glance about the room to find the speaker. The man with the undercut nods as he catches my eye, and I could hug him. He's about my age and large, not especially tall but broad and muscular, with a flexible, expressive face. Two silver piercings and a stud glitter in his left ear. "She's got the right to look for her partner if she wants. I'll help." He gives me a tight smile. "I'm Hutch, by the way."

Brian sighs. He runs a hand over his face. He looks a decade older than he did when he welcomed us onto the bus that morning. "Okay. The three of us will go out again. Everyone else, stay here. We'll have to take the lamp but keep the fire burning so we can see our way back."

Two other figures rise. The severe, blond woman who worked on my hand, as well as the tall, gray-haired man. The woman picks up an old-fashioned lantern from the table, and I expect her to pass it to me, but instead she zips up her jacket one-handed as she approaches the door.

"Well, I'm not going," Steve says. He's sharing a couch with Miri, his arms folded and his legs kicked out in a way that fills the limited walking space. "It's a suicide mission for a dead man."

I suspect Brian would agree, but he just waves Steve off as he wrenches the door open.

Snow pelts my face and tugs at my damp clothing, but instead of shying back, I lean into it.

He's not dead. Not yet.

The five of us step out into the raging blizzard.

5.

The ice in the air steals my breath away. My throat and eyes begin aching again. I didn't think to bring the scarf, and the clothes I did manage to pull on are still damp and immediately begin to sap energy from me as I lurch away from the cabin.

I won't be able to last long out here, I realize. But however much I'm suffering, Kiernan has it worse. The others said I was asleep for hours. I try not to think about what these conditions would do to a man in that time.

Someone touches my arm. Hutch's hair is being whipped about his face. He leans close so that I can hear him yell through the storm. "Do you remember where you last saw him?"

I wish I had a better answer to his question. Wish I'd paid more attention as I wandered. "He was somewhere high," I call back. "I mostly walked downward before getting here."

Brian nods toward distant trees. "We found you coming from that direction. It's probably the best place to start. Everyone, stay close together. Leave clear tracks; you'll need to follow them back."

Our footprints won't last long in the storm, but Brian makes no attempt to set up more permanent markers. He's planning to keep the search as short as possible, I realize. I want to fight that, but any argument is likely to end in him refusing to search at all.

"If you get separated from the group and need to find your way back, look for the pine," Brian adds. He gestures up and I see it: a massive pine grows close to the cabin. Even through the wind buffeting my ears, I can hear it creak. It must be hundreds of years old. Only the highest branches are still intact and green, creating a block of dull color far above our heads. Every branch from the two-thirds mark downward is stripped bare, sharp and jagged angles extending from the trunk. It's probably the clearest landmark for a long distance.

We push forward. Hutch stays close to my side, as though he's taken some kind of responsibility for me. Brian is to my right, with the severe blond woman on his other side, and the shaggy giant of a man past them. It's hard to see what might be ahead. Sheets of snow race across the empty land, blinding us, and I fight to snatch glimpses in the brief gaps between them. Something massive and dark is in the distance. One of the mountain walls?

I should warn them that the cliff edges are hard to see in the blizzard but bite my tongue. If I do, Brian will drag us back to the cabin. And I can't turn back. Kiernan's still out here.

"Hello!" Hutch's voice is deep and strong, but it still vanishes under the deafening pitch of the blizzard. I suck in a deep breath and taste snow on my tongue, then join him in calling for my partner.

"Kier!"

"*Hello!*"

Brian pulls a whistle out from under his layers and fits it to his lips. The frozen steel must hurt, but he doesn't flinch as he blows on it. A clear, high pitch comes out, and it's better than our voices for cutting through the gale.

Our group is slowly spreading outward. I can barely see the blond woman. The taller man has vanished entirely. I strain through the blinding snow, my feet aching each time I lift them to plunge through the ice.

Our voices create a chorus that mingles with the shrill cry coming from the whistle. *Hello, hello, Kiernan, answer me if you can hear me.*

I'm trying not to cry again. The tears will only freeze on my face and burn my skin. But the hope I've been clutching to is beginning to slip through my fingertips. These mountains are so vast, so tangled, that our only chance of finding Kiernan is if we happen to stumble on him. A lone man could be swallowed by mountains like these. Swallowed so deep that not even his bones are ever found.

The wind grows fiercer. It hits me hard enough to make me stumble, and Hutch catches me. "Easy," he calls.

We're nearly at the distant mountain face I'd seen, and our path has to turn right to avoid it. Trees cluster around the rocks, clinging to the shelter, and prickly needles scratch my skin as I push into them. Clumps of snow fall from the branches I disturb but are snatched away by the wind before they even hit the ground.

"We need to turn back."

The voice sends a sickness into my bones. Brian stands a dozen paces behind me, whistle held at his side. He dips his head in the direction we came. "We're not going to find him like this. We'll go back and try again in the morning."

I want to yell, to pull away, to forge forward on my own, but I'm broken. We can't have been out in the storm for more than fifty minutes, but I'm already close to collapse.

"We can leave the lantern," Brian calls again. "He might be drawn to the light. It'll lead him back to the cabin."

I'm too bone weary to do anything except nod.

The severe woman hangs the lantern on an exposed tree branch. Someone else pulls the cord out from the waist of their coat and uses it to tie the old metal in place, so that it won't be pulled free by the gale. Brian scratches into the tree trunk, just below the lantern: an arrow, pointing in the direction of the cabin.

They begin shuffling back. I linger a moment longer. The lantern is battery run. As long as the batteries are fresh, it should last most of the night. I touch the glass side and leave a silent prayer. *Please, Kiernan. Please find us.*

The wind redoubles, as though to spite my wish. The gale rises, and as it whistles through the rock formations, it sounds very much like a man's screams.

6.

It takes a long time to retrace our tracks in the snow and back to the cabin. I am hollowed out, like someone has taken a spoon to my insides and scraped, scraped, scraped until there is nothing left.

Without the lantern, we are nothing but vague silhouettes by the time we reach our sanctuary's door. I can't see how far the building extends, but I don't think it's large. Certainly not the lodge we were aiming for. We push inside, dragging in snow on our shoes and clothes.

The room is darker than when we left it. A small fireplace at the room's back is our only source of illumination and holds the temperature at something survivable.

The others—the ones who stayed—watch us as we enter, counting our numbers. One by one, they look away when they see we've returned alone. The only exception is Steve, the trucker. He chuckles. "Said you'd find nothing."

In my mind's eye, I picture myself striding across the cabin and slapping him. But my legs are shaking and my lungs are raw, and I'm not sure I could even form a coherent sentence in response. Instead, I drop onto the makeshift bed I woke in and begin taking the damp clothes off again. With my left hand bandaged, it's an incremental process.

"There'll be a proper search soon." Brian is shaking snow off his clothes as he surveys us. "They'll bring helicopters in as soon as it's safe."

As soon as the storm recedes. As soon as visibility returns. Soon, soon, soon, but not soon enough.

I drag the blankets around my numb body and sit back against the wall. One by one, the other searchers return to their designated portion of the room. It's the kind of space that might have felt small with three people. With ten of us, it's claustrophobic. There aren't enough places to sit, so many people are on the floor, their backs to walls and their legs awkwardly folded to avoid pushing into anyone else's space.

Miri's mouth purses as she watches me. She gives a resolute sigh, then pushes out of the double couch she shares with her husband and shuffles around to reach me. I feel shivers run through the floorboards as she sits on the floor at my side.

"Come here, hon," she says and nudges me with an elbow. "Life can be mean some days."

She says it briskly and with conviction, as though we're talking about a dropped ice cream and not the reality that the man I love is either dead or suffering horrendously.

"Give her space," the blond woman says. Although she was part of the search party and must be as exhausted as the rest of us, she's still standing, her back to the wall and her arms crossed. It's hard to be sure under the layers of clothes, but I imagine she has a gym membership and uses it. Her eyebrows lie low over blue eyes and her skin is almost translucent. She could be a model. Her body language and the frown that has been a permanent fixture on her face tells me she hears that a lot and doesn't appreciate it.

Miri flaps her hands and makes a vague noise in the back of her throat. "I'm trying to help her. Christy, right? What happened is horrible, but dwelling isn't going to fix anything."

Bile burns at the back of my throat. I reach for something—anything—to change the subject. "What is this place?"

"Not Blackstone Lodge, that's for sure," Blake, the woman with short gray hair, says. She's in a wooden chair to our right, close to the fire, her arms and legs extended to soak up the heat.

Brian nods toward the roof over us. "We were lucky to find it. The bus is designed for the snow, but it still couldn't handle the blizzard. We got the fallen tree moved out of the way just as the storm started in earnest. When you and your partner didn't return, I tried to get the others to shelter, but we lost the road and the bus became jammed in the snow. I thought we might be within walking distance of the lodge. I left to try and find a path to it, but instead…" He gestures to the walls around us. "I found this."

"It's better than the bus at least," Miri says. "Marginally."

"This is most likely a hunting cabin that was left empty over winter," Brian says. "It'll keep us warm and dry for tonight."

A table takes up the room's center. Clutter is everywhere: old books, old CDs, old towels, and bones scavenged from the wilderness and placed about like trophies. Faded paintings hang on the walls, all different sizes, the work of someone still learning the craft. The furniture is handcrafted, even down to the cushions on the couch. Everything feels worn. Whatever this building is, it's been lived in.

"Are we gonna get in trouble for, like, breaking and entering?"

It's the first time I've heard the teenager speak and his voice is unexpectedly deep. He looks like he doesn't want to be here.

"Short answer, no," Brian says. "People in regions like this tend to keep the law of hospitality. If someone's in a dire situation, you don't deny them shelter or food. We'll make sure we leave this place tidy and put a note on the table for when the owners get back in spring."

"The door was unlocked," Blake says. "Almost like they knew some poor souls would need to shelter here."

"It's probably not the first time it's happened." Brian moves toward the fireplace. There's a pot sitting just outside the flames, filled with water. He pours some of it into a cup and brings it back for me. "Whoever owns this cabin has likely had to rely on someone else's hospitality in turn. The weather can turn on a dime in this region."

"As we found." Steve claps his hands on his knees and changes his tone. "Since we're going to be stuck in such close quarters, we might as well get properly introduced, eh? I'm Steve Peltz, and I'm here with my wife, Miri. I'm a trucker. Miri raised all four of our kids, which is as much of a job as anyone could need. Me and the wife were looking forward to a solid two weeks in the wilderness, though this is a bit more than we were expecting."

"We're adapting," Miri says, and pats my arm as though she believes she's some kind of role model.

There's a brief pause. I hold the mug of warm water awkwardly. No one seems eager to go next. Then Hutch rocks forward, one hand flicking out in an abrupt wave. His piercings shimmer in the low light. "I'm Hutch. Hutch Huang. I'm a DJ and can get you all into the best clubs in So Cal should you ever visit."

Steve makes an odd huffing noise. "Didn't think you'd be the kind who'd want to visit the mountains. There aren't any parties up here, you know."

Hutch shrugs. "I'm mixing work and pleasure. At least, that was the plan. I was on my way to the lodge to check it out as a venue for a wedding next year. One groom loves skiing, and the other loves remote retreats, and they have the budget to indulge both. They wanted to confirm that the venue could handle the lights and sound system before they committed and paid for me to do the recon work."

"I wouldn't turn down a free trip either," Blake says. She glances at the rest of us. "Blake Shorey. I work as a 911 dispatcher. Did, anyway. Retired just a few weeks ago. Figured I should see some of this country while my body can still handle it."

"Oh, hey," Steve says, his face lighting up. "I have some first responders in my family. One of them used to serve in the army. You might know them—"

"Simone Wall," the severe blond woman cuts in. The attention turns to her, but she gives no further elaboration—no job or reason for the trip—and tilts her head back against the wall to indicate she's done.

A small voice pipes up to fill the silence. "Alexis Barras."

I lean forward. It's the woman with shoulder-length hair. Her fringe, which is lighter than her skin tone, grazes over her eyebrows. Two moles dot her left cheek. There's something off about her and I can't quite decide what it is. She's no older than I am—midtwenties at the most—but crease lines border the corners of her mouth. She's the kind of person I could imagine talking eagerly and laughing freely, but she's hunched in the corner of the room, between an old bookcase and the seat the tall, shaggy man occupies, her knees pulled up to her chest. Until she spoke, she had very nearly vanished into the furniture. I'm struck by the idea that that was something she welcomed. That she would be invisible if she could.

She's been just as brief as Simone and presses her lips together. Our attention slides to the tall man and the teenager at his side. He sighs, and it's a large sound, like he was holding half the room's air in his lungs. "Denny Olstead," he says, blunt and unwelcoming. "Mechanic. And my boy, Grayson."

Grayson flicks up two fingers in a silent acknowledgment.

"And you all know me," Brian says. His smile is short, tense. "Brian Hernandez. Your guide. I have an active first-aid certificate and qualifications in wilderness survival. I'll be getting you all out of here as soon as possible. You're welcome to come to me with any questions in the meantime. I'm here to help."

"I have a question," Blake says. Her lipstick is shockingly bright in the candlelight. "What happens after this? Not to be insensitive to today's events, but are we still going to the lodge?"

Brian chuckles nervously. He sends a short glance in my direction. "We're going to decide all of that tomorrow, once we can speak to the rescue workers. I'm anticipating that the trip can continue. For those who want to."

For those whose partners aren't lost in the wilderness.

My stomach turns. I pull the blankets tighter around myself, like a wall. We should be out there, looking for him.

It's then that the premonition hits me, stronger than any I've felt in a long time—stronger even than the one on August 8—and I lean forward and close my eyes as a cold sweat breaks out over my flesh.

None of us are getting out of here alive.

7.

The storm won't stop.

It tears at the trees outside our cabin. Sometimes I hear the branches being ripped off, and I can't stop imagining Kiernan, struggling to fight his way through the inhospitable landscape. I wad the blankets up and press them against my ears, but it's not enough to block out the howls.

The others are restless. There's a little food in the cupboard and Brian doles it out, giving us each a serving on a saucer or in a mug: beans and crackers and rice cooked over the fire. I make myself eat. I'll need the energy. The moment dawn rises over the horizon, I'll return outside and search for Kiernan again. I doubt I can convince the others to go out with me again. But if there's a chance—even a tiny, paper-thin chance—I won't give up on him.

People have survived worse. They've dragged themselves across tundras and deserts. They've clung to flotsam in the ocean, sometimes for months. There are even cases of people being revived after being frozen solid.

Kiernan is strong. Not just physically but emotionally. What he went through could have snuffed anyone else's light out, but it only made his burn brighter. He's going to live.

He has to.

Conversations are brief. Some of the guests pick through the books on the shelves, but they're mostly nonfiction and old. Brian sits forward in his chair, his expression open, as he fields questions and gives assurances.

Our shelter doesn't have a bathroom. When we need to relieve ourselves, we're supposed to go outside and walk as far from the cabin as we safely can without losing sight of it. People leave, looking embarrassed as they fumble with the door, then come back in squinting and sour.

There's a clock on the highest shelf of the bookcase. It's small and bronze and hard to read in the firelight. I watch the hands burrow into the morning's rawest hours. It's nearly two when I curl up in the makeshift bed and try to force myself to sleep.

The wind screams. The window above my head rattles, and I almost imagine someone is on the other side, frantically beating their open hand against the glass.

The others have worked on their own version of beds, divvying up the blankets found in the closet and the couch's cushions for pillows. Those who aren't lucky enough to get the prime pickings do the best they can. Hutch lies on his side, a spare jacket bundled under his head. He has his cell phone out and its screen lights up his face. I have a vague memory of Steve yelling at someone about their phone when I was barely conscious. I wonder if that was Hutch.

Sleep teases at me, only to be ripped away each time someone moves. None of us seem able to rest well, except perhaps Simone, the severe woman, and Denny, the giant of a man. Steve and Miri attempt to share the couch, but it's crowded and their grunts and whispered reprimands repeatedly cut through the silence.

The clock slinks past two. Blake, who was granted some of the few blankets, sighs and throws them aside. She gets up and shuffles toward the bookcase, apparently looking for a distraction.

"Can't sleep?" Miri whispers as she passes.

"This is hell on my back." Blake eyes the couch. "Don't suppose there's room for me to sit? Just for a moment?"

Steve groans as Miri shoves him. The pair of them shuffle over, and Blake sighs as she drops in next to them. I can't see from where I lie on the floor, but I know the couch isn't large. Their thighs must be pressed together.

"I used to work night shift when I was a 911 dispatcher," Blake says, her voice soft but the *s* sounds whistling. "I'm still trying to get used to a normal sleep schedule."

"I'm sure this place isn't helping." Miri's voice is sluggish, sleepy. She shuffles, trying to get comfortable. "It's not the twelve-hundred thread count of the lodge we were promised."

"Fingers crossed for tomorrow," Blake says. There's a pause. "I don't mean to sound callous. I feel for that girl, let me tell you. But you learn, as a responder, not to hold on to things too tight."

"Guess you'd have to," Steve mumbles.

I shuffle my legs to make some noise, hoping they'll get the hint and stop talking about me.

"The things you hear on the job could turn a person's blood to ice." Blake seems oblivious. She tilts her head back, sighing. "Especially overnight, and especially on the weekends. Had one not long before I retired where a kid's car went off the road. His entire face was sliced away. The skin just ripped clear off. He was still alive and moving. His friend was in the car and she was the one who called me, and she just kept saying, *I can see the muscles, I can see the bones.* Can't imagine how someone would get past that."

A sour tang permeates my mouth. I'm not sure if it's caused by the story or by the flippant way Blake tells it. Like it's the kind of memory she calls up occasionally so that she can dwell on it. Like she has an entire mental catalog of them: the skin-crawling and the macabre, ready to be reviewed and redigested when she has a quiet moment or two.

Someone—Hutch, I think—whisper-calls, "Just go to sleep already," and Blake sighs in response before climbing out of the couch.

The window rattles above my head. I turn to face the wall, eyes wide and burning. The door creaks open and closed multiple times as people leave to use the bathroom. My mouth is dry. The longer I lie there, the harder it becomes to ignore, so I creep out of bed and cross to the fireplace, where the pot of water sits just beside the coals. I dip my mug into it, then cradle it as I stare at my place beneath the window and the view beyond.

The wind tears the outside world into constant motion. Torrents of snow flash past the window like static, until I can't even see the distant trees.

Brian's place by the fire is empty. He must have needed the bathroom. There's a stack of papers, facedown, where he sat.

The others are all still and quiet, either asleep or close to. I bend down. The papers don't match anything else in the cabin; they're crisp and white. Recent.

I turn one over and see Kiernan's signature.

8.

My hands shake as I carefully spread the papers out on the floor. The familiar name near the sheet's base is achingly familiar: Kiernan Marshall, followed by his tidy scrawl of a signature.

I flip through the pages and see more names. Denny Olstead. Blake Shorey. Simone Wall.

And at last, my own. My signature is slightly shaky. I remember writing it. I'd been both sleepy and jittery, the recently consumed coffee amping my anxiety but without clearing the fog.

We'd signed these papers the previous morning, before boarding the bus taking us into the mountains.

They were the liability indemnification contracts.

Brian must have brought them with him when disembarking the bus. He hadn't thought to take any food, drinking water, or any of our luggage. But he'd brought the forms.

And he'd been reading them. When I was trapped in the fugue of exhaustion, while Simone bandaged my hand and when I'd mistaken Brian's hunched form for Kiernan's, I'd seen him bent over the table, examining something. The papers.

He'd wanted to make sure he had all of our signatures. That the wording, which only took up one page, was watertight.

While Kiernan was dying outside, he was making sure he couldn't be held responsible.

Anger burns deep in my stomach. I'm tempted to throw the contracts into the fireplace. He'll be more eager to search for Kiernan if he no longer has his signature, I'm sure.

I steady my hands and place the papers back onto the floor, facedown, the way I found them. Brian still isn't back. I bring my mug of cooling water to my bed and sit, sipping it, until the fury in my guts cools to something more manageable.

It isn't Brian's fault. I can't blame him for seeking protection when something bad happens.

I did exactly the same once.

Images flash on the back of my eyelids. The churning water. The voices. "Is there anything we can do?"

The blood trailing down my arms.

I can't let myself spiral, no matter how close I am. I have to focus. The floor is hard and unforgiving under the blanket. Daylight will be here in a very few hours, and if I am going to find Kiernan, I need at least some kind of rest.

The storm sounds louder, angrier. It's not subsiding. There can be no official search—no helicopters—until it does.

Somehow, I sleep. Dreams are scattered and angry. I wake anytime the door opens or someone turns over in their bed. The fire is growing low and the room chillier.

When I next open my eyes, a pale light glazes the wooden ceiling above. It's dawn. And that means I can start searching again.

I jolt out of bed and begin struggling into the outer layers I'll need to survive the ice outside. Miri, half-draped over the edge of the couch next to me, mumbles at the disturbance.

"Does anyone know where Brian is?" Blake asks. She looks like she's only recently woken; her short, gray hair is flattened on one side and her lipstick is smudged. She stands next to the fireplace, her shoe almost touching the papers, holding a cup of warm water.

Brian's place is still empty. I scan the room and see the others are stirring. Alexis, the girl with pale hair, looks bloodless. Almost frightened. She's on her knees, hands braced on the floor ahead of her, as she cranes forward to examine the room.

"Probably needed the bathroom," Simone offers. She's in the exact same position I last saw her: back to the wall, legs askew, arms folded. Her head is down, her chin resting on her chest, the angle hiding her eyes.

"I woke earlier," I say. "Hours ago. He was gone then too."

"Weak bladder?" Blake offers, but the words fade out as we glance between ourselves.

The far more likely answer is that he became lost. He encouraged us to walk as far as we could from the cabin to avoid contaminating the area. He'd also emphasized the importance of not losing sight of the light, but that wasn't always easy in the blizzard. He could have become turned around. Taken a few too many steps in the wrong direction. And lost us entirely.

A small thrill of hope passes through me, and I hate myself for it. But there's no ignoring the reality that my companions will be more willing to search the land around us if Brian is missing too.

Already, people are shucking into their outer coats. Denny's jacket must be a XXXL, but it still looks too small on him. Simone tucks her ponytail under her cap. Hutch fights to get his boots on.

All the same people who joined me in my search the previous night. I stare at Steve, and he finally sighs and reaches for his coat.

"Give the guide a minute," Blake says. "He'll be back."

My right hand fumbles with my coat's zipper. My left is still sealed inside its bandage wrap. The back of the hand hurts horrendously, but I can't feel the fingers. I turn my mind away from that before I can dwell on it too much.

Simone is already at the door. I'm surprised to see Alexis, who I thought was a permanent fixture in the corner, is coming with us. Even Miri begins to shake out her coat, though apathetically.

We spill outside. The snow has blown around the door and I have to clamber over it. The winds are still high, funneling tracks of snow across the landscape. Visibility is a shade better than it was at night. I can vaguely see the mountain walls in the distance. I make a note of them in relation to where we are now, knowing I might need as many landmarks as possible to find my way back.

"Where to?" Hutch yells to be heard over the wind.

"Fan out." That's Denny. He turns toward the closest patch of trees. "Look for footprints in the snow."

Our movements are hesitant as we branch outward. I have to bend to search the snow. The parts I can see look unblemished. I wonder how long it would take wind this vicious to fill footprints. Not too long, most likely. Our tracks from the previous evening are gone.

It's dawn, but only just barely. The cabin and my companions are nothing but silhouettes, all sickly ruddy color against the gray-white land. The chill is already stealing my breath and burning my exposed face. I aim toward some trees, thinking, if I were Brian or Kiernan and I couldn't walk any farther, I'd at least try to take some shelter.

The branches rain powdery snow as I shove through them. The trunks sway in the wind. They create terrible noises—groaning, creaking, cracking—as though, any second, they could come crashing down and crush me. I stay just long enough to be sure there are no irregular, huddled shapes around the trunks, and then backtrack.

A small object clings to one of the last trees in the cluster. In the poor light and snow-dense air it takes me a moment to recognize it. It's the lantern we left there the previous night.

Its light has gone out. But not because its batteries failed.

Someone has smashed it.

9.

My heart is in my throat.

The lamp is nothing but a clump of tangled metal and broken glass shards. It's still attached to the tree: the cord we used to tie it in place cinches it there. But it rocks erratically, rattling in the wind, threatening to jar the little remaining glass free.

Did the storm do this?

That feels unlikely. It was strong, but I can't picture it twisting the metal frame like this. It feels more like someone took a rock to it, smashing it in, snuffing out the light. The bulb inside is shattered.

Did one of the people in the cabin do this?

They could have. Plenty of them left for the bathroom last night. I didn't pay any attention to the timing. Someone could have easily spent half an hour outside, breaking the lantern in a fit of rage.

Why, though?

And if not one of the tour group, then who?

I back away from the lantern. It feels like a bad omen. Like something I shouldn't get too close to.

A voice calls loudly. They've found something.

Grateful for the distraction, I turn my back on the wrecked lantern and begin jogging.

Hutch emerges from the trees near the cabin, clutching his hood in place as he wades through the snow. Denny emerges from a different section of the forest and Blake, who was staying close to the cabin, joins me to meet him halfway.

"I found a building," Hutch says, breathless. He points, his thick gloves indicating to the grove he just came from. "A shed or something."

Blake leans forward. "Is Brian in there?"

"I don't know. I don't think so. The door's locked."

"No, then," Denny says. "Keep searching."

We part again, Blake retreating to the sheltered area around the cabin, Denny cutting across the field toward the dark cliff walls in the distance, Hutch back in the direction of the trees.

I turn to circle the cabin and search around its other side. The ground becomes uneven there, the snow disguising jagged rocks. I climb one of them, getting some height, and crane my neck to see the expanse beyond.

The cabin appears to be in some kind of bowl-like valley. That was how I'd stumbled on it before; by following the land downhill, I'd been funneled toward it. I'm grateful I'd wandered into this valley and not any of the hundreds of others that must dot the region.

The land on this side of the cabin is too rugged and too dangerous. Gaps between the rocks, invisible beneath the snow, threaten to twist ankles and break bones. I doubt either Brian or Kiernan would willingly trek through it. I turn back.

The massive pine near the cabin must be close to a hundred feet tall. Standing isolated like that, it's a miracle the wind hasn't felled it by now. The top branches—the only green left on it—whip down and then back under the force of the wind. My eyes trail along its length, tracing the broken and rotting branches leading to its base.

There's some color there. I approach, slowly, eyes squinted against the blinding snow. A smear of vivid red discolors the field of white. It's already been mostly covered by fresh snow, but the color still bleeds through.

It's blood. I try to shut the thought down. It could be many things. Rust from scrap metal buried under the snow, discarded paint, even a scrap of red clothing that was lost out here. It was too dark to see the ground the previous night. For all I know, it might have been here for years.

I ignore the pain in my legs as I crouch to see it better. The massive pine casts its shadow across me. The slow, creaking, cracking reverberations from its wood rise out of the whistling wind and I try not to think about the trunk splintering.

Using my gloved hand, I dig into the snow to uncover more of the color. It's definitely some kind of liquid. It's soaked into the snow and frozen into large, sharp crystals. They crumple when I squeeze them in my palm. I raise a handful to smell, but my nose has lost a lot of its sensitivity. There might be a metallic undercurrent. I'm not sure.

I drop the crimson-tinted ice and take a few steps back. It doesn't seem like a coincidence that it's here so close to the pine. I tilt my head up to search the branches directly above.

There's something there. A shape, roundish but irregular. A bird's nest? No. Large wasp nest? Unlikely in this region. Mistletoe or some other fungal or parasitic protrusion?

It's hard to see from my angle. The rising dawn acts as a backlight, silhouetting it. I shuffle around, trying to get a better angle. The sides are smooth, but the top is ragged, somehow, strands of something delicate fluttering in the wind like fine grass. It protrudes from the end of one of the dead branches.

I take another step and suddenly the image makes sense. My mouth turns dry.

Speared onto the end of the branch is something horrendously familiar. Brian's head.

10.

We're all going to die here.

The head rocks as the wind pulls at it. Brian's hair whips in a loose flurry on top. His jaw is stretched open, the jagged edge of the tree branch pierces through, protruding like a second tongue. His eyes are open but dull, like his skin. Frozen. He's been up there for some time.

There's a muffled, gasping scream behind me. Miri cuts the sound off abruptly, pressing the back of her gloved hand to her mouth. Her eyes bulge, the lids seeming to vanish into the skin around them, then she turns away.

Others heard. Footsteps race toward us. Denny arrives first, Hutch not far behind him, Simone appearing through the gusting snow like a phantom. Still more close in behind her. One by one they approach Miri, then me, asking questions that go unanswered, before following my eyeline toward the tree.

Denny is completely silent as he stares up at the head. Steve mutters an expletive. It's soft, almost reverent.

I feel numb. Disconnected. The initial shock is morphing into disbelief.

Brian is dead.

More than dead. Butchered. Mutilated. Put on display.

It doesn't seem possible. He was here just hours ago, smiling and answering questions and trying to placate. He helped me search for Kiernan. He was working on a plan for today.

The head in the tree *can't* be his.

And yet…it is.

The tree branch enters through his severed neck, stabbing through flesh and muscle to protrude out of his open mouth. Hair dances on top of his head, whipped about and tangled by the wind. Blood smears across sections of his bloodless skin.

Our tour guide left the cabin sometime within the last few hours. And he was killed.

I turn, trying to read my companions' expressions. They're hard to discern in the early light. Miri still won't look at the tree, but she doesn't try to leave either. Steve grips her shoulder, his jaw taut. Grayson's brows rise, stretching his face out and widening his already large eyes. Simone is rigid, veins standing out on her throat and forehead. Hutch has turned away, one hand pressed to his stomach.

Alexis's features are stiff, her eyebrows low, her gaze steely. It's not the reaction I expected from her.

Blake regards the head with an analytical air, her lips pursed—911 dispatcher, I remind myself, though that's less of an explanation and more of a thin excuse.

Steve is the first to break the silence. "Who did this?"

It's as though he expects one of us to raise our hand. *That was me. Sorry for the inconvenience.* No one speaks, but eyes flash from one face to another. I feel more than one set land on me for an uncomfortable amount of time.

"Bears," Miri says. She's ash white. "Are there bears…?"

"Wild animals didn't do this, love," Steve says. His jaw works, the facial hair catching the light. "His head's been cut clean off. This was a human. One of us."

Hutch's head jolts up. "You think someone from our group…?"

Steve stretches an arm out, indicating to the sparse wilderness surrounding us. He's not quite yelling, but his voice isn't calm either. "There's not much alternative, is there?"

"Stop and think a minute." Blake stamps her feet, agitated. "The cabin door was unlocked when we got here. Remember? It just pushed right open."

"I remember," Simone says.

"That's because the owners never left," Blake says. "I'll bet they're still here, somewhere. Staying close by. And they don't want guests."

"It doesn't even have to be them," Simone says, frowning. "There could be other accommodations within walking distance. We don't know how many people might live in this region."

"So…" Steve nods toward the head above us. "Some neighbor was wandering around during a snowstorm, saw a man leave the cabin to take a leak, and decided to cut his head off and stick it on a tree. Is that what you're saying?"

"Stop it." Miri's voice is brisk, but her hands are unsteady as she tugs the pack of cigarettes and lighter out of her pocket. She lights one, then draws on it deeply, almost desperately. Her jaw trembles as she exhales the smoke.

"I can't buy it being the people who lived here either," Hutch says. "We've been here since, what? Yesterday afternoon. What have they been doing in that time? Where have they been staying? They can't be out in the storm; they'd freeze."

Blake shakes her head. "What's the other option? That one of us killed him?"

"We'd have the opportunity." That's Grayson. The deepness of his voice catches me off guard again. He's managed to shake off the stupor but keeps glancing toward the head. "Most of us were asleep. Someone who wanted to hurt the guide could have waited for him to go outside and followed."

"You'd still need a motive," Steve says.

Blake turns on me, her eyes narrow and cold. "He didn't want to help you search for your friend. That seemed to tick you off pretty badly."

That's enough to pull me free from the shock. Heat blooms across my face. My voice shakes, and there's nothing I can do to stop it. "You think attacking our tour guide would get me any closer to finding Kiernan?"

"But if you were angry—"

"I don't care about angry. I care about finding my boyfriend." My voice chokes entirely, and I'm furious at it giving out on me. "Brian knows this region better than any of us. He could have helped. I needed him."

"We all did," Denny notes. His massive shoulders shift. "He was the one getting us out of here."

Silence falls over the group. I don't want to look at the head again, but I force myself to. Small icicles made of blood hang from his jaw and throat. It's hard to see from my angle, but the exposed flesh where the neck was severed looks rough in some places, smooth in others. Was his head taken off in two or three blows? Or sliced through by a skilled butcher?

"We need to know where he was killed," Hutch says. His arms are wrapped around his torso and I don't think it's just from the cold. "Inside the forest? Behind the cabin?"

Blake mutely points to the blood mixed into the ice. I'd assumed it must have dripped from the severed head, but now I realize there's too much for that. It's soaked down deep.

"They killed him right here," Blake says, blunt. "Outside our cabin while we slept. Did anyone hear strange noises in the night? Sounds of a struggle, something like that?"

I was closest to the window. I try to think back. The wind had been intense, sounding like a hundred hands beating against the cabin's walls through the night.

"No one could hear anything over the storm," Hutch says. "And I don't think he could have been killed here. There's no body."

Blake shrugs. "They dragged it away. Hid it somewhere."

"Okay, but *why*?" Hutch is growing agitated. "Not to hide the murder because they left the head."

"People do strange things and for strange reasons," Blake says. "I learned that while taking all those calls. Sometimes it's drugs. Sometimes it's something wrong in the head. Sometimes you can't ever figure out a reason, even if you have a panel of psychologists working on it."

"But—"

"One man called me to tell me he'd drowned his two-year-old son. He was calm as could be. Apologetic almost. It had been a normal day; he and his wife had gone to bed as usual, but a bit after midnight he'd gotten up again, run a bath, and carried that boy to it. I asked him why he'd done it and he just said, 'I don't know, it seemed like I had to.' So, yeah, I can believe this too."

A horrible silence falls over us. My suspicion was right: Blake has a collection of stories she files away for later reflection.

"What do we do now?" Miri's still close to her husband, her face white except for blotches of red on her cheeks. Her cigarette is almost burnt out; flecks of soot dot the white snow around her feet.

Denny raises a hand and points. "Hutch found a shed that way. We need to know if there's anyone inside."

11.

We face the knot of windswept trees behind the cabin. I squint, trying to see through the bowed branches and constant flecks of snow, and think I can make out something dark and hulking in the distance.

"We should wait," Blake says. Perspiration dots her upper lip. "Brian called for search and rescue yesterday. They'll be here any minute."

"They won't." Denny points to the sky. There must be vicious clouds up there, but they're invisible thanks to the blanketing, frenzied snow.

His point is clear. There won't be any helicopters until the weather gives us relief.

"We can wait," Simone says, "wondering if someone or something is hiding in there, or we can open that shed and know for sure."

Steve hangs near the rear of the group. "We don't have any weapons. There could be more than one of them. What if they have a gun?"

Denny is unfazed. "If they did, they would have shot the guide, not beheaded him."

I'm not sure I can share in his conviction, but he's already begun to move toward the trees. Simone follows, matching his long paces. The others hesitate, then begin to trail after in drips.

As we walk, I can't stop myself from stealing glances at my companions. Especially their jacket sleeves and gloves. If one of them was responsible for Brian's death, there should be signs. The murder would have been violent. A lot of blood sprayed free and soaked into the snow.

I can't see any red on those nearest to me, but I don't know how well planned the attack was. They could have worn spare clothes and changed out of them before returning to the cabin. They could have even taken some of the water from beside the fire and washed up. We were all asleep or at least trying to ignore our neighbors. The killer could have taken hours to clean themselves and still not been missed.

It's a strange feeling to know you might be walking beside someone who's taken a life. Technically, the statistics on that are ugly on a regular day: the average person is likely to cross paths with three to ten murderers in their lifetime, including not-insignificant odds of having one inside their broad social group.

Still, that's better than what I'm facing. The possibility that one of the eight people around me is a killer.

A memory pushes into my mind. August 8. I see the man's face again. Reddish-blond hair. Wild eyes. He was so young. My skin turns cold and I put my head down.

Tree branches crackle as we enter a narrow passageway between the trunks. I can see the shed more clearly now. It's wood, like the cabin, and not much smaller. There are no windows, just a door, set squarely into the building's front. A padlock seals it closed.

We form a loose semicircle around the doorway. Denny rattles the lock, but it holds solid. He grunts and turns aside, riffling through the snow, and returns a moment later with a rock the size of his fist.

I know it's coming, but I still flinch when I hear the snap of stone against metal. Denny raises the rock again and brings it down a second time. I'm transfixed by the way his body moves under his coat. Muscles swell the layers of padding. He would have no difficulty severing a head or dragging a body away.

A third blow. The metal snaps, the sound cracking around my ears. The cabin's hasp shears away, its screws pulled out of the wood, and Denny pulls it out and tosses it aside.

"We need a weapon," Steve repeats, but Denny has already opened the door.

His huge body blocks the entrance. I'm frozen, my hands limp at my sides, as I watch with mounting anxiety. I'm afraid his head is about to burst apart, a well-aimed bullet cutting through bone and brain. Or that there will be a heavy, meaty slap as an ax gouges into his flesh. He leans forward, hands braced on either side of the doorway, and huffs. "Anyone have a light?"

"Here." Hutch steps forward. His hands are shaking, but he's brought his cell phone out of his pocket and switched the flashlight on.

Denny takes it and angles it into the room. I still can't see around his shoulders, except for glimpses of wood and metal surfaces. Then Denny steps inside.

He fades into a distant shadow as he swings the light from side to side. The shed is longer than it is wide, and he presses deeper into the tangle of contents.

Simone follows behind him. She pulls the door back and checks behind it, and the movement is so smooth that I wonder if she's had practice. Hutch hesitates, sending a tense glance back at the remaining group, then steps inside as well.

Sounds echo. The thump of boots. Heavy, panting breaths. A clatter: something metallic being knocked over.

I can't stand it any longer. I push past Miri and step up to the doorway.

12.

The space is far more cluttered than the cabin. A lifetime accumulation of items fills nearly every available inch. I see gardening tools; the snow must melt enough during summer to allow for it. Wicker chairs, some broken, some discolored, are stacked into a cluster that throws nauseating shadows against the walls.

Shelves are stacked about, a meek attempt at categorization. They hold pumps, motors, machines. Most so dusty and rusted that I doubt they would work any longer. Near the back of the shed, items have simply been left in piles, like the midway stages of hoarding. Tarpaulins are draped over sections to protect them from dust.

Denny has completed a loop of the shed, clambering over one of the piles to make it back to the door. "Empty," he confirms.

Reactions are mixed. Miri pats her chest to indicate her heart has been racing. Blake nods, a quick, perfunctory movement. Grayson scuffs his shoe in a motion that could be interpreted as disappointment.

Alexis, who has been clinging to the back of the group, keeps her head down. I can't see her eyes under her fringe. I don't like that.

Denny waits until we're all outside, then pushes the door closed again. There's nothing to do about the broken lock. It will have to stay open until the owners return.

"What now?" Miri asks. She glances behind us, toward the cabin. "I mean, what are we supposed to do next?"

I don't think any of us knows. There's no handbook for what to do when your companion is killed during a remote vacation.

"There's no reception out here," Hutch says, pocketing his phone. "I already tried last night. And then again just now. Zero bars."

Simone speaks. "Help's on its way. We're going to stay here until rescue services arrive."

I can see Miri's throat bob as she swallows thickly. "Can we at least get Brian's head off the tree?"

It's a horrible question, but one that's been lurking at the back of my mind since I first saw him. I already know the answer and close my eyes as Simone delivers it.

"That's a crime scene. We can't touch it."

Miri makes a faint, unhappy noise. "It's right outside the cabin, though—"

"And if you lay your hands on it, you'll be implicating yourself." Simone's tone brooks no arguments, and Miri drops the question.

For a moment, we stand there, our shoulders hunched against the icy wind. Then Simone speaks, her voice ringing loud. "We don't know what happened to Brian. But this is obviously no longer a safe location. We're returning to the cabin. No one will be allowed to leave until help arrives. Understood?"

There are weak mutters of assent. One at a time, the others turn to march through the trees to the shack we're staying in. My heart catches in my throat. I jog to catch up to Simone. "I have to search for Kiernan."

"No one's leaving," she repeats, sharp and unforgiving.

"He's out there. He needs help. I can't abandon him."

Blake, just behind me, lets out a barking laugh. "Maybe *he's* the one who killed Brian. Revenge for being left behind."

I send her the harshest glare I can. She just laughs more.

Stay calm. Focus. Kiernan needs you. Getting into fights won't save him.

"If you won't come, at least let me go alone," I say to Simone. "It's morning now. Visibility's better. This might be my last chance to find him."

"If you do, a hundred-to-one odds say you'll be finding a corpse."
Simone is taller than me by half a head, and it feels like more. Her glare
softens a fraction as she stares down at me. "I'll give you two hours."

I don't know why I'm accepting time limits from a woman who
shouldn't have any authority over me, but I'm too desperate to turn
anything down. "Sure."

"Hang on." It's Grayson, the teen. Long black hair trails down to his
shoulder blades. He's wiry, thinner than his father, but he inherited some
of his height. Unlike Denny, Grayson slouches to mask it. He glances from
me to Simone, his sunken eyes conflicted. "What if she did that to Brian?
She could be trying to escape."

"Realistically," Simone says, turning back to our walk, "if she *did* kill
someone, would you really want to keep her inside the cabin with us?"

That ends the discussion. I return to the cabin with the others, but
instead of tugging off my outer layers, I grab Kiernan's scarf from the wall
and loop it around my throat.

"It's a suicide mission," Steve says with faint amusement as he
watches me.

I ignore him.

Then Denny approaches. "Girl," he says, to get my attention.

I swallow a lump in my throat. "Christa."

A slight roll of his shoulders suggests he doesn't care to know my name.
He holds up a scarf. It's come from the cabin's cupboards, I suspect; not
quite thick enough for these temperatures, it's designed to be draped over
shoulders or used to tie hair back. It's dyed a deep crimson.

He waits to see I'm watching, then picks at one of the many loose
threads on the side and pulls. A strip of fabric tears off cleanly, about a foot
long. He passes me both the scarf and the loose end.

"Tie strips around tree branches as you go," he says, already turning
from me. "So you can find your way back."

"Oh." I clutch the material tightly. He was one of the few to help search for Kiernan the previous day, I remember. "Will you help me? We can go in opposite directions—"

"I'll look for someone for as long as there's hope they're alive." That's all he says, but I understand his meaning as he crosses to his chair.

As far as he's concerned, Kiernan is dead.

They're wrong to give up on him. His odds might be slim and dropping with every passing hour, but Kiernan is a fighter. He's survived worse than this.

I leave the cabin, pulling the thick knit scarf up over the lower half of my face as I return to the frozen world outside. Miri calls out, "Good luck!" and I think the phrase is echoed by Alexis, though she's too quiet for me to be certain.

My hip still aches and the multitude of bruises make my limbs stiff, but I set up a fast pace as I move away from the cabin. Kiernan's scarf still smells like him. Tears prick my eyes.

The storm hasn't abated, but it's slowed enough that I can make good headway. I pass the crushed lantern tied to the tree. I know the road back to the cabin from there, so I mentally designate it as the first marker. Then, just as the lantern is fading at the edge of my visibility, I stop by another tree and tie the first strip of the crimson fabric there, angling the knot so that it points in the direction I need to travel.

The scarf is very red. My mind returns to the pool of blood underneath the tree. I close my eyes, trying not to dwell on it, then drag a gust of biting air into my lungs and move forward.

I spend more than four hours out in the wilderness. Every few minutes, I call Kiernan's name and wait to see if I can catch even a faint, distant response.

I can't give up that small slice of hope that keeps me moving, keeps me *breathing*. But I'm not searching effectively. I stumble over hills and into valleys, my path blocked by cliff walls and threatening drops at every turn. My lines aren't straight, no matter how hard I try to make them. I'm walking blind, trailing my way across the mountainside like an ant wandering lost through a kitchen. The environment is vast. For all I know, I could be covering ground I've already walked over.

Tears freeze on my eyelashes as I tie off the final, scant strip of red fabric. I'm exhausted already. Frustrated with myself. Frantic and hollowed out all at once.

Focus. I run my tongue over my lips and taste tacky froth. *What can we do better?*

I need a map and a compass. I need to mark off areas that have been searched. Break the region into a grid. Try to pick the most likely locations first—valleys and crevasses—and work out from there. No matter how frantically my heart beats in my chest or how pressing the desperation becomes, I can't fling myself about wildly. Kiernan has the best chances if I'm careful about how I search.

As I follow the thin trail of red markers back toward home, I cling to the idea that I haven't completely wasted precious time. He might stumble onto the markers. He might understand that he needs to follow them. I leave them where I tied them.

My throat gave out before I was halfway through the walk, and now, on the return trip, I can't even call for Kiernan. Brian's whistle would have helped. If we'd found his body, I might have been able to salvage it. I grimace, hating myself for the thought.

Afternoon shadows pool across the valley as I come out through a narrow pass and find myself within eyesight of the broken lantern. The storm is easing. Not as fast as it needs to, but each hour the visibility gets slightly better, from four feet to ten to twenty to forty.

My legs shake. My lungs are raw and I'm desperate for a drink as I push myself toward the cabin. The firelight plays through the windows, and for a second it almost looks like a Christmas photograph: wood cabin, unblemished snow coating all surfaces, golden light in the window.

Then I hear the voices. Raised, yelling. Something breaks inside the cabin. Someone screams.

13.

The door shudders as I reach for the handle. Simone's voice barks over the noise, "Stop!"

I wrench the door open. A tangle of limbs and hair and snarling teeth writhes on the floor. Grayson and Hutch are fighting.

Miri screams as they rock too close to her. She's pressed tight against the wall, disgust distorting her features, Steve standing beside her with one arm held out in front of her.

Denny reaches for his son, to pull him out of the fray. There's the electric snap of tearing fabric and then Grayson rolls out of his grip.

Simone yells again, and it's more a bark of anger than any coherent word. She dips in, trying to separate them, then steps back with a grunt as an elbow hits her shin.

"Get them apart," Steve yells, but he still doesn't move from his place by the wall.

Over the fighting bodies, I see Blake. She's on the other side of the table, leaning forward, her eyes wide and eager, the corners of her mouth twitching upward.

Then Denny reaches into the fight and gets his arms around Grayson. He hauls back. The teen is a ball of rage, a writhing wildcat, all bared teeth and hisses. He fights to get free, but Denny's grip tightens so much that I'm frightened I'll hear cracking bones.

Hutch scrambles back, one hand pressed to his face. Spots of blood spurt from between his fingers.

"Get that kid under control!" Steve yells.

He doesn't need to. Grayson is growing still, his energy spent. His long black hair hangs across his face, wet with spittle and possibly tears.

"What the hell," Hutch manages. He drops his hand to see the blood, then presses it back into place.

I feel small, trapped. The room's atmosphere is toxic. No one pays any attention to me as I close the door behind myself and edge along the wall.

"Sit down, boy," Denny mutters, finally dropping him. Grayson uses his sleeve to swipe the sweaty hair out of his face. His lip is split; a trail of red smears away from it. He limps as he crosses the room, putting as much distance between himself and Hutch as possible before slumping down against the wall.

Simone crouches in front of Hutch to examine his face. He moves away from her, reaching for something small and silver on the floor. My stomach twists. One of his studs was pulled out during the fight.

I need to know what happened. Simone is simmering, though, bright fury gleaming in the sweat on her face. Steve and Miri whisper to one another. Blake has settled back against the opposite wall, but her eyes are still large and keen.

Alexis stands next to the bookcase, half-hidden in the shadows. She's the least-threatening person here. I creep past Steve and Miri, and Miri gives my arm a quick squeeze to acknowledge me before going back to Steve.

"Hey," I whisper as I stop beside Alexis. "What happened?"

Her eyes are a dark color, not quite black but close. The two moles on her cheek bob as she gives me a tense smile, and she scratches her forehead, pushing part of the fringe away. "I don't really know."

She pauses, her eyes darting to the others. Grayson is sitting, surly and angry, and Denny looms over him, talking in a quiet but unforgiving voice. Simone has given Hutch a cloth to press to the cuts on his face and is boiling water by the fire. Alexis clears her throat and leans a fraction closer to me. "Grayson and Hutch were talking. I think Hutch made a joke, and it set Grayson off."

"Oh." I file that away. Grayson is volatile and possibly sensitive about certain topics.

Alexis glances aside and clears her throat again. "I'm sorry. I didn't get to say it earlier but—I'm sorry about what happened to your partner. Were you married?"

"No." The question creates a deep ache. Twenty-four hours ago, I thought we might be close to an engagement. I try very, very hard not to crumple into myself. "He's my boyfriend."

"Ah." She shuffles, and her mouth twists. It's an expressive mouth. Once again I get the impression that she would be the lively friend in any group. The bubbly friend, the one who laughs and claps and is the first to suggest going to the dance floor. It's hard to reconcile that mental image with the woman next to me: quiet, anxious. Trying to hide herself inside the shadows.

She sends me another glance and her tongue works at the inside of her mouth. She's chewing something over, trying to decide if she should speak. Then she presses her lips together and turns away.

I take the cue and leave her, crossing to the fireplace to get a drink before returning to my space under the window. Someone took my blanket while I was gone. Maybe they didn't expect me back. I sit on the floor, my knees pulled up to my chest.

Simone's finished working on Hutch. I wonder why she's the designated first-aid person; she tended to my hand the day before too, even though Brian made a point of bringing up his first-aid certificate.

I fidget with the edges of the bandages. The red spots have dulled to a rusty brown. I try to flex the fingers underneath and feel a deep soreness in my bones.

Hutch is restless. He paces the cabin, picking up objects and then putting them down again. A square bandage is taped to the side of his face, covering the torn skin. Denny sits, perfectly still and silent but as full of potent fury as a storm, with his son at his side. Grayson is hunched, his arms crossed over his raised knees and his head buried behind them.

The atmosphere is as poisonous as it can get. I'll stay just long enough to rehydrate and find a map, if possible, and then return to the search. They're all so distracted that they might not notice me leaving.

"How much longer till these rescue people get here?" Steve asks. He wasn't involved in the fight but he's absorbed the room's sour tone. And there's perhaps something else. Something that's been simmering there since the previous night and is only growing worse.

He wants a drink, I realize. He was banking on a beer or maybe something harder when we got to the lodge, and now he hasn't had anything in more than a day.

My stomach turns. I'm glad the cabin doesn't have any alcohol. In a place as big as a lodge, Steve would be easy to avoid, but there's nowhere to hide in our current shelter.

"The storm's getting lighter," Simone says. "They should have arrived by now if they're coming by helicopter. Did Brian tell them there was a man missing and possibly dead?"

There's an uncomfortable kind of silence. Simone clears her throat. "Did anyone hear him place the call?"

"He didn't on the bus." Miri speaks carefully. "I was the last off and he came down right after me."

Alexis pipes up. "When he said he placed a call, he pointed to that radio over there."

Our attention turns to a small gray plastic box on the table, half-lost inside the clutter of dirty plates, discarded books, and jars.

Hutch picks it up and turns it over. He fiddles with some dials, then forces the back open with a dull crack.

"We can call them again," Miri says. "Call everyone. Call the news.

There are nine people stranded in the mountains. Some media heat will get people moving."

"Are we sure Brian pointed to this when he said he'd called the emergency responders?" Hutch's face is hidden behind the radio as he examines it.

"Yes," Alexis says, but she's looking less certain.

"I remember it too," Simone adds.

"Okay. And did anyone actually *hear* him make that call?"

There's silence.

Hutch lowers the radio. His face has grayed out. "Because this is broken."

14.

Simone crosses the room in quick steps and takes the radio from him. She goes through the same motions: pressing buttons, turning it over, opening its back. She swears.

"Are you serious?" Steve rises from the couch.

Simone tosses the radio back onto the table, her delicate features set as hard as granite. "There's no way Brian could have thought it was working. Its insides have been gutted."

My body turns cold. I start picking at the bandages faster.

"He thought we would panic." Miri lightly touches her lips with the tips of her fingers, her eyes peeled wide with shock. "So he lied. He lied to make us think we were safe and to buy himself some time to figure out an actual solution."

And his time ran out. From my angle, I can't see the head on the tree, but I can picture it. Mouth forced wide to accommodate the branch's tip. Eyes wide and unseeing. Frozen.

"Not necessarily." Blake's eyes are growing keen as she hunches in the shadows. "One of us could have broken it after he made the call."

I pull harder at the bandages, peeling up one edge. She's right. Someone could have pulled the wires out while we were asleep last night. Or even used the fight between Grayson and Hutch as cover. For that matter, I can't remember if all nine of us participated in the search for Brian that morning.

I need to be more alert. Count our numbers more often, keep track of who leaves and for how long. But it's hard to stay that focused all of the time. I haven't eaten since the previous night's beans and rice. I'm short on sleep. Everything has grown fuzzy around the edges, dulling the instincts I normally rely on.

Simone shakes her head. "Or it could be that the cabin's owners were pulling it apart to make repairs and left it here when they cleared out. We don't know. But"—she gestures toward the window—"the sun will be down soon and no one's come for us."

Miri moans and slumps down. Her brown hair, without a dryer or brush, is becoming limp and clinging to her skin. "What are we going to do?" she asks.

Steve pats her back twice, then turns on Simone. "Well? What's your plan?"

She sighs and presses the fingertips of one hand to the bridge of her nose. "The bus is still out there. The roads won't be friendly—we've had a lot of snow—but we might be able to get somewhere."

Alexis is already grappling into her outer coat. The others watch her struggle with it for a second, then begin reaching for their own.

"We need a map." My voice fades into the rustle of clothes and soft grunts as the others prepare to leave. I lick my lips and try again. "We should have a map. Unless one of you remembers the roads back?"

They hear me that time. Hands fall still as they glance one to another. "I might..." Steve starts but fades away.

"We should look for a map." Every part of the cabin—from the handcrafted furniture to the amateur paintings of local fauna—speak to owners who have a deep pride in their remote hideaway. I cross to the bookcase. "This cabin feels like it belongs to the kind of people who would have one, even if it's just a topographical map."

"Good call," Simone says. "Everyone, look."

I don't tell her that I need the map for Kiernan. That I have no intention of accompanying them down the mountain. I'll make sure they have directions to get out, but then I'll return to my search. For as long as it takes.

We rifle through the shelves. There are countless travel guides—many worn and dog-eared—for locations like Lagos and Bali and Taiwan. Our hosts had high ambitions for their travels. I wonder if that's where they are now—escaping to some faraway country for the winter, the appropriate book tucked into their luggage.

When someone finds a map, they throw it down onto the table. We scour it, trying to determine if it covers the local area before discarding it. The first map we find is of a small Ohio town. The next, the California coast. After that, one of the British Isles.

Slow down. Think it through.

Piles of books are forming on the floor as we empty the contents of the bookshelf. The cabin's owners loved to collect maps, apparently, so where would they keep one of their local region? Not tucked away with every other map. No, they're passionate about their home in the mountains. It would have to be somewhere more significant. Somewhere more visible.

My eyes drift toward a broad corkboard attached near the bookshelf. It's full of a flurry of colorful items—Christmas cards, birthday cards, tabs of paper with phone numbers, postcards from far-off locations. There's a blank space near the middle, about the size of my head, as though something significant belongs there.

I cross the room to stand in front of it. The cards and papers overlap where the missing item belongs, but I can see where it used to be. The surface elsewhere is pockmarked from the press and removal of hundreds of pins, but the empty square is pristine save for four small holes at the corners. The cork underneath is a slightly deeper shade of golden, richer than the board elsewhere. It was sheltered from the fading effects of the sun. Something rectangular was pinned here and stayed in place for years, possibly decades.

"This is where the map was," I say, and the others slowly stop rifling through the bookcase's contents to stare at me. I gesture to it, trepidation slowly building in my stomach. "Did anyone see if there was a map on the corkboard when we arrived?"

"I—I can't remember." Alexis glances toward her nearest neighbors. She's retreating back into herself, shrinking down to appear smaller.

"Damn it," Steve mutters. He pushes in beside me to examine the blank space on the corkboard. "So, no map, then."

Apparently not. Pain swells inside of me: frustration at the waste of time, frustration that the search is yet again hampered. The clock on the highest shelf inches past five in the afternoon. Kiernan has been missing for exactly twenty-four hours.

"There might be an alternative." Simone shoves an armful of books back onto the shelf haphazardly but leaves the rest on the floor. "Hernandez would have brought a map. Even if the area is familiar, even if he'd made the drive a hundred times before, he's a tour guide and they tend to have backup for exactly this kind of scenario."

"Right." Hutch's bandage is darkening, pink spilling across the cotton. The patch runs from his cheek to his jaw. I wonder how deep the scratches went and how badly they'll scar. "Where would it be? Inside the bus?"

"Either that or on his body." Simone reaches for her coat. "We won't know until we look."

All nine of us are at the door in under a minute. I wear Kiernan's scarf again. It feels right to have something of his, to take it with me as I leave. We push through the re-forming snowdrift around the cabin's edge and press outward.

I don't know exactly where the bus is. I haven't crossed it on any of the searches I've been on before now. I stay near the back of the group. Simone is at the head, barely visible as she presses into the endless white.

The sun is growing low. I try not to fixate on it. No one wants to stay another night in the cabin. But the drive up the mountain took hours; it will be well and truly night before the bus reaches any kind of human habitation. And that's if it can traverse the snow-packed roads.

Simone turns past the trees with the broken lantern. I watch for any kind of reaction from the others, but they don't seem to have noticed it.

There's a gap in the pines that I haven't seen before, just wide enough for a car, and Simone leads us down it.

My feet sink up to my knees in the snow. The wind is still relentless, dragging at us and robbing our balance. The figures ahead fade in and out of sight as flurries drive between us.

The walk's longer than I expected it to be. By the time the charter bus emerges through the snow, I'm breathless. Its windows are dark. The company's name is barely visible under the frost caking its sides. It's buried past its wheels in snow, and I realize, with a sinking sensation, it will need to be dug out before we can even think about driving it.

Then Denny voices a slightly more urgent issue, and we all come to a halt. "Keys."

I glance from Simone to Hutch. Brian would have had the keys. I didn't see them near the fireplace, where he'd left his scant belongings—including the contracts. They must be on his person, inside one of his pockets or in the satchel he wore.

Simone presses through the rising snow and grasps the bus's door. She heaves, and the metal groans as it wrenches open an inch at a time, exposing the dark, stark interior beyond.

She turns back to us, her teeth bared in a snarling grin. "He didn't lock it." Her voice is hoarse, desperate. "Get in."

15.

Bodies jostle me as they shove past. I catch myself on the bus's threshold, torn. I can't leave Kiernan. But the premonition pushes at the back of my mind, insistent, terrifying.

We're all going to die here.

"The keys aren't in the bus," Simone says, feeling around the driver's console and flipping down the sun visor. "They must have been on Hernandez when he was killed. Which means the person who killed him probably has them now."

"Does anyone here know how to hot-wire this thing?" Steve cranes to see past me. "What about you, kid?"

Hutch is already on the bus. It takes him a second to realize Steve is speaking to him. "What?"

"You're one of the young ones. I'm sure you've raised hell in your day." Steve's gaze slides to the remaining piercings in his ear. "Ever hot-wired a car?"

Faint disgust pulls at Hutch's mouth. "Are you serious? I run my own business."

"You play music for kids who don't have a curfew, and it shows."

"Sure, I DJ at clubs. Is that a problem for you?"

Steve tilts his head back, his whiskers bristling as his mouth works. "I know kids like you. You stand on the shoulders of hard workers and complain that life is still too difficult. I bet you've never considered what *you* give back to society."

A vein throbs in Hutch's throat. He steps down from the bus, and I'm reminded that, despite his gentle face, he's built, muscles thick underneath his coats. "Sure. Let's do this. I carry naloxone to reverse overdoses at the clubs I work at. I've taken teens into my home when their parents kicked them out. Last year I spent three months helping build homes for immigrants who had nothing. But I guess none of that counts as *contributing to society* in your eyes, since it's not the kind of society you like to be around."

He and Steve stand nose to nose. They're nearly the same height, and although Hutch is simmering, Steve's eyes are narrow, calculating. They're going to fight. Someone needs to stop them. I glance around, desperate, but no one moves in. Alexis is frozen, eyes wide. Grayson, his hair over his eyes, watches with evident anticipation. Simone, most likely to take authority in this situation, is still inside the bus, observing with the barest flicker of interest.

Steve takes a breath to speak.

"Lay off it." Denny isn't loud, but his voice cuts through us. "The bus isn't going to start."

I seize on the distraction and press past Steve, bumping him to break him out of the stalemate. "Why not?"

Denny grunts and kicks something on the ground.

Gray shapes are scattered around the bus's front, half buried under the snow. At first I took them for rocks. As I draw nearer, though, I realize I'm looking at metal. Engine parts have been stripped out and discarded.

"I could repair it if they were intact," Denny continues, and I'm reminded that he's a mechanic. "But someone broke them up pretty good."

The metal is twisted in places, dents marring the smooth finish. It's an echo of the broken lantern, crushed in an apparent fit of rage.

Simone has come down from the bus. She frowns at the half-buried carnage, her delicate lips pressed tightly together. "Then we don't have an option. We're going back to the cabin."

Miri turns away from the bus and takes out her pack of cigarettes. Her eyes are red and exhausted. "Are you trying to say we should just give up?

As far as we know, no one's looking for us. And they won't miss us until we're due home, and that's not for another twelve days, at least."

"You're welcome to sit out here as long as you like," Simone says, kicking a piece of the now scrap metal to make her point.

"We can take our luggage back with us." Alexis's voice is very small. "Brian probably brought some food too."

Food. There's an empty ache in my stomach and a weakness in my legs that redoubles at the thought.

The others must feel the same. We cluster at the storage compartment in the bus's side. Luggage cases come out. Some are already caked with snow. I spot Kiernan's case: purple with black stripes. He joked that they were racing strips and would help him pull it faster. It hurts to turn away from it.

I find my own luggage and pull it free from the group, then stand over it like a guard dog. It's not like me to covet my possessions so jealously, but this luggage is the first thing I've had since arrival that's *mine* beyond the clothes on my back.

Sighs of relief break out as boxes of food are discovered behind the luggage. Miri claps. There's not a lot. Less than the eleven of us would have needed for the two weeks we were scheduled to stay at Blackstone Lodge. This store was probably an emergency backup, I realize; Brian most likely had a separate delivery of fresh foods scheduled.

Still, it will fill us, at least for a night or two. We leave the water—frozen inside its plastic jugs—and divvy up the burdens; all of us carry our luggage, and those of us that have extra strength take some of the food as well.

Walking through snow is a challenge. It's so, so much worse with the luggage. The wheels bog; the clamshell cases become stones to drag in our wake. We cling to the path we forged when walking to the bus, taking advantage of the compacted snow. Even so, the trip back takes so long that daylight is fading by the time we see the cottage.

My muscles are cramping. I have to hold my portion of the food awkwardly in my bandaged hand. Still, right on the doorstep, Simone stops us.

"There won't be enough room for the luggage inside," she says. "Leave it out here."

Faint complaints come up, Miri most prominently. "My bag won't take up that much room."

"Leave it outside." An edge enters Simone's voice, and my stomach turns. "You can get anything you need out of it, but otherwise we're only bringing the food into the cabin."

Luggage thuds as it lands in the snow. We line our cases up: nine of them, one for each of us. Irrationally, I wish I'd brought Kiernan's with me. He'd appreciate having it once I find him. Moisture floods my nose and eyes and I turn away, angry with myself.

We shove the maps and books off the table and drop our containers of food on the clear spaces, then paw through them like hungry animals. A box of energy bars; they're ripped open. There are only eight. I don't get one. Alexis's hands are empty as well. Someone must have taken two. I look around but can't see who.

Other boxes contain cans of vegetables and bags of dried fruits. This time, I get a handful of the latter. I check that Alexis has as well, then push the apricot halves into my mouth. They're frozen solid, and my teeth and gums ache as I try to chew them. I shudder, holding them in my mouth as I wait for them to thaw enough to swallow.

Then there are dry foods. Rice and oats. Miri pulls out a bag of rice and carries it to the fireplace. The coals are down. There's no wood left in the holder. Miri pulls a pot off the rack above the fireplace. "Can anyone get me some wood?" she calls over her shoulder.

"There was some in the shed," Denny says, rising. He taps his son's shoulder on the way past, and Grayson stands, arms crossed around himself as he follows his father outside.

Miri ventures outside just long enough to fill the pot with clean snow and place it on the coals to melt. The dried apricots have finally gone down but they've only scratched at the hunger inside, waking it up. I gravitate to the window to distract myself.

The glass is sheeted with frost, disguising most of the outside world. Light is fading fast. I can barely make out the silhouette of the massive pine tree. Brian is still there, somewhere, though it's impossible to see him through the fading light.

Something on the windowsill catches my eye. Small shapes are lined up on the outside, crusted in fresh snow. I lean forward, frowning, doubting what I'm seeing. My breath condenses on the glass.

The shapes are pale white, with spots of deep crimson.

Those are…

Recognition hits me. I reel back, one hand pressed across my mouth as I try not to scream.

16.

"What is it?" Alexis takes half a step out of her alcove. "Are you hurt?"

I double over, one hand on my stomach, the other clutched across my mouth. I'm dizzy. Queasy. Can't speak.

Hutch moves toward me, one hand held out tentatively. "What's going on?"

I force my gaze back up to the gory display on the windowsill, praying rather than believing that I've made a mistake. I haven't.

"Teeth," I manage.

The others move in, clustering around me. Heat radiates from their bodies, stifling and moist. It's pushing the nausea back up again. I duck between them and cross the cabin's length in a few short paces, then shove through the cabin's door just as Denny and Grayson appear on the other side.

I don't answer their querying looks as I stagger past the luggage cases to see the windowsill from the outside. A clearer view doesn't reduce the horror.

Someone has left a row of human teeth on the windowsill.

They're crusted in frozen blood. Some still have nerve endings attached.

I drag shallow breaths in as I take stock of the scene. They were placed in a line, starting at one side of the sill and ending near the other. Their tips jut up in crooked directions, like a macabre art display.

"The hell," a familiar voice whispers. I turn. Steve stands just beside me, scratching under his woolen hat as he squints at the teeth. More bodies cluster in behind him, barely visible in the low light. The group is all there. I count to be sure and realize I was wrong: we're one short—Miri.

Grayson turns from the teeth on the windowsill to stare up at the huge pine tree. Slowly, we all follow him, stepping closer and squinting up at Brian Hernandez's head.

His mouth is jutted open. It's hard to see from this far away and with ice crusting his features, but I'm certain I can see his teeth surrounding the jagged wood.

I turn back to the windowsill. The little white shapes, pressed firmly into the snow, ringed in frozen red, send my stomach squirming.

"How many teeth are in a human mouth?" Alexis asks.

Blake's response is instant. "Thirty-two."

I count them. The display is one short. I count again to be sure. There are thirty-one teeth on the windowsill. Eight incisors, four canines, seven premolars, twelve molars. One premolar is missing.

This time, I really do lose the contents of my stomach, stumbling along the side of the building and spitting bile. There's a ringing sound in my ears that won't subside. I slap the side of my face, trying to break myself out of the spiral, but it's only getting worse.

The others are still talking, their voices seeming too loud. "We're sure they're not from an animal?"

"No." Blake again. "Those are definitely human."

"How do you even get teeth out?" Steve asks. "Intact, I mean? You could use pliers, but wouldn't they shatter?"

Denny says, "Not if you're careful."

My stomach heaves again. I dip lower, mouth open, and flecks of snow connect with the thin layer of stomach acid on my tongue. There's nothing left to bring up.

Kiernan only had thirty-one teeth. He was missing a premolar, something that never grew in after his baby teeth came loose. You couldn't tell, not even when he smiled, unless you knew where to look.

A deep, furious, howling misery rises inside me. My throat is too tight to voice it. I press my hands to my face, the bandages rough against my skin.

It doesn't have to mean anything. My internal voice is desperate, panicked. *They don't have to be* his *teeth.*

Hope was already so thin it had been tearing in places. I'd clutched at its edges, fighting to keep it together against every voice of doubt, but now, the emotion I'm clinging to is less hope and more delusion.

Something touches my shoulder. I flinch, only to see Hutch crouched next to me. The cotton gauze on his face crinkles as he frowns, concerned. "You okay?"

I can't explain the teeth to them. Can't tell them about Kiernan's missing premolar or the way the gap felt under my tongue when we kissed. That was our secret. So I force myself to say, "Sure."

I'm not sure he believes me, but he doesn't press. Instead, he gives a gentle smile. "Let's go in. It's cold out here."

He puts his arm under mine and helps lift. I find my feet. The others are already gone, with only the indents of their shoes to mark where our group once stood. I stare at the teeth again as I pass them. I can't stop myself. Thirty-one teeth caked in blood. A quick swipe of my hand would send them spiraling off the sill, to fall gently into the snow. My fingers flex, but I can't bring myself to do it.

I hope he was already dead when they were pulled.

Inside, the cabin is quiet. Everyone's returned to their separate corners, as far apart as possible but still so close that we can smell one another's body odor and hear our neighbors' breathing. Miri crouches over the fire, stirring the pot of rice. She alone didn't come out to see the spectacle.

The space under the window waits for me. I don't want to have to sit there, below the row of teeth, but I don't have much of an option. There's so little room in the cabin that anywhere else would be invading another person's space. I drop down, my back to the wall, and try to shut my mind off.

Some of the occupants retrieved items from their baggage and are now sorting through them. Fresh clothing. Books. Steve fiddles with a pair of reading glasses.

"Does anyone have a phone?" Grayson asks.

Hutch raises his cell phone, which he's been fidgeting with. "No service up here."

Grayson snorts. His hair was bordering on greasy when the trip started; now, it's starting to tangle. He lets it fall over part of his face to hide the swelling around his lip. "Whatever. Dad didn't let me bring mine."

"It was in the brochure." Steam dampens the front of Miri's hair as she stirs the food. "Something about unplugging from technology and experiencing nature."

"We're getting our share of that, eh?" Steve laughs. No one else joins in.

My own phone is in my luggage somewhere. Kiernan and I agreed to stow ours away before leaving the hotel. I know there won't be any reception, but there's still the temptation to find my phone and try.

Miri empties cans of peas and corn, liquid included, into the pot of rice, then pulls it off the heat. We all gather around, our cups and bowls and saucers held at the ready as she slops the food into our receptacles. There's not enough cutlery, so I end up eating with my fingers. The food's hot enough to burn my skin, but I don't stop. I need something to replace the taste of bile. To settle my empty stomach.

The pot seemed enormous when Miri put it on the fire, but as we go back for seconds and thirds, it quickly diminishes down to nothing. There are only two more bags of rice and two bags of oats. They won't last us long.

The others must be thinking the same. Simone puts her empty plate aside. Her face seems longer, paler in the fire's light. "We need to start planning," she says. "It's clear we're going to be here for another night. We need to figure out how we're going to survive."

17.

Outside the window is dark. I'd planned to search for Kiernan again before night set in. I've lost my chance. Not that it matters much now, I suppose. My fingers itch. I pick at the edge of my bandage to distract myself. The material's become damp from being repeatedly exposed to the snow.

Simone leans against the wall. She sighs heavily, her eyebrows low, her arms folded. "One of us died last night. It might have been an outsider—someone with a grudge. Or it might have been one of us." Her gaze lingers on each of our party in turn. "We can't ignore the very real possibility that we're still in danger. We need a night watch. Two people at a time."

Steve tilts his head, digging his fingernails into an itch in his beard. "It's not a stupid idea. But I can't help but notice how you've started giving the orders around here. How do we know you didn't kill Brian, and now you're acting all imperial to distract us?"

Her glance is sharp. "You don't. None of us do."

"Huh." He keeps scratching. His fingernails need trimming. I imagine them digging through the wrinkles, scraping layers of skin off. "You know, it would help if we knew a bit more about you. Like why you came on this trip, for instance. Or why you've made yourself in charge of first aid. For all we know, that girl's hand could have an infection now."

That girl means me. I glance down at my bandage. The rusty red stains on the back are spreading in the moisture, branching out like cracks in shattered glass.

Simone lifts her eyebrows, appraising as she glances about the group. We're all watching her. And I'm fairly sure we all have the same questions as Steve.

"Simone Wall," she says at last, her tone clipped. "Currently between jobs, though I've worked at a host of them, including a car rental and as a courier, and before that, I was in the army. I learned practical wound dressing there. Had to. I was supposed to spend two weeks at Blackstone Lodge with an old friend, but she canceled the day before we left. Is that enough?"

"Army, eh?" Steve's disposition shifts subtly. He drops his hand and leans forward, his posture more open. "I see it now. It's in how you walk. I can respect that. I have some relatives in the army. You might know them—"

"Doubtful." She turns aside. "I left years ago. Are we all agreed on a watch?"

Heads nod.

"Good. We'll need two shifts, with two people at a time. Are there volunteers?"

There's a second's hesitance, then Blake sighs. "Sure, I guess. I always used to be awake at this hour when I was a dispatcher."

"Good. Who else?"

Hutch shrugs. "I can do it." I suspect he's volunteering now so that he doesn't become stuck on a watch with either Steve or Grayson.

"That's our first set." Simone turns slowly. "They'll be on guard from now until two thirty. Then we'll need a second watch to carry us through to dawn."

Denny raises a hand. "Me and my son."

Simone hesitates a second. "I want unrelated persons. You and I can do the second watch, Denny. That okay with everyone else?"

Vague noises of assent rise from the gathered. Simone slouches down against the wall, reaching for her jacket. "Good. First shift, wake me at two thirty. Denny, try to get some rest. You'll need it for later."

We gradually settle in for the night. Steve pushes extra wood onto the fire to keep it burning. It's not as warm as any of us would like. Several people, myself included, make pilgrimages outside to riffle through our luggage. Since my blankets were taken, I'll need to find a new way to sleep. I drag in puffy jackets and sweaters and scarves—as many as I have—and use them to form a nest. I'd worried I was overpacking for two weeks. Now I wish I'd packed more.

I roll a scarf up under my head and try to close my eyes. At that angle, facing into the room, I can't see through the window, but my mind keeps drifting to the horrors outside. The head on the tree, slowly crusting over with ice. The teeth. *Kiernan's* teeth. My heart aches.

When we first started dating—just a month after that first awkward encounter where he approached me at the library and asked for help with his university course—I'd feared that I was going to kill our relationship. My anxieties and the crippling doubts and the everyday struggle would wear on him, drag him down, slowly drain the joy he seemed to hold in life.

When I looked at our future, all I could see was a toxic end. So I began pulling back. Testing the relationship, seeing if I could disentangle us without leaving scars. He must have felt it. But instead of being hurt or trying to cling to me, he instead asked if we could take a trip together. And he took me to visit his mother.

Thinking of her brings up the memory of bleach and old furniture and the distant ring of phones. Kiernan led me through a care facility to a woman who sat quietly in front of a television in the common room, watching an old movie with very little recognition in her face. She smiled when she saw Kiernan and repeated my name when I was introduced but very soon faded back into herself, facing the television, unresponsive.

On the drive home, he told me about his life. Not the broad strokes, which I already knew—studying English literature at university, sharing an apartment with an old friend, dreams of writing a novel. Instead, he told me about the pieces from his past he hadn't dared voice before. How his teenage brother had died in a hit-and-run. His father's suicide six months later. How his mother had crumbled into a person who barely resembled the vivid, laughing figure from his childhood.

And I'd looked at him with new eyes. He wasn't the unblemished, naive figure I'd imagined. He was weathered by pain. Aged by suffering. And despite it all, he had learned how to reforge his joy. How to use the pain to construct his life.

We were more alike than I'd imagined, only he was a better, fuller version. The person I had been striving, and failing, to become. He gave me hope. More than that, he became someone I could trust. Someone I could let myself love.

Now, lying in the overlapping pieces of my luggage, moisture burns at my eyes. I'll have to visit his mother. How am I going to tell her that her only remaining son is dead?

I'm exhausted, but like the previous night, it's nearly impossible to fall asleep. As the fire collapses lower in its grate, I keep my gaze on the two guards: Hutch, close to the fireplace on my right, and Blake, on the other side of the table. They sit, hunched, wearing layers to ward off the growing night chill. They look tired. I don't blame them. I'll just be grateful if we can get through to dawn without problems.

Slowly, sleep claims me. The dreams are fragmented and tense. I imagine the cabin door opening again and again, letting in gusts of snow and perhaps something else. Something dangerous, blowing in on the icy wind.

The thought circles like a vulture: *We're all going to die here.*

The dreams change, spiraling to the one day I don't want to remember. The rain. The voices, calling, "Can't we do something?"

And then, "Where is she?"

My dream splinters apart at the edges. My eyes creep open, but my limbs are still heavy with the numbing effects of sleep. The voice repeats, nearer and louder and horrifically real.

"Where is she? *Where's my Miri?*"

18.

The heaviness doesn't want to leave my limbs. My vision is hazy. The room is dark. It's still predawn; our only light comes from the fireplace, which is down to coals.

Voices overlap: short, staccato questions, asking what's happened. Simone yells for light.

There's a second of chaos and then the beam from Hutch's phone cuts across us.

It's a cold light, very different from the glow of the fire's coals. I squint as it flashes in my eyes.

Simone snatches the phone from Hutch. She's more deliberate with it, moving the light over everybody in the small room. I count as we go. Hutch, Blake, Denny, Grayson. Steve stands, strands of spit clinging to his beard and his eyes wild. Alexis crouched in the corner. She's holding something—her book, I think—but the light moves on before I can be sure.

Simone and I make eight. We're missing one—Miri.

"Where is she?" There's a frantic misery in Steve's voice. His jaw quivers. "Where's my girl?"

The light flicks toward the clock on the high shelf. It's after four in the morning. Simone draws a hissing breath in through her teeth. "Why didn't you wake me?"

The phone turns back on Hutch. Perspiration pearls on skin that appears grayed out. "I'm sorry," he manages. The words seem to cost him.

"Sorry for what?" Simone strides toward him. Hutch flinches back and his shoulders hit the wall. He shakes his head. Simone repeats herself, her voice booming. "Sorry for what?"

"I fell asleep." The admission is a whisper, thin and pale.

A furious hiss escapes Simone before she swings toward Blake. "And you?"

Blake stands near the back wall, her arms crossed, her features as hard as granite. Her pupils contract as the light flashes across them, but that's the only reaction I can sense. "I barely got any rest yesterday."

"Are you saying you also fell asleep?"

She lifts her chin. "My back's been killing me. I needed to lie down."

The door slams. We all flinch. The light wavers as it passes over that half of the cabin. Steve has left.

"Move." Simone shoves past Hutch to get to the door. I grapple for my coat, my bandaged hand more of a hindrance than a help as I tug it on. There's a flurry of activity as others reach for boots and warmer clothing.

My mind spins, trying to keep track of everyone. Alexis seems pale and grim. Denny is unreadable, Grayson surly. Hutch is frantic as he searches for his clothes, as though rapid action now might undo his mistake. They shove through the door in quick succession, still pulling hats and neck warmers onto grimy skin as they go.

I'm one of the last out. My heart is in my throat, beating uncomfortably fast. The earliest traces of light flush across the horizon, leaving the mountaintops as dark, jagged knives piercing into it. The light hasn't touched our valley yet. I can see Simone to the right, the phone's glow swinging in broad arcs as she moves into the hazy predawn with frightening speed. The others are nothing but dark blurs through the gloom.

"Miri!" Hutch calls. His voice is strained, cracking. "Miri, answer me!"

I follow in Simone's wake. We're aiming for the same landmark. The massive, heavy pine tree with its rows and rows of jagged, dead branches.

A voice yells behind me. The words are lost under the wind. *We shouldn't be split up like this.* It feels too dangerous to let anyone out of my sight. I can't keep track of who's where or what they're doing. A tall, spindly figure moves to my right. Grayson, I think, but it's strange to see him without Denny at his side.

The tree looms out of the darkness. Its bark flashes in polarized shades as the harsh LED light darts across it. Deep shadows, sharp whites. The snow crusted over it is almost blinding.

Panting, I stagger to a halt beside Simone. Her lips twitch as she whispers to herself. The light moves in short, sharp flicks, crisscrossing up the tree. There's something dark above us, about the size of a basketball.

"No," I whisper to myself, willing it to not be Miri.

The light finds it. The head, severed at the neck, pierced onto the branch, shivers as the icy wind whips at it. The skin is crusted in sparkling white frost as though someone dipped it into a bowl of jewels. Gray flesh and dark-red gore shimmer beneath.

My throat is dry. I force myself to swallow. It's not Miri. It's Brian's head, still attached to the tree despite the storm's ferocity.

Simone begins to move the light higher, moving from branch to branch, searching each exposed tip.

Howling, keening cries rise in the distance. I squint, trying to see through the haze. Simone flicks her light in its direction, but the beam isn't strong enough to pierce more than twenty feet.

The cry breaks into a scream. We lurch forward, struggling through the snow. More bodies join our race. We fight our way through the empty land, following our steps back through the snow. The scream chokes out into something lower, harsher. My lungs ache. My muscles hurt. Running through the snow is like trying to run in a nightmare, where every movement is slow, sluggish. My arms reach out and claw against the white powder as I try to drag myself forward.

A dim shape emerges through the haze. It's rounded, like a boulder in the snow. It shivers. Simone stops ten paces from it and extends the phone, the light angled at the form as she slowly circles it.

Different aspects are cast into view as the light moves. Creases in fabr. The edges of an arm. Then the head lifts, revealing Steve's face, blotchy and wet. Strings of fluid cling to his beard. The distended skin under his eyes is swollen and red.

His arms stretch toward the patch of dark snow ahead of him. He moans, a deep, aching sound that comes from low in his stomach. "Look what they did to her."

19.

Simone angles the light and the dark shape on the ground begins to take form.

I recognize Miri's hands first: gloved fingers cast out to her sides, as though grasping at the snow.

She's wearing her thick outer coat. Her legs are askew, one knee pointed inward while the foot is tilted in the opposite direction. She's sunken several inches into the snow, until the rise of her chest isn't much higher than the surface. It's not snowing, but the wind works to bury her, driving white flecks across her clothes.

I drag my eyes upward, toward her head. The space where it should be. It's been cleaved off, just like Brian's. A glut of red blood sinks into the field of white, slowly mixing with it and turning to ice.

Steve lurches forward. He's sobbing so deeply that he's almost retching from it. His hands fumble over her body, pulling her arms back in to fold them over her chest.

"This is a crime scene," Simone says, but none of us try to stop Steve.

Slowly, Alexis creeps around our group. She stops at the only clear space, opposite the rest of us, then crouches down and removes a glove. She reaches for Miri's neck and touches a patch of clear skin, just underneath the coat's collar, where the blood hasn't dripped.

"She's probably been gone for a few hours," Alexis says. She pulls her hand back quickly and replaces her glove. "Steve, you didn't hear her leave at all?"

"No, no." He rocks, huge tears dripping onto his wife's coat. "I just woke up and saw she was gone."

Alexis remains crouched but shuffles to see the severed neck. Her face contorts as she leans close to it, then she ducks back again, blinking rapidly toward the sky.

I'm queasy at the idea of looking closer, but I have to. I need to under-stand…how this happened, *what* happened. I crane to see past Miri's collar.

The neck is a mess of flesh and muscles and a sliver of white bone, but it's all coated in the oozing, vivid-red blood. The edges of her skin appear smooth, like a cut of meat at a butcher's. Does that mean it was done with a sharp knife? Or a single blow from something larger, like a machete?

The pool of blood has spread wide and sunk quickly. I look past its edge. Droplets of red mar the snow for at least a foot beyond. I bend low as I walk around them, trying to see them through the fresh snow being blown across the surface. There are a lot of droplets. I don't know much about crime scenes, but it looks to me like her head was removed quickly, while there was still enough blood pressure to cause the liquid to spray.

Miri was wearing her outer coat, which meant she left the cabin willingly. Someone could have lured her outside—maybe with the promise of private information that couldn't be shared in our cramped quarters—or maybe she left to relieve herself and was ambushed. If it was the former, she must have trusted whoever she accompanied. If the latter, it could have been anyone.

I gaze about the snow. There are fresh tracks—ours—scattered across the empty field and converging at Miri's body. But I can see older prints as well. Scuffles of them are around Miri's body, then more distinct prints leading away at an angle. They must be from the killer; unlike our own tracks, which are fresh and jagged around the edges, the older channels have been softened by the beating wind. I can't read any of their details—not the make of the shoe and not even their size. Within another six hours, they'll likely be filled up again.

We've disturbed the ground around Miri's body too badly for me to make out any sequence of events. I can only see the one trail, leading away and to the right. That could have been the killer arriving. Or it could have been the killer leaving. I squint, trying to guess where the tracks go and see the massive pine's silhouette against early dawn.

My breathing is labored as I push through the snow to reach the tree. It's still too early to see clearly, but enough light has broken through the mountaintops to make out the pine's shape without the help of a flashlight. Brian's head is still there. The rest of the tree is growing easier to see as the world grows lighter. I tilt my head back, squinting as I search each branch.

I find her above Brian. The dead branch angles upward. Miri's head has been impaled on it. The flesh around her face is slack, her mouth barely open. Blood leaks from the corners of her eyes. Her hair, brown but with an inch of gray at the hairline, whips into a flurry around her blanched white skin.

Simone and Alexis followed me. Alexis doesn't say anything—she just looks—but Simone swears under her breath before swinging back to the cabin.

We shouldn't split up. I'm trying to keep track of where each of my companions are, but they're growing more fragmented. Hutch is still crouched beside Steve, who cries over Miri's body. Blake is shuffling back toward the cabin. Denny and Grayson have vanished.

We're all going to die here.

Bile rises in the back of my throat. I turn away from the tree and cross to the shelter, stepping inside just after Blake. Simone stands in front of the fireplace, her hands hooked into the loops of her pants and her mouth a severe gash as she stares into the flickering coals.

I stop by the window. Thirty-one small red dots mark the sill. The teeth are gone, though; all that's left are small spots of blood.

One of my companions must have cleared them. We weren't supposed to touch anything that might count as evidence, but they were probably as disturbed by the violent display as I was.

My instincts snag on something. I wind back. The teeth were there when I went to sleep the previous night. We were all woken by Steve, and the following minutes were much too chaotic for me to pay attention to my surroundings.

I wasn't perfect at keeping track of who split off in which direction, but I don't think any of them went close to the cabin's window.

The teeth were removed during the night.

Ice runs through my veins. If the teeth were taken during the night, it was most likely by the same person who placed them there. The same person who killed Miri. I lay directly beneath, asleep and unaware, as the butcher picked the teeth off the sill above me, one by one.

The door creaks as more people enter. Denny, huge and hulking, followed by Grayson, Hutch, and Alexis.

I run my tongue across my lips. I can't afford to let my voice quiver. "Hey, who cleared the teeth away?"

A few weary heads turn toward me, but they only shake in response.

Stay calm. Stay natural. "I just want to say thanks. They were bothering me. We should keep them as evidence for the police, though."

I glance over the group. I don't know what I expect to see; the blush of a guilty conscience? Averted eyes? Agitation?

They're only tired and irritable. Denny begins feeding fresh fuel into the fire.

Steve is still outside. I feel as though someone should be with him. That feeling isn't enough to drive me toward the door, though. Two deaths have occurred outside. I don't feel safe turning my back on any of my companions.

The killer doesn't have to be someone inside the cabin, I remind myself. We had other theories. Someone living nearby, perhaps, targeting the tourists who were unlucky enough to stop in their region.

That theory feels thin, though. The attacker left marks in the snow. I didn't see any leading away from the cabin or toward the road. Though, I have to admit, I didn't search very hard.

Someone joins me at the window. Simone's long blond hair hangs over her shoulders. It's the first time I've seen her wear it down. She gazes into the distance, and I search the bleak scape outside to find what's drawn her notice. A shape in the distance is barely visible through the haze. Steve, still kneeling over his dead wife.

"Is it just me"—Simone sends me a sleek, questioning glance—"or does that feel performative?"

She doesn't give me a chance to answer. She turns and steps away, her voice ringing loud as she calls for attention. "We're going to search everyone here."

The words send ripples through me, but I still can't move from the bloodstained windowsill, as I watch the distant figure of Steve rock and shake his head.

20.

"Step away from your belongings," Simone calls. "All of you. Immediately."

"You have no right to search us." Blake stays at her space by the wall, her jaw working. "We have a right to privacy."

"You lost that the moment we had a second death." Simone moves toward Blake and grasps her arm. Blake cries out, a pained whine, as Simone drags her to the cabin's other side. "By the door, all of you."

"That *hurts*."

Simone doesn't respond. Her ice-blue eyes dart across us, and I find myself pressing close to the others in the doorway, my shoulders and back brushing against their thick coats.

One at a time, Simone goes through us, feeling around our clothes and digging her hands into our pockets. She pulls out a receipt from Grayson's jacket—he purchased it just before the trip, evidently—and a tube of lipstick from Blake's coat. Nothing else.

Finally, she removes her gloves and makes us do the same. She examines our hands, prying around our fingertips as she searches for signs of blood. I watch my companions closely as they're searched but can't see anything obvious.

"Right." Simone's breathing deeply. "Here's what we're going to do. We'll go to each person's possessions one at a time. That person isn't allowed to touch anything, but they can watch. Search thoroughly. Our suspect might have hidden evidence in unexpected places."

We start at Steve and Miri's couch. Miri brought her purse back with her from the bus. It feels sacrilegious to paw through her lighters and gift vouchers, but we do, turning out the bag's contents until they're thoroughly vetted. Steve has relatively little besides clothes, but we still feel through all of the pockets multiple times.

Next, my own nest. I'm made to stand with my back to the table as the others shake out my scarves and jackets. I have nothing to hide, but it still feels deeply invasive. They examine every stain and every spot on my clothing, even tugging on Kiernan's scarf as they feel for anything hidden inside the wool.

Then, Alexis's space. Hutch flips through the journal while Blake searches her small bag.

"Weird journal," Hutch says.

Alexis's face has turned a heavy red. "It's personal."

"Knife." Blake twists toward us, a furious smile stretching her red lips. "She has a knife."

Held up in her hand is a small metal shape. She presses a button and a blade flips out. It's no more than three inches long, but it doesn't look cheap, either. Alexis's color deepens. "That's for my protection."

"Give it to me." Simone carries the knife to the window and holds it up to the light. She spends time turning it and squinting at the different angles, the knife held just centimeters from her eyes.

"No sign of blood," she says at last. "I've looked in the creases and joins. If she cleaned it, it was a remarkably thorough job."

"I didn't need to clean it because I've never had to use it." Alexis's voice is almost a whisper. I detect both shame and anger in the quiver. "I'm a girl traveling alone. I'd be an idiot not to think about my safety."

The idea didn't cross my mind, but only because I was with Kiernan. If I'd been on my own, though, I'm fairly certain I would have brought a pocketknife or a can of pepper spray as well.

Simone tosses the pocketknife back into Alexis's bundle of clothing, Hutch gives her a tight-lipped smile and replaces the notebook too.

Next are Denny and Grayson. They move as a unit as they stand back from their belongings. I'm one of the four assigned to search them. I peel back flaps on the duffel bag Grayson brought, feeling faintly dirty as I paw through the contents. It's mostly spare clothes. Some are old and tattered around the edges. Others appear unworn. I reach into one of the pockets and feel something soft and damp.

It's not uncommon for our clothes to be wet; we drag more than enough snow in with every trip through the door. But a small pang of uncertainty unfolds in me as I pull the wet material out and drop it on the floor.

It's a handkerchief. Damp with blood. The liquid doesn't quite spread from edge to edge, but it's enough to leave a trace of crimson on my fingertips.

Activity around me falls horribly still as the others stare at the material.

"I was in a fight." Grayson's voice is tight. Panicky. "My lip got busted open."

I glance at him. His hair hangs half over his face. With shaking hands, he pulls it back.

His lip's still swollen from the struggle with Hutch. So is the space just under his right eye: a blood blister has formed there.

Would he have bled enough to fill the handkerchief? My throat is dry as I swallow. *Would it still be damp after being in his jacket's pocket overnight?*

It's a water-resistant polyester design. Draped the right way, it probably could have stopped air from circulating around the material. And I never got a good look at Grayson or how much he was bleeding after the fight; more than anything, I was trying to avoid him.

Denny shifts forward. His eyes are as dark as a shark's. "I can vouch for my son," he says. "That's his blood there."

"We'll need to keep it," Simone says, holding out a hand. I dutifully place the handkerchief into it, trying not to touch any of the crimson dampness. "Forensics will want to test it."

"I didn't hurt any of them." Grayson is breathing fast. "Why would I? I don't even want to be here."

"We're not leveling any accusations." Simone carefully folds the handkerchief and places it under the broken radio on the table. "But there's a good chance one of us is responsible for these killings. We've got to take extra precautions until we know."

Simone's own possessions are next. She hangs back, unfazed and aloof, while we explore her belongings. There's nothing of note except a lighter—no cigarettes—and the partially used first-aid kit she took from the cabin's stores.

Then it's Blake's turn. I find two wrappers from the energy bars we were supposed to share the previous night. A part of me wants to make a scene but I swallow that impulse. It's not worth it. Not when we have two heads outside the window.

Hutch is last in the procession. Alexis scrolls through his phone while the rest of us search his bed. He must have taken a lot of videos; short clips of audio blare out of the tinny speakers. "Hey, fam, guess where I am? The Rocky Mountains, baby! Right now—"

"I took that the afternoon we arrived," he explains. "Before things... got bad. It was for my socials."

"I've looked through the recent videos and photos." Alexis addresses this to Simone. "But there are thousands more. I don't want to waste too much battery. We might need a phone."

"Sure," Simone says.

We drop everything, including the mobile, back into a pile. Then, under Simone's instruction, we file outside, to the travel cases.

The process there is a bit more streamlined. We're all assigned a case that doesn't belong to us. I'm given Alexis's. It's surprisingly sparse. I find spare clothes and toiletries, but not much else I'd expect a person to bring on vacation. No novels, no technology, not even a pack of cards. Even I brought cards.

I pile it back in and zip it up once I'm done. The others are still working through their respective assignments. I flex, relaxing stiff muscles, and stare across the emptiness surrounding us.

It's not a surprise that we can't find anything. Someone who's patient enough to line up teeth in a neat row and then clear them away again the following night is going to be careful about how they work. There are ample locations they could hide their items or a spare set of clothing. Patchy pine trees cluster around the cabin, offering plenty of alcoves. The ragged rocks on the cabin's other side are full of nooks and crevices. We haven't even fully searched the shed.

A body moves through the hazy white. Steve. His walk is shambling, unsteady. He's been out in the cold for a long time. His muscles are probably stiff. But Simone's words return: *Doesn't it feel performative?*

His face is blotchy. Simone leaves the cases to meet him partway. I can't quite hear what she says to him but can guess she's explaining what we're doing.

"Fine." He pushes past her after a few words. Ice crusts his trimmed beard and the stubble that's begun to develop. "I want to know what we're going to do about this."

He stares at each of us, challenging us.

Simone exhales heavily, a plume of condensation rising from her. "I think it's obvious that we can't stay here. I'm going to try to walk to town. Anyone who wants to come is welcome to join."

21.

I feel my eyebrows rising. The bus ride took hours. I can't imagine how long it would take on foot.

But then…

It's growing painfully clear to all of us that no one is coming. Brian lied about the radio. With no way to contact the outside world, we won't be missed for another twelve days, at least.

Maybe walking to town is our only chance.

Hutch shrugs. "I'm game. Even if we can't get to civilization proper, we might be able to find a home or get a phone signal."

"I'm not leaving Miri." Steve's body quivers. "She's out there and—and we need to bury her—"

Simone casts a hand behind herself, gesturing to the swollen mounds of white. "Where, Steve? In what part of the snow are you going to bury her?"

He doesn't answer. Doesn't even look at her.

"I'm not going to pretend the walk will be easy or even safer than staying here," she says. "It won't be. It's up to you to judge whether that's a risk you want to take. Anyone who prefers to stay can. We'll send help back for you. But I'm leaving in about three minutes, for those of you that choose to come."

"Okay." Hutch tugs at his gloves, anxious. "I will."

"Grayson and I are going." Denny turns toward the cabin.

His son works his jaw, his hands in fists at his side. "I want to stay here."

"Grayson." It's a single word, but there's a lot of weight in it. A command to fall in line.

The teen doesn't buckle, but he doesn't meet his father's eyes either. "I don't think any of us are getting anywhere by walking. We need to stay. There might still be a rescue."

It's hard to read Denny's expression. His brow is heavy and his beard disguises the angle of his mouth. All I know is I'd feel real fear to have that gaze directed at me.

"The boy can make up his own mind," Simone says. "I'm not bringing someone who doesn't want to go."

Denny turns away.

"I'll stay too." Alexis isn't looking at us. She's facing the tree.

"My back's acting up," Blake says. She glances at the cabin's dark window, and her lips twitch. "If my choice is between sitting here and waiting to be picked off, or wandering into the wilderness to die, I guess I'm going to stay. At least we have food here."

"No one's gonna die," Hutch says, but his voice falters on the last word. One of our party has already been lost to the white-blanketed peaks.

The Rocky Mountains stretch for thousands of miles. With no map and no compass, we'll be walking blind, hoping to find signs of a road we can follow and then hoping that that road will lead us to civilization before we drop from exhaustion.

I flex my good hand. The injured one still won't move.

Staying means having to watch my back at every turn. It means looking up at the heads of my companions whenever I pass the window. It means fighting off sleep lest I feel a knife against my throat.

Leaving means straining my aching muscles. It means being trapped in layers, cold and burning hot at once. It means risking the wrath of nature. And potentially perishing from it.

I gaze at the distant rock walls rising out of the horizon. I hate them. I fear them. But they also hold something I dearly, desperately need.

Answers.

What happened to Kiernan?

That's the thought that propels me toward Simone. The odds are small that we'll find anything, and the chance that I'll like the answers even slimmer, but I still can't let him go. "I'm in."

She gives a short nod. "Take some bright clothes from the luggage to mark the path. And bring a water bottle, if you have one. Wear it under your clothes. That will stop the water from freezing."

I have an empty bottle in my luggage, thankfully. The bag's contents are disorganized after the search and I have to dig to the base to find it. Even its cap was removed as they looked inside. I try not to feel irritation. It's not like anyone else was treated more lightly.

My cell phone is in my bag too. Its battery is three-quarters full. I can't stop myself from checking for service bars but, of course, there are none. Still. I tuck it into a pocket, on the small chance we can find reception farther down the mountain.

Hutch is already kneeling by the pot at the fireplace, filling his own water bottle. He gives me a wry smile as he tips the pot to pour some lukewarm water into mine. "How do you like our odds of actually finding someone?"

Telling him how I really feel won't help either of us. "We won't know unless we try."

"Mm." He smiles, crinkling the bandage on his cheek. Like mine, it's growing damp around the edges. "That's a good attitude."

Four of us leave: Simone, Hutch, Denny, and myself. The others— Alexis, Blake, Steve, and Grayson—stand outside the cabin to see us off. Grayson still won't look at his father.

We follow the same path we took the previous day, when we found the bus. Our footprints from then have already been erased, and I have to rely on the landmarks to track our progress. At least the weather is clearer. A white haze still permeates the chilled air, but I can make out distant rock formations.

We set a good pace. My jacket is a little too tight with the water bottle underneath and I find myself adjusting it often to keep it from chafing.

Denny leads the group. His thick legs carve through the snow. The rest of us follow in a single file, taking advantage of his slipstream, so to speak.

The morning was still fresh when we split from the cabin. We left no more than an hour after dawn. I can feel time trickling away, though, moving faster than we can afford as the shadows slowly tilt and new facets of the distant rock walls come into light.

We find the bus at the entrance to the valley. Simone and Hutch spend a minute searching inside while Denny and I open up the luggage compartment, hoping to find any tools that could help us. After five minutes, Simone hops back down. "Nothing. No map, no compass, no two-way radio."

"Nothing here, either." I pile the abandoned luggage—including Kiernan's—back into the bus.

"He should have brought something." Hutch wears a neck gaiter that covers his face up to his eyes. The skin around them is creased as he squints against the wind. "Those things are all basic gear you'd bring for two weeks in the mountains, right?"

He's right. Either Brian was wildly, dangerously underprepared—and he didn't strike me as that sort of person; if anything, he took pride in how thoroughly he stuck by the books—or someone else came through and cleared any important items out of the bus.

That would have most easily happened on the first night, when Brian was killed. There was no watch then; none of us were too alert. The killer could have been gone for hours without being missed.

If they came from inside the cabin. I still can't discount the idea that they're an outsider, someone darting in each night to pick us off opportunistically.

We return to our path. Now that we're past the bus, we start tying colored strips of fabric to the trees to mark our path. Denny still leads, but Simone calls out directions. She's trying to retrace the path the bus took to find the cabin. From what I understand, Brian was trying to get them all to the lodge before coming back to search for Kiernan and me. But the roads had faded under the snow and the bus became bogged, and it was a small miracle that someone was able to see the cabin through the storm.

That means there's a road nearby. We just don't know where. Natural channels have been carved through the rock, and with the snow coating every surface, they do a good job of imitating man-made paths until you hit a dead end or a crop of trees or rocks that are unpassable.

Simone seems to have a plan, though. She leads us through narrow ravines and across uneven ground that shifts beneath the snow. My mouth is dry, but I try to moderate how much water I drink. Even Denny's breathing grows labored.

Then, pushing through a cluster of trees that could in no way have fit a bus, we break into a channel that looks like it once carried cars.

We stop for a moment, panting, as we examine the space. A ribbon of clear land extends in both directions. Trees and boulders mark its edges, but the snow in its center is unblemished.

"Hey," Hutch says. I can hear his smile, even if I can't see it. "Looks like we found our road."

Simone turns left. She only makes it two paces before stopping. There's something about the rigid angle of her shoulders that I don't like. I move up behind her, cautious, straining to make out what's disturbed her, and then I see it.

There's something dark on the road ahead. It's between the rocks on one side, shielded from the wind, but, even though it's partially covered by snow, it's still unmistakably human.

Kiernan.

22.

My lungs feel empty, like the air has been sucked out of them. My legs, which were steady until now, falter as I stumble toward the form. He lies on his front, half-hidden between jagged rocks. One arm is reached overhead. One is cast out to the side. Limp.

My mouth won't work. I reach for him. My hands touch the familiar thick jacket over his back. I wait, trying to see if I can feel him breathing through the material. There's no sense of warmth underneath. No sense of movement. I press down a fraction and realize he's stiff.

"Hey." Hutch has come up behind me. His hand shakes as he touches my shoulder. "Maybe step back a bit. Maybe, maybe don't touch him…"

My eyes follow Kiernan's body up to where his face should be. There are his shoulders, slim but strong under the jacket. But there's no head.

"Come on." Hutch tries to loop a hand under my arm, to pull me away, but I shake him off. Noise whistles in my ears. My eyes aren't focusing like they should. I reach toward where his head belongs, certain I've made a mistake. My fingertips touch the severed ends of his neck. It's cold and solid, like a slab of meat from the freezer.

The whistling noise grows louder. I feel as though I'm breaking, imploding. Something has been torn out of me and it's left a gap where it belongs, a hole so deep that it sucks everything into its emptiness, tearing my body into shreds through its sheer intensity.

My mouth hangs open, but I can't scream. Can't even cry. There's nothing left. Just pain, so sudden and overwhelming that it robs me of every other motor function.

I knew this was the most likely outcome. The words reverberate, cruel and heavy. *I knew that if I was going to find answers, I wouldn't like them.*

"Give her a moment, Hutch."

Simone's words are barely audible under the whistling, but she sounds tired. I crumple over Kiernan's body, placing my head on the back of his jacket, and hold him.

I'm wearing his scarf. It still smells a little bit like him. Lying there, with his scent in my mouth and his body under my head, I can almost imagine we're back at home, watching a movie, while I feel the rise and fall of his rib cage under my ear.

Why did we have to come here?

An irrational kind of desperation falls over me. The idea that I might still be able to fix this somehow. Unwind the badness. Repair the damage. If I can only *understand.*

I pull back from his stiff body. My hands run over him, trying to find the familiar planes underneath the layers of winter gear. My voice shakes, but not as badly as I was expecting. "I want to know what happened to him."

There's a second of silence. Then Hutch, uncertain: "We all do. If we can get the police—"

I begin pulling at his body. "Help me turn him over," I say.

"Christa—"

"*Help* me."

Simone comes up on one side and Hutch on the other. Together, we pull Kiernan out from between the rocks and roll him faceup.

A small, green item that was sheltered under his body falls free. Pangs of recognition zip through me. It's my glove. The one Kiernan pulled off my hand while trying to catch me. He kept it. He'd wanted to return it when he found me. Because until his last moments, that was all he'd tried to do: find me again.

It's a punch to my stomach, and I double over from the ache.

I don't want to look at Kiernan's torn skin, but I force myself anyway, crawling around to see his neck. Like Brian and Miri, the skin has one or two ragged places, but the slices are as smooth as a butcher's.

"What happened to his hands?" Hutch asks.

I was so focused with his upper half that I didn't notice the damage to his fingers. He's not wearing the beautiful, thick gloves he owned. The skin is shredded. Torn away in strips until the white of the bones are exposed.

Nausea rolls through me. I close my eyes as I wait for it to pass.

"Some kind of carrion animal," Simone says. She stands slightly apart from us, her arms crossed. "Maybe a wolf."

I remember the last time those hands touched me. On the bus, brushing against mine, asking to hold me. Then later, as I fell from the precipice, clutching at me, trying to save me.

An animal makes the most sense. There's plenty of wildlife in the Rocky Mountains, and animals will take anything during the scarcer months of winter. But there's something not right about the image. I can feel the wrongness deep in my stomach, even if my mind can't pick up on the same clues.

I stand, breathing hard. Kiernan's body left a line in the snow where we dragged him. I follow it back to the rocks he was propped between, then stop.

"He didn't die here," I say.

"What?" Hutch follows me.

I stare at the pristine snow. "No blood." Miri and Brian both left a slick of red where they fell. That should have still been visible, even with fresh snow falling on top. I dig my gloved hand into the powdery substance, turning it over, searching for even a drop of red. I can't find any.

What does that mean?

He was killed somewhere else. Then dragged to the road. Why? So someone could find him? Frustration builds in me as I turn to gaze down the road. The person killing us hasn't tried to hide their activities so far. It's as though they *want* people to see what they've done. Heads displayed on trees like trophies. Teeth propped on the windowsill for us to discover the following morning.

And somehow, they found Kiernan lost in the wilderness. And it wasn't enough to just kill him. They wanted their victory to be seen. To cause pain. So they dragged him to the road and left him propped between the rocks, where he would be sheltered from the snow but visible to anyone passing by.

It's an incredible amount of effort to go through. There's no trace of blood nearby, no drops left around his severed neck. He was dragged far enough that his body bled out long before he'd reached his final resting place.

"We need to keep moving," Simone says. "Our only goal right now should be to reach town before dark."

Hutch makes a thin, pained noise. "We can give her a few more minutes."

"No. We really can't." Simone's eyes flick to me, and they're as harsh and unforgiving as the environment around us. "Our time is already drastically limited. You can mourn while you walk."

Denny turns toward the road. Hutch hesitates, sending me a questioning glance, then also stands.

I stare down at the man I loved. It feels wrong to just leave him there, lying on the side of the road, as though he's been forgotten. Left exposed for the weather to tarnish and the animals to pick at.

No.

My breath stings in my aching throat. I've finally realized what bothered me about his hands. They were torn to shreds, as though a scavenger animal had ravaged them. It made sense. Animals will go for the easier, exposed parts of a body first.

But then, why was the bare flesh at his neck so pristine?

23.

"Wait," I say to Simone.

She doesn't respond, but I can feel her eyes on my back as I crouch down beside Kiernan and feel around his body.

The way his hands have strands of flesh and muscle torn off is consistent with a carnivorous animal—or even a herbivore like a deer pushed to starvation. The familiar creases are all gone. So are the freckles that I loved to trace. My stomach aches as I stare at what's left: slivers of red flesh wrapping around exposed white bones.

The neck, however, is almost perfectly preserved. Ice particles crust over solid muscles and tissues and exposed vertebrae. Nothing has tried to eat there. And that would have been the most attractive part of his body, even more than the hands: no skin to tear through to get to the desired fresh meat.

Then, what happened?

His head could have been removed well after death. Maybe Kiernan succumbed to the blizzard on the first night, like I feared he would. Maybe hungry animals then attacked his hands, his eyes, the tongue inside his mouth. The most vulnerable parts. And a day after that, our tormentor— the butcher—might have found his body and decided to desecrate it further by carving the head away to claim Kiernan as one of his or her own victims.

It would make sense that the body was dragged far from its original resting place: there are no scraps of flesh or spots of gore on the pure white snow. Scavenging animals would have left plenty of those.

Though…

I return to his hands. The remaining slivers of pale skin have been bleached an unnatural shade of white by the freezing temperatures.

Could these wounds have been made by a knife?

Defensive wounds, possibly?

I imagine Kiernan fighting for his life, using his hands to shield himself from the blows that would ultimately claim him. A knife slicing into those hands again and again, until they were stripped to ribbons.

My teeth ache from how hard I'm clenching them. I turn away from the hands before they can infect my mind with any more ugly thoughts.

The question could be solved by searching his body for any other injuries. Bruising that wasn't caused by settling blood post-death, cuts across his clothing.

I'm half-wild from the raw, aching need to *know* what happened to Kiernan, as though that will somehow help him. I feel over his jacket, hampered by the bandaged hand, as I look for tears in the fabric. There's something solid there, near his stomach. I pull the jacket up but underneath is only the knit sweater he put on the morning we left the hotel. Inside the pocket, then. I unzip it. A small, dark object falls free.

My heart feels as though it is about to break. I slump back into the snowbank, my legs limp, my body numb. Ahead of me, sharp and crisp in its bed of white, is a small midnight-blue velvet box.

I know what it means.

Tears blur my vision and then snake down my skin to absorb into the scarf as I reach for the box. It's intricately made. A small gold latch holds it closed. I flick it up and open the box.

The engagement ring is beautiful, delicate. The diamond in its center almost certainly cost more than he could afford.

Keening cries build in my chest, only to smother in a throat that's too tight to let out anything more than a painful gasp.

This was the reason for the trip. To take me somewhere he cherished. It's also very likely the reason he pulled me away from the group, to search for a lookout with views of the wilderness below. The perfect place to ask me.

We would have had fourteen days together as a freshly engaged couple. Fourteen days to kiss and to hold and to go on walks and to build dreams for our future.

All shattered in an afternoon.

The others are silent, but I can feel their eyes on my back. They can't afford to wait much longer. I bend across Kiernan's chest one final time, holding him, telling him how achingly sorry I am. I can't even kiss his forehead. Can't close his eyes. Can't cover his face. There's nothing left to do but to kiss the familiar jacket and then to pull back, the box and its precious ring clutched in my hand.

"I'm done." It escapes me as a whisper. They hesitate for a fraction of a second, then turn, following the path as it leads downward.

Hutch glances back several times, making sure I'm still with them. He looks like he wants to help but doesn't know what to say. Solitude is the best thing he can give me. I place the little felt box into my jacket pocket, closest to my heart, which feels as though it's been shredded. Each pulse that pushes blood through my limbs is an obligation it despises. It would shut down if I let it.

The temptation is there. Leave the group silently. Walk until I can't be found again. Strip off my layers one at a time and then lie down in the snow and let the cold eat me alive.

I can't, though.

Someone hurt Kiernan. They carved his head off. Removed his teeth. Shredded his hands. He hadn't done a single thing to harm them, and they mutilated him so badly that it's not even possible to have an open-casket funeral for his mother's sake.

I'll find out who they are.

And I'll hurt them like they hurt Kiernan.

24.

The others were affected by Kiernan's remains in different ways. Hutch is jittery and uncomfortable. Simone seems to have grown tenser. Denny, on the other hand, shows almost no reaction. I watch his back as he leads us through the snow. He rocks slightly with each step, his head so high above us that he nearly brushes the branches overlapping our path.

The road is easy to follow at first. It trends downward in broad sweeps, and we stop tying cloth onto the trunks to mark our path.

The clear ground doesn't last long, though. Soon, trees begin overlapping the road in ways they shouldn't. Trunks emerge in the center of the path. Boulders encroach on what should be empty ground.

Simone's tenseness increases, but she pushes us onward. We make it another ten minutes along what we'd mistaken for a road before a cluster of white-coated firs barricade our way.

"No car's coming through here," Denny says, matter-of-fact.

Simone swipes a hand over her face. Her pale skin has become pinched and sunken. "We must have missed a turn. Let's go back."

Our path is still visible in the snow, at least. We hike uphill until the passageway grows clear again. Simone leads us in different directions, searching for a continuation of the path. If there is one, we can't find it. Soon, our footprints weave over one another in chaotic patterns, lines gouged through the snow so often that it's hard to keep track of where we started.

"Back," Simone barks, her teeth bared. "If we can't get out this way, we'll go in the opposite direction."

Hutch is bolder than I am, and voices what we're all thinking. "Won't that take us higher into the mountains?"

"This road has to lead *somewhere*. The lodge, maybe. That was where we were trying to get before this whole mess." Her gaze is steel fury. "There'll be some way to contact the outside world there."

The theory is good, but only as long as we're actually on a road. And the more I see of it, the less certain of that I become.

When we first drove up the mountains I remember seeing freshly plowed snow on either side of the path. The piles were high enough to look like guardrails. Even after the blizzard and the brutal winds, those clumps of hard snow should still be visible, if only as a rise in the landscape. But the only visible edges to our path are where the clear land ends and the pine trees begin.

More likely, what we're on is some kind of riverbed or a channel gouged by a landslide. Something with smooth bends that doesn't allow for tree growth.

It's impossible to be sure while the snow covers the land. It blurs everything, sapping away distinct features under its unifying layer of white. Simone wants to believe we're on a road. I have no alternative plan or better suggestion. All I can offer is doubts. So I keep my mouth shut.

The walk uphill is hard. The incline isn't steep, but it's unyielding. My water bottle is empty, so I fill it with snow and tuck it back under my clothes, knowing the chill against my skin is going to be hell but that it will still be better than dehydration.

We pass Kiernan's prone body by the side of the road, and it feels heartlessly callous to glance at him and then keep walking. I doubt Simone would tolerate another delay, though. She leads the group now, ahead of even Denny, forging through the snow with brute determination. Our breathing sounds like saws being pulled through wood. Gusts of condensation leave our mouths like cigarette smoke.

The sun has passed its zenith and is sliding downward. The passageway grows narrower, trees pushing in on either side, but still Simone won't abandon it. It's grown steeper too. Instead of walking, we're climbing. I see hazy gray sky ahead and know we're aiming for some kind of precipice.

"Slow down," I call, but Simone ignores me.

My muscles scream. I push them for one final burst, clambering past both Hutch and Denny, and snag the collar on Simone's jacket.

I pull her back just as we burst through a final layer of trees. The ground ends abruptly ahead of us, plunging downward for at least a hundred feet. There's nothing ahead except empty air and a hazy view of distant mountain ranges.

Simone, panting, hangs there for a second before stumbling back and clutching one of the trees.

Denny and Hutch come up on either side, moving cautiously. Snow tumbles over the cliffside, vanishing into the void below.

Weak laughter escapes me in gasping bursts. The edge doesn't frighten me. After today, I don't think much can. But it's spectacular in the truest sense of the word. Overwhelming. The cold stings my face and the wind whistles in my ears and the crisp tang of snow and pine lies over my tongue. And the view, stretching for as far as I can see, shows endless valleys and gulfs and mountain peaks spiking and collapsing toward the horizon.

It's the most alive I've felt since I lost Kiernan.

"Sky doesn't look good," Denny says.

The clouds above us are the same angry steel gray as the afternoon we disembarked the bus. There's no snow on the air yet, but I don't expect that to hold true for more than a few hours.

"There's nothing here, is there?" Simone's still gazing at the valley below, not yet willing to give up on the idea that the path was leading us to Blackstone Alpine Lodge. Her mouth twists. "We've been hiking to nowhere."

"Do we go back?" Hutch asks. "Try again?"

I fumble my phone out of my pocket. No cell service. It's nearly three in the afternoon. Regaining our lost ground will take us precariously close to sundown. Pushing on farther will almost certainly guarantee a night spent outside. We don't have any kind of shelter beyond the spare coats we all brought. No food, either. Even if we get through the night and the impending storm intact, we can't hike indefinitely on empty stomachs.

Simone slumps against her tree. One hand is looped around it to hold her steady. She's always been a force of grit and calculated decisions. Now, she looks empty. Lost.

"We'll have to go back," she says. "Maybe we can try again tomorrow, but…"

But for now, to have the best odds of survival, we'll return to the cabin. And perhaps, to the killer inside.

25.

Night has set in by the time we pass the bus.

It's a relief to see the broad, white shape. I'd started to think we'd lost our way. Twilight robbed us of our depth perception and sapped any color out of the landscape. We hadn't been able to find the last three strips of fabric we'd tied up to mark our path.

At my back, Hutch groans as he sees the bus. It's a relieved sound, I'm pretty sure. I wasn't the only one afraid of being lost in the mountains at night.

We leave the trees and strike out across the empty land leading to the cabin, using Hutch and my phones as flashlights. Snow has begun to fall. It's only light but threatens to get worse.

My light catches on a dark mark in the nothingness. Miri, still lying prone, slowly being covered by falling snow. Not the burial Steve would have wanted for her.

The massive pine tree rises out of the gloom. I can't stop myself. As I draw near, I trail my light over it. The beam isn't strong enough to reach the highest branches, but I can see Brian's head not far out of reach and Miri's head about fifteen feet above him. Nothing else, unless it's well hidden. The killer hasn't added Kiernan to the tree. Yet. I don't think I could have survived it if they had.

Dull light glows from the cabin window. The fire must be burning low. I hear movement around the building's side and signal to my companions. Slowly, wearily, we follow the sounds.

"You're back, are you?" Steve asks as he sees us.

Alexis, Grayson, and Steve are grouped around a boxlike shape at the cabin's rear wall. Steve props a hand on his hip, disappointment pulling broad creases over his expression. "Don't suppose help is on the way," he says.

"We're going to try again." Simone turns, deliberately putting her shoulder to him and cutting him out of the conversation. "Has anything happened here?"

Grayson's hair hides most of his expression, but he doesn't appear happy to have his father back. Alexis, for her part, seems relieved as her eyes dart over us.

I crane forward and recognize the object they're working over. A generator mounted to the wall. "We found some fuel in the shed," Steve says, forcing his way back into the conversation. "When it became clear you weren't getting us any kind of rescue today, we figured we might try to get some proper lights in the house. Only the damn thing is broken."

Denny steps forward. He bends over the generator and then pulls on something. It rattles. "You have air in the fuel system," he says. "I can clear it out. Provided I have the tools."

"The shed might have what you need," Simone says.

Denny grunts and stands, dusting off his hands on his pants, then moves away from us.

Simone runs the back of her hand across her forehead. She looks bone weary. "While Denny works on that, the rest of us are going to get some wood for the fire."

There are small noises of assent from the group as they split off in different directions. Steve shoves past me, bumping my shoulder, and I catch a tang of alcohol. Some of my relief to be back fades. It seems he found more than just gasoline in the shed.

Alexis snags my arm before I can follow the others. She offers a tight smile, then nods to the side, wordlessly asking me to walk with her.

A cold, gnawing kind of trepidation starts in my stomach. Walking off

to speak with someone in private is very likely how Miri died. I want—
need—to know who killed Kiernan and what he might have suffered
before then, but I can't willingly make myself the next victim.

And Alexis has been acting strangely since we first arrived at the cabin. I
rarely see her without her journal in hand. She's made no effort to befriend
anyone, not even on the bus, before things went wrong. I've had the sense
that she's hiding something. I just don't know what.

Alexis catches my hesitation. "I want to tell you something," she
whispers. "It's important."

She's small. I'm fairly sure I could fight her off for a few seconds to
scream for help if it comes to it. As long as I don't let her lead me too far
from the cabin. I nod.

We walk a dozen paces, Alexis glancing behind herself to make sure
we're not being followed. She stops first, and we're within yelling distance
of the others. It's very probable she has the same concerns I do. I still don't
let my guard down.

Her arms are folded across her torso. The wind buffets her short, flax-
colored hair around her face, uncovering the moles with every strong gust.
She leans her upper body toward me, and I bend slightly so that our heads
are at the same height.

"I think I can trust you." Her words are breathy and hot in my ear.
"Which is why I wanted to talk to you alone. There's something you
should know."

I glance behind us. Silhouettes move in the distance. Our companions,
scavenging for firewood. "What?" I ask.

"While we were working on the generator, Grayson and I started
talking." Alexis shuffles her feet. She's nervous. Her eyes scan the trees
nearby, searching for movement between them. "I found out why he and
Hutch fought. They'd been talking right before, right? Apparently, Hutch
made a joke about mothers. And it set Grayson off."

"Did he say why?"

"Yeah. His mother died recently. Only about six months ago."

Grayson's here with his father. I'd assumed it was some kind of bonding experience for them. Learning how to become a man or similar. I don't know Denny well, but what I've seen strikes me as a severe, no-compromise kind of personality. I can't imagine he approves of Grayson's hair or his slouch or his attitude.

Now, I start to see things in a different light. The vacation might have still been planned as a bonding experience but with a goal to bring what remains of their family together. Denny's not a paternal figure. He's more the sort of person who spends long hours at work and interacts rarely when he's at home. Even though he's kept Grayson at his side for the whole trip, their body language suggests they're nearly strangers.

Most likely, it was his wife who formed the core of their family. Without her, Denny might have felt his son drifting away and, realizing Grayson was very close to adulthood, recognized his window to make things right was closing.

Grayson, meanwhile, is acting out from grief he has no healthy way to express. His father's stiff demeanor doesn't invite any sort of intimate sharing. He hasn't made any secret out of the fact that the trip was forced on him. From his perspective, the trip is too little too late.

I try to reel myself back. I'm making a lot of assumptions about a family I barely know, who are trying to survive under horrible circumstances. I could be wildly wrong.

"Anyway—" Alexis breaks off, flinching, her eyes darting toward some sound she heard in the trees. It's a struggle to see through the falling snow. I crane my neck, squinting, but can't make out anything beyond the first few trunks.

Alexis clears her throat and leans closer to me, the words rushing out of her faster. "This is the part I really wanted to tell you about. I asked Grayson how his mother died. And he didn't say anything for a really, really long time. He just stared at me. And then he said, 'I think my dad killed her.'"

26.

My mouth tastes sour. I can't feel the bandaged hand, but my good hand has grown numb and tingly. At the edge of my vision, I see Denny bent over the generator, working on it.

I lean toward Alexis, my voice low. "Did Grayson say what happened?"

"The police ruled it a suicide. She left the house early one afternoon. She ran a red light close to their house and was hit."

"Okay." I hunch. A drop of moisture clings to the tip of my nose. "That doesn't sound like it was murder, though."

"Yeah. Supposedly the brakes failed." Alexis gives me a significant look.

"And Denny's a mechanic," I whisper.

"Exactly. Grayson says he maintained that car meticulously. It was the one he usually drove to work, but that morning he had some convoluted reason for why he couldn't take it. Something about the trunk space. So he took the family car to work that morning and left his wife with a vehicle she didn't know was broken."

"Huh." Doubt creeps through me in painful increments. "And the police didn't find him suspicious?"

"Apparently not. But Grayson said there were a lot of arguments between his parents in the weeks leading up to it. She was talking about leaving and taking Grayson with her. And…" Again, Alexis glances behind us, making sure there's no one who could be listening in. "Grayson thinks there might have been another man involved. He thinks she was going to visit him on the day she died."

A new image forms: Denny, a man rigid in his life, content with what he has, suddenly threatened by an outside force. The woman he thought was devoted to him says she wants to leave him for someone better. Simmering jealousy. A refusal to let her be happy anywhere except in his home.

"It's only what Grayson said," Alexis adds. She shrugs, hunched and nervous. "I'm not sure if even *he's* certain about it. But he had enough doubts to share it with me. Anyway. I thought it's something you should know. Just in case."

I remember the look on her face when our group returned. Relief. She'd been worried not all of us would come back.

There's a whirring noise behind us. I turn. Light shines from the cabin's window. It forms a rectangle of illumination on the ground, just barely grazing the base of the butcher's tree. They got the generator working.

Alexis gives me a final, tight smile then begins hurrying toward the light. I stand outside for another minute, letting the revelation flow over me like ice water.

The tinny whistling noise is back in my ears, setting my nerves on fire. I've spent the day walking beside Denny. For a lot of the time, I could have reached out a hand and touched his back.

Did he kill Kiernan?

He's massive. Easily six foot four and built with muscles. He could overpower even a fit man like Kiernan without too much trouble. He could have taken Brian out before the guide even had a chance to draw breath.

But why? What motive could he possibly have to purchase a vacation package for himself and his son and then begin murdering the other attendees?

Blake's whispered caution reverberates in my ears. Sometimes there's no reason. Sometimes not even a panel of psychologists can explain why a person does something.

And if I needed a reason, grief or anger is a powerful motivator. It's not only Grayson who's repressing his emotions. Denny's wife passed very recently, whether by his hands or by accident. And it's likely he hasn't been given a space to talk about what he's feeling on the inside since he was a child, if even then.

It's not proof of anything, I remind myself as I turn back to the cabin. No more than the knife in Alexis's bag or the bloodstained handkerchief in Grayson's. But *someone* has committed atrocities against our companions. And the kills are so efficient and terrifyingly precise that it's hard to believe the butcher has never taken a life before.

The cottage is brighter than I expected. The overhead light is on. Alexis has returned to her corner and is scribbling in her journal. She keeps her head down, avoiding both my gaze and the eyes of the room's only other occupant.

Denny sits in his seat against the opposite wall, his forearms resting on his knees and his hands limp between. His head is bowed, his shaggy hair limp. The cabin feels almost empty with just the three of us.

"Where are the others?" I ask.

Denny just shakes his head. Alexis speaks up, her voice tentative. "I think they're out at the shed."

The door bangs open behind me. Steve is laughing as he and Hutch drag in two heaters. "Look at what we found," he booms. "No more fires. No more smoke!"

They're large, waist height, and look at least a few decades old. I eye the rust crusting around their bases as Steve drags one toward the bookcase. As he passes me, I catch another gust of alcohol. He's in a good mood. Bordering on manic. He finds a power outlet and plugs the heater in.

"Yeah," he crows as the machine rattles to life. "*Hell* yeah."

"This one works too." Hutch has set his up at the room's opposite side.

It clicks softly as it begins to heat. I can only pray the rust hasn't damaged either of them enough that they start leaking or catch on fire.

"If we're going to be stuck in hell for another night, we'll do it on our own terms!" Steve is speaking a decibel louder than he needs to. When he sees me watching, he sweeps his arms out wide, as though to draw me into an embrace. I duck away, pretending to be interested in making my bed instead.

"We're gonna be warm inside and out," Steve booms. He reaches into his coat and pulls out two bottles of whiskey, confirming my fears, and slams them onto the table. One of the bottles is half-empty. "We'll drown our sorrows and lift our spirits all at once. A drink to Miri. A way to remember her!"

The word *performative* rings in my ear again. I don't dare speak as I hunch into my nest of clothes, aching legs pulled up to my chest.

Steve's cheerful at the moment, but I've seen how quickly a person's temper can shift with alcohol. My own father would start out jolly. He'd talk about the toys and sugary treats he was going to buy me and my brother. Goad us into raucous games. I learned to humor him when he was in that bright phase and be quick to hide as soon as I sensed that subtle turn an hour in, when he became sour and cruel instead.

I can credit my father for a lot of things. A hyper-developed ability to read others' body language, a hatred of hard liquor, a mistrust of people who indulge in it.

"We should go easy on the drink," Hutch says. He eases past Steve to hand me a bowl. It's full of warm food from the fireplace pot: the same blend of rice and canned vegetables we had the night before. The rice hasn't been cooked quite long enough and is crunchy at its core, but I still eat it gratefully. Hutch gives Steve a meaningful look as he passes again. "We're going to want to stay alert."

"Not like staying alert last night did us much good," Steve sneers. Deep color builds over Hutch's face.

The door pushes open, revealing a windswept Simone in the entrance. "Hutch is right." Her voice is cool, measured. If I hadn't spent so much time around her the last few days, I might not have picked up the undercurrent of exhaustion. "You can drink if you want, but we've lost two of our party across the last two nights and I don't intend to let it happen again."

Steve snorts. "Just don't put this one in charge again."

"Sure. That's fair." Hutch's color deepens. "I'm going to see if I can find a third heater or something."

Simone shifts out of the way so that he can leave. Her cool eyes follow him as he goes, her jaw working. The door hasn't quite closed before she catches it. "None of us should be outside alone," she says. "I'll go with him."

She didn't ask for volunteers to accompany her, but Denny rises and shambles to the door regardless, leaving Alexis and me alone with Steve.

"Well, they're in a sour mood." Steve unscrews the top on one of the whiskeys and sips straight from the bottle. If he'd been my father, this would be the point where I would try to slip, unseen, to my room. His eyelids seem to sag as he gazes from me to Alexis. "You're both young girls. Don't you like to have fun?"

Alexis puts her book aside. "I'm going for a walk," she whispers, crossing the room the long way to keep the table between herself and Steve. She hesitates at the door. "Christa? Want to come?"

"Yeah." I'm already grabbing for my jacket. I don't even wait to put it on before stepping outside. Alexis shuts the door firmly behind us and releases a long, strained sigh.

Standing on the cabin's front porch, struggling to pull the jacket over myself one-handed, I stare through the falling snow. It's grown denser. Even with the light from the cabin, I can only see a sliver of the butcher's tree. The bark looks strange in the distorted light. Almost as though it drips with blood.

We shouldn't be spreading out like this.

Grayson never returned to the cabin after we converged around the generator. For that matter, I last saw Blake that morning.

They know better than to be alone, especially after dark. At the same time, I can't blame them. We're grating on one another in the small cabin. The extroverts—Steve, Hutch, and to a lesser degree Blake—may be able to endure it better, but the constant pressure of unwanted company is wearing on all of us. I'd give a lot to just have twenty minutes on my own.

But privacy is a luxury we can't afford. Especially not now that night has set in. The heavy clouds and dense snowfall bring visibility down to nearly nil.

Alexis seems content to lean against the door, her face pinched against the cold. I adjust my jacket as I step away from her and pull out my phone. "I'm going to round up the others," I say, hoping she won't hear the nerves in my voice. "Meet you back here in five."

27.

Fresh snow crunches under my boots as I force my way out from the cabin. If I were even a little smarter, I would have stayed with Alexis in the doorway, close to light and safety. Trying to bring the others back together puts me in the same situation I just criticized them for: alone and vulnerable in the dark.

But maybe that's where I want to be. Just a little. A lamb in the snow, waiting to see if they can draw the wolf out of hiding.

I doubt Alexis would lend me her knife. If she did, she'd be a lot less intelligent than I've pegged her as. And I have no weapon of my own. I might be able to find something in the shed. A screwdriver, a sharpened stake. Anything that can be driven into a body to stop its approach.

I switch my phone to flashlight mode. The snow looks strange under the LED. Tracks already crisscross the space ahead of me, marking where people have made the journey to the shed and back. One spears off to the right, though, an aberration leading toward the sparse pine trees in the distance. I follow it.

The snow has a strange dampening effect on noise. All I can hear are my own breaths, kept light, and the sound of snow crushing beneath my feet. I keep alert, straining to hear any other presences nearby. Except for the cabin that's now growing faint in the distance, I could be alone out here.

A spark of light flickers ahead. It's a single coal, burning at eye height. A monster in the dark, hellfire glowing in its skull. My throat is dry as I cover my phone's beam, plunging myself back into darkness.

The light flares, growing brighter. I cross to it as silently as I can manage. The coal fades, then there's a deep, aching sigh, followed by the scent of sweet smoke on the air.

I raise my phone. Its harsh light cuts across ice-crusted trees. A figure between them flinches back. I push my advantage, stepping closer, my light held ahead of myself like a priest's cross.

"That's in my eyes," Blake says. Her voice is shaky. I lower the light and find the coal that drew my notice. A cigarette, held carefully between her fingers. Dark ash mars the snow at her feet: two other cigarette butts, already extinguished.

"I didn't know you smoked," I say.

She swallows, flicking the cigarette. "I've been trying to quit, but you can't hold this against me. Not after what's happened."

I don't remember seeing any cigarettes when we searched her belongings. The carton and blue lighter clutched in her spare hand are matches for the ones Miri used to carry, though.

It's not worth an argument. I nod back toward the cabin. "I came looking for you because we're not supposed to be splitting up. Especially not after dark."

"I need a few more minutes, okay?" Her mouth twists. "Being in there is going to send me mad if I don't get some space. The entire time you were gone, the truck driver talked about his wife. The same stories again and again, like a broken record."

I begin to turn away.

"You know," she says. I stop, waiting. She takes a pull of the cigarette and holds the smoke lovingly in her lungs before expelling it. "Despite all those years as a dispatcher, I've never seen a dead body before."

I have. I don't tell her that.

"I've spoken to plenty, though." She tilts her head back. Her red lipstick must have been recently applied. It stains a clear ring on the cigarette. "Right before they died."

The wind catches at the exposed back of my neck, prickling the hairs there. I turn away, leaving the small smoldering light to flicker in the darkness.

This time, I follow the edge of the sparse needled trees as I move back toward the shed. That's where Hutch, Simone, and Denny were supposed to be headed. I can tell before I even reach it that they're not there, though. There are no lights among the trees.

I slow my gait and soften my breathing as I step into the narrow channel of churned snow that marks where my companions trekked between the trees. My ears catch every creak and shudder as the wind picks up, tugging at the branches. Snow falls, raining onto my shoulder, and I flinch.

Sacrificial lamb. Bait to lure the wolf.

I flex the fingers around the phone, wishing I had something sharp to hold instead. There's a sound behind me that might have been sloughed snow or might have been a footstep. I turn. My light refracts off a thousand ice particles and endless cracked bark. It's hard to see through the branches. I think I'm alone. Impossible to be sure, though.

The shed rises out of the darkness. Its door hangs open, the broken hasp lock loose. I can't hear any sounds coming from inside but call out, just in case. There's no reply.

As I creep nearer, my light shines over the broken chairs stacked just inside the shed's entrance. Faces seem to rise out of the gloom beyond. I adjust my hold on the phone, straining to make sense of the overlapping slices of wood and metal.

If a stranger was staying near the cabin with the intention of picking us off one at a time, the shed would offer them shelter. It's close. It's full of tools they might need, gardening implements that are dangerously sharpened. Rope and twine. Potentially even a sled, to make transporting heavy burdens easier. It's where I would stay.

I'm at the doorway. The flicker of reflected light is disorienting, as though a dozen eyes gleam back at me through the darkness. It's enough to make me paranoid, convinced that I'm being watched. My shoes scrape over the threshold as I step inside.

The wind's low howl fades. My breathing suddenly sounds louder, until it's all I can hear. The light shakes as it travels over the space's dense clutter.

Something shines at my side. I bend over two crates to see it. There, tucked into the room's corner, away from easy view, is an ax. The wooden grip leans against the wall, the heavier metal head propped on the floor. I stretch my phone forward, bringing the surfaces into stark relief. The blade is clean. But traces of color cluster around where the metal joins with the wood.

Rust.

No. Blood?

It's hard to get a good sense of its true shade with the LED washing it out, but the pattern looks like someone may have tried to clean liquid off the ax and failed to get it out of the cracks. Exactly what Simone had been looking for when she examined Alexis's pocketknife.

My mouth tastes acidic. My pulse is in my ear, rushing and sick. I stretch my fingertips toward the ax, wanting to pull it closer, wanting to see it clearer, but afraid to touch it. The blade is so large. Wider than a neck, easily, and curving out from the handle. It's a vicious thing. Wicked.

A heavy hand lands on my shoulder.

28.

I shove myself backward, legs kicking. My shoulder hits the leg of a workbench. Boxes crowd under it and on either side, blocking my retreat, trapping me.

Oh, little lamb, you should not have let your guard down.

Denny looms in the shed's doorway. He's so massive I can barely catch any glimpse of the falling snow behind him. Shadows cling around his eyes. Emotionless eyes. Unfeeling pits, staring down at me.

He takes half a step toward me. I pull away. My back presses into the corner I've blocked myself in.

"I'm looking for Grayson," he says.

My mouth is dry. I give a small, tentative shake of my head. "He's not here."

Denny's eyes slide toward the ax hidden in the corner. There's no trace of surprise or curiosity in his expression. He already knew it was there.

"Dried tree sap," he says, and I realize he's talking about the red staining around the metal's edge.

It's not sap. No chance. Not with that consistency, that flakiness. But I'd be a fool to argue with the man who blocks my escape. "Yeah."

His eyes turn back to me. Measuring me. The silence is unbearable. Then he says, "Keep watch for Grayson," and turns and shambles back into the night.

Energy drains from me. I feel like a small animal being dropped from the jaws of a wolf. Shocked to be intact. Still not quite certain that I'm alive.

There's no proof that Denny is the butcher, I tell myself. He's only one of the seven people I need to be wary of.

But I don't like how unconcerned he was by the ax.

Or the way he stared at me. As though he was weighing up a choice.

I get my feet back under myself. My legs shake like paper in the wind. I need a weapon. There's not much a screwdriver will do against an ax, if that's truly the weapon that cost Brian and Miri their lives, but it's that or be defenseless.

I find a tool belt hung on the wall. There are no knives, but a row of worn screwdrivers jut out of the leather. My hand drifts toward the longest one, but I stop myself. A longer weapon will be harder to hide. Harder to palm in an uncomfortable situation. I take one of the shorter ones. Its metal section is only three inches long. That will still cause enough damage in an emergency.

My eyes linger over the ax. I'm far enough away that the discoloration—sap or rust or blood—is no longer visible.

I don't want to leave it where it is. But the idea of touching it is now more than uncomfortable; it's repulsive. And the shed no longer feels like a safe place to be.

The wind scrapes across my exposed skin as I leave. The gale's grown harsher. I have to lean into it to keep my balance as I navigate my way back into the cabin.

Heat wraps around me as I enter the room. It's almost shocking in its intensity. Both heaters are set to high and angled to radiate warmth across the space. For once, my companions have stripped out of their layers of fleece. Steve wears a shirt that he's left unbuttoned. It exposes a strip of curling, bushy chest hair and flushed skin. He sits on the edge of the table, legs swinging below, and holds one of the whiskey bottles. It contains significantly less than when I last saw it.

"Chrissy," Steve crows. He raises the bottle toward me: a toast. "I'd about given you up for dead. Come and have a drink."

Dread runs through my veins like poison. It's a very different kind of fear to the sharp tang of terror I felt in the shed with Denny. This is slower, slicker. The kind that clouds my head instead of clearing it. Numbs instead of energizes. I'm not sure what I say, but I mumble something as I slink along the room's edge, trying to keep myself small and insignificant.

I'm an adult woman. My father has been dead for nearly ten years. But old scars sometimes peel back open and weep fresh blood.

Outside, the wind intensifies, as though warning us that we won't be escaping anytime soon. Something—a loose branch, probably—bangs against the cabin's back wall. It sounds uncomfortably like a person knocking to be let in.

Steve's attention doesn't stay fixed on me. He talks to the room, his voice booming, his bottle raised and skin blotchy. "Total smoke show when I met her. Served at the rest stop a lot of us truckers used. They all flirted with her, but she blew them off. My buddies…my buddies said I had no chance. But I asked her out anyway. And I was the first and only guy she said yes to. I took her to a real nice restaurant and she ordered a huge steak with pepper sauce, and that's when I knew she was the only girl for me."

I slide down the wall to nestle in my bed, my sanctuary. This doesn't feel like grieving to me. It feels more like feigning grief while taking advantage of being the center of attention.

The branch beats against the wall, shredding any trace of calm I try to clutch around myself.

People grieve in different ways, I remind myself. When my father passed, I didn't speak his name for nearly four months. Any outsider would have read that as callousness. But there was too much there. Love and anger and resentment and longing. I couldn't explain that the words physically choked me.

And after August 8…

Images flash across the theater in my mind. The rain. The roar of rushing water. The pain. The boy's terrified eyes.

A voice, yelling: "Can't we do something?"

After what happened late on the night of August 8, I barely left my apartment, quitting my job and spending my savings on grocery deliveries.

I don't know if that's something I should be ashamed of. That I grieved for a stranger more than for my own father.

Steve has launched into another story. He was going to be an airline pilot. Paid for the training and nearly got his license before a near-miss accident soured him on it. Miri only features in the story once: as the person who told him he was a fool after the crash.

The room's too hot. I've stripped out of as many layers as I feel comfortable losing and it's still stifling me. To my left, Alexis flutters her sweater's front to circulate air underneath. Simone seems unconcerned by the heat but leans back against the wall, her arms crossed and gaze directed toward the ceiling.

Hutch is folded over, a rolled-up coat between his head and the wall, as he tries to sleep.

Two of our party are still missing, I realize with a jolt.

"Hey." My voice interrupts the start of another story, and Steve raises his eyebrows, the skin across his face going slack. I lean forward, making sure I have everyone's attention. "Blake and Grayson are missing."

Simone grimaces. Creases form across her delicate skin, concentrating around her nose. I feel as though she knew but was willing to ignore it as long as no one spoke up. "Okay. When was the last time anyone saw them?"

"I passed Blake maybe half an hour ago." The sense of wrongness, of danger, makes it hard to get the words out. "She was smoking. But she should be back by now. There's a storm—"

The loose branch thuds against the cabin's wall to punctuate my point.

"Grayson goes on walks sometimes," Denny says. He sounds muted, defeated. "Sometimes in the rain. Sometimes in the snow. He won't be back for hours."

The cabin's support beams creak as the rising storm applies pressure.

I lower my voice. "We can't just leave them out there."

My final words are drowned under a heavy rattling. I flinch, staring at the door. It shudders, then draws inward. A heavily bundled form shuffles through. Blake flips her hood off her short gray hair and shakes herself out.

"See?" Steve, still on the table's edge, has begun to slur, his words dragging out. "She's fine."

"Well, you've found a way to make the place a sauna at least." Blake realizes we're staring, and her eyes narrow. "I wanted to get some fresh air."

A sluggish kind of relief enters me. Blake shuffles to the couch Steve and Miri used to share and slumps into it, a heavy sigh escaping her as she begins to untie her shoes.

"And Grayson?" I try.

"You won't find him if he doesn't want to be found." There's frustration in Denny's tone. I can imagine nights spent cruising the streets looking for his missing son.

I don't like it, but I tell myself Denny knows his boy better than the rest of us. I try to relax back against the wall as sweat beads on my skin from the heat. The loose branch hits the wall again, muffled but persistent.

"What the hell is that noise?" Blake asks. She kicks her shoes aside.

The question leaves us silent. My mouth turns dry. I was so preoccupied by the more pressing threats—Steve, the alcohol, my missing companions—that I let the sound fall into the background, dismissed as a broken branch.

But it's not. It's too loud, too heavy.

It repeats. Banging against the cabin's back wall, not far from where Denny sits. A slow *thud, thud, thud*. Like a dead man knocking to be let in.

29.

I'm the first up. The room is so hot that I carry my jacket until I get to the door. Behind me, Steve calls, the words running together as he grows irritable. "What're you doing going out there again?"

There's movement at my side. Hutch pulls his cap down over his dyed hair and gives me a short nod. I turn my phone's flashlight on.

We shove out into the blizzard. The snow's growing deeper. I'm panting within a few paces. Voices mutter behind me; some of the others have joined us. I try to see them, but they're a blur beneath the driving snow.

My gloves scrape frost from the wood walls as I circle the cabin. Pine trees grow close to the building's back, their branches spreading over parts of the roof. Something glitters on one of the nearer trunks. Liquid, a vivid red in my light. I press the tip of my gloved finger into it. It's nearly frozen, but a smear of color comes away under pressure. My heart sinks.

I step back, raising my light. The liquid trails across multiple trees in thin ribbons. Drops glitter on the snow around our feet. Someone—Simone?—whispers a string of curses behind me.

We can't stop now. I feel the bite of the screwdriver against my hip as I step forward. Branches graze my jaw and my exhaled breaths condense into crystals against their frost-coated tips.

The noise repeats. Deep, slow thuds. I face toward it and my light shimmers over an unnatural shape among the harsh lines of bark and branches.

I make out the hand first. Palm facing toward me, fingers slightly spread. The glove is gone, but I think I see it in my peripheral, half buried in the snow nearby.

There are no legs beside the hand. I trail my light up the arm, Grayson's puffy jacket reflects the beam back at me. I find the torso. It's oriented wrong, the split of the shoulders occurring below the narrowing of the hips. The legs stretch high above, clamped together by lashings of rope.

He's hanging upside down.

My light shimmers down again. The space between his limp arms is empty. As before, the head was taken. All that remains are slick icicles of blood and spinal fluid clinging to the stump of neck.

The blizzard gusts around us. Grayson's body moves like a pendulum under its force, his arm and back thudding into the cabin wall with each gust.

There's a soft crunch behind me: heavy shoes on the packed snow, pressing it into ice. I step back as Denny moves past. He doesn't make a sound, but there's a drawn emptiness in his slack face that sends pain through me. His massive hands reach out. They touch Denny's chest, unbelieving.

"Cut him down," he whispers.

My light traces over the rope tied around his leg. It rises over the closest pine's high branches before looping back down. The other end is fastened to a trunk less than ten feet from us.

Simone steps forward. "Denny—"

"Cut him *down*." Denny's voice booms like a cannon. We all pull back. He swings, his shaggy hair sticking to his forehead, lips peeled back from teeth in a grimace. "Girl. Alexis. You have a knife."

She's frozen, her limbs locked in place. Her eyes remind me of a deer in headlights as Denny advances on her.

"Here." Hutch moves forward. He pulls a rusted, serrated knife from his pocket and advances on the rope. He tries to cut it, but the knife jams on the fibers.

Denny takes it from him and begins sawing in earnest. Even through the storm, I'm certain I can hear the faint snap of the cords giving out as the rope frays. Grayson's body shudders down an inch, then, all at once, falls.

We step back as Denny cradles his boy's body. Neither rigor mortis nor ice have been able to claim him yet, and Denny lays him on his back, his arms folded over his chest and his legs together. Then he kneels beside his son, arranging his clothes. Gently tugging the creases out. His hand flutters to where Grayson's head should have been and I know he wants to brush his hair back.

Once he's done with his clothes, Denny stays hunched beside him for several minutes. The temperature is dropping as the blizzard coats the region, but none of us dare interrupt the giant. Denny finally stands. His expression is unreadable, but there's a slackness about his cheeks that I haven't seen before. He doesn't speak to us or even look at us as he walks past, returning to the cabin.

I glance at those who are left. Hutch, Simone, and Alexis. Steve and Blake must still be inside.

"Where did you get that knife?" Simone asks. Her gaze is distant, her eyes clouded, her voice dangerous.

Hutch clears his throat. "In the cabin. In the bottom of one of the drawers. I figured the place's owners must have kept some for cooking, but this was the only one I could find." There's a second hesitation, then he follows it up with, "I only got it this evening. It's for self-defense."

"All right." Simone turns. Her movements seem very measured. "Fine."

As she passes a tree, she hurls her fist at it. The crack rings out through the freezing air. Simone keeps walking as though nothing happened, even though I can see flakes of broken bark crumbling from the impact.

Hutch's breath comes out shaky. He shoves the knife back into his pocket and avoids our eyes as he follows in Simone's wake.

The wind funnels fresh snow across Grayson's body. Alexis's eyes catch my phone's light as she watches me. "Are you coming in?" she asks.

"You can go." My throat is tight. "I'll follow in a minute. I want to see if I can figure some stuff out."

The body lies ahead of me. My mind is filled with memories of people leaving the cabin and returning.

Somewhere in this dark, icy cluster of trees I'm going to find my answers. The killer has left more evidence with this death than with any before. It has to be enough.

Surely.

30.

Alexis tilts her head, a soft exhale slipping from her lips. Her eyes dart across the trees around us, searching for movement in the darkness. Then she crosses to Grayson's body and crouches down by the stump neck.

"Another clean cut," she says, using her gloved fingertip to scrape away the forming snow and ice crystals. "That means a large blade was used. Like a machete or a sword."

"Or an ax," I say.

"Potentially." Alexis sends me a questioning glance. "He died in these trees. There's too much blood on the bark and on the ground for anything else. Which means the attack must have killed him fast, before he could make any noise."

Small mercies, I think.

The alternative would be that his throat was slashed open and he struggled, voiceless, while he bled out.

I move outward from the body, examining the snow. Like I thought, Grayson's missing glove is half buried only a few feet from his body. It's crusted with partially frozen blood.

Did it come off in some kind of struggle? Or while his body was being dragged to its final resting place?

I move back to his hands. Denny laid them over his chest and I try not to disturb the arrangement as I search the exposed skin. It's also smeared with blood. I picture Grayson clutching at his neck as blood gushed through his fingers.

"Look under the fingernails." Alexis has crept up to my side. Her pale hair clings to her damp skin. I can feel the heat from her small body.

I raise Grayson's hand. The nail bed's not clean, but then none of us have had a bath in days. Alexis uses her pinkie finger to indicate them. "No chips or breaks. No scraps of skin under the nails. No obvious signs of a prolonged struggle."

That compounds what I'd already started to believe. That the attack came as a surprise: sharp and sudden and over before Grayson really knew what was happening.

"You know a lot about what to look for," I say.

Alexis can't quite meet my eyes. "I fell down a true crime research spiral recently."

This isn't the first time I've felt like she's only giving me part of the story. I could press her on it, but the mystery in front of me is more vital, and I don't want to be outside any longer than necessary.

"Can you tell how long he's been dead?" I ask.

Alexis feels his hands, moving the joints experimentally, before placing them back on his chest with a frown. "Only as much as we already knew. He's still warm but cooling quickly. He would have died somewhere within the last two hours, since we last saw him at the generator."

I trail my light down his body until it stills over his legs. The rope is still tied there, lashing his ankles together. I shuffle closer and lift the material. It's old and rough and dust flakes free when I twist it. It came from the shed, I'm fairly sure. The killer is using whatever's available to stage their attacks.

I train my light toward the branches above. It's not hard to find the one Grayson was strung from. The bark has been rubbed raw where the rope dragged.

"How heavy do you think Grayson is?" I ask. He's tall but very thin. Probably not much more than 130 pounds. Still, that's not nothing.

The men could probably lift his weight. Simone's strong. I might be able to if I really strained. Alexis is tiny, though, and I can't see Blake having the upper body strength.

"They could have used a counterweight," Alexis says. "Anything heavy that could clip onto rope. I'm sure you could find something like that in the shed."

"I was on the verge of trusting you too."

She chuckles. "That would be a mistake. To believe too much in anyone's innocence, I mean."

I hate how much truth there is in that.

Finally, I leave the body. My phone's light shimmers over churned snow and flecks of crimson. I pace back, struggling to read the environment. I think I can pinpoint the place where Grayson was attacked. Between two trees that now bear sprays of red. I crouch and find a pool of blood between the roots. It's not unblemished, like the previous two. It smears, the trail of red thinning as the body drained. The killer began moving the body almost immediately. Time wasn't on their side.

I raise my light. There, to our right, the path to the shed is barely visible between the trees.

A lot of us went back and forward along that path. Steve and Hutch to collect the heaters. Then Simone and Denny. Even I went to the shed in search of a weapon.

I can see the scene from the killer's eyes. He would have stood exactly where I am, crouched over his bleeding victim, possibly even working on fully severing the head. Then, noise. One or more people walking along the track less than twenty feet away. The butcher, so close to discovery, would fall still. As soon as the danger faded, he would grip Grayson's legs and pull, dragging him deeper into the trees and up to the cabin's shelter, where he could finish his work.

Earlier, I left the cabin with the hope of encountering our tormentor. There's a not-unreasonable chance that I was the disturbance. The person who could have looked to the side and glimpsed his bloodied form hunched exactly where I now stand.

I could have stopped this.

"We need to go to the shed," I say.

31.

Wariness darkens Alexis's expression. I squeeze my eyes closed. I'm slipping again. I've begun to trust her and expect her to trust me in return. Her words reverberate: *It would be a mistake to believe too much in anyone's innocence.*

"Sorry," I say. "I need to check something in the shed. And I'd really rather not be there alone. But I won't blame you if you want to go back to the cabin instead."

She watches me for a second, her eyes so dark that they look almost black. Then she says, "Sure. I can come."

The trees have done a lot to shield us from the wind. I hunch as we exit their cover and cross the empty expanse bridging the way to the shed. Its door is still open. Snow has built up and the door strains against it, creaking, as gusts pull against it. My light seems to fade out at the threshold, refusing to touch anything inside.

Alexis's breathing is quick and shallow. She stays close to me. I'm grateful not to be alone, but I'm also very aware that, in the crowded shed, we'll be dangerously underprepared for any kind of attack. I slip my hand under my jacket and rest it over the screwdriver handle.

My light flickers across the room's dusty contents. I raise it, trying to see as much of the floor as possible to search for fresh tracks in the dust and snow. There are plenty; multiple sets loop around the narrow walkway. I can't tell how many. At least some would have been when we first searched the shed. Still more would come from when Steve and Hutch found the heaters. I strain to read individual footprints, but it's impossible to say whether someone else has been through the shed.

Instead, I turn toward the corner. The ax is still there. I crouch, pushing my light close to it.

Alexis takes a short breath. "Is that why you brought up axes earlier?"

"Yeah." I strain to see the staining around the handle. Is there more? Less? Has it been bloodied and cleaned again since I last saw it? Was it sitting in this position, or was it more to the left? Frustration bubbles in me. I should have taken a photo of it. I just didn't expect to need to reference it so soon.

"It's the right size. And the right shape to make those kinds of injuries." She's so close that a loose strand of hair tickles the back of my neck. She swallows. "We should bring it back to the cabin."

I glance up at her.

"Put it somewhere with a lot of eyes on it," she continues. "Make it impossible for anyone to sneak away and collect it."

That's a good thought. I pass her my phone and reach for the ax's handle. It's heavier than I expected. I bring my other hand—the bandaged hand—underneath to help stabilize it and still stagger a fraction as I drag it out of its corner.

"Is there anything else here that could be used as a weapon?" Alexis asks. "Anything we need to lock up?"

Everything. The circular saw. Legs could be torn off the broken chairs and used as clubs. Screwdrivers from the kit I pilfered earlier. The gardening tools. Everything in the room is either sharp metal or heavy wood.

"I don't suppose we can lock up the whole shed," I say.

"Not unless we can find a new hasp." Her mouth twists. "Even then, the wood's rotten. Anyone could break it open again with a little determination."

I adjust my hold on the ax. The idea of getting any closer to the reddish-brown stains makes me squirm, but the weight is too great to hold away from my body. I reluctantly press it against my chest. "This is the only thing I've found that matches the killer's style. It'll have to be enough for now."

We force our way back through the snow. Alexis lets me take the lead, which is only fair. I wouldn't want someone carrying an ax behind my back either.

As we near the massive pine tree outside the cabin, I gaze up its length. The sparse light makes it hard to see clearly, but I think there might be a third shape suspended on the branches. The queasiness in my stomach tells me to turn away, but I need to know. I move closer, eyes squinted against the bitter wind as I fight to peer through the deepening shadows.

I was right. A third head has been affixed to the pine. Not far above Brian's. Grayson's long hair flows like a river, tangling over the long-dead branches and snagging on the bark. The tip of the branch was impaled into his neck and its end juts out through his slack mouth. His eyes are open just a sliver: a narrow slice of whites barely visible beneath thick lashes and the strands of hair coating his face.

Did Denny have to look at this as he passed? Did he stand where I am now, gazing up at what remains of his son? The thought hurts. I turn back to the cabin.

It's only as I'm pushing through the door that I realize how I must look. "We have an ax," I call, and wish I could have found a way to be more casual about it. "Don't panic."

Most of them still rise as I drag the weapon in. I doubt I could swing it properly even if I'd wanted to. At least not without the use of my left hand. I manage to lift it, though, and drop it onto the table's edge, where Steve was sitting the last time I saw him.

"Christa found it in the shed," Alexis says as she enters behind me. Her voice is soft. "We thought it would be wiser to keep it somewhere visible."

Simone seems to be holding a simmering anger in check. She crosses to me, and the look she gives says she's not happy with this choice.

Some of my conviction falters. Instinct tells me to back down and go quiet, but I push forward instead. "It's better than leaving it out there where anyone could take it, isn't it?"

She leans close and her words drop to a whisper that only I can hear. "You have a room full of frightened people, all tired and hungry and pushed to the edge of what they can endure. Two of them are drunk. You tell me if it sounds like a good idea to bring a weapon into that situation."

Two drunk? Steve is on the couch, panting and face slack. He still holds one of the bottles but the other is missing. I scan the room and find it: on the floor beside Denny.

Simone picks up the ax. Unlike my fumbled hold, she grips it easily. She crosses to the closet near the fireplace and wrenches the door open.

There's very little inside. We already scavenged the spare blankets and coats, and now only a metal bucket for fire ashes and a walking stick are left. Simone props the ax inside.

"Hutch." She turns toward him. "You have a knife too."

He swallows. "For self-defense—"

"That's no longer an excuse." Her eyes are deathly cold as they slide over us. "How many of you have armed yourselves?"

"We're being picked off like blind sheep," Blake says. She sits beside Steve, her arms crossed. "We'd be fools not to want to protect ourselves."

"Pass it over." Simone reaches her hand out toward Hutch. Her fingers are very long and pale. "Now. Or I'll take it by force."

He seems frozen for a second, then reluctantly passes her the rusty serrated knife.

"Alexis."

Her skin is white and her jaw a rigid line. "No."

"Your knife, Alexis."

"It's my property! You can't take something I legally own—"

Simone's hand slams onto the table. The sound is like a gunshot. It runs through me, heavy reverberations that shake my bones.

"Give it to me." She's whispering now, and it feels far, far worse than yelling. "Or so help me, I will carve scars into that pretty face of yours."

32.

Alexis stares at the rest of us. Her eyes are wide and frantic, begging us to step in, to say something.

"Come on now." Steve's words drain into one another. He smiles, his cheeks red and his face sweaty. "She hasn't caused any trouble. And you—you know how important it is to be…to be safe. You're one of our country's heroes. You saw active duty, right? So you understand—"

"Bite your tongue, Steve." Simone doesn't move her gaze from Alexis. "For just five minutes of your life, learn the joys of silence. Alexis, you have ten seconds before I lose the last of my patience."

Alexis's skin is normally a rich bronze, but now it's taken on a sickly, blotchy shade. She reaches an unsteady hand into her pocket and passes Simone the folding blade.

"Fine." Simone's intensity doesn't waver. Her focus switches to the rest of us. "Anyone else?"

The screwdriver is sharp and hot against my side. I try to keep my face empty, to not give anything away.

"If you don't hand over what you have, I *will* search you."

She seems to mean it. And I don't want to know the consequences of lying. A lump sticks in my throat as I pull out the screwdriver. Blake hands Simone a carving fork, its tips dangerously sharp. Steve was carrying a paring knife, something that he seems to have brought in case they found a way to open up the frozen lake for fishing.

Only Denny doesn't offer up a weapon. Simone makes the rest of us stand to one side as she searches his belongings and pats down his body but finds nothing. She carries the rest of our items to the cupboard with the ax and places them inside. Then she shoves the door closed.

"You're all adults. I thought I could trust you to use enough common sense and caution to keep yourselves safe," she says. "Apparently, I was wrong. Four bodies now lie in the snow, and still, no one in the outside world even knows that we're in danger. The rest of us will be dead within a day if we don't change something."

Blake hunches, sinking deep into the couch. "We don't know that the murderer is one of us. All you've done is strip our protection away for next time we're attacked."

"You still think the killer isn't sitting in this room right now?" Simone casts an arm out, indicating all of us. "We're in the middle of nowhere. The chances of another building or settlement being close by are so slim, it may as well be rounded down to zero. The chances that those hypothetical settlements hold someone with murderous impulses and who just happened to stumble on us is even smaller. No. One of us is doing this. And I don't know why, but I'm absolutely, unshakably certain that it's a mistake to leave any one of you with a weapon."

My companions are all silent. I count them. Seven, including myself. If Simone is right—and with every passing hour, I grow more convinced that she is—then one of the six people around me is a monster unlike anything I've known before.

"Anyone who tries to find a replacement weapon will be treated as the very real threat they are." She gazes at each of us, making sure we understand the message. "If you leave this cabin for any reason, you'll be searched before you're allowed to reenter. Are we clear on that?"

No one speaks. Simone evidently takes that as assent because she slumps down, her back to the cupboard, and drags her jacket over her knees. She must plan to spend the night there, physically blocking anyone from reaching the sharpened metals inside.

"I expected more from a soldier," Steve says.

"Did you?" Her delicate brows rise up, but her eyes remain distant, detached. "Fascinating."

"You defended this country at one time." His words are still loose around the edges, but he's no longer trying to drink from the bottle he cradles. "You…you know how it feels. The urge to fight or…or to protect."

Simone shuffles her legs out, her shoes scuffing over the wooden floor. "I was eighteen when I joined the army. A recruiter came through my high school just before graduation and told us about this opportunity. A chance to learn practical skills, a chance to forge friendships that would last a lifetime. Challenge yourself, he said. Travel to places no one in your town has ever been. Do something that really, actually *matters*. That was the promise, at least."

I lean forward, attentive to her words. There's a painful rawness to them that sends discomfort crawling through my skin. Simone has never let herself appear this vulnerable in my presence before.

"Four months into my service, one of my closest friends stepped on a land mine. I was so obsessed with trying to stop the bleeding that I didn't hear his final words. After that, I wanted out."

She pauses to take a deep breath, and I hear it rattle as it passes through her throat.

"And that was when I discovered I'd signed a contract that essentially said they owned me. I *couldn't* leave. In any other job, if your boss asks more than you're willing to give, you can quit. But not there." A crooked smile breaks out across her face. "I had to wake up when they decided. Go where they wanted and stay there until they said I was done. And they didn't just control my body. It felt like I'd signed over the rights to my soul. They got to decide my ethics, my limits. What constituted wrong and right. They could tell me to kill another human, a complete stranger, and I'd have to do it."

My mental picture of Simone shifts. She'd always struck me as the kind of person who liked to be in control; with Brian gone, she naturally slid into the leadership position. I'd thought it was just a part of her personality. Some people like to follow directions; some like to give them.

Now, I start to wonder if it's more of a compulsion. Simone spent years of her life feeling like she didn't belong to herself. And now she's willing to fight—furiously, viciously—to not lose that control ever again.

"The army turns some people into heroes," Steve mutters. "Guess it just turned you into a weak-spined pacifist."

"My time there wasn't useless," she retorts. "It hardened me. Sharpened me. And it made it easier to see other people for what they really are." She fixes each of us with an exacting gaze, as though she can penetrate our outer shells. I wonder what she sees in me. "So many of the new recruits were just like me, only there because they didn't have any better plan for their lives. Others joined for idealistic reasons that were quickly wearing thin. And a few…" Her mouth twists. "A few were salivating for active duty. Eager for any kind of enemy to fight. Taking bets on who would claim their first kill."

"You get bad eggs in every job," Steve says. "You think the army's special? It's not. Last year one of the truckers I used to know was pulled in for beating his brother until he died. Bad people will find their way into any career."

I can't help but glance toward Blake. She's stiff and silent, but there's a brightness about her eyes as she absorbs the words.

Steve's right. Insidious figures will worm their way through any kind of profession.

"That's what's happening to us," Simone says. She stares down at her long fingers. The knuckles stand out, white and straining, thin veins wrapped over them like spiderwebs. "Someone here has that hunger for violence. They came on this trip with a plan. To hunt us. And they don't intend to stop until we're all dead."

33.

My mouth is dry. The wind drags across the cabin's walls, whistling along every narrow gap it finds. It rattles the window—a constant, brittle noise that aches in my bones.

Grayson was cut down, so why are my ears convinced that they can still detect the rhythmic thumping of his body against the wall?

The butcher planned this all before we even arrived. It's an ugly thought. But there's some validity to it. One death could be a spur of the moment provocation. Two might have been eliminating a witness or cleaning up loose ends. But four? Spaced apart, timed carefully, the victims apparently chosen according to who presents the best opportunity. It's more akin to sport hunting.

Unbidden, my gaze turns toward Steve. On the bus, he bemoaned the fact that he hadn't been allowed to bring his guns. He'd been eager to hunt. And it wasn't impossible to imagine a man like him might be fascinated by the idea of the world's most exclusive prey: humans.

But Miri was a victim. And it's hard to believe Steve would murder a woman he seemed to love very much.

Did he love her, though?

I turn my head as the question stings me. There's something not entirely authentic about Steve. It's as though some part of his personality compels him to put on a performance, to win our admiration, to win our sympathy.

How much could someone hide under that kind of veneer? Could they conceal their disgust for a spouse that society expects them to adore?

Could a man who wanted his wife out of his life organize a vacation to stage her murder? He must have known that police are quick to suspect husbands in cases of murder. Would he have thought that slaughtering more of his companions might divert the brunt of the scrutiny from him? It would certainly make the attacks appear random, rather than targeted.

But then, could he go through with not just the murder of his wife but also the performance when the time came?

I swallow and taste sourness at the back of my throat.

Very similar questions linger for Denny. His own son was killed. Would he be capable of that?

Perhaps. I've heard stories of people who, when their world crumbles beyond repair, kill their wife and children before leaving to start a fresh life somewhere. A way to purge the past. To clean up unfinished business before starting anew. No matter how twisted that logic is, it makes sense to a certain kind of mind. A black-and-white form of thinking.

Denny drinks deeply from his bottle. The skin around his eyes is slack and heavy, wrinkles draping like loose cloth.

The paranoia is eating at me. I need clarity. If I can't narrow down the list of possible suspects, then at least I need to know which of the six people around me I can trust. Even just one or two allies would go a long way to keeping me alive for another night.

Kiernan could have been killed by anyone and at any time. There was a two-day gap between the last time I saw him and uncovering his body. My mind flashes to the way the flesh was stripped from his hands, and a clammy sickness builds in my stomach. There's not much I can glean from my would-be husband's death except raw, blinding grief.

Both Brian's and Miri's murders happened overnight. If I take Hutch and Blake at their word and believe they fell asleep on their watches, then anyone could have been responsible. Any of us would have had the time, not just to kill but to clean up afterward.

There's one thing to note, though: Steve, Hutch, and Blake were closest to the door. In a cabin as cramped as this one is, where we need to walk over one another to reach anywhere, it's not hard to imagine that the killer might have picked their position carefully.

The most significant murder is Grayson's. That happened as dusk set, while we were all still awake and active. And it occurred during a relatively narrow window—between seeing Grayson at the generator and the first time we heard his body bumping against the wall. That's a window of less than two hours, I'm pretty sure. Still ample time to behead a man, stage his body, and clean up afterward…but there would have been more pressure. Less leeway for mistakes.

I dredge through my memories, trying to recall who I saw, when, and how they were behaving. They're all starting to blend together. I was exhausted after walking for most of the day, irritated by the way people kept leaving the cabin, and not as focused as I now wish I'd been.

Blake was outside for the longest, anxiously smoking among the trees. I remember that clearly. She was gone for almost the entirety of the two-hour window.

Hutch and Simone left with the excuse that they were going to the shed, but when I went looking for them, I couldn't find either of them.

That doesn't have to be suspicious. The cabin's tight confines were grating on us. Like Blake, they might have simply craved a chance to stand alone in the snow for half an hour before returning to the stiflingly hot confines of our temporary home.

Denny spent time outside as well. He shocked me in the shed while I was examining the ax. His excuse was that he was looking for Grayson, but later, when I suggested a search for his son, he rejected the idea.

Frustration builds. I swallow it. If I'd been better at keeping track of time and who I saw at what points, I might be able to exclude people by process of elimination. As it is, I was in my own head for too much of that two-hour window.

But there are still two people who I might be able to scrape together an alibi for.

Alexis pulled me aside to talk to me after we reconnected at the generator, the last time we saw Grayson alive. From there, she went straight back to the cabin. We were inside together until I left to look for the others. I left her standing at the front door, and she was back inside by the time I returned.

There's still a gap. I lost sight of her during the time I found and spoke to Blake and went to the shed. How long would that have been? Twenty minutes? Half an hour?

How long does it take to kill a person and change out of bloodied clothes?

The answer probably depends how prepared they were. Whether their clean clothes were close at hand. Whether they'd practiced the sequence of events until it became muscle memory.

I bite my lip. Alexis is the type of person who could be pedantic and methodical, especially about something high stakes. Even so, the window of opportunity would have been so narrow, and so fraught with risk, that I can't imagine her taking it. Especially considering how much larger Grayson was compared to her. The element of surprise will shift the dynamics of a fight dramatically, but it still has its limits.

The only other person I might be able to trust is Steve. He stayed inside the cabin longer than any of us. Assuming that Alexis didn't wander away from the cabin after I left, Steve wouldn't have had a chance to slip out without being seen. He's also been drinking heavily. This level of intoxication could be faked, but not easily. And it would be a serious hamper on anything that required finesse, like the clean slices to Grayson's throat and the careful knots tying him up.

Steve's not the type of person I would normally choose to have on my team, but my options for allies are so severely limited that I'll take anything I can get.

"We need another watch," I say. Six sets of exhausted, resentful eyes turn toward me. I voiced the thought first, so it's up to me to follow through. "I'll volunteer for the first half of the night."

"Okay." Simone gives a short nod. "I'll join Christa on the first watch, but we'll need two more for the second shift."

"I'll do it," Hutch says.

Steve scoffs. "After last time?"

"You volunteering instead?" Hutch sends a meaningful glance toward the nearly empty bottle.

"Let me do it," Alexis says.

"I'll join you on the second watch." Denny's voice is weary and his bottle almost as low as Steve's, but no one questions him.

The clock is creeping close to eleven. The wind is vicious. Unrelenting. None of us want to go through another night, not after what's happened, but denial won't stop exhaustion from dragging us down one at a time. Each of us is going to have to rest at some point—and hope that we're still alive to see the dawn.

34.

By unanimous decision, we leave two lamps on: one at each end of the cabin. Our own version of night-lights, designed to chase our monsters away. They give every item in the space two shadows, shearing out at competing angles and running up the walls like jagged teeth.

The heaters keep the room warm enough that no one tends to the fire. The last of its coals are going cold and dark.

I keep my back to the wall and my knees up near my chest as I settle in for my portion of the watch. I haven't had a full night's sleep since leaving home. The same could probably be said for everyone else here. I can feel the tiredness like a physical pressure, pulling on the skin on my face, causing everything to droop. At the same time, anxiety prickles like a thousand needles jabbing inside my chest, forcing me to stay alert. I cannot afford sleep. The last time someone lost focus during a watch, it came at the cost of a life.

Simone sits across the room from me, partially hidden by the table. Her back is to the cupboard filled with our weapons. Her head is down and she's so still and quiet that it would be possible to imagine she'd already slipped into sleep, except for the steely glint of her eyes as they shift. She watches everything, including me.

I'm hyperalert to every noise and every hint of movement. Denny twitches, then extends his legs a few inches farther. The motion sends anxiety snapping through me, like a rubber band pulled past the breaking point.

Blake sleeps on the couch to my right, and I can't see her from my angle, but I hear her shuffle, grunting as she stretches the muscles in her back. There's a low, steady scratch coming from Alexis's corner as her pen scrapes across the pages of her journal.

The clock ticks past midnight, but many of my companions still seem resistant to sleep.

I wonder which of them are too anxious to rest and who might be staying awake in hopes of finding an opportunity to corner one of us alone.

I wish I had my screwdriver.

There's a small lump in my coat's pocket. I reach my good hand in under the zipper and slide out the velvet box. It's such a delicate thing. The screws holding the hinges in place are tiny. I unlock it and open the lid.

The ring inside is as pristine as it must have been when Kiernan first bought it. I imagine him leaning over a display cabinet, asking the assistant quick, eager questions as he searched for just the right design.

He never made decisions quickly, but once a decision was made, he settled into it with comfortable conviction. To him, indecision was the worst part of making a choice.

This is hell.

I close the box's lid, careful not to make any noises that could disturb my companions.

Between Kiernan and me, he was the one who deserved to live more. He had more hope. More fight. He could have not only lived a full life but used it to better the world around him.

I've spent the last two years of my life feeling like a doll whose stitches have all come loose, desperately clutching at limbs that are falling off.

It will get better, people kept saying. And I'd clung to that promise for so long that it came as a shock when it actually happened. When I met Kiernan. When I started to let my walls down around him. I began to heal.

And now he's gone.

My world has narrowed into something tiny: the cabin, the stretch of frozen land around it, and the brief window of time that I'm forced to survive here.

I need to find out what happened to Kiernan. To learn who cut his life short when he, out of all of us, should have survived.

It's not possible to imagine what will happen after that. Or what my life will look like now that the one thing that was saving me has been torn away and sawn up and discarded in the snow.

Blake shuffles again, sighing heavily as she settles into a new position.

I tuck the engagement box back into my jacket's pocket. Simone doesn't move except for her eyes, which slide over me, watching my every motion.

The clock shows one in the morning. The weariness has gotten heavier. I'm almost suffocating under it; all I'd need to do is slide to the side, let my head rest against the wall, and let my eyes close, and I'd be gone within a minute.

There's not much I can do to hold on to my alertness. I can't pace, I can't go outside, I can't stretch. Not when those around me are fighting to hold on to sleep. Instead, I tug at the bandages around my left hand. I've barely paid any attention to them in the past two days. There's never been enough time, not when every waking hour was dedicated to searching for Kiernan and trying to survive.

But now, in the depths of night and with nothing else to do, I begin unwinding the bandages. They're no longer the crisp white they were when first applied; days of letting them get damp in the snow has left them wrinkled and discolored. The spots of blood that had marred the back have seeped to create a yellowish stain across most of the fabric. The layers stick together as I unwrap them, and they come away in ragged strips.

The wrist is uncovered first. The skin there is pale and wrinkly, with creases showing where the bandages pressed in. An effect of being trapped and damp for too long.

More of my hand is revealed as I unwind the fabric. Two dark gashes cut across the back, marking the last time Kiernan touched me. The place where skin belongs has been filled in with old, crusted blood. Flakes of it peel back with the bandages. A dot of fresh red beads when I'm too quick to drag the cloth back.

Underneath the outer bandage, each finger was wrapped individually. I uncover them one at a time, and a strange emotion passes over me. I'm overcome by the sense that I'm not looking at my hand any longer.

These fingers aren't mine. The nail beds are too exposed. The skin is foreign. Some stranger's hand has been transplanted where mine belongs.

That explains why the fingers won't respond to my instructions. I turn the appendage over, staring in wonder at the alien limb that has replaced my own. The disconnect is so jarring that I feel dizzy under its weight.

A voice resurfaces in the back of my mind, from when I first arrived at the cabin. *That's frostbite.*

The fingers, from the first joint up, are gray. I try to move them and they twitch, but won't bend on command.

I've seen photos of frostbite before. When the cold gets so deep into the body that it kills both flesh and muscle. The appendage starts out a fierce white—bloodless—before dulling and turning black over several days. I appear to be partway between those phases.

My new, foreign hand barely hurts beyond a vague ache. I lower it to rest on top of my knees. I lost my glove on that first day, when Kiernan and I were separated. If I'd been more careful—tucked the hand inside my jacket, wrapped the scarf around it—it might not look like this. But I'd been half-delirious as I wandered, and I left the hand exposed for hours to the gale-force winds and achingly cold temperatures.

In a strange way, it feels like retribution. The universe, meting out overdue justice.

I hear the metal screaming. Feel the rain on my face. Hear the scream again: "Can't we do something?"

It's been a long time since I let myself fall into the events of August 8, but I fall then and let the spiral drag me down.

35.

The storm fought against my car. My windshield wipers were set on high, slicing across the glass with an intensity that still couldn't keep up with the downpour. My headlights skimmed across streams of water that trailed over the road. The guardrails. The trees.

Even with the car's heat set to high, I still felt cold. The radio was turned up until it was almost deafening as I tried to use the talk show to drown out the pounding rain. The hosts' conversation, punctuated by jarring laughter, was still unintelligible.

The roads would have been busy during the day. My job wasn't exactly in the heart of the city, but close enough to be infected by the traffic and the noise. Now, as the clock on my dashboard ticked past two in the morning, the streets were as good as deserted. Traffic lights changed to green within seconds of my arrival at them. The narrow shops I passed were all vacant, their windows dark mirrors reflecting my headlights back at me.

I hated the night shift. But multibillion-dollar companies, who couldn't afford to lose infrastructure for even an hour, paid well for round-the-clock phone support, and twice a month, I was rostered to fill the five-to-one overnight slot. It paid better than the day shift. And it was usually quiet enough that I could read a book if there weren't any tickets to catch up on. But I loathed the drive home.

The forty-minute trip seemed to stretch out to last an eternity. The roads were vacant, the sidewalks empty, and it left me feeling hollow and unsafe, as though a biological bomb had gone off while I was in the office and evaporated every other human in the country.

My scarce protection against it—the recycled late-night radio shows and audiobooks—were powerless under the storm. I'd driven that route every day for more than a year, but the rain turned everything slick and shimmery and foreign until I barely recognized it.

I pulled up ahead of another red light. The neon glow basked across my skin for a few aching seconds, then turned to a sickly green. I took the turn, aiming away from the city to reach my apartment on the outskirts.

Headlights flashed in my rearview mirror. I glanced back and saw a car several lengths behind me. Even in the second I watched, the space between us seemed to vanish. He was driving faster than was safe in the rain. Faster than the speed limit too. The wheels skimmed across double lines before he corrected.

Drunk? Or drugs? I worked my jaw. I didn't like how close he was driving or how erratically. If there'd been any room, I would have pulled into a parking lot and let him pass, but the street had tightened, guardrails squeezing in on either side, as our road funneled us toward the Pickett River.

The body of water wove through the city, slicing it in half, and the city fought back with copious bridges. It was normally a steady, calm flow of water, but I knew from experience that the last few days of rain would have sent it into a thundering, swollen frenzy.

Sure enough, I could hear it as I drew nearer, even under the pounding rain.

The car behind me abruptly swerved into the oncoming lane. He was going to try to overtake me. And right before the bridge too. My jaw ached from how hard I was clenching it. Even with the roads as empty as they were, it was a maddening decision. He couldn't even wait two minutes for us to get past the bridge?

The engine roared as he sped up to cut past me. Sudden frustration hit me, heating me like a furnace. I couldn't stand the thought of letting him past. I increased my speed too, hoping to force him back into place behind me. The road began to tilt upward as we climbed onto the bridge. His engine was deafening. I turned to look through my window and saw he was right abreast of me, his side window level with mine.

"Idiot," I spat.

He turned to look at me, almost as though he could hear me, and he wasn't some drunk, messy-haired partygoer like I'd imagined. He was young, his face pinched and sunken. Red eyelids and red nose stood out against his pale skin. He'd been crying.

A premonition slammed into me, harsh and painful enough to suck my breath away. *This is going to end badly.* My mouth turned dry.

Then I looked forward again and saw the truck lights.

The next sixty seconds have gone hazy in my memory. I have to rely on the official reports to piece together that precious gap. I braked; they can tell because my tires left marks on the road. Only, the man in the car next to me tried to brake as well.

Our cars were level. We'd been moving fast. There was nowhere for the man next to me to go. In his statement, the truck driver said he blew his horn. I think I remember that: a deafening, mournful tone rising above the rain and the radio and the power of my own thundering heart.

Then the police say the car next to me tried to speed up. To cut ahead of me and slip back into the correct lane. But there wasn't enough space. The truck had seen us too late. The road was slick and slippery. There was nothing to be done.

My memories return with burning pain. I was still in my car, but no longer moving. My hands were so tight on the wheel that I wasn't sure I could pry them off.

The truck was close by. It was turned at an angle, its cab facing the bridge's guardrail. I couldn't see clearly through its blinding headlights, but I thought I saw movement in the cabin.

My hands hurt as they came loose from the wheel. I unbuckled my seat belt. The truck and my own car were still on the bridge, at dangerous angles, blocking both lanes. But I couldn't see the third car. I opened my door and immediately felt the rush of rain across my flushed skin.

They drove away, I told myself. But even as that thought flitted through my mind, I found myself staring at the guardrail close to my car, where an immense force had sheared through the metal and left a six-and-a-half-foot-wide gap.

"Are you hurt?" someone yelled, and I realized the truck driver had come out of his cabin. He took a step toward me, then hesitated and turned toward the guardrail. He swore, then raced back to his truck, hands grasping at the metal as his feet slipped out from under him. A sharp dent marred the otherwise glossy metal bumper.

Rain got in my face, sticking my hair across my eyes. I tried to wipe it free. Pain shot through my shoulder. I looked down and saw blood, seeping through my work shirt and dripping from my fingertips. Something protruded from my shoulder. I reached my good hand for it, but debilitating pain ran through me when I tried to pull it free.

I would later find out it was a scrap of twisted metal from the stranger's car, cleaved off during the accident with enough force to shear it through my windshield and impale me.

At that moment, I didn't know what else to do but leave it there. I staggered toward the guardrail. The drop seemed immense. The streetlights barely touched the rolling, swollen river below.

He's down there. The thought danced through my mind, frantic and unbelieving and strange. *He's drowning right now.*

I was suffering from shock, my therapist would later say. At that time, I felt like I was watching a movie. I could feel the rain on my face. The heat of the blood running down my arm. I could hear the truck driver speaking in a frantic, frightened voice. But none of it felt truly real.

Tires screamed, snapping through my daze. Another car had come across the scene. It was bright and flashy, red with some kind of glossy business name emblazoned along the side in a wrap job that must have cost thousands. A man leaped out of the driver's seat. I couldn't see his face through the dark, only that he was large and that his shirt collar popped out around his neck like tiny wings.

"I thought I saw a car go over." He yelled to be heard over the storm.

I didn't answer. The world still felt detached, unreal. It was a movie. I was powerless to affect it. All I could do was sit back and watch the story unwind.

"Can't we do something?" the man yelled.

Things go hazy again. I never spoke to either person after that—not the truck driver and not the flashy businessman. The police statement says I wandered off the bridge and sat on the sidewalk near the river, which is where they later found me.

The truck driver called the police. The businessman tried to climb down the embankment to reach the river but realized the futility and gave up partway. I was taken to the hospital to have the metal removed and stayed there for two days.

The boy's body was eventually retrieved later that day, well after the sun had risen. He'd survived the plunge over the edge and had tried to open the car door and swim out. He was found washed downstream, trapped in a snarl of weeds and garbage that had collected in a quiet corner.

Liam, they said his name was. Nineteen. He'd had a fight with his girlfriend shortly before leaving her apartment.

There was some uncertainty in the official report about whether the crash had truly been an accident or whether he had been driving recklessly with the intent to cause harm to himself.

That didn't matter quite as much as the other questions in my mind. If I hadn't been irritable with him—if I hadn't tried to speed up to block him from overtaking me—would he still be alive?

Yes, I'm fairly sure. Yes.

No charges were ever brought against me; he'd been in the wrong lane, after all.

But I know the truth.

On the eighth of August, I stole a boy's life.

36.

This is hell.

Using my good hand, I gently touch the grayed-out fingers. They register no sensation. The skin feels strange, unnatural. Too tight and missing the familiar pliability.

This is my punishment. I've been waiting for it ever since the night of August the eighth. Fate, coming to seek payment for my crimes. The slow, grinding gears of the universe calling things back into balance. I caused great suffering. And now I must suffer in return.

For months after the accident, I struggled to even leave my apartment. I still can't drive at night. It was like my life was suspended, waiting for the consequences due to me. But time passed and very little happened. My savings ran out and I found a new job—a quiet occupation, working phone support at a small company—that requires less travel. I met Kiernan. I let myself trust him.

Nearly two years have passed. I thought I could begin to breathe freely. Live again.

But the judge has finally come knocking. And now everything—Kiernan, the butcher, my fingers—are all part of the cost being exacted.

I'm terrified to think of how much more the universe will take before it's satisfied.

There's movement in the dark. My head snaps up, hunting through the long shadows thrown from the lamps.

Alexis has left her nest. She creeps toward me on hands and knees, each movement slow and careful to avoid creating noise. Her bangs hang past her low eyebrows and partially cover her eyes, disguising her expression.

As soon as she's close enough, she whispers, "Can I talk to you?"

"Sure," I say, hoping she won't hear the unsteadiness in my voice. "I wouldn't mind some company. Can't you sleep?"

She turns and puts her back to the wall. Her shoulder is so close that it nudges mine when she leans her head toward me. "Not really. I haven't been able to sleep properly since we got here."

Dark half circles have grown underneath her eyes. She's still alert, though, her gaze darting across the covered forms around us. Watching to see who might be awake. Simone is: I can feel her gaze fixed on us. She's motionless but intense.

"I need to tell you something." Alexis's whisper is lower still. I can barely hear it, my ears straining against the rattling wind and the low, steady snores coming from Steve. Alexis presses against me, her lips at my cheek, and I can smell her breath, stale and sweet, as she admits: "I knew one of us was a murderer before I even arrived here."

Those words are like ice through my body. I feel myself going stiff as I prepare…for what, I'm not sure. A knife into my side, just below my ribs? A hand clamped over my mouth to stifle my scream?

Alexis stays still at my side. Her body is almost uncomfortably warm. She's so close that her features blur, but I realize she's still not looking at me: her eyes continue to dance across the bodies around us, watching for motion.

"This wasn't ever a vacation for me." Her voice falls past my ear in delicate wisps. "I was… It's complicated. I need to tell you about my sister."

I don't dare speak in return, but I give a very small nod.

Alexis pulls something out from underneath her sweater. It's the journal she's been feverishly writing in this whole time. She carefully opens the front and slides out a small image. It's a yearbook photo: a student, posed in front of a blurred background, well lit and smiling for the camera.

"Janet," Alexis says. "She was two years younger than me and my best friend."

I can see the resemblance. The deep bronze skin and paler hair. Eyes so dark that they're almost black. She looks kind and warm. The type of person I could see myself being friends with too.

"She died last year." The photo is tucked back into the book. The movement feels almost defensively fast, as though Alexis doesn't want me staring at her sister for any longer than necessary. "Hung in her student accommodation living room. I found her. She'd… She wrote a goodbye note. She'd been through a bad breakup and wasn't meeting her grades for her college. And the police took it at face value. That she killed herself."

The couch creaks as Blake adjusts her position again. My eyes trail toward the clock. It's nearly two in the morning.

"I think they were wrong." Alexis's tongue darts out to wet her lips. Her words are still quiet, muffled, but she's speaking faster. "There's so much they were missing from the picture. Her grades were bad, but she was working with a tutor to improve them. She'd just started talking to a boy she liked in her class. And we were going to go to a movie that afternoon. That's why I found her. I was there to pick her up. She wouldn't have—she would never do that to me."

She stops, breathing quickly to make up for the lack of pauses in her story. I wait, and in a moment she continues.

"I started digging. I looked at everything I could, searching for discrepancies, and I found a lot. The goodbye note was written on a sheet of paper that didn't match anything else in the building. I read the coroner's report, and it said there was some bruising on her wrist and shoulder. I tried replicating it and it's hard to do to yourself. And she left part of a sandwich on the table. People don't just leave meals half-finished unless they're interrupted."

"You think someone killed her?" I ask.

"I don't just suspect it. It's a fact." She glances at me, then looks away again. "I'm guessing they'd been watching her for a while and knew she'd be alone that afternoon. They somehow convinced her to let them inside and then forced her to write the note. It might have been someone she knew from college. Or someone from her work. Or it could have been a random attack. Maybe a serial killer's active in that area, and she caught his attention. I still don't know. But I know she didn't want to die."

The building seems to shiver around us as the wind tears at it. I don't know what to say, so I give a small nod to show that I'm paying attention.

"The police wouldn't listen, so I started a website," Alexis says. "I compiled everything I'd discovered and added to it when I found something new. And people started paying attention. At first, only people from Janet's college, but soon, true crime bloggers were writing about it. And it led to a breakthrough. One of the residents in that building block came forward to say they saw someone knocking on Janet's door that afternoon. They think it was a man, but they couldn't be sure because their face was blocked by a large winter hat."

We're pressed so tightly together that I can feel the ridged cabling in her sweater even through my own coat. In the distance, the wind howls so ferociously that it sounds like a scream.

"It was enough to make the police reopen the case. They didn't do much except interview the people I'd already talked to, though. But I kept updating the website. Reminding people about what had happened. Making sure Janet wasn't forgotten. And I got involved in the true crime communities, learning as much as I could, trying to add even one or two extra pieces to the puzzle."

I think back to how analytical she was about both Miri and Grayson. Examining the bodies. Testing how warm they were. Analyzing the wounds.

For a lot of people, true crime is a fascination.

She's become consumed by it.

Alexis's voice is still level, but there's a quiver at its edges. "I thought if I could just push hard enough—if I could just keep it active in people's minds—eventually someone would come forward. Maybe the killer said the wrong thing to the wrong person. Maybe someone else's relative was killed in the same way, and there's a connection waiting to be drawn. And..."

Blake moves again, creaking the couch's supports. Alexis goes still and quiet. Her eyes dart, reading each body in the room. She's wound tight. I can feel it in the press of her body: tense, wiry. Like a spring loaded and ready to explode at the slightest tap.

"And I was right," she says. "I got something in the mail a month ago."

Her small fingers reach back under the flap of her journal and pull something out. She passes it to me.

It's a card. The front holds a wreath of pale pastel flowers, drawn delicately. They surround the words *In Sympathy*.

Alexis nods. I open the card and feel my heart go cold.

Inside, written in large, scratchy letters, are the words:

You were right. I killed her.

Let's meet.

37.

I try to read Alexis's expression. We're as far as we can be from both lamps, and the shadows cling to her skin, hollowing her cheeks and gathering around her dark eyes.

"At first I thought it was a time-waster," she murmurs. "There were plenty of those. People who wanted to make a stranger hurt or force themselves into the narrative. But inside the card was a brochure for Blackstone Alpine Lodge and a ticket for a two-week stay."

"If it was a prank, it would be an expensive one," I whisper.

"That's exactly what I thought. Someone who was wasting time might tell me to meet them at a coffee shop and then never show. But I called the tour company and they confirmed the ticket was real and paid up-front. It would have cost thousands of dollars. And the only conclusion I could come to was that it was genuine. That Janet's killer was offering me a chance to confront them. And in exchange, a chance for them to silence me."

Memories race through my mind's eyes. Alexis has been tense and withdrawn since before the trip began. Even on the bus, while most of the other guests were looking forward to reaching our destination, she seemed on edge, her eyes scanning the people around her relentlessly.

I wonder what that must have been like. Knowing that she might be facing her death as the bus's doors creaked close behind her. Fighting to stay awake during that first night, aware that there was likely someone within that small room who wanted her dead.

And I remember her expression as she gazed up at Brian's head on the tree that first morning. Not shock or fear. Just resignation.

"I didn't think they'd hurt other people." There's a frustrated misery in her voice. "Or I would have told the police about the note. But—I just thought—"

She thought the only thing she was gambling was her own life. I remember standing outside the cabin and feeling very much the same way. A sheep on offer. Bait to lure the wolf. The fear of death far outweighed by the pressing urge to know the truth.

"I thought that going to the police might scare them away. This was my one chance to get my sister justice. I couldn't afford to lose it. But now…"

Now, four of us are dead. And as our numbers dwindle, our chances of escape feel increasingly precarious.

I remember something else she said to me. "It would be a mistake to believe too much in anyone's innocence," I repeat. It's hard to read her face. Hard to see how much honesty is in her expression. "So why are you trusting me?"

"Because of that." She nods toward my hand. My fingers, slowly turning black. "If Miri and Grayson had been decapitated with a sawing motion, I'd still be watching you. But the cuts were all made with a few strokes from a large blade. Maybe the ax. It would have to be a double-handed weapon. Heavy. You couldn't get enough force behind them with just one hand."

I try to flex my fingers. They twitch but don't bend.

"I'm going to lose them, aren't I?" It feels almost like a silly thing to worry about when so much else is at stake. Alexis doesn't answer, so I tuck the fingers under my other arm, hiding them.

"I can't prove any of what I've told you." Alexis is whispering faster, her voice husky. "But I can't do this on my own anymore. I've been watching everyone as closely as I can. And—and I'm not a hundred percent sure yet, but I think—"

Alexis breaks off abruptly. There's movement on the room's other side. Simone tilts forward, rising from her position in front of the cupboard. Her eyes catch the yellow light as they flick from Alexis to me and back, unblinking.

Alexis swallows. She presses her lips against my ear and her voice is all hot humidity as she says, "I think I know who it is."

Simone's fingertips graze the table's edge as she circles it. Her feet are light, rolling, barely disturbing the aged floorboards as she comes to a halt ahead of us. She looms forward, bending down until she invades our corner more than is necessary.

Alexis draws back, her arms wrapping across her torso. Her face is shuttered again: cold and distant. Protected. I hadn't realized how much she'd let the mask slip while she was talking to me.

"Your watch will begin in less than an hour." Simone doesn't try to whisper. Her voice would still be considered quiet, but its volume feels like a slap after Alexis's murmured secrets. "You should rest while you still can."

"Sure." A smile twitches over Alexis's mouth and is gone again within a second. She turns to creep back to her corner beside the bookcase.

I catch her sleeve before she can leave me. Her last words have set up a fever in my brain. I need to know like I need to breathe. *Please*, I mouth to her.

She glances at our companion. Simone refuses to move but stands over us, her eyes nothing but ice and refracted light.

Alexis ducks into my side. She presses against me, her hand tight on my shoulder, pinching until the skin hurts and whispers one final word, breathy and tense. "*Surgeon*."

Then she's gone, retreating to her designated space and pulling the blankets around herself until her face is hidden under layers of shadows.

Simone continues to stand over me. Her expression hasn't changed, but I think I can pick up an undercurrent inside of it. Frustration?

Alexis had kept her voice quiet, but the room is small. How much of our discussion did Simone hear?

I meet her gaze, challenging, and she finally turns aside. It's only when she sinks back into her place against the cupboard's door that my mind begins to spin.

Surgeon. That was what Alexis said. But no one inside the room listed surgeon as their occupation. Steve drives trucks. Blake was a dispatcher. Denny a mechanic, Simone between jobs, Hutch a DJ.

My gaze falls on Hutch. He sleeps on his side, and the white cotton pad on his cheek stands out sharply against his deeper complexion. Simone applied that bandage. Just like she treated my hand. Is that what Alexis meant? It's not exactly surgery, but then—

A river of cold runs through me.

That's frostbite. We should amputate.

I remember hearing those words as I lay barely conscious. Someone wanted to saw my fingers off. Would have, if Simone, who was treating me, hadn't refused.

A self-designated surgeon.

That has to be what Alexis means. A code that only she and I would recognize.

The memory of that night—my first night in the cabin, before I'd even realized I'd lost Kiernan—is distorted. I didn't see who was speaking; I only heard their words. And now, as I try to play through that scene in my mind, the voice seems vague and unreal, like a recording played too many times until the audio corrupts.

Was it a man? I'm pretty sure the voice was deep. Clipped and efficient. Denny, then? That doesn't feel right. It doesn't match the way Hutch speaks. Steve?

It couldn't have been Simone. She was the one crouched over my hand, the one who shut down the suggestion before it could sink in.

There are only seven of us left. It must be one of us. But—

Blake rolls over on the couch. A soft moan rises from her as she drags the blankets back over her shoulders. I can't see her from where I sit, but that small noise sparks something in my brain.

It was Blake.

I know it with a desperate, uncomfortable certainty. She stared down at me while I was collapsed and unresponsive, and suggested removing my fingers.

My mouth is dry. Does Alexis truly believe Blake is the butcher? The older woman is stocky but short. And she's not fit, not like some of the other people in the cabin. And she hasn't tried to hide the issues with her back. It's hard to imagine someone who struggles to sleep on a couch would be capable of hauling Grayson's weight or swinging an ax with enough force to cleave a head from its shoulders.

Though, if someone wanted to divert suspicion, repeatedly reminding their companions about a bad back would be a simple way to create an alibi.

I glance at Alexis. She lies on her side, the blankets pulled around her head until I can barely see her eyes. She's still awake and staring blankly into the room.

She must be exhausted. But it's hard to rest when danger feels so close.

The clock ticks past two twenty. The wind screams across the jagged summits surrounding us.

I sense that something's going to happen before it actually does. A prickle of unease across my flesh, raising hairs. A pressure at the back of my skull. The premonition, growing heavier: *we're all going to die here.*

The two lamps on either side of the room—our security, our protection—suddenly flash bright and then die.

The small cabin room vanishes into darkness.

38.

Shivers rush through me like electricity. My eyes are wide-open but there's nothing for them to see. We let the coals in the fireplace turn cold. The storm is so dense that no traces of moonlight can reach through the window. We're blind.

Sounds rise out of the empty world around me. Scratching fingers across rough wood.

Ragged breathing.

A heavy thump to my right.

Blake. She's right there. On the couch, less than an arm's reach away.

My body reacts before the thought can properly sink in. I scramble away, my back dragging across the wall before I hit something solid.

"Everyone keep still!" Simone's voice is sharp and terrified.

"What's happening?" Hutch sounds sluggish with sleep. Then, suddenly, his words quicken as he yells, "Who is that? Who touched me?"

"I said *don't move.*"

A chair scrapes. My head swivels as I try to keep track of the sounds, trying to place each of the bodies around me. Something brushes my shoulder. Fear floods my veins as I flinch back.

I need light. Where's my phone?

I stretch my fingers out, desperately feeling across the floor. It was in my jacket. But where's that now?

"Get back!"

Simone's voice is so close to a scream that I almost don't recognize it.

My fingers close around rough fabric. My jacket. I scramble with it, trying to get my phone out.

Something bangs against a wall, hard. There are frantic noises. A second of sickening silence. Then someone screams: "They have a knife. Hell, *they have a knife*."

Pure panic breaks out. Bodies slam together, feet scraping on the floor for purchase. Something hits the wall behind me so hard that I can feel the reverberations travel through my bones. I clutch my jacket to my chest as I crawl, trying to find shelter.

"Get off, get off!"

A grunt. A scream of pain. Feet pound across the floor, achingly loud. We're like frightened birds trapped in a box with a predator, fluttering and beating ourselves senseless against the walls.

Something hard and bony hits my side. I grunt, dropping over. A body lands on top of me. The weight is enough to drive the air out of my lungs. I push against it, trying to get free, and a hand crawls its way across my throat and up over my mouth.

No. No.

Fingers press into my face. The skin is hot and damp with sweat. It's over my nose. Smothering me. The pressure peels my lips back from my teeth. I scramble against the body, fists beating against a thick jacket. The cabin's door bangs open as someone escapes into the storm outside. Still others are moving, yelling, hands clawing against the walls, the window. Someone trips over my outstretched legs; dull pain blooms where I was hit.

They can't see what's happening to me. And I have no breath to scream.

I open my jaw and let the flesh of the stranger's palm sink between my teeth. Then I bite down.

The skin is sour and tough. My teeth ache from the pressure. There's a gasping, voiceless cry, then the hand tears away from my face.

The pressure across me vanishes. I suck in air, gagging, and crawl.

My sense of the space has been eradicated. I can't tell where I'm facing or how far I can go before I hit a wall, but I don't stop moving, putting as much space as I can between myself and the person whose hand I bit. I still have my grip on the jacket but there's no chance to stop and search it. The storm feels wildly loud. The door must still be open, I realize; freezing air strips the heaters' residual warmth out of the room.

A light flashes on. Stark and white, it only makes the panic worse. The narrow beam moves wildly, flashing across the walls, the floor, the ceiling. Impossible shadows arch out from it. There's no pause, no rest, just constant motion, like a strobe. It reveals untold terrors and yet nothing all at once.

Voices cry out, but if they're using words, I can't understand them. Another body hits me, and I flinch, preparing for a fight, but it pushes away again. The light's too frantic, too jittery, to see who it was. I keep crawling.

My fingers touch snow. I'm at the door. Without even thinking, I stand and lurch through the opening, my shoulder grazing the wooden frame on the way out.

"Stay away," someone—Simone or perhaps Alexis—screams. I can barely hear them. The wind is a gale, driving snow into my mouth and blinding my eyes. I have a sense that someone or something is at my back and rush forward again. Visceral fear floods every limb. I force myself to stop moving after a dozen paces and instead scrabble at my coat, searching for the weight of my phone. I find it in the right pocket and pull it out.

My left hand is useless; I let the coat drop to the ground as I struggle to hold the phone and find the flashlight button. My fingers are numb. They slip as I try to press them against the glass. The button highlights, but doesn't activate.

There's a scream somewhere to my right. I lift my head, my heart in my throat. The harsh, white light from inside the cabin shimmers over trees and driving snow as its owner moves through the door. Flashes of its beam catch over a struggle. Two forms, fighting, tumbling into the snow. They break apart even as I watch, thrashing in opposite directions.

I fight to press my finger against the flashlight again. Another slip, and I almost scream. I try once more. This time, it activates. My own harsh, white beam, almost identical to the other one, cuts through the night.

The snow is close to blinding. The flecks, driven at impossible speeds, look like static as they blur across my light, shortening its reach dangerously. There's a horrible creaking noise at my back. I turn, raising my light, and feel the chill of death pass through me as I make eye contact with a bleached-white, tortured face.

39.

Aged wood creaks painfully. The eyes that meet mine are bleached and covered in a layer of frost. Brian's jaw, forced achingly wide-open by the branch jutting out of his open mouth like a second tongue.

Without realizing, I fled toward the dying pine tree.

Above, additional heads bob. They seem to float out of the endless dark. Phantoms of my dead companions, watching over me, sightless and unfeeling.

My pulse runs dangerously fast as I back away from the tree. I turn, casting my light wide, trying to cut through as much of the blizzard as the weak LED possibly can.

Forms shift through the snow. I watch a figure dart forward, stumble to a halt, then move again. They're trying to force as much space between them and the others as they can.

No. We can't split up. If we split up, the butcher has the advantage.

"Come toward the light!" I yell. My voice feels weak and reedy. I'm still fighting to get my air back after being smothered. But I stagger forward, toward the cabin, the phone held above my head like a beacon. "There's safety together! Come toward the light!"

The other beam—the one that disoriented me so badly inside the cabin—holds still for a second, then begins swaying as it grows nearer. I aim my own light at the holder. Hutch squints under the beam, his spare hand lifted to shield his eyes. I turn the light away.

"Gather at the light!" I yell again. More shapes move toward us, staggering through the snow. I fight to see each face as they draw nearer. Simone is the first to reach us. She looks half-wild. Her hair is loose and tangled about her face. A drop of red blood has been smeared across her chin. It's so small that I wouldn't have noticed it if her skin weren't so blanched.

Denny makes it to us next. Close behind him is Steve, panting, cheeks flushed from the cold. "What's happening?" He has to bellow to be heard over the storm. When he's not given an answer, he pushes closer, his voice rising higher. "Who cut the power?"

"Shut up a moment," Simone barks. Her neck's craned, trying to see through the storm. She's looking for the missing members of our party.

"I thought you were meant to be keeping watch." Steve turns on me, and I realize he's still drunk. "Why weren't you keeping watch? Why did you—"

"I said *shut up*." Simone's hand shoots out, fingers curved into claws. Her nails very nearly rake across Steve's face.

He flinches back at the last second, and his features scrunch into something between shock and disgust. "Hey—hey—the hell's wrong with you? The rest of you saw that, right? She went for me—"

"Stop," I say, but my voice vanishes under the rising war between Steve and Simone. We're still missing Blake and Alexis. And every second they're lost in the perfect darkness of this storm carries us closer to disaster.

Hutch shoves between Simone and Steve, arms pressed to their chests as he tries to push them apart. They're yelling, their voices indistinguishable noise, pale white fury against blotchy red anger as they grapple at each other, and I feel as though my head is on the edge of exploding.

"Quiet," Denny's voice booms. He grasps Steve's collar and hauls him back with enough force that he collapses into the knee-height snow.

Hutch stays next to Simone, his outstretched arm still pressed across her torso, but she's no longer fighting him. Instead, she sucks air through her bared teeth, her fingers clenching and unclenching at her sides.

I swallow and taste the residue from the hand I bit inside the cabin. "We're missing Blake and Alexis," I say, and hate the way my voice catches on the last word. "We have to find them. And fast."

"We're not going to find *anyone* in this storm." Steve has regained his feet. A string of mucus runs from his nose and clings to his stubble. He hunches, arms wrapped around himself.

None of us are dressed for the freezing temperatures. Lulled into relative comfort by the heaters, we're all stripped down to our thinner layers: cardigans and cotton shirts that are more appropriate for a brisk morning than a snowstorm.

He's probably right. I can barely see ten feet, even with my light. But I can't abandon Alexis. Not after what she told me. Not when Blake is unaccounted for as well.

I stride forward, phone held as far ahead as I can. The others can follow or not. But I have the light, which means I have control.

Hutch moves first. He comes up alongside me, his own phone extended into the howling winds. He's shivering, but his expression is resolute.

We're not going to make it even ten minutes out here.

"Alexis!" I scream into the gale.

From my right, Steve's voice: "Blake!"

I glance over my shoulder and count three bodies moving in the darkness behind us. Even though the cabin was close by, no one stayed behind.

The tree is to our left. I turn away, leading us around the cabin's side, toward the irregular rocks pockmarking the blanketing white.

A hand grabs my forearm. Simone's pale face looms at my side, her eyes wide and intent as she stares forward. "Do you see that?" she asks.

I follow her direction, straining to see through the endless blur of snow and suspended ice particles. The dark rocks fade in and out of sight. Something moves among them. Fluttering. Fabric, caught in the wind, spinning like a flag in the dull light.

No. I stagger toward it. My body's turning numb. There's not just fabric, I see, but hair. Shoulder length and pale, it creates a tangled mat across the stark white.

My light isn't strong enough. I push closer, straining my phone higher, until the form resolves.

Alexis, lying prone on the snow. One of her arms is stretched out ahead, as though reaching for something. The rocks, perhaps. The other is trapped under her body. Her legs trail behind her, limp and overlapping. Already being buried beneath the snow.

A burst of red spins out from her head like a halo. The color sticks in her hair, darkening it. There's not as much as with the other bodies. The killer didn't have enough time to fully decapitate her. But it's still too much.

I'm frozen in place. Simone pushes past me, followed by Hutch. They both crouch down beside Alexis's head, their hands prying around the skin of her neck. I feel like I'm trapped in someone else's dream. Everything is hazy. Disorienting. My ears ring, but I barely feel the cold any longer.

Then Simone's voice cuts through the howling wind: "She's still alive. Someone, help me lift her."

40.

The storm steals my breath as we fight through it. I lead, my phone guiding us.

Simone and Denny carry Alexis between them. She's horribly limp. I try not to look back because, when I do, I see the vivid blood dripping from her jaw.

We still haven't found Blake.

My light picks up the dark outline of our cabin ahead. I almost run to the door. It's closed. That surprises me; we were all terrified when we fled. I can't imagine anyone taking the time to shut it behind them.

Unless the butcher was the last to step outside.

The door shoves open, scraping over a thin layer of snow that's already beginning to melt on the wooden floors.

"Clear the table." Simone, breathless, has lost the frantic terror from earlier. In its place is a sharp focus that leaves her voice clear and clipped.

The cabin's lights are still out. I place my phone on the table's corner, its light aimed toward the ceiling, and begin dragging the stacks of books and dirty plates off as well as I can with one numb hand and one that doesn't move at all.

Hutch, close behind me, stops by the nearest lamp. The button's clicks are like angry insects in the dark. He abandons the light and joins me at the table, and together we drag the contents off, dropping them unceremoniously onto the floor. Simone's shoulder jostles me as she and Denny push past and lay Alexis's rag-doll form on the cleared surface.

I catch a glimpse of her face. It's run over with lines of bright red, like veins dragged out of her and overlaid across her skin. Both her mouth and her eyes are open a sliver. They don't move.

Queasiness comes quick, and I turn away, focusing instead on what needs to be done. Alexis had a blanket in her corner. It will be good to cushion her head. I cross the room to gather it, but as I kneel by her small pile of possessions, I hear a slow, rasping noise.

The room is so poorly lit that it's barely possible to see past narrow slices of it. Hutch stands beside Simone, his own phone's light pointed down at Alexis's head as Simone gently manipulates it. The walls around us are nothing but dim clusters of shadows.

Someone breathes in, then lets it out as a low sigh. I follow the noise toward the couch.

"Blake." The word escapes me as something between a gasp and a scream.

She sits there, almost invisible in the darkness, her hands resting limply on her knees. Shadows cling to her like cobwebs. At my voice, she turns her head slightly, her cold, unimpressed eyes assessing.

Are her lips redder than before? Did she reapply her lipstick while we were gone?

Simone only glances toward Blake before returning to work on Alexis. Steve, though, chokes on an exclamation. "How long have you been there?"

"I never left." She sounds uncaring, even slightly irritated. "After you all panicked over hell knows what, you abandoned me here. So I figured I'd wait for you to come back." She nods toward Alexis. "Apparently I made the right choice."

My stomach turns. Did she really stay here the whole time, or is she only saying that because we can't prove otherwise?

I try to remember how many bodies I saw leaving the cabin. At least four. But all six? I was too focused on getting away to pay enough attention.

Pins and needles run through my limbs as they begin to regain some of their lost warmth. I carry the blanket back to Simone, taking the long way around to avoid passing Blake.

"How is she?" I ask.

I already know the answer to my question. Simone's fingers are buried in Alexis's hair. Both hair and hands are streaked in scarlet. Alexis's eyes, which are open a sliver, are glazed and unseeing. One of them is filling with blood.

"Her skull's cracked open." Simone's mouth twists. She continues working, gently feeling around the back of Alexis's head. "Someone hit her with something. A rock. A shovel. Not sure. But she'll need to get back to civilization, and fast, if she's going to have any chance. Someone get me some clean snow. It'll slow the swelling."

Denny wordlessly picks up the fireside bucket and exits the cabin. We all stand in silence until he returns with the filled pail.

I have to turn away as Simone packs the fresh snow against the back of Alexis's head. It must be agonizingly painful. If she can even feel anything. There's no response to any kind of stimuli—no twitch of her fingers, no flicker of eyelids.

We may as well be pushing snow into a corpse's head.

Is this even the right thing to do? Wouldn't the snow carry contaminants that shouldn't be forced into an open wound? I swallow and feel a thick lump stick in my throat. Simone is taking charge because none of the rest of us know what to do. But does *she*?

A tiny spot of red on her jaw catches my eye again. The words tumble out of me before I can even judge whether they're wise: "There's blood on your chin."

Her eyes flick up to meet mine before she mutely raises her hands. The fingertips are turning off-white from the cold. Melting snow and diluted blood streak across the flesh. Her point is clear: there's blood everywhere.

"No." My voice is hoarse. My skin prickles, as though a thousand insects are crawling over me. "It was there earlier. I saw it before we even started looking for Alexis."

She uses the back of her wrist, one of the few clean parts, to swipe the speck of red off her jaw. It's mostly dried and flakes away under the pressure. "Someone grabbed me as I was leaving the cabin. It must have happened then."

I saw something like that. Two bodies, fighting in the snow just outside the door. They broke apart after a second, tearing in opposite directions, both eager to be away from the other.

"Someone had a knife," Steve says. He hangs back, near one of the heaters and what residual warmth it still exudes. "I felt it press against me. I thought I was a goner."

"Oh," Hutch says. He's been quiet, mostly focused on holding his light steady for Simone, but now he lifts his jaw to nod toward the corner behind us.

It's the corner Simone was sleeping in before the lights went out. She'd been keeping the unlocked cupboard closed with her back. Now, the door hangs open.

The small array of trinkets inside glitter under my light as I step closer. Alexis's pocketknife is near the front. I wonder, if she'd been allowed to keep it, would she have been safe? Would the killer be sporting a gash across their face instead?

It's an unpleasant thought. Hutch tilts his light. Behind the pocket knife is my screwdriver, the carving fork, paring knife, and rusty kitchen blade. But that's all.

The ax is missing.

41.

"I can't see with this light," Simone snarls.

"Right," Hutch mutters, adjusting his hold on his phone.

My heart runs painfully fast as I turn away from the cupboard. One of us took the ax. And in the precious few minutes of darkness, they found somewhere to hide it.

Where?

I try not to seem obvious as I glance about the small room. It's full of clutter and hard to see with the limited light, but then, the ax is neither small nor discreet. I don't think it's stored inside. There's plenty of space outside—among the trees, near the shed—that it could have been tucked away. I have a horrible sense that I won't see it again unless it's coming toward my throat.

Simone swears. "I can barely see."

"We need to get the lights back." Steve pulls his jacket over his arms in slow increments, apparently sore. "Maybe the generator ran out of fuel."

"Then go take a look at it." Simone's bloodied fingers leave marks all over the first-aid kit as she opens it and searches the dwindling contents.

"I'll help," Denny says.

"Well, I'm not going." Blake tilts her head back, her lips pursed. "None of you have done a single thing to help me since we got here, so don't expect anything in return."

My blood feels like a tide rushing through my limbs. There are so few of us left. The butcher needed to be cautious until now, picking us off one at a time, waiting for an opportunity. But our dwindling numbers present an ever advantageous scenario to them.

We have to split up. There's no way around it. Simone has to stay here with Alexis; someone else needs to go to the generator.

What do we need to do to stay safe?

"There are six of us," I say. "If we're going to split, it needs to be into teams of three."

Simone nods, though it feels like she's barely listening. "Someone has to hold the light for me."

"I can keep doing that," Hutch says.

Blake already made her intention to stay clear. That means, by default, I must be a part of the group traveling to the generator.

My chest feels too tight as I pull on my jacket. Denny and Steve already stand by the door. Steve's face is heavy and sour as he rubs at the side of his nose. The intoxication is turning to sickening hangover. Denny drank just as much as Steve did, but if he's experiencing any of the stages of drunkenness, he doesn't show it.

I take my phone from the table's edge. Then we press back into the dark and the cold.

Visibility is abysmal. Dawn won't arrive for hours, and with how dense the storm is, I'm not sure if even that will help.

I lead the way, forcing sore limbs through the mounting piles of snow, my light swinging across the cabin's wall and the darkness pressing in on all sides.

The generator is at the cabin's back. Not far from the place where Grayson was hung. I feel dangerously vulnerable in the dark and move as quickly as my aching limbs will allow. Snow flows into my gasping mouth and melts on my hot tongue.

A shape appears. Long, thin, nearly covered by the snow. Grayson's body. The pose that his father chose for him—laid on his back, arms crossed over his chest—now feels unnatural. Especially with his legs still tied together. As though he's waiting for someone to grab the rope and drag him away.

I lead us in a wide arc to avoid the scene, before looping back to the cabin.

The gray metal generator is still mounted on the building's wall. I've never had to use a generator before. I stand back and hold the light as Denny swipes snow off the metal and examines it.

"Ran out of fuel," he says after a moment. Then a grunt. "We gave it enough to last until morning."

"We didn't run out," I say. There's a dark stain below the machine. Our fuel, seeping deep into the snow.

"A leak?" Steve's obviously struggling. He keeps blinking, and his eyes are more bloodshot around their edges than they were when we arrived at the cabin. "Did you forget to screw it shut or something?"

The brittle angle of Denny's shoulders shows how much he resents that accusation, but he doesn't bite back. I don't think any of us truly believe the lost fuel was accidental. We've been in lockdown since Grayson's body was found, but anyone could have come along and loosened a valve before that, creating a slow drip that wouldn't be discovered until we were deep in the middle of night.

"Can we get more fuel?" I ask.

"Maybe." Denny sighs, wiping his gloved hands on his pants. "We used the last of what was in the carton. Might be able to find more in the shed, though."

I don't like the idea of returning to the shed. Not with the giant of a man who may have killed his wife and son. But going back to the cabin with only our phone's lights to keep us safe until dawn doesn't feel wise either.

"We might find candles there," Steve mutters. "Or a battery-powered lantern. *Something*."

I don't know what else to do, so I nod. They weren't waiting for my agreement; they're already forging ahead, following the small trail toward where the trees crowd around the shack.

The driving ice burns my face as I fight to keep pace with my companions. I know my light can't be growing dimmer, but it feels as though it is. I've existed in this small valley for days now, walking this very path multiple times, but the environment feels so unutterably, viciously foreign. And it's not just alien but aggressive. As though there are wolves flanking us, just out of sight, bared teeth at our backs. As though the ground itself is preparing to crumble away, plunging us into voids that close over our screaming faces.

I shiver, my teeth clenched.

We hear the shed before my light can even touch it. The wooden structure groans under the gale's pressure. The door shudders, jammed in place by the snow banked up on either side.

We stop at the entrance. I reach my phone forward, fighting to see into the cluttered, crowded space. Steve leans against the doorframe. Each panting breath escapes him as a burst of condensation that's immediately snatched away.

Denny hesitates for only a second, then lurches forward, the first to enter the storage room. Steve's eyes flick toward me, and in the poor light, they look beady and calculating. Just days ago, we sat a row apart on the bus, talking as though we might be on the verge of striking up a friendship. Now, neither of us is willing to turn our back to the other. Every scrap of warmth and camaraderie has been stripped away into naked desperation.

He rubs his glove across his red nose and finally steps forward. I wait until his broad coat begins to fade into the gloom, then I follow, breathing in short, panicked gasps as I enter the claustrophobic shack.

42.

The screaming wind fades a notch. The shed smells faintly of dust and wood and oil, but scents that I imagine would be pungent during summer are barely detectable in these freezing temperatures.

My attention is pulled to the left, to where I found the ax. A part of me almost expects the killer to have returned it to its place. They've been growing bolder, taunting us, provoking us. Something that brash wouldn't have surprised me.

The corner holds other gardening implements, but the ax is still gone.

"Light," Denny says, and I raise my phone high above my head.

Shadows jump erratically as the shed's darkest recesses are dragged into view. Denny trails through the narrow walkway between shelves, his movements slow as he searches the contents. He's broad enough that his shoulders brush both sets of shelves, forcing him to walk at an angle to fit.

Steve takes the shed's other side, picking up containers to examine their labels before replacing them. I'm left in the middle, holding my phone as I try to provide light for both men.

Three people seemed like enough when I suggested it.

Denny pauses to glance at me over his shoulder. It's a brief look but a calculating one. My mouth goes dry.

It doesn't seem like enough any longer.

He's so much larger than either Steve or me. And Steve's distracted. If he chose to, Denny could probably drop him with a single blow. The only thing he'd have to worry about is blocking the door before I got to it.

We're too far from the cabin, and the storm is unrelenting. I could scream myself hoarse and not be heard.

"Looks like we're going to have some lights after all," Steve says. A tired, strained smile lights his face as he holds up a cardboard box half-full of fat, white candles. "Found some potpourri scented oil too."

Denny grunts as he leaves his shelf to circle the room and meet Steve. "Any fuel there?"

"Haven't found any yet. But this place is a junkyard."

You could hide anything here.

My eyes trail toward the shed's back wall. In between a stack of boxes and an old workbench, a tarpaulin has been draped over something with a strange shape. It's mundane enough and tucked far enough back into the recess that my eyes would have passed over without even noticing it except for the way my phone's light reflects off the shiny blue material. For half a second, it almost looked as though the shape underneath had moved.

"Look for red or black containers," Denny says. He bends to see into the lower shelves. "No one brings *just one* can of fuel to somewhere as remote as this."

No. They wouldn't have. But that doesn't mean they're still here. There are plenty of places fuel could be dumped around the cabin without it being noticed. The plastic jugs might already be buried under the snow.

Even as the thoughts trail through my mind, my eyes stay fixed on the tarpaulin. The material twitches.

It's the light. Making shadows jump, reflecting in strange ways. It's not real.

I move forward half a pace before catching myself. So far, I've kept my back to the door, ready to bolt at the first sign of danger. Steve and Denny are to my right, pawing the shelves. If I take even another step forward, I'll be passing them, making it possible for them to reach the door first and block me in.

All it would take is a second.

I glance toward them. Their backs are to me. Steve moves sloppily, shoving items around as he hunts behind them. Denny's far more methodical.

He pauses again and tilts his head just barely enough to glance at me over his shoulder.

My pulse is hot and fast as it races through my skin.

"Light," Denny says, and I realize I've been letting it trail downward without realizing. I lift it again, my arm muscles complaining, and he turns back to the shelves.

Another glance toward the plastic tarpaulin. Nothing else in the shed is covered like that; dust has been allowed to accrue over tables and implements alike. What item requires special shielding?

And is it shielding from dust or from prying eyes?

It's risky, but I take another step forward. I swear I hear something. Most likely the wind beating at the back wall. But it sounds uncomfortably like a whispered voice.

Something metal hits the floor behind me, making me flinch. Steve swears. I still can't tear my eyes away from the blue plastic as I take another step, and then one more toward it.

There's a stain near its edge, just barely peeking out from the loose hem. Dark brown. Not unlike the color I found around the ax.

The hidden shape is larger than an ax, though. Larger than a crouched human, even. It only comes up to my waist but it's at least four feet wide. As I draw nearer, I see small rocks have been placed around the plastic's edge to hold it in place.

I'm still directing my light behind myself, toward where Denny and Steve are. It leaves the corner ahead to drown in gloom. Whatever liquid has seeped across the floor seems to have been splattered over the tarp too. Not enough to see from a distance, but the tiny drops catch in the refracted light as I approach it.

"That's enough," Denny says, his voice low and chillingly cold.

I turn. He stands, partially hidden behind the shelf, facing me. His overgrown beard hides any emotions his face might have betrayed. All I can make out are his eyes: icy gray and unblinking.

My heart skips painfully. I let myself stray farther than I ever meant to. Now Denny's between me and the door. No matter how fast I run, no matter how much luck is on my side, I have no way to beat him to it.

I'm frozen in silence for a heartbeat. My mind rushes, adrenaline and fear blending into a pulpy mess as I scramble for options.

"There's no fuel," Denny says, and then he turns aside. "Let's go back."

I don't dare let myself move as the giant shuffles toward the door. Steve goes with him, the box of candles hefted under one arm. I wait for the threat to materialize. For Denny to make his move. For Steve to fall, his head cracked open.

They reach the doorway. Denny steps through first and pauses just on the other side. Steve stops and turns, frowning, irritation and tiredness written in lines across his face.

"Are you coming?" Steve calls. "We need that light."

"Yeah." I don't know if either of them can hear the whispered acknowledgment. I take two stumbling steps toward them, then stop.

As I turn my light back toward the tarpaulin, I'm certain I see it move again. Just a fraction.

It's only a distortion from the light, I promise myself. But the words don't ring quite true.

I have to be certain.

I cross to the hunched, covered shape in three long steps.

The liquid seeping out from under the material looks ruddier and sicklier with my light directly aimed at it. I crouch, using the hand holding the phone to lightly touch the stain. It's dry. But recent. There's no dust gathered over it, not like everything else in the room. It was made within the last month.

"Girl. Chrissy." Steve's voice cracks around the edges. "What've you got there?"

His voice drowns out something that might have been the wind dragging across the roof or might have been a whispered word.

I've come too far to turn back. I grip the edges of the tarpaulin. And I pull.

43.

My blood is like a heavy drum, *boom-boom-boom*, pounding through my head. It's all I can hear. All I can feel. The tightness of my veins, the pressure, the endless, unstoppable beat.

Footsteps crunch on the dirty floor behind me. Steve's voice comes again: "You found something?"

My mouth opens a fraction, but no sound comes out. *Hair*, I want to say, but that's not really it. *Bones? Flesh but twisted?*

Boom. Boom. Boom.

The tarpaulin hangs limp from my hand, trailing across the ground. Its top bears a few drops of blood, but its underside is absolutely drenched. It wasn't just used to hide the shapes I now stare at but to drag them here.

Rope. Strips of skin, draped loose like fabric. Cartilage and marrow and intestines.

A sharp cry escapes Steve as he finally comes close enough to see. I'm too thoroughly rooted into place to react. Heavier footsteps trail toward us as Denny catches up.

"What…" he starts, but the word dies into nothing.

All I can do is stare at the two bodies jammed into the narrow gap between the boxes and the table.

Their faces are unrecognizable. They've been almost entirely cleaved away, exposing nasal cavities and chipped skulls. Both of their jawbones are missing.

Hair hangs down, bloodied and matted but mostly disguising the damage underneath. Gray and collar length for the man. Streaky and light brown for the woman. With so much else missing, the hair is the first thing you can really properly identify.

Their arms have been hacked into. Chunks of meat are missing, allowing white bone to glisten in my light. The woman is missing a foot. The man is missing both hands. Their throats were cut deep enough—sawed through, leaving mangled muscle and sinew hanging free—to expose segments of their spines.

They've been propped up, back-to-back, and tied into place with lashings of rope. Their knees are up to their chests. It's enough to disguise the worst of the damage at first glance, but as my hand shakes, the light brings the unpleasant reality into clearer view.

Their chests have been broken open. The sternums have either been caved in or removed entirely. Sharp, spiky rib shards protrude around their knees. Intestines spilled free from their stomachs and were unceremoniously packed back into place.

They're not rotting. Not yet. The temperature has been low enough to freeze them like this: fused together and hidden away in the shed's back corner. The cold is harsh enough that they barely even smell.

"The owners," Denny says, and it's with a plunging sense of horror that I know he's right.

The cabin's door was unlocked when the tour group first arrived. Items were scattered around, apparently miduse, including books propped open and blankets draped over the chairs.

With the owners conspicuously absent, we all assumed they had left for the winter.

We were wrong.

Steve's shoulder hits mine as he turns away and sprints toward the door. Air freezes in my lungs: Why's he leaving? What has he realized? I'm alone in the shed with Denny, and there's a sharp terror that Steve might be sacrificing me to save himself, but then I hear him retching outside the door.

Denny is unmoving, staring down at the bodies, though there is still no trace of emotion about his face.

I don't want to be there for even a second more. I hunch as I move to the shed's entrance. Steve's there, rocking unsteadily, knee-deep in the snow. He dropped the box of candles nearby. I use my damaged hand to awkwardly pull the box against my chest. I don't know what else to do. I just know that I wish I'd never suggested splitting up like this.

It's not safe to be alone with these two men. Not safe to be near the massacred, butchered bodies in the shed, the last remains of the couple who had lived in and loved this cabin.

I feel almost nakedly vulnerable. There's no nausea or howling misery— not like when I found the teeth outside or discovered Kiernan's body. Instead, I feel empty. Shaken but almost uncomfortably alert. That's shock and adrenaline combined, I'm sure. Real emotions, dense and thick and overwhelming, will catch up to me later. Right now, my body is focused on survival. On getting back to the group. Safety in numbers. If I can even believe that any longer.

"We should go back," I say.

Steve mumbles, but the words are so slurred that it's hard to be sure what exactly he's saying.

I move forward, my light held ahead of my body, the box of precious candles clutched to my chest. Even through the howling wind, I can hear my companions following behind: the heavy crunch of snow compacted beneath their boots and the panting, wet breaths.

The cabin comes into view. Steve lurches forward and passes me to reach the building first. I catch a glimpse of his bulging eyes and gritted teeth before he shoves through the door, bursting into the dimly lit room beyond.

"You were right," he yells, his voice cracking, the wind still driving snow against his back. "You were right, damn it. *This was all planned.*"

44.

"What?" Simone asks.

She stands over the table, apparently finished with her work on Alexis. Next to her is an old cloth and a dish of water that she used to wash the blood from her hands.

Blake is still on the couch, reclined back, barely visible in the shadows. Hutch is by the fireplace, trying to light a fresh fire. The small flames sputter as he forces kindling into them.

"Whoever's doing this came here ahead of time and chopped up the cabin's owners." Steve's yelling, even though I don't think he realizes it. "*That's* why this place was empty when we arrived. Not because they'd left. But because someone staked out the cabin and carved them up to make sure it would be empty. The door was unlocked! *The door was unlocked.*"

"That doesn't make sense." My voice is too low for any of them to hear. I swallow and taste the burn of bile. "We didn't know we'd have to stop here. The plan was to go to Blackstone Lodge."

The only reason we're here is because of the tree across the road and because of the snowstorm. That was out of any normal human's control.

Wasn't it?

My mind races. Someone could have felled the tree deliberately. We spent the night before the trip in a hotel in the closest town. Someone could have rented a car and left in the middle of the night to cut down the tree that blocked our path. They wouldn't have been able to predict the snowstorm, but maybe they were banking on being able to delay us long enough to funnel us to the cabin.

I flick my head to break free from the grip of fantasy.

It's too much of a reach. The killer's presence has me twitching at shadows. Their behavior—the spectacle they've crafted—is all designed to invoke terror. The heads in the tree outside our home. The teeth. Cutting the lights during the night. The mutilations.

And I've begun doing exactly what I'm sure they want. I've begun to view them as something more than human. Something preternatural that can predict our moves before we even make them. Something inescapable.

They're not.

They're human, like me. Fallible. They would have relied on planning and practice and, I'm sure, luck.

Cutting down the tree would have taken all night with travel factored in. And they had no way to be certain it would be enough to divert us to the cabin. If the storm hadn't descended so suddenly and viciously, we would have reached the lodge as intended.

What does that mean, then?

Have we been wrong all this time? Is the killer not among our number but an outsider, like we originally feared?

Someone who lived within the region possibly. Who had a feud with the cabin owners.

Who killed them.

And then?

I chew my lip as I rock. Did we stumble into the scene of a murder and not realize it? Is the killer hiding somewhere nearby, picking us off to eliminate potential witnesses?

None of it makes any sense.

The cabin owners must have been killed within the last month, while the temperatures were low enough to freeze their bodies before they decayed. And they were hidden—not especially well, but enough that an entire bus of people could spend days in their house without realizing its owners were dead. The tarpaulin draped over their bodies and the way they had been shoved into the back of the shed suggested they were supposed to be found *eventually* but just not *quickly.*

If those murders were unrelated to us, why did the killer go to the effort of hiding them? They can't have known we would arrive. Why not leave the bodies in the middle of the cabin or on the front doorstep? They likely wouldn't have been found until the couple were called in as missing persons. And that might not have been for months.

Except for our unexpected arrival.

The lack of sleep feels like a rough stone sliding across the inside of my skull, scraping layers off my brain. I can't focus on anything properly. Can't piece things together like I should be able to. I feel as though I have all the answers just within my grasp, but I'm ineffectively banging them together like an overwrought child.

"Can you get off that phone for one damn minute?" Steve yells. He's at the couch, searching in between the cushions for the bottle of brandy, and it takes me a second to catch that he's not yelling at me.

Hutch stands near the fireplace, supposedly tending to the young flames, but his face is lit by his phone screen. He doesn't acknowledge Steve's words. His thumb flicks over the screen as he stares into the display.

"I used to make jokes about kids being addicted to technology. Didn't realize it was so damn *true.*" Steve finds the bottle and wrenches its cap off. I want to smash it out of his hands, to beg him to stop, but he's already tilting it back and swallowing.

"Explain this to me." Simone takes the box of candles out of my arms. Her voice is clipped, efficient, and it's almost enough to hide the undercurrent of exhaustion. "The owners are dead? You found them?"

"In the shed." I'm still lost in thought, trying to untangle threads that go nowhere. "Hidden under a tarp."

"Were they there the whole time?"

"Yeah." Not long enough to gather dust. But long enough to freeze into place. They would have been propped up like that while they were still freshly dead, and the subzero temperatures ensured they wouldn't be movable for a while yet.

"Is it possible one of us killed them on the night we arrived?" Simone asks. "Some of us spent time outside searching for you and your partner, remember."

I let the idea trail through my mind. Images blend together, each one filled with minute clues. The extreme scope of the damage inflicted to the bodies, the specific way they'd been placed. Even the rocks carefully spaced across the tarpaulin to hold it into place. It suggests a murderer who had all the time they could want. "I don't think so. The whole thing must have taken hours. And there would have been so much blood—more than any of the other murders. More than you could wash off or hide on short notice."

The cabin's owners couldn't have been killed in the shed or we would have noticed stains across the floor and walls sooner. They'd been attacked outside, most likely, and then were dragged inside and hidden afterward.

I wonder if the scene of the massacre is hidden under the snow somewhere nearby. Bloodred scars marking the land, covered over by the smoothing, unifying layers of snow. Have we walked over it? Stood on it? Would we have found bone fragments and missing hands if the snowstorm had been a little less intense?

Simone paces the cabin, placing candles and lighting them with an unsteady hand. The feverish brightness is back in her eyes. She seems determined not to leave any trace of darkness to threaten us. She's already lit a dozen candles, placing them on top of the bookshelf and on the table and on the floor, and isn't stopping.

"We should be careful," I say, and fight the urge to wither under her sharp glare. "That's the only box of candles we found. We can't afford to run out."

Simone stares at me for an almost uncomfortable length of time. She doesn't say anything, but she places the matches into the box with the remaining candles and puts it aside.

She doesn't want to think about *later*; she's only focused on the here and now, and the darkness that threatens to blind us. I'm fairly sure we're all running on the fantasy that this will be our last night in the cabin. That tomorrow, one way or another, we'll find our way out.

We need that kind of hope. It's the only thing keeping any of us going.

But it's just that. Hope.

And hope cannot be relied on.

Until now, I've avoided looking at the table and the body lying supine on top. I've been scared of what I'll see.

Simone has draped a clean towel over Alexis's forehead, covering everything from her eyebrows up. It disguises the worst of the damage. A few smears of blood run across her cheek, but there's no sign of the catastrophic damage to her skull.

She's still breathing, and I take in a breath of my own, mingled relief and misery burning on the way down.

Her face doesn't look quite right. It was always alert, intent. Expressive. Flexible lips and eyebrows gave her character, even when she was trying to keep her face neutral.

Now, everything about her is slack. Her jaw is loose, her cheeks sunken, blooms of discoloration forming in the hollows beneath her eyes. Thin, shallow breaths enter and exit through her parted lips. They feel fragile. As though they could end at any second, like a candle struggling to stay alight in a harsh wind.

There's a theory that unconscious people can still hear, even when you don't think they can. Simone is off at the other side of the cabin, staring through the window I used to sleep under. Hutch is still near the fireplace. Denny's in his seat, head down. Steve and Blake share the couch, neither speaking. No one is close enough to hear me.

I bend close to Alexis's ear and whisper, "Stay with us. I'm going to get you out of here. I'm going to fix this. Just hold on for a bit longer."

I don't know if I'm imagining it, but I think I see her eyelashes flutter, just a fraction. I could tell myself it was the flickering candlelight or that I was tired enough to see whatever I wanted to see. But I don't.

Hope cannot be relied on.

But sometimes we still need it to survive.

"Hey," Hutch says. He's still by the fire, but he's been neglecting it. The young flames are withering without enough fuel to keep them going. He doesn't seem to notice. Even as he speaks to us, his eyes are fixed to his phone. The bandage on his cheek billows slightly as he works his tongue inside his mouth. "I think I have something."

45.

I take a step closer to Hutch. His face is intense, his eyebrows lowered. One finger taps on the phone, adjusting something.

"You have a signal?" Steve shoots up from the couch, then rocks unsteadily. "How—"

"No. No signal." Hutch's eyes still don't leave the screen. "This is about earlier. When the lights were cut. I could barely think. I'd only just woken up; people were yelling and I couldn't see anything and—well. I couldn't think except for one thing: if I'm going to die tonight, I'm going to leave behind some evidence."

"And?" I prompt.

"I turned on my phone's video camera."

I cross to him and press against his side to see the screen. He's musky; days' worth of oil and body odor and unwashed hair fill my nostrils. Our jackets crinkle as we push together. Another body moves in behind me, a large hand pressing into my shoulder to hold me still. Denny, craning to see over me. I want to shrink away from him. But I need to see this video.

Simone and Steve are on Hutch's other side. Even Blake is drawn in, morbid curiosity playing over her features as she stretches her neck. The phone is open to something blurry and distorted. A still frame from a video. I can't quite make out what it's showing me. Instead, my attention is pulled to the screen's upper-right corner. A single red line fills the battery symbol.

"Battery's low," Simone says.

"I know. I just got the ten percent warning." Hutch deftly taps the screen and scrolls the video back. "But look."

The video begins playing. I recognize flashes of the cabin ceiling's exposed wooden beams. The camera turns, but it's moving so fast that the images are nothing but blurs. Distorted glimpses, like half-forgotten memories. I catch movement, then the camera swivels again. Two bodies are on the floor. I recognize the lower one's dark brown hair.

I think that's me.

And I think that's Blake crouched above me.

I glance at her. Her mouth twitches, but she refuses to look up from the video. She's been wearing gloves since we reconnected with her in the cabin. I'm increasingly certain that, if she took them off, there would be a red, bite-shaped welt on one of her palms.

The camera's view spirals. It stops with a loud thud and lines of wood grain appear large across the screen. Hutch must have dropped it onto the floor. Or had it knocked from his hands. It stays like that for an agonizing eight seconds, then it's picked up again, and its harsh, white light flashes across the empty fireplace and one of the oil heaters.

Through all of this, the audio has been nothing but chaotic noise. I hear occasional voices shouting, but any words vanish under the thud of footsteps and the shove of bodies. The camera moves toward the door. Hutch came out after me, I remember: I saw his light in the doorway. The scene doesn't stop moving. It's almost nauseating how quickly the blurred scenes blend together.

I can't actually see the doorway as he goes through it, but I can tell when he makes it outside because the lighting changes. There are no more wood tones, only pixelated darkness and the rushing blur of snowflakes. The camera catches flashes of the ground, full of our trampling footprints. Hutch's jacket. A brief glimpse of the cabin's exterior wall. More darkness, more snow. Figures move in the distance as we all try to get away from one another.

The noises grow fainter as we spread apart, until I can only make out the heavy panting coming from Hutch himself and the sound of his boots digging into compacted snow. A distant, strained voice calls out: "Come toward the light!"

He pauses the video. "That's when Christa called us back together. I didn't stop recording for another couple of minutes, but there's nothing noteworthy in that part."

We're clustered so tightly together that our body heat is almost smothering. Denny's hand is still on my shoulder, heavy and hard and uncomfortable.

"What are you showing us?" Simone asks.

"Just wait." He rewinds the video, but this time begins playing at the moment he leaves the cabin. He taps several settings and the video slows down, playing at quarter speed. It doesn't help fix any of the blurriness. Instead, each frame stretches out longer, all distorted confusion. Hutch holds his finger over the settings button and, as his camera peels away from the cabin's wall and turns toward the darkness, he switches it to an even slower speed. Now, the frames are clearly separate, each one staying on the screen just long enough to read them.

I see bodies moving away in the distance, racing to escape the cabin. Snow funnels past, sometimes obscuring the view, sometimes blocking the camera entirely.

Hutch pauses the video. "You see it?" he asks.

I frown at the screen. Two figures are visible in the distance, but they're no more than silhouettes. Part of the cabin's corner can be seen to the right. It's only visible as a dark line cutting through the snow. "What is it?"

"Look at that coat." He points to one of the figures—the one that's farthest away. "See the collar? That's Alexis."

I take a quick breath. Alexis, still lying on the table, wears that coat now. She must have pulled it on before fleeing the cabin, which is more than most of us managed. The collar, made of fake fur, hangs limp under her neck. I glance back at the screen. The figure is so far away that it's nothing more than a silhouette half-hidden behind static-like snow. But yes, I can see the collar, I'm sure: a ragged fringe around the back of her head.

"She's running away," Hutch says, his voice low and quick and tense. His finger moves to point at the second, slightly closer figure. "And this one's following her."

46.

I can barely breathe. The pressure against me intensifies as the others lean closer, their chests to my back, their shoulders wedged to mine, as we all fight to see the screen.

"Who is it?" Steve asks. His voice is husky, almost reverent.

Hutch's jaw works. "I'm not sure. That's why I wanted to show the rest of you."

"Replay that bit," Simone says. "I want to see how they move."

He winds back and sets the speed to normal. The view of the two figures lasts for less than a second. It's nothing more than a glimpse before the camera's view spins away again.

But I think he might be right. The farthest figure is Alexis. And the second body appears to be moving after her. They're headed in the direction of the jagged rocks on the cabin's other side, where we found Alexis just minutes later.

Simone swears. She runs one hand across her forehead, where sweat is blooming. "Again. But slower."

He rewinds and sets it to one-eighth speed. I lean in, not daring to even blink as the frames scroll past.

"They're short," Denny says.

"No." Steve reaches a hand through us to point to the screen. "It's the snow. It's up to their knees. They're taller than they look."

Then Simone, cutting over the others: "Pause it."

Hutch rewinds a third time, then freezes the scene on one of the frames.

Alexis is partially hidden by an out-of-focus snowflake, but it's probably the clearest shot of the figure following her.

"It's a man," Blake says, with conviction. "Not that that's a surprise."

"It could still be a woman," I counter. "We only have their silhouette. As long as they clipped their hair back…"

I trail off. Simone's hair is tied into a severe ponytail again, like it was at the trip's beginning. I'm sure it was loose the previous night, though. When did she tie it back? When we started our night watch? Or was it still down when we began our search for Alexis? I can't remember.

She feels my eyes on her and gives me a quick, unforgiving glance. I look away again, my heart in my throat.

My eyes trail over the figure, fighting to make out details through the blur and the snow and the darkness. The bulky clothes hide most of their frame, including the lower half of their head. With the snowdrifts up to their knees, it's nearly impossible to gauge how tall they might be.

They're familiar, though. I feel it in my bones. My subconscious is picking up on something that my tired eyes are missing; I just wish I knew what.

My gaze shifts from the figure to the landscape surrounding them. Alexis, no more than ten or twenty paces ahead of them. So close to safety. Only one or two minutes separate this footage from the moment she was attacked.

"Wait." My heart leaps into my throat. The cabin's wall is in the frame. And the unknown figure is close. It's hard to be sure, but it looks like they might have just passed it. It wasn't visible in the earlier frames, but for this split second in time, a sliver of light has caught over something protruding outward. "That's the window. Right there."

Simone's head tilts. "Are you sure?"

"I am." I've sat under that window for almost our entire time here. I stared at the teeth on its wooden sill so intensely that the images are seared into my head. And maybe—just maybe, if we're lucky—it might be enough. Words rush out of me in a torrent. "We can measure ourselves against it. Figure out how tall this person is. We just need to—"

The phone's screen goes black.

My final words—*recreate the scene and compare it against the video*—die with it.

Steve's and Blake's voices blend together as they yell at the phone. Simone peels back, her face twisted in frustration. Denny finally moves his hand off my shoulder.

"Yeah," Hutch says, tapping the power button twice to be sure. The phone stays dead, and he drops it onto the chair next to the fireplace. "That's it."

"We can still do it, though," Steve says, eager. "We can go outside and measure ourselves next to the window, right?"

My mouth is sour as I turn aside. I don't have the energy left to answer. Simone speaks in my place. "It only works if we have the original footage to compare it to."

The image is frozen in my mind, but it's already melting, shifting, changing. There were too many quirks that need to be accounted for: the height of the camera when that section of the video was taken, how far the figure was from the house, their body's angle.

We might have been able to recreate the scene with trial and error and a rigid focus on accuracy, but without the original for reference, we have nothing.

I find myself at the table's head, staring down at Alexis. Her chest rises and falls in frighteningly small increments as she struggles to breathe. I want to cry. Want to sit in a corner and howl until I lose my voice. Can't afford to do any of it.

"A power bank," I say, and swing back to face the others. "Does anyone have a power bank? Or anything else that can transfer its charge to Hutch's phone?"

"We were told not to bring electronic distractions on this lovely vacation," Steve says, a bitter twist over his mouth.

"We did, though, didn't we?" Hutch's voice quickens. "I have my charging cable. All we need is something—anything—that can give out energy. The generator—"

"Doesn't have any fuel," Denny says.

"Are you *certain*?" Simone leans her upper back against the wall, hands braced on her hips. She looks bone tired. We all do. But she's picked up on my intensity, and her delicate features are set in hard, eager angles. "Did you search every corner of that shed, or did you give up when you found the candles?"

"I'm not going back in there," Steve says. "You didn't see those bodies. That place is as close as you can get to hell without breaking through the earth's crust."

"If you won't go there, I will," Simone snaps. "And just because none of *us* brought a power bank, doesn't mean one of the other guests didn't. We have their luggage outside. Search it."

47.

The thought of pawing through our dead companions' belongings is an unpleasant one, but we're well past the threshold of squeamishness.

Simone moves to the door. If we're going to split up again, it needs to be into groups of three to ensure no one risks being left alone with the butcher. Denny, reliably the first to volunteer for anything, steps up behind Simone. I watch the others closely. Hutch seems to be attempting to avoid eye contact as he fidgets with his dead phone. Blake never volunteers for anything. Steve has already made it clear he won't go back. Which leaves me. A bitter tang fills my mouth as I move toward the door.

To my surprise, Blake cuts in front of me. "I'll go," she says. Her voice is nonchalant, even bored, and her expression almost matches it. Almost. There's a gleam of eagerness, of anticipation, that she can't quite hide from her eyes.

She *wants* to see the bodies.

I step back, giving her right-of-way. In that moment, I don't even care how distasteful her motive might be. I'm just grateful that I won't have to go back to the claustrophobic, rattling shell of a building.

"We'll be no longer than twenty minutes," Simone says, wrapping her scarf around the lower half of her face. She tucks one of the unlit candles and a box of matches into her pocket to light the shed's interior. "See what you can find here in the meantime."

Simone, Denny, and Blake disappear outside the cabin and turn toward the path leading to the shed, leaving me, Hutch, and Steve to search the luggage.

Traces of early morning light have started to rise over the distant ridges. It's scant, but enough to see where we're going. I turn my phone off to save the battery and return it to my pocket.

Our cases are lined up a dozen paces from the cabin's front-facing wall. They're only identifiable as raised lumps in the snow-covered field. We scrape the coatings off as we hunt for their name tags.

"I got Miri's," Steve says. I can tell by his tone that he doesn't expect to find anything. Miri was committed to the idea of two weeks without technological distractions.

"Alexis's," Hutch says, dragging a blue-and-gold case out of the snow.

I search until I find Grayson's. Glossy black and heavy—I have to strain to haul it clear.

The other two cases belonging to our lost companions—Kiernan's and Brian's—are still on the bus. The trip there and back again would take at least an hour. It will have to be a final resort.

I unzip Grayson's case. As I flip the lid open, the distant tang of male body odor is detectable for a second before the wind snatches it away again. I rifle through the contents—casual clothes, thermal layers, a spare pair of shoes—without luck, before turning to the zippered compartment in the luggage's lid.

There's a handheld game console that has no battery left, multiple charging cables, headphones, and a pouch containing a half dozen USBs. I sort through the contents methodically, examining each one for possibilities before placing it aside. Despite Grayson's obvious interest in technology, he seemed to be relying on Blackstone Lodge for power and any kind of Wi-Fi reception.

As I work through the suitcase's side pockets, I keep one eye on Hutch. He's next to me, methodically searching Alexis's bag. If we're going to find anything, it's going to be there. This was never a vacation for her. She would have come on this trip with the knowledge she was facing her own death. And she had been fighting tooth and nail to prevent it.

Out of all of them…

Alexis was the only one who came into this prepared to meet a killer.

She's the only one who was on guard from day one.

I drop the bundles of clothes. Steve doesn't react and Hutch barely lifts his head as I jog back to the cabin.

My breathing is labored as I shove through the door. Alexis seems horribly exposed on the table, limp as a rag doll and nearly colorless. I squeeze her hand on the way past, just in case she can feel it.

She'd created a little nest for herself next to the bookcase, not far from my own stretch of wall. Blankets and jackets, rolled up to form pillows, are jammed in piles against the wood to keep the walkway free. I dig through them, shaking the blankets out as I search for the small item she rarely let out of her sight.

I find it when I shake out one of the jackets. The notebook flops free, scattering both the photo of her sister, Janet, and the card that housed the ticket to this fateful trip. I take up the items carefully, almost reverently, and cradle the notebook in my damaged hand as I use my teeth to tear the glove off my good fingers.

I flip the book open. Each page contains a date in the upper-right corner. Numbers run down the left-hand side, lined up next to a small, tight scrawl. 13.46; 14.12. It takes me a second to realize they're time stamps.

"Alexis," I breathe. "Thank you."

She's been tracking the group's movements. And not only did she note down every major event, but she also marked the time down to the minute and, in some cases, the second.

Alexis was convinced—or very nearly, she'd said—that *the surgeon* was our killer. That has to mean Blake, the woman who'd insisted they should carve my fingers off. And I want to believe Alexis.

Blake isn't large. She isn't young either, and shows her years of sedentary desk work in the stiffness of her movements. She claims to have a bad back. On the surface, she doesn't appear to be a physical match for the butcher's actions: climbing trees, suspending bodies by rope, swinging an ax with a shocking level of brutality and accuracy.

But Alexis alone has been collecting evidence. She'd seen things no one else had thought to look for. And if I'm right, she documented it all.

I want to be able to gather every other surviving member of our group together and expose the killer in a way that they can't escape. I want to end this right now, before dawn arrives.

The clock above the bookcase reads five in the morning. Time is short. I need to do this in private, away from the butcher's eyes, and I know the cabin won't stay empty for long. I use numb fingers to flip back to the journal's first page.

48.

Icons flood my vision. At first glance, I think Alexis must be using a language I don't know. But if she is, it's closer to hieroglyphs than any actual written language I've seen.

I blink. There's a horse's head next to a set of numbers. A fish. A *t* encased in a box.

She's using code.

I swear voicelessly, then breathe deeply and quickly, trying to calm myself.

Simone said they would be back in less than twenty minutes. My other companions are just outside the window and must be nearly done searching the luggage.

There's no time to unravel a code.

I have no choice except to try.

I start on the first page. It has a time stamp of just after nine. Symbols are arranged in two rows, but their lines aren't completely straight; some wobble. Some rows have three symbols instead of two. There are no words to accompany them or explain what the shapes might mean. I move forward.

There's the *t* inside a box again, next to a clover. An arrow points away from them with the notation *NE*.

Northeast? Nebraska? I move on, turning pages frantically as I search for patches of writing I can understand.

For how much time Alexis spent working on it, the journal isn't long. I reach the last entry—the entry written only an hour or two before the lights went out and Alexis was attacked among the jagged rocks behind our cabin—within six pages.

The time stamp reads 11:43. It simply says *watch*, followed by the *t* in a box and the horse's head.

I have to be able to figure it out. I was present for these exact events Alexis was writing about. I watched them play out with my own eyes. All I need to do is match those events to the code.

Are the symbols word replacements? Take the first letter of each symbol…? No. There aren't enough of them to form words. Only two on this entry. And they're the same two that have been repeating through the journal—

My breath whistles out. Of course. The symbols are *us*. Ten symbols for the ten people Alexis was tracking. That final entry—*watch*, followed by the boxed-in *t* and the horse—designate Simone and me as the first half of that night's vigil.

I hold the book close to my face and struggle to read it through the low candlelight as the code starts to fall into place. The shape inside a box—it's not a *t*; it's a cross. Christian. Christa. That's me.

The horse has to be Simone, then. It takes a second longer to figure out. It's not a horse; it's a pony. On the first day, when we met on the bus, Simone wore her hair in a tight ponytail.

I flip back to the first entry in the journal. The two rows of symbols had confused me, but now I only need to find the cross and the pony in their midst to recognize it. Alexis created a map of the bus and marked where each of us sat. Two rows of seats: eleven people spaced among them. With that, it's not hard to match the remaining symbols to the others in our group.

Kiernan is the clover, sitting next to my cross. He was Irish American and, although his family valued their heritage enough to give him an Irish name, neither he nor his parents had ever visited Ireland. But Alexis hadn't known that when she'd met him; she likely only heard his name and saw the reddish tint to his hair and gave him the clover without a second thought.

Heavy footsteps move outside the cabin. I hear voices and raise my head, but no one tries to enter the room. I turn back to the journal, my pulse running hot and urgent.

At the bus's front is a star. That has to be Brian. Our guide. Guiding star?

Denny's and Grayson's places are marked with a wobbly triangle and a bird. No, not just any bird; the beak has a particular shape. A crow. That would be Grayson: black hair, sour expression. Which means the triangle is Denny. A man built like a mountain.

Steve is the fish; he was hoping to go fishing at Blackstone Lodge. Miri is a pair of reading glasses. On the bus's other side is a circle with a hole in its center, like a thick donut or an overly detailed zero. I'm too exhausted to think clearly, and it takes a moment to remember who was sitting there. Hutch. It's a vinyl disk; he's a DJ. I didn't learn his job until after waking in the cabin following the storm, which means Hutch and Alexis must have introduced themselves before boarding the bus. I could see that easily. Hutch, sociable, might have seen Alexis was his own age and tried to form an early friendship.

The final symbol—Blake's—is a line, thicker at its lower end, that bends awkwardly near the tip. It almost looks like a stick. Because that's exactly what it is, I realize. Blake's bright-red lipstick stands out starkly against her colorless skin. And so lipstick became just *stick*.

I glance down to the entry I struggled with before. The cross and the clover, with an arrow pointing away accompanied by NE. That's when Kiernan and I left the bus. We must have been traveling northeast. At the time, I didn't think to pay attention to the direction we were going. But Alexis did. Because she had to. I thought we were on our first day of a vacation. She was preparing to fight for her life.

It's not a complex code, now that I know what it means. But Alexis wasn't trying to make it impenetrable. She was just trying to create something that couldn't be immediately understood if the butcher stole a glance at her journal or managed to flip it open while she was distracted.

I remember the day we had to search each other's possessions. Hutch flipped open Alexis's notebook. "Weird journal," he'd said. I remember the color rising over Alexis's face before Hutch discarded the book again.

The candles scattered about the room flutter. Shallow, aching gasps rise from the table as Alexis fights to breathe. I feverishly flip back through the pages. I can feel my time running out like sand spiraling out of an hourglass. The answers are here, though. The reason Alexis believes Blake is our butcher. The missing piece of the puzzle. I just need to find it.

Blake's symbol is the stick. My eyes hunt for it as they dance across the small, cramped writing. I find the time Blake left to smoke cigarettes at the woods' edge. The time she told Steve and Miri about her work as an emergency call center worker. How she fell asleep during our first night watch.

Alexis has recorded *everything*. And yet, I can't see what raised her alarm.

My eyes are blurring and aching, as though small needles are being driven into them. I rub the heel of my hand into one, fighting for relief. Alexis's breath wheezes like a rusty gate.

Come on. Alexis figured it out. That means you can as well.

I turn to the journal's end and scan the time stamps, running backward from the final entry, which came just moments before Alexis revealed her secret to me. It has to be here. It has to—

The door slams open. I shove the journal underneath my top, bitter fear sparking across my tongue.

Simone pushes in first, carting in clumps of snow on her shoes and her coat. Her arms are full of cables and some kind of electronics I don't recognize.

"All of you get inside," she says, and her bared teeth are somewhere between a desperate smile and a vicious, violent snarl. "We've found something."

49.

Bodies push in behind Simone. Blake first, slouching over to the couch. Her expression is flat. Inflexible. I can't tell if the bodies in the shed left any lasting impressions on her.

Steve, Denny, and Hutch follow. Their faces are mottled from the cold. Denny carries an orange plastic fuel carton that he leaves beside the door, then stomps as he crosses to the fire and begins working at the kindling we let die out.

I watch for reactions, but none of them pay much attention to me or ask why I'm crouched in Alexis's corner. I may as well be invisible to them.

We're all going through the same mental calculations, I'm sure. Ranking one another according to possible threat. Using every casual comment and unnatural expression as points for and against as we adjust the odds in the virtual theater of our minds.

And they must all be ranking me low. Probably for the same reason Alexis did: my blackening, inflexible fingers.

I cross back to my area while the attention is elsewhere and slip the journal underneath the bedding so that it can't be seen.

"We found exactly nothing in those suitcases," Steve says. He glances at the couch and his expression turns sour. He'd planned to sit there. Blake's taken it over and spreads herself across the space, making it clear that she doesn't want company.

Simone ignores Steve. She's untangling the armful of cables she brought in with her. The cords are coiled up, the bundle cinched by a length of old, discolored string, but the cables are long enough that loops are spilling free and pooling on the floor.

I move closer, trying to identify the three shapes wrapped inside of them. They're an off-white; they must have looked sleek and modern when they were first released, but now their sizes and shapes make me believe they must be at least a decade old. Two of the objects are rectangular and one looks strangely like a microphone.

"What is it?" Hutch is at my side, head tilted as he tries to decipher what he's seeing. His eyebrows shoot up. "Hang on. Is that—"

"A cell booster," Simone says. She lowers herself to her knees and begins spacing the items apart on the small amount of clear floor. "We used them in the military when reception was bad."

A booster. Hope and doubt run like dual currents in my veins, churning as they try to overwhelm one another. A booster could pick up a cell signal that not even our phones can reach and amplify it. It might be enough. We don't need much—just barely enough to connect with the outside world and send out our coordinates—and someone will come for us.

The cabin's owners must have bought it for the same reason we now need it: in case of emergencies.

Though I don't like the way dust has been allowed to gather over the system. It looks like it's been sitting forgotten in the shed for years. Did it ever work? Or did it disappoint the cabin's original owners too?

"We found some fuel," Simone continues. "In a carton behind the shed. The owners probably threw it out because they thought it was empty, but there's a tiny bit left. Not much. Just enough that we might be able to get the generator running for a couple of minutes."

I glance at the orange container by the door. It looked uncomfortably light when Denny brought it in.

"We're going to have to be quick with this," Simone says. "Quick and careful. If we mess it up, there's no getting it back."

I lower myself to my knees, moving carefully so that I don't disturb the tangled cables. "What do we need to do?"

"This part"—she points to one of the rectangles—"connects to the phone. This part"—the second rectangle—"is the booster. It amplifies the signal. It has to be kept inside an enclosed space so that it can form what's essentially an echo chamber. This cabin will be perfect. And that all connects to this." She indicates the part that looks like a microphone. "It's what picks up the signal to begin with. It has to be outside. As high and as clear as we can get it."

I look at the cables. They're long but still limited. Not enough to hike to the bus or climb any of the ridges around us.

"The cabin's roof," I suggest.

Simone nods. "That was my plan. Someone climbs up there and holds it as high as they can. Then we close up the cabin so that the booster has the best shot possible and turn on the generator. If it works, we'll be able to connect to any networks that have even a whisper of signal out here."

"If we're turning the generator on, I can get some charge into my phone too," Hutch says.

Simone works her mouth. "We don't have much fuel. Only scraps. We can't afford to waste it."

"Just turning the generator on will burn through plenty," Denny says. "Charging a phone at the same time won't make much difference."

"Okay, then. Plug your phone into one of the outlets. But turn everything else off. The lamps. The heaters. We can't afford any additional drains."

Hutch, Steve, and I move about the cabin. There are only two power outlets—one on each side of the building—and it's quick work to unplug the equipment around them. We spend an extra minute searching behind the furniture in case we missed anything, but once we're done, I'm pretty certain the booster and Hutch's mobile will be the only active electronics.

"Denny, you'll be running the generator," Simone says. She has nearly all of the cables untangled, and her eyes are quick and sharp as they dart over us. "Don't turn it on until you're given the signal. I'll work with the equipment in here. Christa, your phone still has some battery, doesn't it?"

I pull it out of my pocket and tap the power button. Days in the cabin have whittled it down, but I'm still hovering around fifteen percent. "Yeah."

"Then that's what we'll use to make the call." She holds out her hand. I don't like giving up my possessions, but we can't afford to lose this chance. I pass the phone over.

"Right," Simone says as she places the mobile next to the booster on the floor. "Hutch, you're good with technology, aren't you?"

"I'm an unpaid IT expert as far as my four grandparents are concerned, so sure. If that counts." He chuckles, but Simone's too engrossed in her planning to even force a smile.

"Then you'll stay with me. I know how boosters work, but I'll need help in case we run into problems with the phone." She takes a slow breath. "Finally, we need two more people to make this all work. Someone to stand outside the cabin and relay messages. And someone to climb onto the roof and hold the receiver as high as possible."

There's a beat of silence. Denny will be with the generator; Hutch and Simone inside. Out of the remaining three—Steve, Blake, and myself—it's clear who's expected to do the climbing.

"I'll go to the roof," I say, and I'm grateful that the shaking I feel inside doesn't slip out into my voice.

"You sure that's smart?" Steve nods down at my fingers. I hate the way Blake cranes forward to get a better look at them.

I tuck my hands under my jacket so they won't be subjected to any more scrutiny. "I can still climb a ladder."

Steve shrugs. "Then I'll be the relay," he says. "Let's make this happen."

50.

I take my time pulling on extra clothing. A second layer of pants. A second layer of socks. Gloves, borrowed from Hutch—thick and with cinches around the wrists to keep the cold air out. Kiernan's scarf, wrapped around my neck.

The layers leave me sweltering inside the cabin, but they'll be vital once I'm outside. I don't know how long I'll need to stay on the roof except that I'll be there for as long as it takes.

Simone's preparations are exacting. She prepares every part of the internal setup first: attaching the amplifier to the wall and setting up the broadcaster next to my phone. With Alexis on the table, her work has to happen on the only clear patch of floor, in front of the fireplace.

Hutch plugs his own phone into one of the power sockets just behind Simone. Denny waits next to the door, the carton and its precious scraps of fuel at his feet.

We haven't felt so united in days. The mounting fear and mistrust vanish under the sheer force of our desperation.

This has to work. For Alexis's sake.

For all of our sakes.

"Okay," Simone says. She rocks back onto her heels, her breathing shallow and fast, her eyes darting across her setup for the hundredth time, mentally checking it again and again. "Okay. Go."

Denny, Steve, and I leave. The three of us stay close together as we circle the cabin and return to the shed to retrieve a ladder. There's a wooden one propped against its far wall. Denny examines it, shaking it to test the wood. I wait, trying not to let my eyes drift toward the open shed door.

Or think about the things inside.

Denny huffs a breath as he lifts the ladder, bracing it over one shoulder. Steve and I trail behind him, present only as a safeguard against tampering.

We'll need to split up for the next stage. There's no way around it. I'll be on the roof. Steve on the ground. Denny behind the cabin, with the generator.

I try not to think about that. About how easy it would be for one of them to sabotage the whole affair.

Our only hope is that, with our jobs so clearly demarcated, any tampering will be obvious. It's the only hope we have of keeping the murderer in check.

"Where do you want it?" Denny asks.

I've been so wrapped in my spiraling thoughts that I jolt at his question.

"There," Steve says in my stead, pointing toward the cabin's rear wall. "The ground should be fairly stable here."

"Christa's the one who has to climb it." Denny adjusts his hold on the ladder, grunts. Flecks of snow gather over his dark gray cap and cling to his long beard. "She should choose."

I swallow and taste sour fear. "At the cabin's front. Near the window."

He wordlessly turns and continues walking.

It's hard to explain why being near the window is important to me, except it is. It feels slightly less cut off. Slightly less isolated.

Slightly less likely that the ladder will be taken away and broken while I'm still on the roof.

The wooden rungs dig deep into the snow as Denny puts it down. It's not a long ladder; the highest bars barely reach the roof's overhang.

"You sure about this, girl?" Steve asks me.

I'm not sure I can speak, so I nod.

The three of us return to the cabin's door. Denny takes up the carton of fuel and moves away, aiming for the generator behind the building.

Simone meets me in the open doorway. She passes me the

microphone-shaped portion of the setup. It can't weigh more than a couple of pounds. A long cable runs from it, disappearing inside the cabin to connect to the amplifier.

"You'll need to get as high as possible." She grips my arm, and I can feel the pinch of pressure even through the layered coats. "Right to the peak. And then hold it up as high as your arm can reach. Understood?"

Again, it's all I can do to nod. She exhales slowly, her eyes searching mine, then she gives me a slight push away. "Go. And good luck."

Steve stands beside the ladder, indicating that he's going to brace it for me as I climb. Images flash through my mind: Steve tugging on the ladder when I'm nearly at its top, pulling my support out from under me, sending me plunging back to the ground.

I try to tamp the thoughts down. In my own mental risk assessments, Steve ranks low. But that doesn't mean I can trust him. Not when the consequences of even a small slip in judgment could be disastrous.

"I think Simone wants you at the door," I say.

His eyes narrow a fraction. He's guessed that I'm using an excuse to get him away from the ladder, but he doesn't try to argue as he moves past me.

I cradle the receiver to my chest. It's not heavy, but it comes with a metaphorical weight that I'm not sure I can bear. I'm carrying our lifeline. And I just hope that it's not dead before we even begin.

The ladder shudders as the wind pulls at it, its rungs rattling against the roof. The early morning air is painfully bitter against my skin, but the atmosphere is also clearer than it's been in days. I can see streaks of color across the horizon as the sun rises. Reds. Oranges. Thin bands of gold. After being surrounded by nothing but empty white and the dark, pitted blacks of the tree trunks and rocks, the sight of color fills my chest with a painful ache.

Kiernan would have loved it.

The ladder is right ahead of me. I tuck the receiver inside my jacket to free up both of my hands. Its cable trails behind me, and I feel like an astronaut tethered to their spaceship by a lone cord.

My good fingers flex. The bad ones barely twitch. I'm glad they're hidden under Hutch's glove. I don't want the reminder of how damaged I really am.

I clasp the nearest rungs and lean my body weight into them as I begin to climb.

51.

The wind is in my ears. Screaming. Whirring. Flecks of ice hit my exposed skin and leave pits of stinging heat in their wake.

I reach up with my damaged hand. It can't grip, but I sling it over one of the rungs, bending my wrist to act as a hook to hold myself in place.

The ladder shudders. I'm only four steps off the ground, but it feels a lot higher. The instability is terrifying. I fix my gaze upward, toward the ladder's end and the cabin's roof, and force my leg to shift up another rung.

Wood creaks. Like everything else the deceased owners stored at the shed, the ladder's old. I try not to think about the years or decades it's been sitting there, exposed to the snow and the rain, slowly decaying.

Another rung, and then another. The cabin's roof is just outside my reach. I tell myself not to look down. The ladder shifts a fraction, sliding against its precarious ledge, threatening to unbalance and tip back, plunging me down with it.

I move faster. My breathing is ragged and painful. I'm getting reckless, but I can't stop myself. My bad arm latches around the ladder, holding my body tightly against it as my good hand reaches up to clutch at the cabin's roof.

There's nothing to grip. The peaked roof, white with its frosted cap, is made of logs designed to funnel snow and rain off. My hand fixes around one of them but begins to slide back.

My teeth ache from how tightly I've been clenching them. I blindly pull my foot out from its rung and climb higher. The ladder tips again. I grip the roof harder, trying to pin myself to it through sheer force of will. I'm afraid to breathe too deeply in case it tips me back. Another step up. Then a final one, and my torso is over the ladder's top, both gloved hands clawing through the snow to clear room for my body.

There's still no purchase. And I can't even grip the ladder any longer. There's more than wind in my ears now; fear leaves a high-pitched whistle that blurs out all other sounds.

Clumps of snow spiral over the edge as I force my way through it. I'm off the ladder and onto the roof, on all fours as I fight to stay there. The angle is steep. I can feel my body weight working to drag me down, drag me off. My damaged hand misses a hold and I slide. Terror floods me. I drop onto my stomach and press my body into the wood, crusted snow icy against my face, the antenna an unforgiving pinch against my ribs.

Words travel through the whistling. They're blurred and fragmented. I have no room in my mind except to focus on how steep the slope is and how slippery the ice is and how close I am to the edge.

The words come again, louder this time. It's Steve, his voice cracking in the cold. "You okay up there?"

"Fine," I manage, and finally force my limbs to move.

I creep forward in increments, swiping my arm ahead of myself to push through the snow. Every few inches my hand or knee lands on a patch of ice and I find myself sliding again and have to drop down and cling to the structure. But I don't stop. *Can't* stop. If I do, I don't think I'll have the willpower to move again.

My hand fixes on the roof's peak. My lungs burn and my limbs shake as I pull myself up the final stretch. I sling one leg over it, turning so that I can straddle the beam that runs along the cabin's length like a spine.

I would sit here for an hour if I could, regaining both my strength and my courage. But the others are waiting. I draw thin air into my lungs and call, "I'm ready!"

"Heard!"

I think I can hear the cabin door open a crack as Steve speaks to Simone. Then he calls up to me again. "They'll only need a minute!"

The wind is fierce. I pull at the scarf—Kiernan's scarf—to cover my nose and my ears. Then I draw the antenna out from under my jacket. Its pale gray cord spills away, following the channel I carved through the snow and vanishing over the roof's edge.

Please. Please. Let this be enough.

I lift my head, searching for the early-dawn light that gave me courage before. The sunrise is at my back; ahead, the land still seems stark and cold and empty.

Except for the tree.

The massive, dying pine is to my left. Snow crusts its desaturated branches. They move as the wind drags across them, and my heart fills my throat as I stare into the dead eyes of Brian Hernandez.

It's the closest I've been to him since we lost him on our first night at the cabin. Early light catches on the stiff, bloody icicles around his severed neck. The wood protruding from his mouth is splintered, his eyes wide and bleached and empty.

Brian's isn't the only head. Below, Grayson is barely recognizable. His long hair has wrapped across his face, stuck there by the crust of ice. Through it I can glimpse scraps of skin and his open mouth.

And then there's Miri. She was kind to me on our first day in the bus. It hurts, deeply and painfully, to see what remains of her. Her creased skin is now slack and colorless. Her eyelids are barely open, revealing slivers of white. Her expressive features have been distorted until she's nearly unrecognizable.

The tree of the damned.

The horror and the lack of sleep and the grief all collide. My vision blurs. I feel my balance slipping and grip the roof's peak between my sore thighs.

Between my blurred vision and the low, angled light, the tree's form swims. For a second I think I see my own head there, swaying on the tip of a branch. My own dead eyes staring back at me. Warning me.

We're all going to die here.

I taste blood and realize I've bitten the inside of my cheek. I keel forward, one forearm braced on top of the roof, the other hand clutching the antenna.

Then, in the distance, a deep rumble builds. It breaks through the dizziness and the nausea as the vibrations reach my ears.

They've started the generator.

52.

"Okay!" Steve yells. "Hold it up!"

I already am. I grip the antenna's base in both hands and raise it above my head, straining to give it every inch of height I can manage.

The wind is relentless. It pulls at the antenna, at my arms, wanting to drag me over. The heads move in my peripheral vision. Swinging, almost clamoring, their wide-open mouths and white eyes aimed directly at me. I clench my teeth and strain another inch.

"It's not working," Steve yells. His voice breaks on the final word. "Try another angle!"

I swear. Then I force my legs to unclench from where I'm straddling the roof's peak.

One knee comes up first. Then the other. I'm crouching on top of the building, my legs shaking, my lungs breathless, the distant rumble of the motor and the ticking clock it represents driving me forward.

I stand.

My shoes slip on the curved beams of wood and the layer of ice crusting them. I feel myself about to fall and scramble to stay upright. The antenna teeters above my head as I fight to keep it raised. My heels dig into the rough wood, finding an inch of purchase. And I jam them there, holding myself in place even as little-used muscles scream. All of the tendons on the right side of my body stretch as I extend that arm as high as it will go, the antenna wavering precariously above me.

"We got it!" I can barely make out the words through the tinny fear in my ears, but I can still catch the frantic, screaming note in Steve's voice. "We got something! Hold it there!"

One of my heels slips an inch. I gasp and jam it back down, wedging it between the beams. My grip on the antenna doesn't waver. I hold it high, as high as I can manage, fighting for every millimeter of lift I can buy it.

There are sounds below me, floating through the cabin's roof. Voices. Eager, rushed. No words are clear through the babble, but I can still hear their hope and elation.

Then the motor dies.

My heart plunges. I clench my tongue between my teeth. Even as the distant rumble fades into nothing, I refuse to move, holding the antenna toward the sky as though I can keep it running through willpower alone. Below me, someone yells harsh words. A door slams. Voices fight to be heard over one another. There's no elation in them now—only anger.

Slowly, I lower the antenna.

To my right, streaks of sunrise are bleeding across the cold sky. Mountain peaks form sharp lines across the horizon, like a series of knives silhouetted against the reds and oranges of the fresh sun.

There's a stretch of the horizon that looks different. Just a small patch— barely two peaks—that are smaller and narrower and feel less organic. I squint at them, my legs trembling, my heart missing beats, as the rising sun backlights them.

Simone calls to me, her voice booming to be heard over the wind. "Come down, Christa."

I lower myself back onto the roof's peak, straddling it once again. My body shakes so badly that I can't trust it to the ladder yet. I release the antenna, letting it slide down the cabin's roof and tumble over the edge, then lean forward, focusing on moderating my breathing as I wait for the shivers and the palpitations to stop.

When I finally lift my leg back over the roof, I find there's almost no way to stop my slide toward the ladder. I lay my body flat, breathing hard as I press myself into the wood, and manage to slow it to a creep. My foot finds the ladder first. I move gingerly, afraid that I'll accidentally kick it away, as I lower myself until I can contort enough to get my boot through one of the rungs.

I didn't need to be so careful, I discover as I get my body onto the ladder firmly enough to look down. Hutch stands below me, his face gray and pinched as he holds the ladder in place. I climb down at a reckless pace, eager to get onto the ground. Neither Hutch nor I speak but give each other weary smiles as we return to the cabin.

Simone sits on the floor, the array of equipment—my phone, the booster's box, and the cables—strewn ahead of her legs. She has her back to the wall and her arms folded across her chest.

I feel like she might yell at me if I ask, but she anticipates my question anyway. "I don't know if it worked."

"You mean…"

She rolls her shoulders in a shrug without unfolding her arms. "We got through. An emergency operator answered. I did my best to tell them where we were, but the power died. I don't know how much they actually heard."

"*We're in the Rocky Mountains,*" Hutch says, and I realize he's repeating Simone's words. "*Near Blackstone Lodge. People are dead.* It cut out sometime in that last sentence."

We're silent for a second as we absorb that, running through the phrasing in our minds.

"It might be enough," Steve says. His nose and cheeks are red from the cold.

"That's the last fuel in this place," Simone says. "We won't get another chance to call out. It *needs* to be enough."

I glance across the room's other occupants. Blake's on the couch. Denny has already returned to his place near the opposite wall. Steve is by the door. Hutch is near the fire, feeding fresh pieces of wood into it. He's more withdrawn than normal. He was next to Simone to make the call; I suspect he would have taken the full force of her anger when the engine died.

As part of their preparations to make the call, Simone and the others moved the table Alexis is on. It's now pressed against the back wall, where she used to sit. It puts her directly ahead of my own nest. Part of me wants to shrivel away from the thought of having a dying woman beside me. But it's quickly followed by a sense that this is *right*. I can look out for her this way. Watch over her. Protect her as much as I'm able.

Simone is still simmering. One of her boots jostles as she tries to work out her frustrations. "Maybe if we hadn't plugged the other phone in, the motor would have lasted longer."

"No." Denny doesn't even look up from his place by the wall. "It was a negligible load. Wouldn't have made a difference."

I'd almost forgotten about Hutch's phone. I glance toward where I last saw it, beside the fireplace. That section of the floor is now empty. "Where is it?"

Hutch finally looks up from the fire. His face darkens as he searches the same part of the floor I looked toward. Then he forces his way behind the chair to reach the power outlet. As he lifts his arm back I see he's found the phone's charging cable. He pulls on it, reeling it in like fishing line, until the phone itself comes into view.

The screen is broken. A spiderweb of cracks runs across the glass. Part of the metal frame has popped free, twisting uncomfortably.

My mind flashes back to the lantern we left for Kiernan. How the glass and metal had been broken. As though someone had taken a rock to it, bludgeoning it to extinguish the light.

This is more than accidental. More than the phone being mistakenly stepped on. The damage is deliberate and extensive.

Hutch presses the power button, but there's no response from his phone. His voice escapes as a whisper. "Did anyone see who did this?"

Steve shakes his head mutely, his eyebrows high. Blake glowers at the phone as though it's a snake prepared to strike at any second. Denny shows no reaction. The quiet fury exuding from Simone seems to redouble until it fills our cabin like a miasma.

"If anyone saw who did this," she says, her voice a deadly whisper, "speak now."

There's a moment of horrible silence. Eyes dart as we each take in our companion's reactions.

"I was outside," Denny says.

"So was I," Steve adds.

Hutch shakes his head. "Not the whole time. You all came charging in once the generator died. People were moving all over the place, demanding answers—any of you could have stomped on it and kicked it out of sight while we were distracted."

I feel sick as I sink down onto the floor next to the table and Alexis's barely breathing form. This has confirmed one thing at least. The butcher must be one of us. They weren't able to sabotage the phone call without drawing attention to themselves, but they saw an opportunity to get Hutch's phone out of commission and took it.

It's not a shock to have that idea confirmed—that one of my five remaining companions is a murderer. I've believed it for a while now. But it still hurts to lose that last bit of hope that it might have been an outside force. It leaves me cold and isolated in a way that I haven't felt since I was holed up in my apartment following the night of August 8.

There's one small piece of hope, though. Just like the sliver of morning light I saw when I climbed the cabin's roof: it's small and pale, but when the rest of the landscape is so bleakly dark and void, that sliver of light—of irrational hope—might just be enough.

I lift my head and try to speak without letting my voice crack. "I saw something when I was on the roof. I think we're within walking distance of Blackstone Lodge."

53.

They're all still focused on Hutch's phone. Steve is trying to take it from him, saying something about being good at fixing things, but Hutch doesn't want to hand it over.

I speak louder, my voice wavering not from nerves but from tiredness and cold. "When I was on the roof, I saw something. I think it's Blackstone Lodge."

Finally, Simone turns to me. "What?"

That one word from her—our leader—silences the others. Slowly, faces turn toward me. I'm still on the floor, sitting on my makeshift bed, my legs unsteady and my heart running too fast.

"It's still a distance away," I say. "And I don't know if the terrain between us and it is even crossable by foot. But I saw its roofline silhouetted between the mountain peaks. Northeast of here."

"Why are you so sure it was Blackstone?" Steve asks.

I can only shrug. "Brian was trying to reach it when the storm blocked the roads. That means it has to be close by. And I don't think there can be many other buildings in this area."

Simone rocks forward, one hand braced on her chin as she thinks. "Even if it's not Blackstone Lodge, as long as it's *some* kind of habitation, it should give us a way to contact outsiders."

"We already placed a call." Steve shakes his head. "The worst thing we can possibly do is wander off into the wilderness when someone might be coming to rescue us this very minute."

"Except we have no idea how much of our message they heard or how seriously they're going to take it," Hutch says. "*We're in the Rocky Mountains* isn't enough for anyone to pinpoint our location. Even if someone *is* now looking for us, it might take days for them to reach us."

"How far away was it?" Simone asks me.

I run my tongue across my chapped lips. That's a question I've been asking myself. "I'm not sure. The sun was behind it, and it was barely visible between other peaks. Maybe a few hours? Maybe half a day?"

"I can't walk that far with my back," Blake says.

"There could be ravines in the way," Denny notes. "Or rock walls that can't be climbed."

Simone's eyes grow darker. "I don't like admitting it, but he's right. All it takes is one major obstacle and a half-a-day walk turns into becoming lost outdoors at night."

"We need to at least try, though, don't we?" Hutch asks. "Sure, maybe the call went through. Or maybe no one is coming and we're sealing our fate if we just sit and wait."

"You going to leave *her* here?" Blake jerks her head toward the table and Alexis. I hate thinking about that. Hate the idea of walking away from the cabin and leaving Alexis behind to quietly die. Or worse, to have her wake up and be unable to move, only to find herself cold and in pain and utterly alone.

But there's no question about moving Alexis. Even if we had the strength to carry her across the rocky, slippery terrain, any unnecessary movement could be catastrophic to her head injury.

"No, she needs to stay here," Simone says, agreeing with my thoughts. "We could split into teams, though. Half of us walk to Blackstone. Half stay here. Divide and conquer, so to speak. Whoever makes contact with help first can send a rescue party for the other half."

It's a good plan. Except for one part. We've been breaking into even groups of three for a while now, to ensure that no one ever finds themselves in a one-on-one situation with the killer. But that only works because the two teams are never far apart, and there's security and numbers to run toward in case something goes wrong.

Out in the wilderness, all it would take is one mistake—a back turned for a second too long—to even the butcher's odds. They could use the element of surprise to eradicate the strongest person in the group, leaving the remaining surviving party to fight them alone. Nowhere to run to. No escape. Just an ignoble death in the endless lattice of dark rock and cold snow, and their body would likely never be found again.

"We could send just one person to Blackstone," I suggest. "Leave everyone else here. It achieves the same thing but puts fewer lives at risk."

Steve's eyes turn upward. "Yeah, and then the killer volunteers to do the walking, and they vanish over the Canadian border and are never seen again."

It's a struggle to keep the frustration out of my voice. "You know what? I'd be okay with that. At least it would get them away from the cabin and the people they're trying to hurt."

Steve's face is blotchy and twisted. "And you have all the answers, do you? Why don't you learn to watch your mouth?"

"Enough," Simone says, but even her harsh voice can't drown out Steve's rising anger.

"My wife's dead." Spittle flies from his teeth as he forces jagged words out. "This was supposed to be our time to get our marriage back on track and now she's *dead*. And no one seems to care all that much or even want to listen to anything I have to say."

The frustration is like an inferno inside of me, but I bite my tongue. He finished the bottle of whiskey only a few hours ago. There wasn't enough left to get him properly, frighteningly drunk, but he's not completely sober either.

Simone has closed her eyes. She seems to be going through the same bargaining process I am. After a beat she says, "You're not the only person here who's lost someone, Steve. And you're not the only person who's tired and frightened and hungry. So you can stop yelling and start working on some kind of solution instead."

Denny, near the back wall, has been largely silent through the conversation. He draws a breath now, though, and it seems to drain the air out of the cabin. When he speaks, his voices is low and moderated and almost unnervingly intense. "Take the problem back to its root. We need to know whether the call is going to get a response. And that will decide whether we try to make it to the lodge and, if so, how many people we send. Right?"

"Yeah," Simone says.

"We have an ex-dispatcher right here." He nods toward Blake, sitting back on the couch. "She'd know."

54.

"Oh." Hutch leans forward, eager. "You only retired recently. And you were here for the call too. What do you think? Was that enough to get them to start looking for us?"

We all pull forward slightly, straining to see Blake. Like the rest of us, she's grown disheveled since arriving at the cabin. Her spiky gray hair has lost its volume and lies flat on top of her head. Her skin looks sallow and slightly greasy, the way we've all gone. One part of her is unchanged, though: the deep red lipstick, a bold line of color across her face. She keeps it maintained, even though most of us have given up on any kind of regular grooming.

Those red lips purse. "Took you long enough to ask me."

"We're tired, cut us some slack," Steve says. "I can barely remember what day it is."

She shrugs lightly, then reclines back in the chair, her arms folded. "Well. It depends on who took your call. Lots of dispatchers are absolute sticklers for protocol. And protocol says everything must be logged and looked into."

Hutch takes a deep breath. There's hope on his face. "You think that's likely here?"

"Maybe." She tilts her head back. "Your call barely lasted five seconds. The responder probably would have tried to call back and gotten a dead line. When that happens, we usually send someone to the address. Even if we think it's an accidental call."

"Could they find us, though?" Simone has leaned forward. She's listening with rapt focus. "They can't trace an address from a cell phone, can they?"

"They can triangulate it to the nearest towers. If they have enough time." Blake flicks a hand. "Five seconds is nowhere near long enough for that."

Denny grimaces and turns away. Hutch runs a hand over his face, crinkling the tape holding his bandage in place. "We *did* give them a location, though. We told them we were near Blackstone Lodge. That should be enough for them to start searching the area around it, right?"

"Sure." Blake takes a slow breath. "Maybe. If they follow protocol."

I don't like the way that sounds. "What are the odds that they don't?"

She looks at me, and there's a depth to her gaze that is both magnetic and horrifying. "I wouldn't have."

Hutch looks incredulous. "That's your job, though! You're an emergency dispatcher. People calling you are going to have emergencies—"

"Sure. That and a mix of everything else. Butt dials—there's a constant stream of those. Toddlers playing with their parents' phone or a kid who just learned how 911 works. Drunks asking for a ride home. The mentally unwell. Or even just average people who want to complain about their neighbor or tell us about the raccoon they saw in the garbage or ask what to do after cutting their finger with a paring knife. Some nights, you get everything *but* real emergencies."

"So, what?" Hutch's voice cracks. "You just…ignored any calls you didn't like? Hoped the problem went away?"

"Sometimes," she retorts. "And you know what? Most of the time it *didn't* matter. And I got to free up the line for *actual* problems."

"And it's a miracle you didn't cost anyone a life," Hutch snaps. He turns away, pressing both hands into his face. He's breathing fast, trying to calm himself.

Blake adjusts her position on the couch, sighing slightly as she tries to take pressure off her back. She seems largely unfazed by his words. "Look, I'm trying to give you an honest answer. If the person who took your call was doing the right thing, they'd log it. Report it. Try to get someone out looking for us. I can only tell you the reality I saw: the call didn't give them much to go on, and not everyone stuck to the rule book all the time."

For a moment, the only sounds I hear are the cracks and pops from the fireplace and the grating rattle of the window shuddering under the wind's assault. We're all lost in our own minds, trying to judge how honest Blake's assessment is. What our odds of rescue might be.

Then Blake clears her throat and addresses Hutch. "For what it's worth, you're right. I don't regret much. Most of those calls were garbage and didn't deserve my time. But I *did* make a mistake. Once. And it ended up costing a life."

"You're kidding," Steve mutters.

Blake's lip curls. "It's a part of the job. Can't save everyone, no matter how good you think you are."

"Huh." Steve scratches at where stubble has formed on his cheeks. "What happened?"

"A kid called me when his car went off the road. He said he was in a river. I thought it was a joke. Or he was drunk." She draws a slow, deep breath. It rattles on the way down. "It was after midnight and I could barely understand him. He was yelling, and whenever I told him to calm down, he started yelling louder. So I hung up on him. I'd done that plenty of times before. Whenever someone got too belligerent or was trying to have a laugh at my expense. But this time...I guess the call was real."

There's an eerie, sickening silence. Blake doesn't seem to realize the impact she's had. She stares into the distance, her expression limp and vague and, for the first time since I met her, lost.

"They fished his body out of the water the following day. There was an inquest. The recordings of the boy's call were pulled and played in court. I thought they were going to sue me for negligence, say that I caused that boy's death by hanging up on him, but it never came to anything. It was the end of my career, though. All of my calls were monitored from that point on, and last year, my boss pushed me to retire early. So I did."

My skin is on fire. My breath is labored, tight, painful.

It's not.

It isn't.

But…

My tongue won't move. It's weighted down by a question that's dense and sickening and poisonous, like a coiled snake ready to sink its fangs into me.

Someone else asks it instead.

"That call…" Hutch is a deathly shade of pale. "That boy who drowned…that happened in August two years ago, didn't it?"

55.

Blake's eyebrows rise.

I stare at Hutch. How could he know? How could either of them *possibly* know?

This is hell. The thought spins in a loop through my mind, a horrendous echo, leaving me broken and aching inside. *You're in hell. This is your punishment. Your payment for that day.* That's *how they know.*

There's a strange, strangled noise from the room's other side. Steve's face was already slightly slack from the alcohol, but now it's broken open entirely. His jaw hangs, his lips twitching. Red color blooms across his ears and in his eyes as he stares at Blake.

"It was storming," he says. "Miri and me were on our way home. We were tired. There wasn't much of anyone on the road… I was going too fast…"

The truck. I see the lights coming toward me as I enter the bridge. Hear the screaming horn.

"You were there." My words are strangled.

The night was so dark and the rain so heavy and the shock so intense that none of my memories are very clear. But I remember the truck driver getting out of his cab, silhouetted by his headlights as he staggered toward the broken railing.

Another, more recent memory resurfaces. Miri, on the bus, saying *you've got the kind of face that feels familiar.*

She was inside the truck. She saw it all. And she remembered me. Even if she couldn't place when or how.

I turn toward Hutch. He meets my eyes, and there's a connection between us all of a sudden. Like we've been shifted from strangers to intimate acquaintances in an instant.

"I was coming back from a DJ gig." His voice is shaky. "It was after midnight. I didn't see the crash, but I heard it. Pulled off the side of the road. Tried to climb down to where the car was, but…"

I remember. The man in a suit, yelling *Isn't there anything we can do?*

It was too far away to see his features, but I watched as he scrambled down the sharp incline, trying to reach the water, before giving up halfway.

"That was you," I whisper.

He points to his head. "Hair wasn't dyed back then."

Blake. Hutch. Steve. Miri. And me. We're tied together by the night of August 8.

That's not a coincidence.

I turn to look at Simone. "You weren't there."

She stares back at me, her expression as hard as granite, her eyes wide and wild, her jaw fixed tight. For a beat, I think she's going to stay silent. Then she says, her voice barely a whisper, "After leaving the army, I hopped through a lot of jobs, trying to put my skills to use. One of them was as a rescue worker. Two years ago, I helped haul a car out of a river the morning after it crashed. Didn't know many details. But there were rumors that the owner had died."

My heart feels leaden, as though it's losing the fight to keep blood pumping through my limbs. I can barely breathe as we all turn to look at Denny.

"You?" I ask.

He leans against the wall, shaggy and massive and reserved. As our focus turns to him, he only shakes his head. "I was never involved in anything like that."

What does that mean? He's not related? But the rest of us…

"You're a mechanic, aren't you?" Steve asks.

Denny shifts his head in a shallow nod.

"What kind of vehicles? Cars?"

"No. Heavy vehicles. Commercial trucks and vans, mostly."

Steve swears. He staggers to the seat by the fire and slides into it. "I bet you serviced Armadale's truck fleet, right?"

There's a pause, then, "Yes."

"I drove an Armadale. That night? August 8? The emergency brakes failed." Steve swipes the back of his hand across his mouth. His lips have turned red. He's trying not to cry, I realize. "The regular brakes take my truck about three hundred feet to stop. But the emergency brakes? It's a fraction of that. And…and they failed. They told me that as part of the inquest. Said it wasn't my fault." He turns to Blake. "That must have been the same inquest you were on."

And the one I was a part of. The driver that blocked the car, the truck coming in the opposite direction, the 911 operator who hung up on the call. All of us judged by a court searching for wrongdoing, all of us ultimately cleared of fault.

And a boy, drowning as he tried to escape his car, his body washed away. No one was found responsible for it.

This isn't hell.

I lift my head, staring at the survivors around me. "This is revenge."

56.

I pace alongside Alexis's table, my exhausted mind struggling to piece it all together. "Someone brought us here. Someone connected to that night. That accident."

I think back through the others we've already lost. Miri. She was a passenger in Steve's truck on that night. Grayson. He was Denny's son, if that is enough of a connection.

What about Brian, the tour guide, though?

Kiernan?

They might have some connection to the accident as well.

Or they might have just been collateral damage.

I wouldn't have come on this trip without Kiernan. Maybe, if not for me, he would still be alive right now.

That thought hurts so badly that I can barely breathe.

I turn. Alexis lies on the table at my side. Pale. Slack. Her breathing shallow, spots of red showing through the cloth draped over her forehead.

"Alexis is here because she thinks someone murdered her sister," I say. "There's got to be a connection there. She was sent a ticket to the retreat in the mail, with a note from the killer inviting her to meet them."

Blake exhales sharply through her teeth. "I got my ticket as a gift too. It came with a card signed *as thanks for your many years of service*. I thought it was maybe from one of the other dispatchers, trying to show that they'd miss me."

"We got our tickets through a raffle," Steve says. His eyes are wide and unseeing as they fix on the floor. "Got a call about it one day. Neither Miri or I remembered entering a raffle recently. Thought it was weird at the time. But who's going to turn down a free trip?"

"My friend had the tickets," Simone says. "I don't know where or how she got them. But she had to drop out at the last minute. Stomach flu. I figured I should still go. I needed a break." She chokes on ragged laughter. "Guess the joke's on me."

Denny simply says, "Envelope under the door. Thought it was a neighbor, trying to do something nice for me and my boy after my wife passed."

"I was meant to be scoping out Blackstone Lodge for a wedding." Hutch looks quietly stunned. "One of the grooms paid for this whole trip just so I could figure out the lighting and music system."

"Did you meet either of them?" I press. "A video call, a phone call?"

"One phone call. He sounded friendly and professional. But I never saw his face, no." A weak smile forms, then immediately fades. "I guess the wedding story was just an excuse to get me out here."

"This was all planned," I say. My legs feel close to collapsing, but I still can't stop pacing. "Someone related to the night of the accident. This was never a retreat. We were being invited to march into our graves. Because of what happened on August 8."

"Does anyone know who that boy was?" Blake asks. "It's been so long, I can't remember his name."

"Liam." His death became such a core part of my life that I don't think I could ever forget it. "They never told me a surname."

"Does the name *Liam* mean something else to anyone here?" Simone asks. Her question is met with silence.

Wind rushes around the cabin, rattling the window and door. I'm ice cold, even under my layers.

"Hutch." I turn to face him. "That man you spoke to on the phone. Was it *definitely* a man? And would you recognize his voice if you heard it again?"

"I mean…" He frowns. "It was a guy, sure. But I don't know if I'd recognize the voice. I can't remember him having an accent or any very distinctive way of speaking, but then, the line was fuzzy."

I nod as I turn away again. Hutch probably would have recognized the speaker if it had been Denny; the man's voice is deep and gravelly and not easy to forget.

But then, I'm jumping to conclusions. The butcher planned this trip so methodically and so perfectly that they probably didn't leave much to chance. They might have asked a friend to make the call. Or even hired someone to do it. If that's the case, the butcher could still be anyone, even one of the women.

They're related to the crash, though. How? One of Liam's parents? A partner? A very close friend? His death must have wounded them so deeply and so irreversibly that they spent literal years planning this retribution.

And they were willing to stake everything on it. Risking a lifetime in jail or even their own death. They must have known, when this week started, that there was a chance they wouldn't come out the other side.

And it was still worth it to them.

I rub at the back of my neck. The muscles ache, almost as badly as my tired eyes sting. All of the people inside the cabin claim to have had some hand in the crash that night, either an unwilling participant—like myself—or a bystander. Any of them could be lying about that, though. Claiming a connection to diffuse suspicion.

There are two people I can account for, at least. Steve, stepping out of his truck to gape at the hole in the railing. And Hutch, scrambling down the steep incline as he tried to help. Neither of them could have known Liam before that night, which means they're unlikely to be the butcher.

Though…can I truly trust what they've said?

The rain was dense and the night dark. I couldn't see either Steve or Hutch clearly enough to let me recognize them when I met them on the bus. Which means I can't be completely certain that either of the two men I'm speaking to now are the same ones I saw that night.

The butcher could very easily step in to adopt someone else's identity. All they'd need is to be a similar height and body size to one of the bystanders and they could essentially assume their role in this pantomime, pretending to be a target of revenge like the rest of us. It would give them a powerful alibi.

Stop. Stop it. This is paranoia.

But then, maybe paranoia is called for in a situation like this. The butcher has had months to plan. It's not unreasonable to think they would have given themselves an airtight cover story.

An aching groan escapes me. My mind is in knots. None of the others are faring well. Steve, sitting near the fire, has his head in his hands. Soft, almost inaudible sobs escape him. Blake stares resolutely at the ceiling, her lips pressed into a thin line.

What was it that Denny said? Reduce the problem back to its basics? We need to get out of here. We need to survive. That's all it comes down to.

"Blackstone Lodge," I say, and finally stop pacing. "I'm going to try to walk to it. I'll go alone. The rest of you should wait here in case there are searchers looking for us."

"That's not a good idea," Simone says. She sits on the floor, long legs askew ahead of herself, her expression blank. It almost looks as though something inside of her has broken.

Her voice was so soft and mild that I'm not sure I even understood her words. "Sorry?"

"Look." She flicks her gaze toward the window. I turn and feel my heart sink.

It can't have been more than an hour since I returned from the rooftop, but in that time the rising sun has been lost under thickening clouds. I step close to the glass, my breath misting in the chilly air, and stare helplessly as flecks of snow are snatched up and funneled across my view.

This morning, we had clear air and visible skies. I thought we were through the worst of it.

But fresh bad weather is sweeping in faster than I'd imagined it could.

"Stay here a few hours," Hutch says. He's come up to my side, to stare through the window with me. "It'll fade again. Just give it time."

Time is something we don't have. The more I grow to understand the butcher's plan for us, the more I realize how intricately—how deliberately—this trap has been laid. They won't be willing to leave things to chance. If we have any opportunity out of this—any at all—we have to seize it.

"You haven't slept in upward of a day," Simone says. She's still lounged against the cabin's opposite wall, hands limp in her lap, her face heavy. "Nature's giving you a chance to rest before you try to kill yourself walking into the wilderness. I suggest you take it."

I grind my teeth together. At my back, Alexis wheezes. I can barely hear her over the wind battering at the walls around us.

They're right. I won't make it far in another storm. I remember the burn of exhaustion and the sense of growing futility from that first day lost in the blizzard. I couldn't even tell which direction I was walking. I'll be just as lost again if I try to leave now.

"Okay." I finally step away from the window. "But I'll go as soon as it clears enough to see the landmarks."

No one argues with me. I drop down into the messy pile of bedding material. Sleep will be invaluable if I'm going to reach the lodge. But before that, there's an even more pressing matter.

I slide my hand under the blanket as I feel for Alexis's book. My fingers touch nothing but rough wooden floor and limp fabrics, and my breath catches in my throat.

The journal is gone.

57.

It's a fight to keep my emotions off my face as I slowly turn back to face the room. Steve still has his head in his hands. Simone glowers at the floor. Hutch crouches over the fire, working on filling our communal pot with dry food from the bus.

None of them pay me any attention.

But one of them took the journal.

How did they know I had it? I was so careful not to let anyone see…

Unless…

The killer might have tried to retrieve the journal from Alexis's corner themselves. When they found it was missing, they would have guessed someone else got there first and went searching through our belongings.

There's a very narrow window where that could have happened. The time between me leaving the cabin to carry the antenna onto the roof and returning. That couldn't have been more than twenty minutes, and the cabin had at least three people inside it at all times.

Whoever took the journal was quick. And discreet. And managed to do it without raising any questions from their companions.

Before placing the phone call, Hutch helped me search for any additional power sockets that might be energy drains. It's possible he did another lap once I left. That wouldn't have seemed too unusual.

Then, Blake was on the couch next to my bed the entire time. Hutch and Simone would have been entirely focused on the call for the few seconds the generator was working. They might not have noticed Blake reaching over the side of the couch to search my items.

And I spent a few extra minutes on the roof before coming back down. There were noises during that time: yelling, arguing. Hutch said the room was chaos. It was busy enough that no one noticed his phone being broken and kicked behind the furniture. They might not have noticed the journal being taken, either.

I could make a fuss. Announce that the missing notebook contained clues about the butcher's identity and that the killer now has it in their possession.

It might be enough to force another search of our possessions. But then, I doubt the killer would be foolish enough to keep it on their person for exactly that reason. They'd have found somewhere else to stash it: a corner, a cupboard. In among the stacks of books moved off the shelving.

Instead, I sit with my back against the wall and force my expression to stay neutral. More clues can be gained by waiting. By watching. If the butcher has even a little bit of curiosity, they'll want to know what's written in the journal, to know how much Alexis might have pieced together. They'll look for an opportunity to be alone: maybe leaving for a bathroom break that lasts a little too long or maybe finding some excuse to search the shed for tools. I just need to stay alert for the signs.

"Here." Hutch passes out food in whatever containers are available. I get mine in a small saucepan. A spoon has been stuck in what looks like oatmeal. Hutch gives me a grim smile. "This is the last of it."

I repress a grimace. This will be our final meal until we're rescued. And it's nowhere near enough to be filling. Still, I eat gratefully, lingering and savoring as much as possible and scraping the last dregs out of the saucepan.

Outside, the storm sweeps across us. I lie down on my bed, facing the room, with Kiernan's scarf under my head as a pillow. It's approaching noon and a cold, muffled light comes through the window. It gives the guise of safety, and no one tries to establish a watch, even though others lie down to rest.

Simone, usually the most alert, lies on the floor with her back to the room and a heavy coat over her body. I'm so used to seeing her leaning against the wall as her glinting eyes rove across us that it's uncomfortable to have her turned away.

She values control above all else, but these last few days have stripped even the illusion of power away. No matter how many watches and how many plans she's established, we continue to die. This might be her new tactic to regain control: to stop caring.

Denny sits heavily in his chair, his forearms braced on his knees, his head down. Except for the brief burst of emotion when he found his son's body outside, he's barely shown any effects from it. That might just be the way he lives, I remind myself. Too many men were raised by families that expected them to hide their emotions at all costs. He might not be physically capable of grieving for his son.

Hutch stays near the warmth of the fire. He holds his phone in his hands, even though the battery is dead and the screen hopelessly broken. I watch him run his fingers over the array of buttons, trying and trying again to breathe some life back into it, like he's doggedly performing CPR on someone who is cold and mottled.

Blake rises from the couch and crosses to the stacks of books. My whole body tenses as she passes my resting place, but she barely glances at me as she picks through the cabin's offerings. Whatever she was looking for, she doesn't find, and sighs heavily as she goes back to the couch.

Steve is on the edge of sleep. He sits in the corner, his arms folded over his chest. Every time his head falls forward, it blocks his breathing and he jerks awake. The third time it happens, I want to tell him to just lie down properly, but I know he'll take that as an invitation to start a conversation, and I can't handle talking right now.

I drift off in bursts, only to start back to awareness anytime one of the others clears their throat or shifts their positions. My body is desperate for proper, deep sleep, but I can't afford it. I keep my nerves tight and my awareness close to the surface. Listening. Watching. Snapping awake at the slightest movement. It's agonizing. But it's necessary.

Sometimes, people leave to use the bathroom. I keep track of when they go and how quickly they come back. No one stands out as suspicious, but as hours trickle by, the names and times start blurring together.

Not that long ago, Simone had threatened to search anyone who left and reentered the cabin. She's apparently given up on that. Her back is still to the room, her shoulder rising and falling in increments as she breathes.

Steve finally wakes from his broken rest against the wall. He mutters something under his breath and shambles to the door. A flood of chilled wind and snow gusts in as he forces his way outside.

Sleep is pulling me back down again when another body moves. Simone rises from her place against the wall. I watch her through half-cracked lids. Her movements are smooth but rapid as she crosses to the door and exits.

Dreams and reality blur together as my half-unconscious mind reacts. It's not safe for two people to be outside at the same time. No one else has noticed, though. They're all lost in their own worlds. My mind is sluggish as it spins uneasy thoughts through the dreamlike haze it's trapped in.

Something's not right.

Not right.

Not right.

We're all going to die.

Before I realize what's happening, I'm on my feet, my breathing ragged and my head swimming. Something's not right.

Steve has started to scream.

58.

"No," I gasp, stumbling to the door and wrenching it open.

Ice crystals hit my face like tiny razor blades. I flinch against them, putting my head down and lurching forward. The snowdrifts are up to my mid thighs. Moving through them is like wading through mud. I stumble and stagger, panic forcing my limbs into motion even before my mind can identify where that energy should be focused.

I tried to stay alert. I tried! It can't be happening again.

The subfreezing air burns my lungs and scorches my throat as I gasp it in. I can't see anything. Not the old pine tree and its macabre display. Not the mountains around us. I raise a hand to shield my eyes as I force my half-asleep mind to work.

I heard Steve scream, I'm almost certain of it. The sound was distant and muffled and gone before I could reach the door, but I don't think it was a dream. Now, though, there's nothing on the air except the howling wind and my own drumlike heartbeat.

Footprints. They'll have left footprints. Follow them.

I put my head down, searching the ground around me. It only takes a second to find what I'm looking for. A channel has been carved through the snow: two sets of feet shuffling through the same blanket of white, leading to my right.

There are voices at my back. Denny and Hutch, I think. They're asking questions, wanting to know what I heard. I don't have the energy to answer. I push forward instead, following the tracks. It's easier to walk in the valley they create. I break into a staggering run.

The field of broken, jagged rocks rises out of the emptiness. Dread coils in my stomach as I see it. I wish we could go anywhere else. The trees. The shed. But I'm trapped following the trail left for me, and it unerringly carries me toward the treacherous, pockmarked landscape.

I try to call out. There's no answer. My eyes sting under the storm's onslaught as I search the land ahead. I can't see much. Sharp rock peaks rise out of the white, only to vanish as bursts of snow funnel across my field of vision.

There's movement, though. Just a flash of it. Half-hidden behind one of the rock formations. I force myself forward, my breathing coming out as gasps, my pulse a flood of raw heat in my head.

I see blood first. Just a drop of it, marring the snow in front of me.

Then more drops.

Then a spatter, arcing across one of the rough stone faces.

I round the formation, my voice dying in my throat.

Steve lies on his back. His arms are spread out at his sides, palms upward, as though he lay down there to rest for a moment.

Simone straddles his chest. She grips a rock between her hands. It's nearly as large as her head and covered in sharp, jagged edges. She lifts it high, her teeth bared in a primal snarl, then brings it down.

My voice breaks as I launch myself toward her. I'm too late to stop the impact. The rock drives home, vanishing into Steve's face.

What's left of it.

This isn't the first time the rock has come down on him. I collapse, my knees sinking deep into the snow, as I become aware of the carnage around us.

Flecks of blood and bone and brain matter spread out in a halo around where Steve's head once was. As Simone lifts the rock again I see it's plastered in red. Streaks of blood drip down her forearms and stick to her face. She's basking in it, unafraid to taste it as drops decorate her bared teeth.

There's nothing left of Steve's head. Nothing but a crumpled circle of paste and bone shards.

A large figure barrels past me. Simone turns as she senses Denny coming, her face contorting from thrill to fury. She lifts the rock, turning it toward him, but he's faster. He hits her, knocking her off Steve. Both of them collapse into a heap of loose snow and sharp rocks.

Hutch darts around my side, staggers as he sees what remains of Steve, then quickens his pace again as he rushes to help Denny. Simone yells something, but it's lost in the howling wind and the rushing in my ears.

She and Denny wrestle, and although Denny has an advantage thanks to his size, Simone's wiry muscles and sharp reflexes make her more dangerous than I'd expected. The rock rolls away as she releases it. One of her bloodied hands swipes toward Denny's neck, but he twists just enough that her fingers dig into his jacket collar instead of his skin.

She rears up, her mouth open in something that might be a scream or might be a gasp. She's trying to bite him, I realize. Teeth aimed at his ear, his nose, any vulnerable and sensitive scrap of skin.

Denny shoves her back. He's breathless and red in the face. Hutch darts in and out at the side, looking for ways to grip Simone without making himself vulnerable.

My legs don't want to work. I climb to them anyway and stagger around Steve, avoiding the carnage as much as I can.

The struggle abruptly ends. Denny has an arm braced over Simone's chest, pinning her down. Hutch manages to press himself into her other shoulder, holding it still.

All at once, as though a button has been pressed, Simone goes limp. Her head drops back, her eyes turning up toward the sky, the furious grin vanishing as her mouth goes slack.

"Well," she says. The words come out between gasps. "I guess that's it."

59.

Simone is the butcher.

The thought doesn't feel real. Nothing does. Not the cold, the blood, the storm. I stand in the middle of it all, staring down at the woman who I just watched murder Steve, and I still can't believe it.

She doesn't seem terrifying any longer. Just sad. Broken. Her hair has come out of its tight bind and sticks to the blood on her face. Her fingers, held outstretched by the pressure Hutch and Denny apply, twitch. They're caked with blood. Not just from Steve, but from Alexis, earlier.

I trusted you.

I shouldn't have. I knew it was dangerous to have too much faith in anyone, but Simone, the leader, the woman who always had a plan, the woman who seemed to be fighting to keep as many of our number alive as possible...

Her eyes slide toward me. I see her mouth, painted red with gore, twitch into a smile.

"Get me something to tie her with," Denny grunts. There's a fury simmering under his surface, and I know he must be feeling the same shock that I am.

I fumble with my jacket. It has a cinch around its waist, and I pull the cord out and offer it to Denny. He's not gentle as he wrenches Simone forward and pulls her hands behind her back. She neither flinches nor tries to resist.

Hutch doesn't let her go until Denny binds her wrists together and checks the knots. Then he slumps back, one hand on his knee to brace himself, the other gently touching the bandage on his cheek. Simone applied it, I remember. Days ago, after his fight with Grayson.

"Why?" Hutch asks, staring toward Steve's body. When he turns back to Simone, his eyes are red. "Why'd you do it?"

"Doesn't matter." She closes her eyes. I can't believe how calm she is. After the reckless fury I just witnessed, it's like every ounce of anger has left her. She's at ease. Even...happy.

A voice comes from just behind my shoulder, and I flinch. It's Blake, huddled in her thick jacket, her face sunken. "What're we going to do with her?"

There's a beat of silence, then Denny says, "The shed. We'll lock her up there."

"She'll freeze, though." Hutch blinks rapidly as snow funnels over us. His voice shakes. "It might still take days for a rescue team to get here, let alone the police—"

"She won't freeze." Denny's face is as cold as ice as he glares down at Simone. "Not as long as she's wearing insulated clothes. There's no wind inside the shed. She'll be cold, but she won't die from it."

To my surprise, Simone chuckles. "Sure. That's a good plan. Let's do that."

A vein twitches in Denny's jaw. I wonder how many of his thoughts are lingering on Grayson right now. And how much willpower it takes to keep him from driving his fist into Simone's head. He turns to Hutch and me. "Search her."

Denny holds Simone still, a hand on each of her shoulders pressing her into the ground, as Hutch and I feel through her pockets. Hutch chokes on laugher as he pulls out Alexis's pocketknife, the one Simone refused to let her keep. "Yeah, okay," he says as he places it to one side.

There's something solid under her jacket, over her stomach. I have to put myself uncomfortably close to Simone to unzip the outer layer. I can smell the blood, sweet and metallic. Can feel her hot breath gusting over the back of my neck. I try not to flinch away from touching her, but being so near to her leaves me clammy and repulsed. As I reach under her jacket, I feel like I'm stretching my hand into a nest of coiling, venomous snakes.

The zipper peels down, and a small book falls into the snow. The journal. The shock barely registers. I'm just grateful to have it back. I clutch the book to my chest, then tuck it and Alexis's knife into my own jacket. None of my companions object.

A strange atmosphere has fallen over us. There's shock, and horror, and anger, and betrayal. But there's also a sense of being cleansed. As though we've been queasy for days, and we've finally thrown up the sickness from our stomachs.

Denny. Hutch. Blake. And myself. The final four conscious, surviving members of our deadly trip. The word *friend* has been forbidden until now, but I let myself voice it, silently, inside my own head. My friends.

There's nothing else in Simone's other pockets or under her layers of jackets and thermal pants. We return her clothes to the way they were, zipping the coats up. Hutch is right. We don't know how many more days might be needed to get out of the mountains. And however long it takes, she'll have to survive until then.

To be arrested. To be tried. To be convicted.

It's still a long way from any kind of justice. I think of Kiernan's body, stiff and mutilated in the snow. Brian's head, the branch forced through his stretched jaw. At my back, Steve is rapidly cooling in the snow, his arms outstretched as though waiting for a hug.

No court proceedings or life sentences can provide *justice* in any meaningful way. But it might bring answers. Some kind of closure for the dead's family and friends.

Something.

There is so little else to be gained from this situation. We will have to accept the scraps we can take.

Denny hauls Simone to her feet. She puts up no resistance or argument. I half expected her to try to plead her innocence, to try to convince us we've made a mistake, that she deserves to be trusted. But she doesn't.

I suspect the killings were like a game to her. She established rules. Roles. She played her part so perfectly that she was able to force us around the game board like pieces she controlled: taking our weapons away, subjecting us to searches, assigning us tasks. She appeared frustrated, powerless. She was far from it.

But now, she's lost her own game, according to the rules she set. She knows it. And she accepts it.

She's not the kind of person to beg or cry or try to weasel out of it. Emotional manipulation of any kind must be repulsive to her. And so, instead, she holds her head high as Denny forces her through the storm and toward the shed.

I follow, my hands numb and my head spinning.

This is it.

We won. We lived.

I should be glad. Or if nothing else, relieved.

All I feel is sick, thick dread.

Somehow, I know.

This isn't over.

60.

The storm is so thick that we can barely find our way around the back of the cabin. All previous trails have been erased. It's frightening how quickly and readily the storm will wipe our existence out of sight.

I'm only certain we're going the right way when we pass the frost-mottled scraps of rope hanging from the tree that was used to suspend Grayson. We move in single-file, Simone at our head with Denny pressed close behind her. He keeps one hand on her shoulder and another on her bound hands at the small of her back, prepared in case she tries to break away. She doesn't. She accepts her fate calmly and resolutely, even as the shed finally comes into sight.

The howling, screaming wind fades as we enter the shed. Its presence is replaced by the low creak of the loose door, the sudden dimness of our surroundings, and the musty, damp smell that I now realize must be at least partially created by the bodies pressed against the back wall.

Did Simone kill them too?

She must have. That would mean traveling out here and taking a car into the mountains in the weeks ahead of the formal trip, ambushing both owners, killing them, and then dragging their bodies back into the shed to hide them.

It feels like something Simone would, and could, do. She's detail oriented, relying on deep planning and preparation instead of impulsive actions. This level of forethought—preparing the cabin, ensuring it was empty for our arrival—is something she would have relished.

But that's the one part I still can't understand: how she was able to waylay us from Blackstone Lodge and force us into the cabin in the first place. It's possible she could have driven up the mountainside and felled the tree the night before, while we were all supposed to be resting in the hotel at the nearest town. But she couldn't have predicted the storm. Or that Kiernan and I would become lost. Or the difficulty Brian had removing the fallen tree.

All of that feels more chaotic and reactionary than anything Simone would be comfortable with.

There are chairs in among the shed's cluttered storage. Denny leaves Simone with Hutch and me while he drags out the heaviest, sturdiest chair and sets it squarely on the floor.

Simone takes her seat without even being told. Her eyes are hazy and distant. Her hair hangs across her face in limp clumps. She doesn't seem concerned by anything as Denny retrieves additional ropes from the shelves and uses them to lash Simone in place.

He takes no chances. Knots go around her ankles, binding them together, then he fixes those to the chair's legs. More connect her already-tied hands to the chair's back. And then still more, around her waist and chest. As a final measure, he ties the chair in place between two of the shelves, ensuring she won't even be able to tip it over.

"Overkill," Simone says, startling us all. As her lips move I see her teeth are still stained red from Steve's blood.

Denny only grunts and ties the ropes tighter.

"We'll check in frequently," he says, as much as a warning to her as it is planning for us. "Every few hours. If I see signs that you've tried to get out, you'll get more rope. And a lot less blood flow to your limbs. Understood?"

"I'm not going anywhere," she says, and closes her eyes as she tilts her head back.

Denny exhales a breath through his nose, then turns and leaves the shed. Blake follows closely behind him, and Hutch lingers only a moment more, staring into Simone's face with something between repulsion and morbid curiosity before he, too, vanishes outside.

As their footsteps fade into the storm, I'm left alone with Simone. With the butcher.

"Tell me." My mouth is dry and my skin too hot, despite the bitter temperatures. I move to stand directly ahead of her. Not quite within reaching distance but close enough to see strands of Steve's hair stuck to her gore-drenched clothes. Close enough to see the tiny wrinkles around her mouth and eyes.

"Tell you what?" There's a lazy drawl to her voice. She's not at all intimidated by me. And I don't believe there's anything within my power to change that.

Why did you do it? For what purpose? How did you know Liam, the boy who died, and how deeply must you have cared for him to massacre so many people in cold blood?

Those are all questions fighting for dominance, but one slides to the front. The most pressing. The most painful. "Tell me what happened with Kiernan."

One corner of her mouth quirks up. Slow, lazy chuckles escape her. We could almost be having a friendly late-night talk if not for the violence still on display across her clothes and skin. "What makes you think I'm going to give you closure, little lamb?"

Little lamb, begging for answers from the wolf. Frustration builds in me like bubbling lava. I fold my arms so that she won't see the way my limbs shake from stress and cold and exhaustion. "At least tell me this. Was he always intended to be one of your victims? Or…did he only die because I was here?"

Her smile fades. Her eyes open. She gives me a slow, appraising look, then says, "I don't think anyone's going to answer that call we placed. You wanted to walk to Blackstone Lodge. That's a good plan. You should do that."

Begging feels inhuman, debasing. But this might be my last chance to know. "Please."

She closes her eyes and tilts her head back again, refusing to even speak.

I turn and leave before she can see the tears spilling out of me.

Both my body and my mind are numb. As though the life has been sucked out of me. I did what I'd promised Kiernan: I found his killer. I stopped her.

There's no gratification. Just a hollow emptiness. A loss of purpose. Of hope.

Warm air stings my skin as I push through the cabin's door. It's still daylight outside but pale, and someone's lit the candles to bring extra light into the space. It sends shadows darting over the walls like quivering, frightened animals.

"There she is!" Hutch calls as he sees me. He spreads his arms out, inviting me forward, his smile wide. "The woman of the hour."

My mind is still back in the darkness and cold of the shed, with Simone. I blink, not fully understanding. "Sorry?"

"You heard Simone leave. None of us would have." Hutch puts a hand on my shoulder and guides me deeper into the cabin. It's strange, how close and familiar we've become with one another since Simone was caught. It's been a long while since anyone's deliberately touched me. "I was asleep," he continues. "Left just to me, I wouldn't have noticed either of them had left. We probably wouldn't have known Steve was missing for hours. It's thanks to you that the deaths stop there."

Denny doesn't speak, but he claps me gently on the shoulder and hands me a mug of warm water as he moves past. Blake has found a novel somewhere from the stack of books and sits on the couch as she reads it, but she still gives me a quick nod when Hutch sends her a meaningful glare.

I mutter my thanks to Hutch, then slink back to my corner. There's something in the praise that makes me uneasy. Maybe it's that the attack happened in broad daylight. Before, every death came at night or when we were separated or confused. The opportunities were picked carefully. Judiciously. This time? It's almost as though Simone wasn't even trying to hide it.

Stop. There's no need to be paranoid any longer.

Simone might have felt pressured to act faster. She knew I'd read at least part of the journal; maybe she thought I was close to piecing together her identity. It might have pushed her to take risks she never normally would have considered.

I can tell myself that, but it doesn't change the sinking feeling in my stomach.

Alexis lies on the table. Someone—Hutch, I presume—has added an extra blanket over her legs. She's fading. I can tell even before I hear the thin, rattling quality to her breathing.

And that seems wrong, somehow. As irrational as it is, it feels as though catching Simone should have fixed everything. Saved us. But Alexis is still unresponsive. Kiernan is still dead.

And we are all still trapped in this small box of a cabin.

This doesn't feel like a victory.

Simone's words echo in my head. *You wanted to walk to Blackstone Lodge. That's a good plan. You should do that.*

Taking advice from our killer feels like a dangerous gamble. But there was no malice or trace of cunning in Simone's voice. She plays physical games, not mind games.

And I'm not sure we have many alternate options.

"We should vote," I manage. "Whether to walk to Blackstone Lodge today. And if so, how many of us should go."

61.

Our small group turns our eyes toward the window. There's nothing outside except white. I'm struck again by the idea that this is some kind of purgatory, that the real world has ceased to exist, that reality has narrowed itself down to this little cabin and the shed behind it and the torments they contain.

But it's not. I was on the roof. I saw the sharp cut of a building barely visible between the mountain peaks around us. There's life out there. If we can just reach it.

"I'm not going anywhere," Blake says. Her lip curls. "I can't walk with this back. I'd only slow you down."

Denny makes a faint noise deep in his throat, then sighs. "Storm's still ugly. Christa, how far away did you think the lodge was again?"

"Maybe a couple of hours." I can't tear my eyes away from the window and the emptiness beyond. "Maybe half a day. It wasn't easy to tell."

"If it's only two hours, we might be able to get there while there's daylight," Hutch says. "Any longer and we'll be traveling in the dark. And we only have two phones, and one of them is dead."

I slip my own cell phone out of my pocket and tap the power button. I'm down to ten percent. That's dangerously slim, but it will only get slimmer the longer we wait.

"I vote to wait until morning," Denny says. "The call might have been enough. People could be trying to reach us but just can't get through the weather. We should wait a little longer."

"Yeah. I'll second that vote," Hutch says. "The storm might have cleared by morning too. There's not much to be lost by waiting. If no one's found us by dawn, the three of us can aim for Blackstone Lodge. Blake can stay here with Alexis."

I nod slowly. It feels like the safest plan. Simone will have to spend the night in the shed, but I feel very little pity for her. The walk to Blackstone will be on an empty stomach, but that can't be helped. Our best chance of success hinges on having daylight for as many hours as possible. And waiting out the night allows us to gain some desperately needed rest.

We sink into our separate corners: Denny on his chair against the wall opposite me, Hutch next to the fire where he can feed some of the last remaining logs into the flames, Blake on the couch, and myself on the floor beside Alexis's table. Hutch tries for a few bouts of cheerful conversation, but none of us have the emotional energy left to keep up, and we soon drop into silence.

"I suppose I can tell you now." Blake's voice startles me out of my reveries. She leans back in the couch, the book neglected on her lap, her eyes distant as she stares at the room's opposite corner. "I broke the phone."

There's a second's pause, then Hutch's incredulous "What?"

"It was an accident." She lifts her shoulders into a halfhearted shrug. "I stepped on it. And then I knew you'd all accuse me of trying to destroy evidence, so I kicked it under the chair. So sue me."

Hutch looks like he doesn't know whether to yell or laugh. A grin finally wins out, and he rubs his knuckles into the corners of his eyes. "Whatever. Guess it doesn't matter now, does it?"

She could be lying, a dark little voice in my head whispers. Maybe, instead of sitting on the couch when the lights went out like she'd said, Blake ran outside and was captured in the video's footage. I'm pretty sure it was also her hand that pressed into my face, smothering me.

Neither of those things are evidence that she was trying to kill anyone. They could have both been accidental actions. But with our paranoia at catastrophic levels, even those two small events would have been enough to make her look guilty. I could very easily see Blake breaking the phone and covering her bitten hand with gloves to keep herself out of the spotlight.

But then, like Hutch said, it doesn't really matter any longer.

I pull Kiernan's scarf around my neck. The cabin's warm enough that I don't need the extra layer, but it's a small way to feel close to him. I close my eyes and breathe in, trying to catch a trace of his scent. It's been too long and I've worn the scarf too much. It no longer smells like him but like me instead. That's a painful realization.

I know I should lie down and sleep, but the adrenaline still hasn't faded. I can't stop thinking about Simone. The rock raised high above her head. The bared teeth. The wild, intense focus on the pulp that had once been Steve's face. I frown.

Why did she use a rock instead of the ax?

Because she was desperate. Because it was daylight and there was a limited window to attack Steve and because retrieving the ax would have wasted precious time.

It's an explanation. But an imperfect one. The rock was vicious. Bloodier. She was sprayed with gore by the time Denny tackled her. There would have been no quick way to clean that off and return to the cabin.

An ax could result in blood spatter too. But not in the same way the rock did. It's more controlled, more contained. The killing can be done at arm's length. With care, there might not be any cleaning up required.

And compared to the almost surgical precision with which the other heads were removed, the rock feels almost barbaric. The butcher thrived on the spectacle: the heads poised in the tree, staring down at us. The perfectly cleaved necks. The posing of the bodies. The teeth on the windowsill. Everything prepared and displayed with an almost artistic eye for the shock it would create.

There was very little left of Steve's head by the time Simone was done with him. Nothing to pose, nothing to display. Almost a betrayal of everything that had come before.

I need something to stop these thoughts. To confirm that we have our killer. That we weren't somehow mistaken.

A lump presses into my stomach, just below my ribs. I reach under my jacket and retrieve Alexis's journal. Simone was one of the three people inside the cabin when I climbed onto the roof. Not only that, but she'd been setting up the two internal components: mounting the booster onto the walls and running cables across the room. She could have very easily stolen a few seconds to search first Alexis's and then my own belongings under the guise of checking her setup.

I flip the pages open. Before, I was convinced that Blake was the surgeon. She'd offered to cut my fingers off, after all. But although I wouldn't call it *surgery*, Simone had been active in treating our wounds. Patching Hutch's face. Bandaging my frostbitten hand.

That must have been what Alexis meant.

Surely.

I turn the pages, searching for the horse's head that signifies Simone. It appears again and again, and I trace every entry, comparing it to the time stamps and my own memories. I reach the journal's end, then wind back through the scant few pages, reading those same entries a second time, and then a third.

There's no smoking gun. No obvious point where Simone's guilt can be established. At least, not one that I can see.

There must be something. *Alexis was close to certain in her suspicions. Whatever she noticed must be in the journal…and I'm missing it somehow.*

I turn back to the first page. This time, I don't skip just to Blake's or Simone's entries but read them all in chronological order.

It's a strange feeling to see my own activities logged down to the minute. The time I spoke to Alexis about Grayson's suspicions. The time I went searching for the others outside. My participation in the failed attempt to walk out of the mountains.

And then I find it. The smoking gun. The piece of evidence that fixed Alexis's focus onto a single suspect.

My blood turns to ice.

62.

On the afternoon Grayson was killed, there was a very narrow band of time for the butcher to strike.

The hiking team had just arrived back. We'd all seen Grayson alive near the generator. Alexis had taken me aside to share what Grayson had told her, and his suspicions about his father being connected to his mother's death.

Then, we'd gone back into the cabin. Steve had found the bottles of whiskey. He was drinking; the atmosphere was bad. People left. Blake spent some time smoking in the forest. Simone, Denny, and Hutch supposedly went to the shed, though I had the sense they split up once outside, desperate for some space and quiet. When they didn't return, I went looking for them, leaving Alexis at the cabin's door and Steve, drunk, inside.

I find all of our departures noted in the journal, down to the minute. As well as the time stamps of when we arrived back and first heard the sound of Grayson's body knocking at the cabin's rear wall.

For a long time after that, I considered both Steve and Alexis to be lower on the scale of potential threats. Steve had been inside the cabin both when I left and when I returned. Alexis had been standing in the doorway. They'd essentially created alibis for one another during that precious window.

At least, that was what I'd assumed.

Two minutes after the time stamp says I left to look for our missing companions, Alexis writes a new entry. There's an image of a fish—Steve's icon—followed by the note: *Left. Not drunk??*

My good fingers shake from how hard they're clutching the book.

This all happened the afternoon after Miri's death. I remember Simone's comment about how *performative* Steve's grief had seemed while he was crying over his wife's body. And once she'd noted it, I couldn't stop seeing it. How he almost appeared to relish the attention her death brought him.

No two people grieve in exactly the same way, and a man can be attention-seeking after his wife's death, even if he hasn't killed her.

But that time stamp, and the note alongside it, is alarming. Steve left after I did. And something about his behavior made Alexis believe he wasn't as drunk as he was pretending to be.

His return time stamp says he arrived back thirty-six minutes later. And unlike the rest of our notes, there's no reason given for the departure.

What was he doing outside during those thirty-six minutes? Why did none of the rest of us see him during that time? Steve, more than anyone in the cabin, was social. He wasn't likely to want a minute alone to himself, like Blake or Simone. He wasn't trying to escape a toxic environment, like Hutch. If he was going to leave for any reason, it would be because the cabin was too quiet and he wanted company.

But he never found any of us. Never called out or tried to follow us to the shed or even mentioned that he'd gone looking for us once we returned.

Slow down. There are other explanations.

He might have wanted to relieve himself and gotten briefly lost. Or he might have wanted to change his underclothes. We had our luggage lined up outside the cabin at that point, and none of us had changed in days; he could have taken the opportunity when there were fewer eyes around. It's a solid theory.

But then I see those two words again and feel sick to my stomach. *Not drunk??*

I flip through the rest of the journal as my blood rushes through my ears. This time, I focus on the fish icon. Again and again, it's unaccounted for during the times when one of our group was killed. During the first night, when Brian was killed, Alexis notes that three people left the cabin. One of them was Steve. And he's the only one without a return time noted.

It's likely she fell asleep, despite her best intentions to stay awake. The journal's entries don't resume until the following morning, after Brian's body is discovered.

But even with that considered…

My mind turns back to the word Alexis whispered into my ear later that night, when she'd tried to share her suspicions with me. *Surgeon.*

That doesn't coincide with Steve in any way. He was a truck driver. At no point did he try to bandage or tend to anyone. It was Blake who suggested amputating my fingers, not Steve.

Alexis couldn't possibly have been talking about him when she gave me that clue.

Unless…

"Oh, Alexis, no," I whisper under my breath as I realize the truth.

She wasn't trying to warn me about a surgeon.

She said *sturgeon.*

On the bus, Steve had worn an embroidered vest. The decal on the back showed a fish leaping out of the water, a hook in its mouth, a distant fisherman standing on the shore. It wasn't just any carp or trout, though. The long body and ridges along its back belonged to a sturgeon. And that was the reason for the fish icon in the book. That was Alexis's code for him.

Sturgeon.

She couldn't have made her clue more difficult or convoluted if she'd tried. But then, she hadn't known she would be attacked that night either, and left vulnerable and voiceless on the table. She'd thought she'd have time to explain her theory to me, to work out a plan.

She'd just never gotten a chance to get that far.

What does this mean?

I stare at my companions. They're all quiet, trying to sleep now that they're reassured that the killer is no longer in the cabin. Denny leans back in his chair, his head propped against the wall. Blake has folded herself over in the couch. Hutch lies on his back, a spare jacket across his chest, one arm behind his head as he stares at the ceiling.

Were we wrong?

Simone had the journal. And she read it. I noted that she lay with her back to the room, facing the wall. It hadn't made sense at the time, but now I realize she was positioned that way so that she could read the book under the jacket she was using as a blanket—without any of us noticing.

She saw the entry about Steve. She came to the same conclusions I have.

And when he left to go to the bathroom, she followed him.

"I'm going for a walk," I manage, standing abruptly. Hutch, nearest the door, gives me a small smile and a nod. He's the only one to acknowledge me as I pull on my coat and step outside.

63.

Ice stings my face. I'm breathing hard and fast, but it feels as though oxygen isn't entering my lungs.

Steve was the butcher.

How is that possible? Simone...

I watched her beat his head in with a rock. Days of rage and frustration and terror compounding until she decided the only way to keep her surviving companions safe was to kill the man responsible.

She didn't try to share any of this, though. She could have told us to read the journal. Explained that Alexis, before her attack, had been trying to warn us about Steve.

But no, that's not Simone. She doesn't beg. She doesn't make excuses.

We chose to lock her in the shed until we could be rescued. And she accepted that fate.

After all, she *had* killed a man.

Simone has an unflinching set of morals. She probably agreed with our decision that she should be separated from the main group, even if her actions had been in pursuit of justice. She had blood on her hands, both metaphorically and literally. She could accept being locked up until the police could perform the necessary forensic tests to exonerate her from the rest of the killings.

She believed she'd killed the butcher. She'd saved us, even if we didn't know it at the time. There would be plenty of chances to set the record straight and mend broken trust once we escaped from the mountains.

You wanted to walk to Blackstone Lodge. That was a good plan. You should do that.

I'm close to hyperventilating as I stop just inside the field of broken rocks. Ahead lie Steve's remains. We were so focused on containing Simone that we barely spared any thought to his body; we simply left it out here, exposed in the field of white.

Already, it's nearly covered by the storm. Patches of dark clothing and small spatters of gore show through the fresh layers of white. I can see the upturned fingers of one hand. Not much more.

Was Steve the butcher?

Alexis seemed to think so. And Simone was prepared to take her word on it.

But Alexis wasn't entirely convinced, even with her rigorous notes. She'd said she was *almost completely certain* she knew who it was. But even at that point, as she whispered her secrets into my ear late that night, she hadn't been prepared to announce them to the rest of the group.

She'd wanted to recruit me to help her watch Steve. With two people keeping eyes on him, he would have had almost no chance to attack our companions…at least, not without giving himself away. She'd likely hoped we could either gather enough evidence to convince the rest of the cabin or keep us all alive until we could get help.

It had just been too little too late.

What if she was wrong?

I stare down at the bleached-white fingers protruding from the fresh snow and feel my stomach turn. It's the same uneasiness that's dogged me through this trip. The fear that I'm miscalculating. The knowledge that any mistake, no matter how small, could cost all of us our lives.

Alexis was probably right. She'd had more than a year to dwell on her sister's death and possible killer. She'd been on the lookout from the moment she met us outside the bus. If anyone was capable of identifying our killer, it was her.

She was almost entirely convinced.

Almost isn't good enough.

I turn away from Steve's body and rush through the snow. There's one other person I can talk to about this. Simone. Her suspicions about Steve had already been raised after watching him cry over Miri. But she might have had more.

A confession wrenched out of him a moment before she killed him.

Or other clues gathered over the previous days that create a watertight case against him.

I can only pray that she had more than just the journal.

The storm is easing in fragments but still not as fast as I need it to. It's a struggle to move against the wind's force. I squint, fighting to keep my footing. The sun must be close to setting. The valley's eerie, white emptiness is growing less blinding, more heavy and grim. It makes it difficult to locate markers in my environment. I find myself at an outcropping of trees and have to backtrack as I search for the shed.

Please, Simone.

She has to know. She has to be able to help. If I can just convince her to talk.

Ahead, I see a dark, blocky shape through the trees. I had pushed the shed's door as far closed as possible before leaving Simone in there, but it must have come free in the wind. It swings, screeching on its hinges, banging every time it hits the shed's walls.

I reach out my gloved hand as I near it, catching the door and halting its furious momentum.

The sun's angle has dropped too far. I can't see inside any longer. Beyond the door I can make out part of the floor, covered in snow, and a few of the nearest shelves. Beyond that is just a wall of darkness.

"Simone?"

My voice is thinner and reedier than I'd like. Simone must be able to hear me, but she doesn't answer.

I step into the shed, letting the door creak closed behind me.

"Simone, I read the journal."

Still no answer. I bring my cell phone out of my pocket and tap the power button. Nine percent battery. I can't afford to fritter it away, but then, the LED light doesn't use much. And I can't stand speaking to the darkness any longer.

I press the button. The light flashes on, harsh and bright and cold. I've grown used to the yellow glow of the candles. The LED feels almost painful by comparison.

The light forms a severe circle on the floor ahead of me. I raise it slowly. There's Simone's chair. Lashings of rope surround her legs, holding her in place. More connect the chair to the nearest shelves.

I lift the light still higher. Her clothes are still coated in glistening blood. Higher still, past her shoulders.

A strangled cry bubbles in my throat. I lose the last of my strength and drop to the floor.

Simone's head has been carved off.

64.

She sits pin straight in the chair, held there by ropes. The highest bindings, the ones that wrap around her shoulders, are just inches from the raw and red stump of her neck.

It's a clean cut, I think through the rushing terror that drowns out all other thoughts. *A single blow.*

Her blood had drained out from her severed neck to spill over her clothes, the ropes, and the floor. The drips form a halo around where she sits, tiny pools that are already beginning to freeze solid.

My good hand holds the phone ahead of myself, the light shaking as I try to focus it on the room. My other arm is pressed over my face, covering my mouth as I fight against the urge to be sick.

I don't want to imagine what her last moments would have been like. The butcher must have entered through the same door I did and stood right where I now am. Simone would have known death was coming. She would have realized it the second she saw the ax.

And the shed is so far from the cabin that we wouldn't have even heard her scream.

My eyes sting. My heart is doing a strange thing where it thumps heavily, then misses its next beat.

Simone's head is missing from the room. I know where it's going, though.

The pine tree.

One more for the collection.

That thought sends jolts through me. I haven't been out of the cabin for long. I stood over Steve's resting place, but not for any more than five or six minutes.

The blood on the ground is fresh. Still liquid, mostly.

The butcher is close.

I fumble with my phone, desperate, and turn the light off. I can't afford to advertise my position. Our killer is most likely searching for me. That makes the most sense. Wait until I leave the cabin, then strike while our small group of survivors is separated and at its most vulnerable.

Alexis was wrong. Simone was wrong. *I* was wrong. It wasn't Steve after all. His greatest crime was being in the wrong places at the wrong times and having his absences noted in the journal, nothing more.

There's a sound outside the shed. Footsteps, growing nearer. My heart freezes entirely.

They're looking for me.

I scramble backward, away from open door. My back hits the tools in the shed's corner—the same corner where I found the ax. They clink under the impact. The storm disguises most sounds; I can only hope it's enough to mask me now.

The sounds grow nearer. Snow crunching under heavy boots. They're slow steps. Measured. The butcher isn't in any kind of hurry tonight. They got us to drop our guard. Now, they can pick us off at their leisure.

The door whines, swinging on its rusted hinges. A final crunching footstep comes from the shed's open doorway, and the banging door abruptly falls still.

They're there. No more than four paces away. I press my arm across my mouth, muffling my breathing, and shrink even further into myself.

Stacked boxes and implements form a flimsy barrier between me and the door. My clothes are all neutral colors that blend into the clutter. Neither of those things will be enough to hide me if the killer decides to search the shed in earnest.

For three painful heartbeats, neither of us moves. Then there's a soft click. A light comes on, a beam starting at the door and shining a circle of light directly onto Simone's body.

Until now, we thought the only light we had left was my phone. Of course, we were wrong. The butcher would have brought resources that they hid around their killing field. The ax. The flashlight they now wield.

The beam stays centered on Simone for too long. I realize they're admiring their work. The pooling, slowly freezing blood around her. The way her body hasn't slumped even an inch. Given enough time, she'll freeze solid in that seat, the place where we pinned her and left her to die.

Then the flashlight moves. It glides to the right, shining over the shelves and broken furniture and cluttered boxes. Searching. For me.

It pans to the far right, then turns back. Shining across Simone's body again. Before moving closer and closer to my own hiding spot.

My heart is in my throat. I'm rigid, unable to move as the circle of light draws closer. My mind flashes across every conceivable weapon. The screwdrivers? Too far away. Broken furniture? Unwieldy. I'm surrounded by farming implements. They're my only real option. Large, clunky, unlikely to do any damage even if I'm able to land a blow.

And the butcher has an ax.

The light stops just feet away from me. I'm certain it must be enough to illuminate the edge of my shoes. My arm is pressed so tightly over my mouth that my teeth ache from the pressure.

Then there's a click, and the light turns off.

They didn't see me.

Or maybe they did, and they're pretending they didn't.

I don't dare move. Not even an inch. Not even to take the arm away from my mouth and unmuffle my breathing. They're still right there, in the doorway, waiting. Listening.

Who is it?

Denny, the man accused of killing his dissatisfied wife?

Blake, who pinned me to the floor and pressed her hand across my mouth?

Or Hutch, the man who tried to save a drowning boy from a swollen river but gave up halfway?

Hutch has been nothing but warm and helpful to me. But then, the butcher would know that the social game would be just as important for their plans as their impeccable preparation. It's easier to get close to people when they trust you. Easier to sway their opinions and shift their minds. I've wanted to walk to Blackstone Lodge twice now. Both times, it was Hutch who gently persuaded me to rest first.

I press my eyes closed. I don't want to believe it's Hutch. I don't want to believe it's *any* of them. This was supposed to be over. We *won*.

How are we still dying?

The figure in the doorway steps back at last. I hear their footsteps. Steady, heavy, as the snow crunches beneath their weight. The sound fades before I can track it far at all, and I finally let some of my rigid muscles fall loose.

I'm alive.

But the butcher is moving again, and I think I know where to.

The survivors in the cabin.

65.

My hand fixes around the wooden pole of a rake. It's not a good weapon; one blow from an ax would cleave it in half, leaving me defenseless. It's hard to hold with one hand, but my other fingers are stiff and inflexible. I have to press it to my chest just to keep it steady.

There's no time to find anything better.

I creep toward the shed's exit. The door swings in the wind again, banging each time it hits home. A fear lingers in the back of my mind that the killer might not have actually left. That the light grazing across the edges of my boots might have given me away. That the butcher only pretended to leave and now stands just out of sight, ax raised in preparation for me.

It's almost enough to paralyze me. I shuffle forward inch by inch, watching the gap every time the door swings wide. Snow gusts past. It's growing duller, darker, as the sun falls behind the mountain range. There are no visible shadows to help me get my bearings. I have to take a risk.

I lunge forward, my head low and shoulders hunched, and stumble into the empty snow. There's no figure pressed against the cabin's wall. No killer waiting for me.

Which means I'm running out of time to save the others.

Rake held against my chest, I jog into the trees. There's a channel in the snow: the path we took after locking Simone away. The path leading back to the cabin. It's hard to be sure in the fading light, but it looks like a fresh set of prints mar the snow.

I avoid the channel, instead moving wide, darting through the trees. I'm less at risk of being ambushed this way. But the snow is thicker, slowing me down. My heart feels as though it's about to explode. I think I hear the crack of a broken stick behind me and swing the rake instinctively, but all I can see are rows of dark, crooked pine trunks, fading into the snow and gloom.

Fast. Faster!

It's a race, and I hate how much of an advantage the butcher has over me. I burst out from between the trees and into the clearing. The storm rings in my ears. I can't be far from the cabin, but the wide sweep away from the familiar path has led me to an area I don't recognize.

I'd see better if I could use my light, but that kind of visibility would only paint a target on me. I stay low as I move across the white field, toward the area I know the cabin must be in. I've strayed farther off course than I thought; I can't see any of the familiar landmarks, let alone the cabin's peaked roof.

A strange sound rings out through the empty world. I freeze, teeth clenched, as I try to orient myself. Was it coming from ahead? Or behind? It seems to echo before fading out. It was a human voice, I'm almost certain, but any words were scrambled and dashed into a blur of nothing by the wind.

I keep my body low in the snow. My clothes are all too dark for me to blend into the white, but as long as I don't stand straight, I won't be instantly recognizable from a distance. It might be enough to let me appear as a rock or a tree stump or even a shadow in the snowdrifts.

It's a fight to stay moving. The wind blows straight into my face, forcing me to squint and burning my skin. I want to slow down. Pause for a second to breathe. Instead, I push myself faster.

The butcher's tree comes into sight. Which means I'm close to the cabin. It's impossible not to glance up the tree's towering length as I pass it.

A new head has been added. Simone's. Her branch sways as the storm buffets it. I'm not close enough to see her expression or how badly her jaw has been forced open by the wood skewer, but that's not any kind of comfort.

Worse is the sight ahead. The cabin's there, facing me head-on.

Its door is wide-open. A single candle flickers inside, a dance of golden-yellow light across exposed wood. I can't see far inside, but there's no sign of my companions.

Run, my instincts whisper. *Don't stop. Don't look. Just run.*

But I can't.

I won't abandon them.

66.

The cabin's door swings under the wind's force, scraping through the snow, an eerie imitation of the shed. There's no sign of life inside. No one tries to shut the door; no voices call out. There's only the single candle, out of sight, casting a thin yellow glow across the small room.

I adjust my grip around the rake's handle. My hands are numb. My body feels as though it's not entirely under my control.

My legs drag as I force them forward. The snow outside the cabin's door is churned after days of feet stomping over it and compacting it into ice. My own shoe prints are mixed in there from when I left to come to grips with the journal's content. I don't even *have* the journal any longer. I think I dropped it in the shed, when my light grazed over Simone, but the events are already blurring.

I strain to hear any kind of sound coming from inside the cabin. The creak of a floorboard. The rush of harried breathing. I can't make out a single sound over the wind's howls. I'm going in blind, fully aware that the butcher may be present, may even be *waiting* for my return.

I don't have a choice. If the others are still alive—even just one of them—I can't abandon them here.

As I near the open door, I lower my body farther. It makes me vulnerable, exposing my back, but I'm banking on the idea that any attack will be aimed for my head. Being low might buy me a second. Maybe two. And that could make all the difference.

I'm at the threshold. There's a whisper of sound inside the cabin, but I still can't hear it clearly. It could be a voice, murmuring. It could the fire, guttering. Or it could even be one of the tree branches scraping against the back wall.

My eyes burn from a lack of blinking. I lean forward, through the entrance, straining to see.

There's blood on the wall near where Denny used to sit. My heart misses a beat. The pattern is sprayed in an arc, thick droplets sticking to the wood and running down to the floor.

I force my eyes away from the blood. Furniture is disturbed; the couch has been pushed aside, the chair by the fire overturned. The dirty cups and bowls, stacked near the fire, were knocked over. Many are broken. I picture them being trampled as figures wrestle.

Now, though, there's no sign of any of my companions. Denny is missing from his seat. Hutch has left his place between the door and the fireplace. And Blake is no longer on the couch.

Only one figure remains. On the table near the back wall lies Alexis. I can't see her well. I don't know if she's been hurt. I can't tell if she's still breathing.

I rise out of my crouch and shift my hold on the rake. This cabin has been my home for days. The furniture, the rough walls, the stacks of books and the odd collections of knickknacks have become almost painfully familiar to me. Now, the space is in disarray. Everywhere I look, familiar patterns have been disturbed. My own bed has been kicked out of place. The window has a large, angry crack running through its glass. The more I look, the more I find spots of blood. Dripped onto the floor. Scattered across the walls. Soaking into the discarded clothing.

There's the sound again. The one I thought I heard when I was in the doorway. Breathing, rough and sickly. Coming from the far corner, hidden behind Alexis's table.

I move slowly, carefully. Placing each foot deliberately to avoid making noise and keeping my back to the wall and my access to the door open. I crane as I try to see around the table. The drops of blood are more plentiful on that part of the wall. There's a smear across the floor, as though something was dragged. A pair of legs come into view, stretched out and skewed. They shudder as the sound repeats. Acidic fear coats my tongue as I take a final step and the form comes into view.

Hutch sits in the room's corner, wedged behind the table. He sits with his back to the wall. One of his arms is limp at his side, rivers of blood running down it.

The other is clutched over his chest.

Trying to hold it together.

He draws another low, rattling breath, and I realize his front has been sliced open. A deep red gash runs beneath his hand, splitting both his jacket and his body.

I make a sound that isn't quite human as I rush to him. I can't get close with the rake so I drop it, then scramble into the corner on my hands and knees. "Hutch—I'm so sorry, I'm so sorry—"

His head lifts a fraction. He's pale, his jaw gaping open as he fights to breathe. He's not entirely there.

I grab for a blanket that's been discarded nearby. It's dirty, like everything else in the cabin, but possible future infections are the least of my worries. I press the blanket into the wound, pushing it around his hand and applying pressure. He twitches, and I make soft, apologetic noises.

"This is okay. We're going to stop the bleeding. We're going to…"

I don't even know how to finish that thought. The injury is horrendous. He likely has shattered rib bones, possibly punctures in his lungs. The gash is nearly as long as my forearm.

The length of an ax's head.

Blake and Denny are both missing. They'll be somewhere outside, in the snow. One of them might already be dead. I can't think about that or about how near I must be to the same fate as I adjust my hold on the blanket, desperately trying to stem the dripping red.

"Who did this?" I ask, even though I don't expect an answer.

Hutch's eyelids flutter. He seems to see me. His hand, wet and red, reaches forward. It grips the collar of my jacket tighter than I'd thought he would be capable of. His lips work as he fights to speak.

I lean closer, meeting him halfway. His skin is horribly clammy and cold as it brushes against mine.

He whispers one word.

"Run."

A floorboard creaks behind me.

67.

I turn.

The cabin's open doorway has been filled. A massive, hulking form stands there, wild gray hair tangled about his face.

Denny.

His hands shift, and the wicked ax glints in the candlelight.

My voice dies in my throat. I'm frozen in place, a prey animal transfixed by the stare of a predator. Hutch's hand clutches at my collar, wet and desperate.

I can't leave him.

But staying will have only one possible ending. Death.

Denny moves faster than I imagined could be possible. He crosses the space in three long steps. I lunge for the rake. Denny gets there first, one swipe of his shoe kicking it away and sending it skittering into the broken bowls and cups.

The ax comes up. I'm wedged into the corner with Hutch, who is making desperate gasping noises as he fights to speak through the blood.

His last word echoes in my mind again and again and again.

Run.

I throw myself backward.

The ax comes down. It narrowly misses my head. Instead, the wickedly sharp corner slices through my upper arm, just below my shoulder, before sinking into the wall beside Hutch.

Fiery, burning pain shoots through my arm. Red blood flows, flecks of it hitting my face and spattering across the wood behind me.

Pure terror overrides the pain. I throw myself under the table that holds Alexis, squirming to get out of the corner I find myself trapped in.

Denny makes a low guttural noise as he wrenches the ax free. I'm nearly out the table's other side, a trail of red running down my arm and off my fingers. He bends, his massive hand swiping to catch at my shoe. It fixes around the leather. Terror floods me as I feel my whole body being dragged backward. I kick. My shoe slides out of his hold. I claw my way forward, out from under the table, ending up in the pile of bedding that used to be my resting place.

To my left is the couch and, past that, the open door.

Against my better judgment, I glance back toward Hutch.

He can barely move, but he's grasping at Denny's pants. Trying, with what little strength he has left, to hold him back. To buy me some time.

Denny steps out of his hold as though he can't even feel him. His eyes are dark pits as they fix on me: empty, emotionless. A shark's eyes.

I run.

My legs feel as though they belong to a stranger as I vault over the couch. My elbow hits the doorframe as I slip through. Denny is close behind. I hear the whistle of the ax cutting through air just inches behind my ear.

I bend forward, my mouth open as I try to drag in air to fuel my limbs. I'm flying faster than I ever have before, cutting through the snow, blind in the near dark of sunset and the tempest winds.

Denny makes no verbal noises, but I hear his boots pounding through the snow behind me. The ax must weigh nearly as much as a child, but he wields it as though it's nothing.

I can't protect Hutch.

I can't protect Alexis.

I can't protect Blake.

But I might be able to buy us all some time.

I can lead Denny away from them and away from the cabin.

We have very little hope that the call will result in help arriving. But I have to cling to it because, without it, we have nothing.

If a rescue is underway, I can give them a chance to get here. Pray that Hutch hasn't lost too much blood by the time they arrive. That Alexis is still breathing.

The butcher's tree casts a long shadow over me as I pass beneath it. The ghoulish head display rattles, long hair whipping in the wind, eyes frozen open as they stare down at me.

It's most likely the last time I'll see it.

My legs burn. My lungs ache. Hot blood continues to seep from the vicious line of pain on my upper arm. It's all I can do to keep moving, furiously, desperately, because even a second's pause will seal my fate. Denny is larger and heavier than I am, but it doesn't slow him down.

I realize, belatedly, that I'm running toward the field of jagged rocks where Steve's body was found. The ground is too unstable. I make to correct my course, to travel toward the trees, instead.

A thought flashes through my fear-emptied mind.

You wanted to walk to Blackstone Lodge. That was a good plan. You should do that.

I doubt I can get as far as the lodge before Denny catches me. But I can try. At the very least, it's a goal, and that's better than being trapped in aimless flight through the mountains.

To travel toward the lodge, I'd need to go through the field of brittle, sharp rocks.

And so I do.

My ankle threatens to turn on the first patch of unstable ground. My mind screams at me, begging me to slow down, to test my steps. I can't. Not when I can hear Denny's heavy breathing so close behind that he could be leaning over my shoulder.

I fix my eyes on the ground as I fly through the broken field. There's only barely enough time to watch the ground I travel over. No room to plan my path, no room to take precautions. I slip. My foot plunges into a gulf between two rocks. I wrench it free, ignoring the way my ankle stings as the rocks score off a strip of skin beneath my insulated pants. And I keep moving.

The gap between myself and Denny is increasing, I realize. I've got nothing to lose. He can't afford mistakes. His balance isn't as solid as mine; he has to slow.

I press my advantage, scrambling over boulders recklessly. I'm still wearing Hutch's gloves and Kiernan's scarf. I'll need them. The sun has almost entirely disappeared. The landscape is growing hazier, dimmer. Desperate, I pull my phone out of my pocket and turn on its flashlight. I catch a glimpse of the battery—seven percent—then aim the light forward.

The field of broken rocks ends. Ahead is a bank of trees, leading up into the mountains that surround the cabin's valley.

My limbs shake, but I can't rest. I've managed to put some space between myself and Denny but nowhere near as much as I need. I've bought seconds, not minutes. All it would take is a cliff wall blocking my path to end me.

I fly through the snow, toward the trees, aiming for the widest gap between them I can find. If I'm lucky, I might discover a hiking trail or natural passage through the mountain walls rising around me. I try not to think about what will happen if I'm not lucky. The butcher's tree would gain one more head, most likely.

My phone's light acts like a beacon in the deepening twilight. I don't try to turn it off, though. Without it, I'd be blind. And there's no opportunity to hide from Denny when my trailing footprints would lead him right to me.

The trees grow denser as I push through them. Clumps of snow rain from the branches, slapping over my shoulders and back. The wind's roar softens between the trunks, at least. It makes it easier to hear my pursuer. He's audible only by the steady thuds of his boots.

My light glints across the dozens of frost-coated trunks around me. It's a maze, and one I'm rapidly becoming disoriented in. I can't see the mountain range, and without that, I don't know which direction to face to reach the lodge.

No time to stop. No chance to get my bearings. I plunge forward, low branches slapping my face and outstretched arm as I tear through them.

Cliff walls rise to my left. I adjust, moving away from them, only to realize more walls have appeared to my right. I'm being funneled into a natural wedge in the mountain's face, and it's already too late to back away.

I'm wheezing as I let my steps slow. My mind spins, furiously searching for any escape, any chance I might have. Can I backtrack? No. Denny is already closing the gap I gained. Can I climb the trees? None of the lower branches could support my weight. Nowhere to hide. No chance of scrambling up the steep walls, even with adrenaline fueling me.

My light lands on a strange shape ahead. It's dark and huddled in the snow, like a rock, except the surface shudders under the gusting wind.

No, not a rock. That's fabric. A familiar jacket: Blake's. She lies in the snow, unmoving, and I feel my heart sink.

A branch snaps behind me. I'm out of time.

I race toward Blake.

68.

The angled cliff walls merge together, seeming to create a corner. Blake lies in that narrowing section, facedown. Her arms are stretched ahead of her, the hands nearly together, like a swimmer midway through the butterfly stroke. The pose must be agony on her back, I think.

But then the obvious sinks in. She's not in pain. Not now. Her head is gone. The arms stretch around the space where it should be, a place that's now just white snow and stray drops of blood.

It's only when I notice how little blood is scattered around her that I realize why she's posed like that; her body was dragged, possibly as retribution after she tried to flee from the cabin and from Denny. She'll have left a long, bloody brushstroke in her wake, one that is now nearly invisible under the snow and the failing light.

I raise my phone. Its LED ghosts across the cliff walls ahead.

And…

A gap.

It was impossible to see from a distance, but the narrowing cliff walls don't perfectly meet. There's a passageway between them: a narrow pass, barely wide enough for a person to fit through.

It's straight ahead of Blake's outstretched arms. Her body almost forms an arrow pointing toward it.

And in the opening is a small, too-familiar shape.

Denny left Blake's head in the chasm's entrance. Embedded in the snow, faceup, slack-jawed, and wide-eyed, she stares at me. I'll be forced to step directly over her if I want to get through.

Her short gray hair is limp as it tangles into the snow. Her vivid-red lipstick is smeared around her mouth, showing that she struggled before she died. It blends in with the fresh blood streaking across her severed neck.

Not quite the same shade. But very close.

Denny's almost on top of me again, my advantage squandered. I'm out of options. Out of *time*. I dash forward, leaping at the last second to jump over Blake's head.

My shoulders brush the chasm's rough walls as I land. I have no idea how deep it goes or whether I'm running into a dead end. All I can do is keep my phone outstretched as I fight to read the landscape ahead.

The gap has filled with snow but not as much as I feared it might be. I'm able to push through it with less effort than the open fields created. The chasm only stays narrow for a moment, then widens, giving me room to sprint forward at full speed.

Denny is still in pursuit. I'm the only one left, I realize with a jolt. Simone is dead. Blake is dead. Hutch and Alexis are locked in place by their injuries, waiting to either be finished off or to succumb to the cold and blood loss.

I'm the last of us.

And he doesn't want to let me go. Not when he's so close to the end.

I drive forward, dangerously and recklessly. The chasm turns repeatedly, hiding its path behind sharp corners. Sounds echo in the space. My ragged breaths. My feet. My heart.

Denny.

I can't see him. The tight walls distort noise, and I have no idea how close he is behind me. But he's there, a voiceless, ferocious pursuer. Relentless. I remember how empty, how cold his eyes were.

What would it take to make a man snap that badly?

How did he know Liam, the boy from the river?

Was that his other son, perhaps?

His marriage was on the verge of falling apart when he killed his wife. Two years of grieving over a child lost before his time would strain any relationship.

Two years spent planning revenge.

Denny would have known he'd have no way to return to his home and his family after the events of this week. Maybe he intends to die out here, with us, in the snow. Or maybe he plans to escape—over the border into Canada, possibly. Somewhere he won't be recognized.

Either way, his old suburban life would be over. And a man as rigid as Denny would not like leaving either his wife or his son behind. He'd want to tie up loose ends.

Maybe Grayson was supposed to die in the car crash that took his wife. Or more likely, Denny always planned to bring Grayson on this trip with him. It might have even been a test. It's possible he wanted Grayson to go on the run with him, to somewhere they could start a new life together. He'd just wanted to ensure his boy could stomach that future first.

But Grayson had betrayed him. Grayson had revealed his secrets.

And so Grayson had ended up hung from a tree, bleeding out like a freshly killed animal.

The thoughts move through my head at the same pace as the storm whistling above the channel's walls. I'm flagging. The adrenaline can only carry me so far. And the road is no longer flat either. The passage continues to widen—now wide enough to drive cars along it—but it's begun to tend upward as well. I still can't see where it lets out. Or if it even does.

Can't stop. Can't slow.

Every step I can lead Denny forward is a step removed from the cabin and another few seconds of grace I can buy the two souls inside.

But the slope is now so steep that I have to scramble, using my hands as much as my legs to pull myself forward. Rocks jut out of the snow, as ragged and vicious as the field behind the cabin was.

How far have I come? How long since I left the valley behind?

It feels like just seconds. It also feels as though it's taken hours. My sense of time is distorted. So is my sense of direction. I've lost my context for where the distant roofline was; unless I can find a landmark to orient myself—and that's growing very near to impossible now that deep night has set in and I only have my phone's light to guide me—then I'll be in the same situation I was the first night of the storm, when I was separated from Kiernan. Lost. Close to blind. Stumbling through the snow with very little hope of rescue.

The storm is growing louder again. That must mean I'm nearing the end of the crevasse. I risk a second to turn, throwing the light behind me. I can see my footprints in the snow, a tumbling, uneven mess, looping down the slope.

For a second I both dread and hope that Denny has given up. I can't hear him. Can't see him either. Then, right at the edge of my light, I catch a glint of metal. The ax, swinging mercilessly as he paces in my wake.

The sight gives me a fresh jolt of adrenaline. I take advantage of it, dragging myself up the final, steepest section of the climb, my lungs burning and my body trembling from exhaustion and stress.

Denny's not using his flashlight to follow me. I guess he doesn't need to, since my own light both guides the way and marks my location.

Though he probably has another reason for moving in the dark, I realize. It's easier for him to catch up if I can't see him coming.

My numb, damaged hand hooks around rocks as I pull myself higher. I'm very near collapsing. Strength is dripping out of me like water through cupped hands, and there's nothing I can do to stop it. Not even the imminent threat of death can buy me any energy now.

But then, suddenly, my outstretched hand lands in empty air. The climb is over. I'm out into a clear patch of land again, far above the valley where I started.

Stringent winds buffet me. Flecks of snow and freezing air smart across my eyes, blinding me, but the outside world isn't completely impenetrable anymore. There's a gap in the storm. Scraps of thin, struggling moonlight break through.

Ahead of me is a clear stretch of land. Images fade in as I fight to see through the dark and the ice and the mist.

There's something flat and broad with a ring of dead plants surrounding its edges. A lake. To my right and left and into the far distance are patches of trees, very similar to the ones surrounding the cabin.

And ahead...

It's barely visible. But moonlight skims over the edges of it, revealing sharp planes and a tall, multifaceted roofline. Even in the dark, even from such a distance, I recognize the outline from the brochure I clutched in my hand just days before.

I've found Blackstone Alpine Lodge.

Sounds echo. Rocks, torn out of the ground, tumble down the steep passageway behind me.

I'm breathless. Broken. So tired that I can barely move.

But the lodge is close. And with it comes a new, vital promise. Phones. Wi-Fi. Connection to the outside world.

The moon's just barely bright enough to show me the path forward. I turn my cell phone off to save the last scraps of its power, then break into a sprint.

69.

Blackstone Alpine Lodge was first built in the eighties. Back then, it really was only a small building: four bedrooms, housing up to ten guests who were expected to bring their own food and bedding.

Sometime over the following decades, the roads into the mountain were improved. Blackstone built a name for itself thanks to the picturesque landscape, nearby lake, and game hunting in the summer months. A developer saw potential.

The lodge was expanded, refined. Luxury sheets were added to the bedrooms. A laundry room and industrial kitchen ensured spaces could be turned over and guests fed in the most efficient manner possible. There was equipment rental for those who wanted to hike, canoe, or fish.

The massive, rustic-themed retreat saw its peak months during spring and summer. Although the mountains had more than enough snow for skiing and snowboarding during winter, the landscape was unfriendly to beginner sportspeople and the weather was too unpredictable to put up permanent infrastructure. Come winter, the industrial kitchen was shut down and housekeeping staff dismissed, and the lodge was then only rented out to private tour groups.

Like ours.

These factoids run through my mind as I fight my way toward the silhouette rising out of the landscape.

I read them in the brochure I had on the bus ride into the mountains. That was the last time I remember feeling normal. Safe. Kiernan was at my side, and he held my hand when he sensed I was growing anxious. The people around me were strangers but not unkind. We had something to look forward to. Two weeks at this breathtaking location, surrounded by nature, and with enough creature comforts to fill even the longest days. A library. Game rooms. Massive TVs with DVDs available to compensate for the poor reception.

There's no hunting or fishing during winter. The lake freezes over and the wildlife migrates lower down the mountains, where there's still food to be found. But there are endless hiking trails if you can find them under the snow. I pass a sign pointing to one. It's advertising a lookout two miles away, I think, but it's hard to be sure under the spiked frost clinging to the wood surface.

Instead, I focus forward.

The building's made of stone, with large wooden support beams at the corners and around the roof to add to the wild atmosphere. Every step closer makes it appear drastically larger. I can't even count the number of windows reflecting cold light back at me. It's three floors tall and sprawling, none of the wings or extensions quite symmetrical.

As the building's shadow falls over me, I pause to throw a glance behind myself.

Denny stalks across the empty field. The moon is at his back, leaving his face obscured. His gray hair whips out behind him. He's no longer rushing but is steady, methodical, as he eats through the distance between us.

I clamber up the slope leading to the main entrance. It's only when I reach toward the door that it occurs to me: the lodge is going to be locked. Brian would have had a set of keys with him. My only hope to get inside will be to break something—a window, if I can find one low enough to the ground.

Still, the entrance is right ahead of me. Double doors, arched into a point above my head, not unlike a monastery's. I reach for the handle. And I'm shocked when the latch clicks, allowing me entrance.

The lodge is supposed to be closed over winter. Did I get that wrong? Is there someone here?

There's no time to question it. I force my way inside, then slam the door closed in my wake.

Any question of having company in the building vanishes. There's not a single light in the space. The air is still, undisturbed, and icy cold. The wind's howls are muffled by thick walls, leaving the space inside almost eerily silent.

I am very much alone here.

Brian said something about buildings in remote areas leaving their doors unlocked. To give shelter to lost travelers in life-and-death situations. The law of hospitality. It's why we thought the cabin was unoccupied when we first arrived.

If I'd owned the lodge, I'd worry about thieves. But the sheer remoteness would dissuade anyone looking for an easy payout. Nature itself might have been a more powerful barrier to ransacking than any number of locks.

This must be the foyer. I can barely see; patches of light come through the windows, but all they reveal is scraps of wooden floor and the corner of some kind of furniture. I take my phone out while pressing a hand into the stitch that's formed in my side.

Four percent battery. Zero bars of reception.

The lodge must have some kind of Wi-Fi system. It *must*. We know there's reception in the mountains because we were able to connect our boosted call for a few precious seconds. But the lodge would have its own system and that would be reliant on power.

There are no power lines running through the mountains. Which means Blackstone will have a generator.

I just need to find it.

70.

My phone's battery is dangerously low. But without it, I'm utterly blind.

I thumb the flashlight button and let its bulb illuminate the space around me.

It's a foyer, like I suspected. My light doesn't reach as far as I want it to, but it glazes over shapes that feel both familiar and alien at once.

Massive wingback armchairs are arranged around a grand fireplace to my right. A reception desk is ahead and to the left, cleaned and organized in preparation for reopening in another few months. Fur rugs drape across sections of the floor, enhancing the rustic-hunting-lodge theme. The space is larger than any lodge I've seen before, though. A chandelier, ringed by a wreath of antlers, is suspended high above my head, cold and dead as it waits for power. Ahead, past the reception desk, a massive, curved staircase leads to the upper floors.

I turn my light toward the double doors at my back. They have a mechanism designed to hold them open for when guests arrive: metal pegs that fasten into holders on the walls.

And as I hoped, there's also a large metal bolt for keeping the doors closed.

I lean my weight into the bolt, driving it home. It slams into place with a satisfying echo.

There's no way to keep Denny out permanently. Failing all else, he'll break a window, just like I was planning to.

But it will get me an extra minute or two.

Where would the generator be stored?

My eyes turn toward the reception desk. I jog toward it, clenching my teeth at the way my strained muscles resist any kind of movement.

There's barely anything on the desk's surface: holders with pens, dead computer monitors and keyboards, trays for papers. Below that are drawers, though, with their keys left in the locks. I wrench them open, phone held above my head with one hand as I sort through.

I get lucky on the second drawer. Three pen-sized flashlights roll about in a tray, in among loose paper clips and rubber bands.

I mutter thanks under my breath as I click the first flashlight's button and it turns on. Then I power off the phone, saving what's left of its battery.

Sounds echo from outside the lodge. The main doors shudder viciously as Denny tries to open them. I freeze, tongue clamped between my teeth, staring at the wooden structure. There's a pause, and then a booming thud as something slams into the wood.

If the doors aren't locked during winter, then when was the last time the bolt was used? How secure is it? How much can it keep out?

My heart knocks against my chest. My eyes burn as I keep them fixed on the doors, watching, waiting. There's a second of silence, then the heavy booming sound repeats. The doors shake, their hinges rattling. Scraps of snow slide in through the gap beneath.

The bolt holds.

I wait to see if Denny will turn aside and leave to try another entrance. There are two windows on either side of the door—narrow, thankfully, too thin for a person to fit through—but there's no sign of movement behind them.

Then the heavy slamming noise comes a third time, deafening. Its echoes set my bones on edge.

Something has come through the wood. A sliver of cold metal. Less than an inch of it. I wouldn't have even been able to see it if my light hadn't shimmered over it.

I'd thought he was trying to drive his shoulder into the doors or kick them down. I was wrong.

He's using the ax.

He's going to cut his way inside.

And that might just work. The bolt itself is solid metal, but its bracket is made of wood. Denny only has to break through that.

Tacky fear coats my tongue. I put my head back down as I focus on the desk drawers. A frantic kind of desperation runs through me. After everything, after all of this struggle, I cannot falter now.

Bang. Shudders run through me. I fight against the impulse to look up.

Drawers scrape as I drag them open. There's no time to be careful. I dump their contents on the floor, sorting through them, shoving loose papers aside as I hunt for the one thing I desperately need.

Bang. I upend another drawer. Thick markers scatter everywhere. I clasp the small flashlight between my teeth to hold it steady. The gloves make it hard to flip through the loose papers so I tear them off.

The fingers on my left hand are entirely black now, the color bleeding down to the knuckles. Dead.

I keep working. There's another *bang*, and this time I hear wood splintering. I drag another drawer out.

There, right on top of the pile, is a binder. A label has been affixed to it: *Operations Guide.*

Air whistles around the flashlight in my mouth as I flip the binder open. There are pages and pages of text, with headings of all sizes and occasional diagrams.

Bang. I keep flipping. And finally, I find it. Near the back of the book. Four pages, stapled together in the corner, their edges worn from decades of use.

A floor plan of Blackstone Alpine Lodge.

Wood shudders as the ax slams home again. I lift my head. The damage to the door is visible now. Splinters arc inward, showing just how deeply the ax has dug. I'm certain, if I held still for just another few seconds, I would see Denny through the narrow hole he's carved.

Instead, I drag the floor plan out of the binder and run.

71.

I don't go far. Just enough to get out of the foyer and, I hope, hide my light.

Wheezing, I press close to a wall and hold the flashlight between my teeth as I flip through the floor plan.

Each sheet is dedicated to one of the lodge's levels. I see endless bedrooms, clumped around winding hallways. The library. The game room. The trophy room. The dining hall. Even a small rooftop garden.

The harsh beam bleeds out the thin lines of ink, making the drawings hard to read. I turn the pages back until I find the ground floor. There, at the lodge's front, is the foyer. The papers are out-of-date. The reception desk is in a different place now.

If the generator is going to be anywhere, it will be on the ground floor, close to where the employees work and stay. I hunt through the rooms, identifying the kitchens and the laundry area, until I find a space simply called *maintenance*.

It's not a guarantee. But with no clear sign indicating a generator elsewhere on the page, it's my best chance.

The heavy, ferocious bangs ring out behind me. I drop the light back into my hand as I press down the narrow hallway. I'm into the staff areas, the places the guests aren't supposed to see. Doors hold signs saying as much: *restricted area*, *private*. Shiny gold locks near their handles show they're intended to be kept sealed. They're all open now, though, leaving the hallways stretching ahead of me.

Most likely, these staff areas are the last to be emptied when the lodge closes for winter and the first to see foot traffic when it's to be reopened. The doors would be kept open for convenience, allowing for power to be turned back on without too much time lost fumbling with locks.

I hold the map and light awkwardly in my good hand, following the path. It's not as clear as it looked on paper. My heart kicks up another notch as I'm forced to backtrack.

Then, finally, I find the door I need: *Maintenance room.* Just like the others, it's been left open, a hook fastening it to the wall to prevent it from slamming closed with any drafts.

Tools hang on hooks along the walls. Pressure cleaners. Wires to force down clogged pipes. Tool belts and clippers and crowbars.

And taking up the entire back half of the room...

A massive, unbelievably powerful generator.

It would need to be big to supply power, air-conditioning, and hot water to the multitude of rooms. I still didn't expect it to be quite *this* large. Or complicated. There's a dashboard with an array of buttons and a display screen that's currently dormant.

Dread coils deep in my stomach. I don't know how to start it. Or if it needs fuel. Or what to do with the dashboard.

And without it, I have nothing. No phone. No way to call for help. It will be just me and Denny, trapped in a lightless maze of a building. The hunter and the hunted, with only one inevitable conclusion to our confrontation.

I can no longer hear the slamming noises coming from the foyer, I realize. The blows of the ax were so rigidly regular that they'd begun to fade into background noise. Now, they've fallen silent.

Denny's inside.

My hand shakes as I dart the flashlight over the control panel and massive machine, searching for any clues about what I'm supposed to do.

There's one button that stands apart from the others: large, round, and black, it's unlabeled but looks important.

I have nothing left to lose. I press it.

There's a heavy thud, then a shudder. Deep, mechanical whirring fills the room, nearly deafening for a second before fading to a more manageable level.

And miraculously, the lights overhead flash on.

Choked, gasping laughter escapes me. It worked. One button, and the generator came on.

My elation fades as I turn to look back at the door.

Until now, I've been operating with only the pen-sized flashlight to guide my way. It revealed glimpses of the space around me but never enough to see my environment clearly.

In the doorway, a drop of vivid-red blood shimmers on the tile floor.

Another one lingers not far past it, in the hallway.

And still more, at my feet.

I look at my arm. Through the cold and stress and fear, the gash became just another ache in my exhausted body. Just one more thing to endure and ignore.

But it's been bleeding. Not rapidly, but enough to create a trail of blood. Leading Denny right to me.

72.

My body turns numb. The generator rumbles at my back—not loud, but loud enough to disguise any sounds outside the maintenance room.

Rows of tools line the walls. Between the building plans and the flashlight, I'm already overburdened with my single working hand, but it would be pure stupidity to pass up a chance at defense while I have it. I reach for the harshest but lightest item I can see. The hammer.

Images flash through my mind. Sinking the metal into Denny's head again and again. Creating a small hole each time, like puncturing through drywall.

I feel sick and clammy as I fight the thoughts away. I'm not sure I could go through with it if the time came. But if it's a choice between that and dying...

Denny could still be in the foyer. Or he could be right outside the maintenance room's door. Without being able to hear him, I have no idea how close he might be. But I can't stay, not with a trail of blood droplets marking my path.

I put my head down and bolt for it. My good arm stretches the hammer out as I dart through the open door, preparing to swing it at any shapes that linger outside. The hallway is empty. I turn away from the direction I came and run blindly, my lungs raw and gasping.

I take the passages wildly, trying to be unpredictable. I don't stop moving until I find myself in the kitchen.

The space is massive, designed to cater to the hundreds of tourists that flock to the lodge in the warmer season. The rest of the mansion clings to its rustic, wood-and-stone decor, but here is nothing but shining stainless steel stove tops and meticulously clean prep stations. You could easily fit a dozen chefs around the center table.

My arm continues to drip. Blood runs down the damp sleeve and off my wrist. I need to stop it. I turn, my feet light as I dart through the kitchen, craning as I search for a towel, a cloth, anything. The room's bare. They must have all been taken to the laundry before the lodge's closing.

I pull Kiernan's scarf off over my head. It's been my talisman this whole trip, a memory of him, something precious, something that makes me feel less alone. And it's thick. I wrap it around the cut on my arm, gripping one end in my teeth as I tie it as tightly as I can withstand.

It won't stop the bleeding. But it will keep it from dripping. For a while.

There's a sound somewhere in the distance. The slam of a door being closed. Shivers trail down my spine. I start moving again, taking one of the kitchen's other exits.

The lights in the staff areas were on, but the new passageway I find myself in is pitch-black. I shuffle the hammer around to get a better angle for the light. It shines over rows of dining tables, each carved out of enormous slabs of wood and surrounded by at least twenty chairs. The dining hall.

It's a fight to keep my breathing quiet as I smooth out the floor plan against the nearest wall. I aim my light at it, searching until I locate my current position in the thin, crisscrossing lines.

Denny doesn't have a floor plan. This is my advantage, slim as it is. I need somewhere to hide. Somewhere remote, somewhere private. Somewhere I can place my call without Denny hearing and finding me.

Metal rings on metal and I bite the inside of my cheek. I can picture exactly what would cause that noise. The head of an ax scraping across stainless steel kitchen appliances.

I shove the map inside my jacket and dart through the dining hall, keeping my body low. My flashlight glances across the lowest steps of a staircase: another access point for guests to get between levels. My first instinct is to shy away from it; going to one of the upper floors essentially corners me, putting me farther away from any kind of exit.

But maybe that's exactly what I need. Denny's not a fool. He'll be loath to leave the front door unguarded for long.

The dining hall has tall, narrow windows set into one wall. They'd probably provide ample natural light during the day, but at night and with the sky overcast, they barely let through a glimmer.

I turn my flashlight off just as I reach the stair's base. Keeping my footsteps as light as possible, I take the stairs, hunched forward and with my hand extended to feel the ground ahead.

The stairs curve. I follow them until I'm certain I'll be out of sight of the dining hall, then I crouch down.

It only takes seconds. Slow, heavy footsteps press into the aged wood below me. They pause, then I hear the click of a flashlight. Shallow light flushes across the ceiling above. I can't see Denny, which is good, because it means he can't see me. I keep perfectly still. Perfectly silent. And hope that Kiernan's scarf around my arm has been enough to keep me from leaving a trail of blood.

The light moves, and I know what's happening. Denny is searching under the tables. It only keeps him busy for a few seconds, then there's a click and the dining hall is plunged back into near perfect darkness.

My heart is in my throat. The stairs press into my hip and shoulder, painful, but I don't dare shift. Instead, I wait. Time seems to stretch on. It's agonizing. And then, at last, the footsteps begin to move again. Slow. Ponderous. Trailing away from me and through the dining hall's other entrance.

I count to sixty, then carefully raise myself off the stairs and continue to climb, keeping my movements as close to silent as I can.

The only way I know I've reached the second floor is when my hand feels for the next step and finds only air. I still don't dare turn my light on.

Instead, I stretch my hand out to my side until I find the wall, then use it as a guide as I move forward.

The wall dips out, then in, repeatedly as I pass doors. They must lead to bedrooms. I wait until I reach a corner and pass around it before turning my light on, and even then, I hold it under a lapel of my jacket to mute its glow.

Shining bronze room numbers glimmer through the shadows. I look for the handles, and feel my heart sink as I see modern key card readers, in spite of the old-fashioned theme of the rest of the building.

I'd wanted to find somewhere quiet and secluded. Somewhere that Denny was unlikely to have time to search, even if he continued roving the hallways. But the key cards are all downstairs near the reception desk, and I'm unlikely to get into any of the rooms up here without one.

I keep moving until the hallway takes another turn, then carefully lower myself down, placing the hammer on the floor at my side. From where I sit, my back wedged in the corner, I can see down both passageways. I'll be able to tell if Denny's coming. And I'll have somewhere to run. It's not exactly secure, but it's the closest I'm likely to get.

My phone is cold. My gloves are still downstairs, discarded from when I was searching for the floor plan, and the fingers on my good hand are turning numb. They struggle to press the right buttons as I switch my phone on.

The screen comes to life. My eyes dart to the upper-right corner. Four percent battery. And two service bars.

73.

My hand shakes uncontrollably as I lift the phone to my ear. It rings, then there's a click, followed by a woman's voice. It's one of the best sounds I've ever heard.

"Nine-one-one, what's your emergency?"

I speak quickly, knowing my time's limited. I start with the essentials. My location. The fact that people are dead. That there are likely to be more deaths if help doesn't arrive urgently.

Partway through, I start crying. I can't help it. After everything—every failed escape attempt, every night watch that failed to prevent more deaths, every moment of believed victory followed by defeat—a part of me thought there would never be any escape.

You're all going to die here, the premonition had said, and I'd started to believe it.

Now, though…

Even if I never get out of the lodge—even if Denny wins—at least my body won't be lost out here, forgotten. Someone knows what happened. And that counts for at least something. Tears trickle down my cheeks, dripping off my chin and landing on my knees and the carpet below.

The dispatcher's name is Natasha. I confirm the lodge's location with her multiple times. Then I start providing as many details as I can. The names of the dead: Brian Hernandez. Miri and Steve Peltz. Grayson Olstead. Simone Wall. Blake Shorey. Kiernan Marshall.

I tell her about Hutch and Alexis, still in the cabin, with the potential that at least one of them might be alive.

And I give her the butcher's identity: Denny Olstead, the man who killed his wife and his son and a tour bus of strangers, all because a boy named Liam died two years ago.

The whole time, I fight to maintain my voice barely above a whisper and keep my eyes darting down each of the two hallways ahead of me, on watch for movement. I don't know how far sound will travel in the lodge. Or whether Denny might have already heard me.

Natasha breaks in occasionally with questions. Her voice is clear and calm, speaking steadily so that I can understand her. She's taking me seriously, though, I can tell. There's the clatter of a keyboard as she types furiously in the background.

"Help's on the way, Christa." She keeps using my name. It must be a technique to keep me calm, even though I still haven't raised my hushed voice. "Stay on the line with me, okay?"

"I will," I promise, then squeeze my eyes closed in a grimace. "For as long as I can. My battery's almost dead."

"Okay. I understand. Is there any other phone you can reach?"

"No." Not without breaking into one of the rooms or trying to get back to the staff areas of the lodge.

"Are you in a safe location right now, Christa?" More typing on the keyboard. "Whereabouts in the building are you?"

I open my mouth to answer, but my voice dies in my throat. A sound comes from the hallway to my left. Subtle. Still far away. But unmistakable. The creak of a floorboard.

My heart hurts from how fast it runs as I rise, silently, and press the phone against my chest so that Natasha's voice will be muffled. I can't see anything down that length of hallway and my small handheld light can't reach more than a dozen feet.

There's a beat of silence, then the soft, barely there scrape of heavy boots against the wooden floor.

I clutch the phone and flashlight against my chest as I begin moving down the opposite hallway, keeping my feet as quick and as quiet as I possibly can. I don't know where I'm going. I just hope that the hallway doesn't close into a dead end.

Natasha didn't say how long the rescue might take. The roads are hopelessly blocked; if they're going to get to me, it will have to be by helicopter. But the wind is still vicious and nightfall makes it harder to navigate. Natasha promised that help was on its way, but I'm struck by the horrible thought that she might have just been *saying* that and the dispatch would be nixed before anything left the ground.

I pause just long enough to take the phone away from my chest, hoping I can ask Natasha, but the screen is dead. Tapping the power button can't bring it back. I shove the mobile into my pocket to make it easier to hold the light and keep moving.

That's when I realize: I've left the hammer behind. I put it down to make the phone call and never picked it up again. I clench my teeth, silently cursing.

I have the floor plan, but no chance to examine it thoroughly. Any attempts at hiding—in a closet, in a staff room—will leave me trapped and vulnerable if Denny manages to find me. My best chance is to keep moving, looping through the endless hallways, trying to stay ahead of Denny at all costs. And hope help arrives before the exhaustion becomes completely overwhelming.

The passage turns, and I pass a window before the rows of doors resume. Frost clings to the panes, a sickly off-white in my flashlight. I can't see anything beyond that, but the view would probably be breath-taking on a sunny day.

I hesitate, my frantic pace slowing to a standstill. Do I really need to stay indoors until rescue arrives? Outside is brutally cold and unforgiving. But at least out there, I wouldn't be in danger of backing myself into a corner.

The lodge is surrounded by trees. All I'd need is to get into a thick enough cluster and crouch there to wait. If I pick my location carefully, I could watch the lodge's front doors so that I'd know if Denny tried to leave.

Even just the thought of returning to the storm sends chills down my back. It will be painful. But it's the safest option I can see. Safer than trying to navigate a foreign building's layout in near darkness. And it means that, when rescue *does* arrive, I can run straight for it without having to get past Denny first.

That means I need to get back to the ground floor. Preferably the foyer. I pull the floor plan back out from under my jacket.

The paper crinkles as I unfold the pages, and I grimace. I raise the light as I try to get some kind of bearing on where I might be.

Then I hear it.

Footsteps. At my back. No longer soft and careful but booming, each pace a sledgehammer colliding with the floor.

Coming straight toward me.

74.

My legs move before I even have the chance to draw breath. I lurch forward, no longer trying to stay quiet but simply trying to *move*.

Denny's breaths are deep and ragged and furious. They echo through the passageway, a background to his booming, loping pace.

I don't look back. Don't even dare to blink. Just run.

Ahead, the hallway splits. There's no time to weigh my options; I swing to the left as I reach the turning point.

Ten paces on and the passage ends in a door. A gasping scream strangles in my throat.

No chance to go back. Denny will be at the split before I can even reach it. But the door ahead isn't like the guest rooms; it's a double, with glass panes above old-fashioned handles.

I drop the floor plans as I clutch at them, desperate. It's unlocked. I throw myself through, swinging the door closed behind myself.

An ax slams into the wood right where my middle back would have been. The whole door shudders and begins to sweep open. I shove on it, and as the latch clicks closed again, I turn the dial to lock it.

Then I back away, barely able to breathe.

Denny's massive form shifts just beyond the opaque glass. A monstrous shadow, staring in at me.

I turn. I'm in the movie room. Couches are arranged in rows facing a large plasma TV, a bookcase full of DVDs below it. There's even a folding table and dormant popcorn machine against the back wall.

And there's a door in the room's opposite side. I haven't cornered myself. Not yet.

Glass smashes behind me. I don't stop to watch, but I can hear as an arm reaches through the broken pane and unlocks the door.

I'm already at the opposite exit, though, and slip through, slamming it behind myself. There's no external lock. I leave it as I race along the hall.

The hammer's gone. So is the floor plan. With only one working hand, I've had to juggle my resources and I've lost all but the most vital—the small flashlight. I can't defend myself with it, but at least it can keep me moving through the dark halls.

There's another split in the path ahead. This time I turn right just as I hear the movie room's door bang open behind me. Taking a gamble, I press my damaged hand's palm over the flashlight, blocking the glow, and follow the passage blindly.

Denny's been relying on my light to find me. Now, I do my best to limit it. When I start to lose context of where I am in the hall, I peel my palm back, just a fraction, to let the smallest sliver of refracted light out. It's enough to see a few feet ahead, not much more. I cover the light again and keep moving, my ears straining as I try to sense how close Denny might be.

Sounds echo behind me. The smash of a fist hitting the wall. A door being wrenched open and slammed again.

I've lost him. For the moment.

It comes at a cost of being sightless. I creep forward, breathing as shallowly as my aching lungs will allow. One step. Then another. Denny seems to be growing farther away, the sounds of his anger becoming muffled.

Then, when the darkness becomes too much to withstand for even a second longer, I shift my palm again to let out a sliver of light.

Just ahead and to the right is a door. It's discreet, designed to blend into the hall and not draw attention. The metal doesn't mesh with the lodge's rustic theme.

There's a reason for that. A small red triangle is positioned at head height. *Fire Escape.*

I cover the light again and reach forward. My fingers ache from the cold metal handle. It whines as I turn it, and I grimace, breath held, as I listen. I can no longer hear Denny. I don't know if that's because he's moved too far away or because he's returned to being silent as he stalks me.

The door hasn't been opened in a very long time. Its hinges groan as they're forced to move, and I cringe at every sound, my heart in my throat. There's no turning back, though. I get the door open just barely wide enough, then slip through.

My light glimmers over a dark, spiraling stairwell as the door falls closed behind me. Dust clings around the corners and on the railings. Very few expenses were spared on the rest of the building, but the fire escape is as bare-bones as it can be while still functioning.

But it's leading down, and that's all I ask from it.

I take the steps quickly. Part of me is terrified that I'll hear the creak of the door above me as Denny opens it; the other half is terrified that he'll have guessed my plan and is moving to meet me at the ground level. Either of those fates can be warded off with speed. I move as fast as I dare, my feet flying over the steps recklessly, every bone in my body jarring as I half-run, half-tumble around the bends.

Then, before I'm even ready for it, I'm at the lower door. If I hesitate, I'll never have the courage to open it, so I reach out a hand and shove through.

Dull light bathes over me. After being trapped in the dark upper passageways for so long, it's almost disorienting.

The fire exit lets out into the foyer, close to the staff exits I ran through before. Ahead is the ransacked reception desk, papers and pens still scattered over the floor. Past that, the curving staircase leading to the upper floors, then the couches arranged around the empty fireplace, and then…

The front doors. Snowflakes spill in through a cavity carved in them. Splinters of wood jut out at angry, dangerous angles, cleaved through by the ax. Denny fit through, though, which means I can get out the same way.

Tears sting my eyes as I creep forward. My impulse is to rush for freedom, to burst out through the doors, to escape. But my greatest chance at safety exists if I stay quiet. If I make sure Denny doesn't guess that I've left. If I don't give him a chance to follow.

Only one light in the foyer is on: the chandelier suspended high above. Yellowed bulbs are surrounded by an intricate mesh of antlers. It's more for show than for light and doesn't reach far. Sconces exist around the room's walls for actually lighting the space, but none of them came on with the generator.

It leaves the room shadowed and uneasy. My eyes dart about as I slink through the space, hunting for any sign of movement, any chance that Denny might be lurking in wait.

I can't see him. Or hear him. And the door's close. A gust of icy air blows through, smarting at my skin. I reach for it.

Then, from above and behind, I hear a soft, muffled thud.

My heart misses a beat. I turn, my mouth dry.

The sound came from the top of the stairs. I think I can see something there, but the space is cloistered in the shadows thrown from the antlers.

The thud repeats, like a distant fist knocking at a door.

I'm frozen. I didn't want Denny to see me leaving the lodge. But I can't turn back. Not when I'm so close to the door.

Another thud. And then another. They're faster now. Something's coming down the stairs. About the size of a soccer ball but heavier, it bounces on each step, creating the awful thudding noises, tumbling down toward me.

I can't breathe. Can't think. My eyes fix on the shape as it spirals and spins, pounding on each impact, rolling closer.

It hits the polished wood floor and continues to roll. Nearer and nearer, until it finally comes to a halt less than six paces from me.

My mouth opens, but no sound comes out.

I can only stare at the decapitated head.

Denny's.

75.

Denny's eyes are sightless as they stare up toward the chandelier. His skin's already turned bloodless, his lips pale and parted. The shaggy, gray hair spreads around him, limp on the floor.

He hasn't been dead for long. Fresh blood continues to ooze from the cleaved neck, trickling across the wood.

There's another sound on the stairs. Footsteps.

A figure slowly, calmly descends. Hiking boots step over the thin trail of blood Denny's head left. Each step brings the form out of the shadows, revealing another sliver. Long legs. Pale hands. The torso, covered in a rugged coat. And finally...the face.

Kiernan smiles at me.

This can't be real.

He's exactly as I remember him. His hair, close to needing a trim, brown but infused with a hint of red. His eyes, a pale green that's very nearly gray, warm and sparkling as they meet mine. His face, thin but expressive.

Weak legs carry me forward. I can't speak, can't think, but desperate, choked sounds escape me as I reach toward him.

Kiernan's smile widens, showing his beautiful teeth. He reaches his arms out as we meet at the base of the stairs. I collide with him, and he's solid, he's warm, he's real.

Kiernan lived. He found shelter. He's safe.

I bury my face into his chest. I'm surrounded by his scent. I thought I'd never experience it again after the scarf lost its last traces.

It's every prayer, spoken and unspoken, answered. Every desperate hope. Every hour of aching loss, soothed in an instant.

And yet...

There's a twinge of discomfort in the back of my mind.

I push it aside. Kiernan is here. Kiernan is alive. That's all that matters.

"I thought you were dead," I whisper.

"No, not yet, my dear Chrissy." He dips his head to rest his lips on the top of my head, the way he always used to, and my heart sings.

"I found...your *body*..."

The words feel painful, but Kiernan's arms are still around me, still warm, still comforting.

"That wasn't mine." He chuckles. "It was wearing my clothes, sure. But it wasn't me. Can you guess who it was?"

The twinge returns, sharper. I frown into his jacket.

"That was Brian Hernandez," he answers when I don't. One of his hands rubs at my back, encouraging. "We look a lot alike, don't we?"

On the first night I woke in the cabin, when I saw Brian bent over the table examining the papers, I mistook him for Kiernan. They have the same lean body type. Nearly the same height. The most obvious difference is their hair color.

But the body we found on the side of the road didn't have any hair. It didn't have any *head*. Because Brian's head was on the tree outside the cabin. His was the only one where we didn't find the body elsewhere. And I now understand why.

The twinge is louder, unignorable, like a rubber band snapping over and over in my mind.

No. Stop. Kiernan is here. Kiernan is safe. And he protected me. He killed Denny, the butcher. He...

There's a sickening lump in my throat. I pull back, away from where I've buried my head in Kiernan's jacket, so that I can see his face properly.

My mouth is dry, my voice cracking, as I gaze up at him. "Denny wasn't the butcher, was he?"

His eyebrows rise a fraction as his smile widens.

He doesn't answer. He doesn't need to.

I stagger backward, out of his arms. Pulling away from him as wave upon wave of horror washes over me.

"You're figuring it out, huh?" His tone is so light, so happy.

I keep walking backward. My heel hits something. Denny's head spins away, the gray hair tangling over his face and flecks of blood scattering in his wake.

It's all I can take. My legs have carried me so far, but now they crumple like paper, and I collapse to the cold floor.

Kiernan still stands at the base of the stairs, his posture easy as he admires the effect the revelation has on me.

"But—" My voice catches, raw. "Denny chased me. He—"

The ax, swung with intent to kill. The hatred burning in his eyes.

Kiernan crouches down, balancing on the balls of his feet, his forearms braced on his knees. His voice doesn't lose the warm, encouraging tone even for a second. "Think it through, Chrissy."

"No—"

"I watched it all happen. It was actually quite perfect." He dips his head. "You left the cabin to visit Steve's body and then check in on Simone. But you were gone for too long. Denny got worried and went to look for you. Leaving just Hutch and Blake inside the cabin. Three would have been too many, but two...two I could handle."

I shake my head. It's impossible to believe the words coming out of his mouth.

"Denny went to the shed and found Simone. He rushed back to the cabin only to find you crouched over a bleeding, dying Hutch. What do you think that looked like to him? You and Denny were the final two survivors from the bus. And just like you assumed he must be the killer..."

A lump in my throat chokes me.

"Denny thought *you* were the killer," Kiernan finishes. "He thought you'd murdered his son. He was trying to stop you."

Memories resurface. Hutch, collapsed in the corner of the cabin, fighting to speak through the blood in his lungs. Grasping at Denny's pants. I'd thought he was trying to slow the mountain of a man down. To buy me some time.

I was wrong. He was trying to warn us both. Trying to stop our terrified, panicked fighting long enough to tell us who was really responsible.

My mouth tastes like ash. "The ax—"

"I left that for him. Just outside the cabin." Kiernan makes a small noise that might be a chuckle. "Just like I left Blake's body to point you toward the passage leading to the lodge. I was hoping you'd find your way here. It's the trip I promised you, after all."

My body has turned cold and clammy. Kiernan speaks candidly, with no trace of deceit, but it's still hard to believe even a single word he says.

"Why?" is the only thing I can ask.

He takes a deep, slow breath, then lets it out. "Do you remember how, about a month after we started dating, I took you to meet my mother?"

Speaking feels impossible. I give a short, dizzying nod.

"I told you that my younger brother died in a hit-and-run." He's still smiling, but there's real sadness around his eyes now. Real grief. As raw and as painful as the endless ache I felt when I thought I'd lost him. "That was close to the truth. But not its entirety. I changed the details so that you wouldn't realize just how connected you and I were. But, yes, my brother *did* die in a car accident."

"The boy on the bridge," I manage. "Liam."

Kiernan nods. His lips are pale. "Did you know I was the last person he spoke to? When his car went into the river, he tried calling 911, but the operator thought it was a prank. Water was already gushing into the car when she hung up. So he called me."

Blake. She'd been investigated for negligence. It had ended her career. But even retelling the story in the cabin, she hadn't expressed much regret. Just disappointment at how it had turned out.

"He was still on the phone with me when he tried to open the door. He was going to swim to the surface, he said." Kiernan's voice breaks at the end. He swallows heavily.

He doesn't need to describe what happened after that. The next time Liam was seen was when his body was found in the trash-riddled weeds far downstream.

"I told you the rest of my story when we visited my mother," he continues, his voice calmer. "And all of that was true. Six months after Liam died, my father took his shotgun into the garage and never came back out. My mother…crumbled. She stopped speaking. Stopped eating. I quit my job to look after her, but there wasn't much I could do."

I remember his mother in the hospice, sitting in a chair and watching a television show that had to be at least thirty years old. She didn't seem to be aware of much around her. She repeated my name but without seeming to understand it. Talking to her had been like speaking to a shadow: present and yet not.

"I don't think she even heard me when I made her a promise," Kiernan continues. "I'd spent months researching my brother's accident. Learning what had led to it. All of the names involved. And I found it wasn't just one person's fault: it was a collective crime. A group of strangers who, with utterly minimal consequences in their own lives, had torn my family to shreds." He takes a long, slow breath. "And so I made my mother a promise."

"Kiernan…"

He smiles at me. "I promised her that I would make them all suffer."

76.

My heart thunders. Against my will, my eyes trail toward Denny's head, growing cold on the ground a half dozen paces behind me.

"This has been in the works for a long time," Kiernan says. There's no anger or ugliness in his voice. It's very much like the conversations we used to have in my apartment when he'd explain the plot of one of his stories to me. He's open and friendly. Warm. "You thought I was enrolled in college—and I was. But I never attended. Those hours away from you were spent piecing this trip together in the background."

I can barely speak. "How long…"

"A year and a half now," he says. "Six months after Liam drowned. It wasn't always this elaborate; I started by going after the names on my list one at a time. I tried to make their deaths look like accidents. And it worked. For a while. I killed Karim Abadi by making him sit in his car at gunpoint while fumes filled the vehicle. Oh, you don't know him. He was one of the emergency responders who pulled my brother's car from the river. Simone Wall was the other. She hopped from job to job a lot, you know, but I think it was Karim's death that made her leave *that* one."

My mouth works, but I can't bring any sounds out. I feel as though I'm suffocating.

"There were mistakes, though. I altered the brakes on Denny's car but, for the first time in months, he took a different vehicle to work. His wife died instead. That was frustrating. I would have left her and her son alive otherwise."

Kiernan rocks on his heels. He's clasped his hands together. One thumb picks at loose skin around the other. A habit he has when he's lost in thought. "And then came the most difficult setback. Janet Barras."

The name catches in my mind, and it takes a second to place it. "Alexis's sister."

My voice is so thin, so reedy, that I don't think Kiernan can hear it. But he still nods. "The Barras sisters, yes. Do you know how they were connected? Janet used to date my brother. He visited her the night he died. They had an argument. I never found out what about...but he was hurt enough to drive too fast, too recklessly, trying to get home."

I remember that split-second glimpse of his face when our cars pulled up alongside one another. His pale skin. His red, blotchy eyes.

When Alexis told me about her sister, she mentioned the end of a relationship six months before Janet's own death. How the police had used it as part of their suicide theory.

Alexis also mentioned a neighbor's sighting of a man entering Janet's apartment hours before she died.

"Using a gun and threats of worse pain, I was able to force Janet to write a suicide note and take her own life," Kiernan continues. "I thought it was clean enough to not attract attention. And it was. At first. But then her sister started a blog. And it began gaining traction. She refused to leave it alone. And I realized that, if I continued to work through the names one at a time, eventually *something* would break. If not Alexis's blog, then DNA left at some scene or some attentive officer realizing my family's name comes up in relation to multiple deaths. I couldn't keep it up. Certainly not long enough to complete the list."

The wind beats at the lodge. The door behind me rattles as gusts of cold air race through the hole Denny carved. Kiernan and I are very likely the only living souls for more than a hundred miles in any direction.

He takes another breath and lets it out slowly. He's still watching me with the same fondness he always had for me before the trip. It's causing a painful dissonance. His beautiful, kind face. The raw horrors falling from his lips.

"I decided my best chance was to take down as many of them as I could in one go. And so I began to plan this trip."

My voice is still a whisper. "How did you know the bus would get trapped at the cabin?"

"Ha!" He snaps his fingers. "That's the fun part! I didn't. I picked this time of year because the storms tend to get bad, but everything else was accidental. The plan was always to have the rest of you reach the lodge"—he brings one hand out to indicate the space around us—"while I stayed in the cabin, only a short walk away but otherwise invisible. We ended up having a role reversal. I won't complain. I used to visit this lodge with my father when I was growing up. It was tiny back then—only really a shack—but the area has some powerful nostalgia for me. I've enjoyed staying here the last few days."

I shake my head, unbelieving.

"Part of my preparations were to get rid of the cabin's owners," he says. "Remember last month when I left for the weekend for my cousin's wedding? That was actually to get my camp ready. Dispatch the Kennedys. That was their name—Grant and Lucy Kennedy. This lodge had a custodian too. Someone to keep the pipes flowing during the winter months. I had to remove him too. But that wasn't hard." He shrugs. "It worked out surprisingly well."

It explains why the door was open on my arrival. I wonder where the custodian's body has been stored. In one of the guest rooms? Out in the forest?

"It wasn't just nostalgia that made me stage the plan here," he continued. "It was a convenient location for quite a few reasons. Far enough from civilization that there's no cell signal without a booster. No easy way to walk out once the bus's engine was broken. And you can't see the lodge from the cabin or vice versa, but they're closer than you might think. That narrow channel you followed through the mountains cuts the trip down to an hour and a half. It made it relatively painless to stay close by and take advantage of opportunities as they presented themselves."

Opportunities. Brian, stepping out of the cabin briefly. Miri, going outside to smoke. Grayson, wanting to be left alone for half an hour.

He sabotaged the generator, cutting our lights during the night. He left the heads on trees. Staged his victims.

Because he wanted us to suffer.

"I spent most of a year planning and preparing," Kiernan continues. "I sold my family's home. A lot of that went to my mother's care. But the rest...I hired Brian's company and rented Blackstone Lodge for a private tour. And then I passed tickets out to my list."

"Steve and Miri" is all I can manage.

"The Peltzes, yes. The truck that cornered Liam and gave him nowhere else to go. Then Denny Olstead, the mechanic who serviced the truck and failed to notice the issues with the emergency brakes. Hutch Huang, who was at the scene but gave up before reaching the water. Blake Shorey, the 911 dispatcher who hung up on my brother. Simone Wall, the emergency responder who took her time pulling his car out of the river. And Alexis Barras, the sister whose investigations had been a thorn in my side for months."

"Brian," I say. "Grayson."

"Unavoidable collateral damage." Kiernan tilts his head, as though considering it. "I needed Brian to make the trip convincing and to transport us here, but his knowledge of the area was too much of a liability after that. And Denny wouldn't have come without Grayson."

"You knew all along," I manage. It feels stupid, selfish, infantile to be focused on this point the most, but it's the one that really hurts. "You knew I was involved in your brother's death the entire time we were dating."

"Oh, Chrissy," he murmurs. "Yes. You were my largest target. My most important one. You were the car that drove Liam off the road. But you were also the trickiest. I wanted you here—I needed you to hurt—but I knew you wouldn't take a spontaneous trip into the mountains, even if you were gifted tickets. The only thing that would make you go was something personal." His mouth quirks up into a smile. "An invitation from someone important in your life."

A sound escapes me. It might be laughter. It might be a strangled moan. I'm not sure.

"I followed you for a long time. I knew your routine; I knew your interests. That's how we met. At the library, remember? I asked you for help with some fictional coursework, then paid for coffee while you explained the answer to me. It was easy from there. I decided I could be the perfect partner for six months. And I was, wasn't I? I was everything you wanted. Everything you needed. You barely even hesitated when I asked you to visit the mountains where I grew up."

I didn't. He's outlined every facet of me correctly: I never would have accepted a trip to Blackstone Alpine Lodge…except that Kiernan asked me.

The ache in my stomach redoubles. This is worse than anything. Worse than being lost in the blizzard. Worse than thinking Kiernan was dead.

"I wanted you to really feel it," he continues, and leans forward slightly, shifting his weight. "The same pain I felt while listening to my brother drown. I wanted to pass that on to you as wholly as I could. Did you find the teeth on the windowsill? Did you think they were mine?"

I don't even have the strength to lie. I nod.

He seems pleased with that. "Those were from the Kennedys. And you might not have found it, but I hid an engagement ring on the body you thought was mine."

Memories resurface, painfully clear. Finding the body dressed in Kiernan's clothes. Leaning over it. *Crying* over it. Feeling like my essence was being torn apart.

The hands had been shredded. At the time, I'd questioned whether that might be wild animals or self-defense wounds. I guess I have my answers now. It's because they weren't Kiernan's hands. The rest of Brian's body was disguised under thick winter clothing that was hard to remove, and the skin's tone was turned gray-white by death, but Kiernan had guessed that I might try to remove the gloves and discover that the hands didn't belong to the man I loved.

I knew them intimately. The shape of the knuckles. The placement of the freckles. And so Kiernan had shredded the corpse's hands so that I wouldn't have that final clue.

And I found the ring. My mind is heavy and aching, but I can still remember where I put it. I reach into my jacket's pocket. My fingers brush metal before fixing around velvet.

"Yes! That's it!" Kiernan seems genuinely thrilled with me when he sees the box. "Oh, I'm happy you got it. I really didn't think you would."

Everything has been a lie. When the bus stopped to clear the fallen tree, Kiernan led me away from the group not to propose to me, but to fake his own death. In doing that, he became a phantom that could dart in at will, picking us off one by one, while our paranoia and infighting grew. To deadly levels.

My tongue darts out to wet, cracked lips. "Simone killed Steve."

"She did. I was hoping something like that would happen." He rocks on his heels again. "Ideally, she would have gone for Denny instead. He was difficult to bring down, even after catching him by surprise. Such a big man. Still. Simone definitely made this final stage easier."

She tried so hard. Fighting to keep us safe. To protect us from a threat she couldn't even see.

"A lot of my work happened in the background, out of sight," Kiernan continues. "Brian was supposed to have an assistant, Uma. She was going to follow behind in a backup vehicle with your food and other supplies. I punctured one of her tires at the hotel the morning before we left. That bought me enough time get Brian's phone and text her to say the trip was canceled. She's lucky she took that message at face value."

The words are moving past me faster than I can get a hold of them. "When—"

"When did I get his phone? After killing him on the first night." He's so calm, so matter-of-fact about it. "I lured him outside by waving a flashlight in the distance. He must have thought he was going to rescue me. He had both the cell phone and the bus's keys in his pockets, which was lucky."

I resented Brian for not wanting to search for Kiernan. For spending time examining the indemnity paperwork. But he was as much a victim as the rest of us. Perhaps even more so. He was just trying to do his job.

"I'm making it sound simpler than it was." Kiernan chuckles and dips his head. "Nothing was easy. There were other people on the list. Gabrielle Patel. She was the emergency dispatcher *I* called after my brother opened his car door and I lost his signal. Mike Andre: he saw the scene of the accident but decided to keep driving. Grant Muller, Liam's school counselor. They all got tickets but never claimed them. I suppose I was lucky to get the acceptance rate I did. People tend to be wary of free things, even if you try to tailor the offer to their personalities."

Hutch was hired to scout out a wedding location. It would have been Kiernan on the phone, I realize: pretending to be a wealthy groom with an interest in the outdoors. Steve and Miri were told they won their tickets in a raffle. Simone got her ticket from a friend who canceled at the last moment. I wonder if Kiernan had a hand in that or if it was pure coincidence.

And, of course, Alexis received a personal card from her sister's killer. Not because she'd been involved in Liam's death, but because she'd frustrated Kiernan enough that he'd wanted to hurt her too.

Finally, me. I was the only one allowed to meet our killer before the trip.

"What happens now?" I ask. My mouth is parchment dry, tacky and sick. "You're going to kill me, aren't you?"

77.

Kiernan's eyes crinkle up around the edges as he smiles. "That's the obvious next step, isn't it? You're the last one alive. The final name on my list."

The ax will be somewhere nearby. Not easy to find—not somewhere I could just stumble on it—but close at hand.

"It might look like I've planned every moment of this trip," Kiernan says, "but most of it has been purely opportunistic. I'd hoped you would live until the end, but there was no way to guarantee it. Or to be sure that my presence would go unnoticed. I did my best to funnel the group in certain directions—like placing Blake's body to help you find your way toward Blackstone—but mostly I had to make choices on the fly, when the chance presented itself." He works his jaw. "My point is, now that we're finally here, I haven't thought much about what I want to do next."

"You didn't know if you'd even survive this long," I whisper.

"Exactly. I had to get close to my victims to kill them, and ambushes are hard to stage. It was risky. Anyone could have fought back. And I was prepared for that; my mother's care is assured and I have no other family. I went into this aware that I might die before the end."

He lifts his head, inhaling deeply. Snow continues to spiral through the gap in the door, dropping the foyer's temperature. My gloveless hands are like ice.

"Everything from here on out is hazy. I could cross the border into Canada. Or hitch a ride into a different state. Start again under a new name, I suppose. That's what people usually want to do in these kinds of situations, isn't it?"

He's asking me as though my opinion carries any weight at all. I let myself droop, exhausted.

His expression softens. "Don't look so sad, Chrissy. If it's any comfort, our relationship wasn't a complete lie. I did actually grow fond of you, especially in the latter months."

I can't meet his eyes. I feel as though I'm going to be sick.

Kiernan's voice grows lower, huskier. "You were…different from the others. You were suffering. I saw that every single day. My brother's death was eating you up almost as much as it had for me. You wouldn't drive at night. Wouldn't leave the house if there was a storm. Couldn't watch movies with car accidents in them." His lips twitch, showing just a hint of his teeth. "I noticed. And I appreciated it."

It's voiced as praise, but it feels like venom.

Kiernan's meaning is that the others did not feel the same sense of guilt I did. That my months of agonizing penitence have gone some ways to absolving my crime.

That's so wrong.

None of the others—Steve or Blake or Simone—deserved to die.

There was not a single person inside that cabin who I could call truly *good* or *blameless.* Every one of them was speckled with flaws: glimpses of spitefulness, of selfishness, of anger. Some worse than others.

But never enough to justify what was done to them.

And if they didn't deserve to suffer for what happened, why do I?

It's strange and faintly heartbreaking that this revelation has to come so near the end. Because it *is* the end. Natasha, the emergency dispatcher, promised help was on the way, but it hasn't come. And I can't stall us any longer.

Kiernan rises out of his crouch. With me still on the ground, he seems to tower. There's a strange emotion in his eyes. He stares down at me for a long moment, and it's hard to tell what he's thinking.

Then he says, "Beg."

My voice cracks. "What?"

"Beg me to let you live." He tilts his head, eyebrows raised as he watches me. "Do a good job and I'll bring you with me when I leave here."

Can I? There's an uncomfortable hollowness in my heart. Am I capable of begging if it means the difference between death and life?

Yes, I decide. Yes. My pride isn't powerful enough to override this chance I've been given. No matter how humiliating it is.

I slip the engagement ring back into my pocket, taking care with it. Then I begin to crawl toward Kiernan. "Please. I want to live."

He smiles, and it's the first time he's let an unsavory emotion slip into his expression. There's true delight for him in debasing me.

I fight to keep the repulsion off my face as I shuffle closer on hands and knees. "Please. Please, Kiernan."

"Good job," he whispers as I stop at his feet. He lowers himself and hooks one hand under my chin, lifting my head so that I'm forced to meet his eyes. "Very well done, Chrissy. You may come with me."

"Thank you," I manage.

Cold steel burns my hand. He still hasn't noticed it.

When I felt for the engagement ring's velvet box, my fingers brushed something metal in my pocket. Until that moment, I'd forgotten about Alexis's pocketknife. I took it from Simone when we subdued her following Steve's death. It's been in my pocket since then, but its existence had slipped from my mind. Until now.

Kiernan bends forward to kiss me. I wait until his eyes fall closed, then bring my fist up, the pocket knife extended in it, and drive it into his chest.

78.

A gasp is forced out of Kiernan, short and strangled. His eyes widen. His face is just inches from mine as he stares at me, unbelieving.

I can feel the knife in him. Felt the pressure and soft give of his flesh as I pushed it through. Felt it scrape over his ribs.

Alexis might be limp and lifeless in the cabin, but she's taken part in this moment. It's her knife I hold. Her knife that's now stained red with hot, seeping blood.

Kiernan's hands fasten around mine. They're strong. Crushing. His expression shifts from shock to anger. He pushes back, forcing my hand away, dragging the knife out of himself.

I've never seen him angry before. *I decided I could be the perfect partner for six months*, he said, and it wasn't an exaggeration. He never raised his voice at me. Never grew short or irritable. I'd thought he was simply incapable.

I was wrong. Cold, calculating fury bleeds over his face, and I'm shocked by how natural it looks there.

"That was a mistake," he says.

He shoves into me. He has not only a height advantage but also strength. I fall, gasping as my back slams into the hard floor. Pain blooms.

The knife's still in my hand. Slick with blood, slippery, only a few inches long. Good for concealed carrying, but not large enough to cause irreparable damage with a single blow.

Kiernan stands over me. One hand is pressed to his chest, and dribbles of blood flow out from between his fingers, but there's not as much as I would have thought.

He lifts his boot and brings it down on my hand.

I scream. The knife clatters out of my grip as Kiernan lifts his foot again, and he effortlessly kicks it aside.

"I really was going to take you with me," he says, dropping down. One of his knees shoves into my stomach and I retch, crumpling over from the pain. His hands slink in, faster than I can prevent, and fix around my throat. "What a waste."

Pressure tightens. I try to claw at his grip, but one hand hurts too much to feel what I'm doing, and the other is blackened and useless.

He leans over me, filling my vision, as he chokes my air away. Veins run across his forehead. His mouth is open, his teeth exposed, as he breathes heavily, and his gray eyes are full of bitter fury and cruel satisfaction as he watches me squirm.

This is his real face, I think. *This is what he's been underneath all along. Under the mask.*

I can't breathe. Can't escape from under his crushing weight.

But I'm still not done.

I lift my bad hand and drive the blackened fingers through his open lips and into his mouth.

It's enough to shock him. He jerks back but can't escape me without releasing his hold on my throat.

He bites down on the fingers.

I feel the pressure, but only through the way my skin stretches. The nerve endings are long gone. The flesh is necrotizing, dying while still attached to my hand. The fingers are black. Lifeless. Impervious to pain.

I shove them deeper, into his throat.

He gags. His hands, hot and sweaty, let go of me.

I kick and crawl, digging my way out from under him as Kiernan doubles over, spitting onto the floor. I must have scratched the sensitive skin inside his mouth; blood is mixed into the saliva. Or maybe it's from the wound to his chest.

Alexis's knife is no more than five feet away. It glitters under the chandelier's light, all sparkling red blood and silver steel. Pain radiates through every part of my body. I shove the sensations aside as I throw myself toward the blade.

Behind me, Kiernan draws a heaving, retching breath. "You're not done suffering, are you?"

His hand lands on my back, shoving me into the floor again. I'm so close to the blade. Instead of fighting with Kiernan, I throw my arm forward, reaching for it.

His fingers dig into my shoulder, through the layers of his scarf, to where Denny sliced me open. I scream. And my fingers fasten around cold steel.

"I'm glad I saved you for last." Kiernan's voice is almost unrecognizable. It's raw and rough and filled with more malice than I thought a person could contain. "I get to take my time with you. I get to look into your eyes as you die."

His hand wrenches on me, rolling me over. He's right on top. Looming over me. Spittle drips from his mouth, clinging to his jaw. His eyes are wide and haunted and furiously angry.

He was too focused on hurting me. For the second time, he didn't see the knife.

I swing it up. Not to stab this time but to slice.

The blade snicks across his throat.

I'm not strong enough to cut right through. The knife is sharp, though, and it burrows in deep enough to split something vital. Blood sprays. Kiernan chokes, gasping, as he reels back.

This time, I don't hesitate. I follow him, slicing the knife in again, and again, and again.

He took my friends' heads. So that's where I focus now: on the thin skin across his throat.

Blood spits across my face. Into my hair. Between my lips. I taste it: sickly sweet and full of metal and nausea. I can't see. Can barely think.

I loved this man. I fought for him. Searched the mountains for him when no one else wanted to. I grieved for him.

Now, the only person I have left to fight for is myself.

My hands shake as I drop the knife. I crawl backward, breathing hard, my whole body shivering uncontrollably. His hot blood is rapidly cooling as it trickles down my face.

Kiernan lies in the center of the foyer, not far from Denny's head. He shudders. His hands twitch, first reaching toward his butchered throat, and then into the air.

He's not dead. But blood is flowing too fast for him to survive long without help.

Hot, frightened, angry tears trail down my face. There's shame in them for what I had to do.

But there's also relief. Cathartic, miserable, painful, powerful relief.

My senses return slowly. I catch the bubbling gasps of Kiernan trying to breathe, not unlike how I left Hutch.

And I hear something else.

Slowly, I pull myself to my feet. Every muscle and joint in my body aches. I'll have bruising across my back, across my stomach, and over my arms. My hip hurts, making it hard to walk. But walk I do.

Icy air steals my limited breath as I approach the gap Denny carved through the door. Snow flows around my hands as I reach through and painstakingly pull myself out of the opening. My legs sink deep into the winter snow.

Flakes continue to trail around me: no longer a blizzard but a soft dusting, dampening the night air and filtering the moonlight.

The world isn't quiet, though. In the distance comes a slow, rhythmic thudding. Like drums beating over the mountaintops. I lift my head just as the first helicopter rises over the trees.

Natasha came through for me.

A spotlight fixes on Blackstone Lodge's door, with me in the center. I shield my eyes and raise my other blackened and bitten hand to hail them. A whirlwind of snow spins in all directions as the helicopter descends toward me.

Tears continue to fall, and I don't try to stop them. As tired and aching and scarred as I am, there's still work to be done.

I don't know if Kiernan will survive.

If he does, he'll face the courts. He'll answer for what he's done.

There were nine other people on this trip with us. Each of them has families, friends. People who deserve answers. Who need some kind of justice. Kiernan can be the one to pay that fee for the remainder of his life.

For my own sake…I don't want to ever see his face again. Though I suspect I'll never forget it, in the same way that I never forgot his brother's face from the night on the bridge.

But that's not what's important right now, as the blinding light grows nearer.

Right now, I only care about two names.

Hutch. Alexis.

They might not still be alive. They might already be past the point of saving.

But we can at least try.

Don't walk alone, or the Stitcher will find you.

Abby Ward lives in a town haunted by disappearances. People vanish, and when they're found, their bodies have been dismembered and sewn back together in unnatural ways. But is it the work of a human killer...or something far darker?

Don't stay out late, or the Stitcher will take you.

She and her younger sister live by a strict set of rules designed to keep them safe—which is why it's such a shock when Hope is taken. Desperate to get her back, Abby tells the police everything she knows, but they claim their hands are tied.

Don't close your eyes, or the Stitcher will remake you.

With every hour precious, Abby and her friends are caught in a desperate game of cat and mouse. They have to get Hope back. Quickly. Before too much of her is cut away. And before everything they care about is swallowed up by the darkness waiting in the tunnels beneath the home they thought they knew.

1.

The air was rotting. Biting cold and heavy with moisture, it filled Jan's throat with every inhale, so dense that it felt as though it was suffocating her.

She crawled through the dark. Sharp rocks scraped her palms, her knees, her shoulder blades. She flinched and dropped lower, hunching to fit through the narrow tunnel, her hands feeling blindly to find a path forward.

How long had she been down here, in the dark and the cold and the damp?

Days?

Weeks?

She couldn't stop moving. The thing in the dark would come back for her soon. And she didn't think she could survive the next time.

Her fingers touched something delicate and disgusting. Threads, criss-crossing the darkness ahead of her. They were as fine as spiderweb and slimy from the damp. When she tried to swipe them away, they refused to break.

She couldn't see them, but she knew what color they were. Red. It was always red threads. They trailed through the maze, gathering drops of moisture from the air, tangling over the rocks and one another. They bit into Jan's flesh when she tried to force her way past them. Cutting into her throat, into her face, into her numb fingers.

A distant sound broke through the background noise of dripping water and her own uneven, echoing breaths. Jan's heart pitched, jittering in her chest. She clamped a hand over her mouth, fighting to muffle her breathing.

It couldn't see well in the dark. The maze held no light; Jan had been staring into the nothingness for so long that she'd started to hallucinate things moving around her. Unnatural shapes danced, taunting her, only to vanish when she looked at them directly.

The sound repeated: hands grasping at rocks as it pulled itself closer. The shift of flesh against flesh. A dry, hollow exhale.

It couldn't see well, but it could hear and smell.

It knew where she was.

Terror overwhelmed common sense. Jan threw herself forward. She didn't feel the rocks cutting into her palms or the drop of blood trailing down her cheek. But she felt the threads as they snagged around her, tightening.

She'd rushed right into them. Jan fought, thrashing like an insect in a spiderweb as she tried to break free. Some of the threads snapped. They gave her just enough room to drag herself forward another inch, then another foot, until she was nearly on the other side of the web of red threads—

A cold hand fastened around her leg. Jan had just enough breath left to scream. Then the thing in the dark dragged her back to join it, and her voice cut out into nothing.

ACKNOWLEDGMENTS

No matter how solitary a writer's work seems, the final book is never a single-person project. Two of the biggest influences behind *Dead of Winter* were Rachel Gilmer and Mary Altman, who acted as plot-straighteners, sounding boards, and the hard polishing stones this story needed.

My gratitude goes to the Sourcebooks and Poisoned Pen Press teams and everyone in them who had a part in bringing this book to life. Special thanks to Gretchen Stelter and Mary Moore, who cut through confusing sentences and repaired continuity errors; Jessica Thelander, for proofing the final files; and Erin Fitzsimmons and Stephanie Gafron for creating this gorgeous cover.

I can't finish an acknowledgments section without also thanking Mandy Chahal and Sean Murray, who have been tireless champions of my books over the last three years. And finally, you, the reader, who made all of this possible. Thank you.

ABOUT THE AUTHOR

Darcy Coates is the *USA Today* bestselling author of more than a dozen horror and suspense novels. She lives in the Central Coast of Australia with her family, cat, and a collection of chickens. Her home is surrounded by rolling wilderness on all sides, and she wouldn't have it any other way.